FALSE
ASSURANCES

BEN PORTER SERIES – BOOK ONE

CHRISTOPHER ROSOW

FALSE ASSURANCES

For information about this title or to order other books and/or electronic media, contact the publisher:
Quadrant Publishing, LLC
354 Pequot Avenue, Southport, CT 06890
QuadrantPublishing@gmail.com

Library of Congress Control Number: 2020905690

ISBN: 978-1-7347147-0-8 (print)
978-1-7347147-1-5 (eBook)

Printed in the United States of America

Cover and Interior design: 1106 Design, LLC

AUTHOR'S NOTE

WHILE THIS STORY IS constructed in the real world, including but not limited to referencing actual companies, places, news outlets and articles, events, and things, it is a novel, and it is a work of fiction.

However, it's not entirely far-fetched.

PREFACE

CREATED AS ONE OF THE responses to the September 11, 2001 terror attacks, the United States Department of Homeland Security (DHS) includes seven subagencies: the US Citizenship and Immigration Services (USCIS), the United States Customs and Border Protection (CBP), the United States Immigration and Customs Enforcement (ICE), the Transportation Security Administration (TSA), the US Coast Guard (USCG), the US Secret Service (USSS), and the Federal Emergency Management Agency (FEMA).

The Federal Bureau of Investigation (FBI) operates independently of DHS, as does the Central Intelligence Agency (CIA).

The places, the technology, and the deficiency in American border security that are exploited in this narrative—all exist. By and large, the government, and the hard-working and dedicated people of Homeland Security, are *very* well informed, and not only do they protect the borders of the United States, but they also try to anticipate threats.

This one, however, slipped through the cracks.

And those cracks remain wide open.

PROLOGUE
TUESDAY, JULY 4, 2017

THE NORTH ATLANTIC OCEAN: 43°53'N, 35°15'W

THE STEADY, INCESSANT THRUM of a low-torque diesel engine created a constant vibration throughout the small ship as it plodded westward, rolling and pitching gently on the Atlantic Ocean swell. In the wheelhouse, with eyes half-closed and arms folded across his chest, a sole figure idly watched the compass and the autopilot. Below, in the galley area, two men sat at a coffee-stained Formica table.

Exposing blackened teeth, a dark-haired man spoke in halting English: "This is for the mission?"

Across the table, a gray-haired man with a matching, full, gray beard nodded distractedly, squinting through round, owl-shaped glasses as he carefully soldered a wire that linked two devices: one a cylindrical shape, the other more squarish, more rectangular. A tendril of light-gray smoke drifted upward from the tip of the soldering iron as he pulled it from a precisely-formed, silvery metal connection. Setting the iron aside in a cradle, he leaned in, carefully examining the bond with the exactitude of a jeweler inspecting a gem.

Satisfied, the gray-haired man sat back, removed his eyeglasses, and twirled them absently as the dark man opposite spoke again, "It is one of the bombs? It is very small."

"No. Not a bomb. A detonator."

"Oh. Yes. I see," replied the dark one. He considered the contraption on the cracked, discolored table, the precision of the wiring, and the newness of the devices incongruous on the mottled surface. "It creates the explosion?"

"Exactly. It will create an inferno," the bearded man answered. He slid his eyeglasses back onto the bridge of his nose and bowed toward his work as the other man lapsed into silence.

As the ship thrummed west, the bearded, bespectacled man reminded himself that he had a week to complete his preparations. He carefully dry-fitted a wire to a terminal before picking up the soldering iron with a practiced confidence. He was in no hurry.

PART ONE
TUESDAY, JULY 11, 2017

CHAPTER

1

MY NAME IS BEN PORTER. I'm twenty-seven years old, and I work for the Federal Bureau of Investigation.

Cool, huh? I'm guessing you're thinking, yup, I know the type. G-man. Clean shaven with a crew cut; a trim, athletic build; a sharp, navy-blue suit; and a pressed white shirt. Striped tie. Aviator sunglasses. A Fed.

Yeah . . . Ummm. No. Not exactly.

It usually goes like this. I'm at a bar, hanging out with my friends. I meet someone new. They say, "What do you do for a living?" I work for the FBI, I tell them. They cock their heads a little, their gaze wavers as they assess the view in front of them. They ask, "Oh, really? Are you an agent?"

I've gotten used to that. Everyone automatically assumes that if you work for the FBI, you're an agent. Out undercover, running drug busts, or investigating nefarious criminal acts, backed up by high-tech data centers and black helicopters. It's the glamour life they see on TV shows and in the movies. Don't they realize the FBI is a huge organization? Thirty-five thousand people work for The Bureau, and we're not all agents.

So, I tell that new person, "No, I'm not an agent. I'm an Information Management Specialist." I try to say it importantly, as if I'm capitalizing the words as I say them.

It rarely impresses. Either you're an agent, and you're cool, or you're a . . . *whatever*. And if you're a whatever, you're clearly just a cog in the machine. A secretary, or a coffee-maker, or a mailroom clerk, or an information management specialist. No caps. It's like people assume there's nothing between an agent and a mailroom clerk.

I know, I sound a little bitter. I wanted to be an agent, but the training is really extensive and takes a really long time. Honestly, I didn't think that I could pass the fitness training tests at the FBI Academy in Quantico, Virginia, and I realized that the administrative staff positions didn't require a twenty-one-week trip to Quantico. I'm pretty good with computers, and I've never done anything remotely interesting, so passing the background check was easy. I bet the agents reading my FD-140—the exhaustive personal information form we all fill out—fell asleep half-way through the paperwork.

Trust me, I live a boring life.

And, truth be told, I'm not exactly the physical specimen that you might have pictured. I'm not the worst-looking person in the world. It's not like I am some sort of troll creature, living in the shadows. But I'm a little overweight, not very tall, and I'm missing the chiseled features of a proper G-man.

Well, since we're being honest, maybe I'm a *tad* more than a little overweight. But I'm not fat. Let's be clear on that.

Let's just go with . . . husky.

Thank goodness for Lasik, otherwise, I'd be in real trouble in the looks department. With my poor eyesight requiring thick glasses, but with my round face limiting my frame choices, I had a perpetual problem: I could never find glasses that fit well and looked good on me. Naturally, I tried contact lenses. I don't know how people jab themselves in the eye over and over again every day or week. My eyes become a bloodshot mess. I looked like a husky werewolf. It was awful. So, my first big splurge, after I had saved enough money from my FBI salary, was not a cool car or an average house with a nice hardwood floor, but Lasik surgery.

In fact, right after the procedure, I bought nice sneakers and joined a gym. Figured I'd get in shape finally.

That lasted a couple of weeks. Turns out, the gym is hard work. People who go to the gym, when I can go, before work, know the routine.

They're driven. It was kinda stressful for me. Besides, I don't need to get a six-pack at the gym. I keep one in the fridge at home.

Oh well. I got the Lasik, but I'm still out of shape. One thing at a time.

I've been working for The Bureau for almost five years. After graduating from Regional High School in nearby Quahog, Rhode Island—where I grew up with mom, dad, older sister, younger brother—an average family at the outskirts of what counts for a big city in New England—I attended Boston University. Once in Boston, I loved it. Even though Boston is less than an hour's drive from my hometown, it's a different world. Such a cool town. Dynamic, historical, fun, colorful. All great adjectives to describe it.

At the BU job fairs my senior year, I applied to every financial district job I could. I didn't make much progress. And by that, I mean none, really. It was tough competition for those jobs, and I didn't get one. The cool kids got all those gigs.

So, when I saw the FBI table at one of those events, I checked it out. Like I said earlier, I quickly learned that the path to becoming an agent seemed like a real pain in the ass, and since there was not much competition for the nonagent administrative jobs, I got one. I started right away after BU's graduation. And I'm still there now.

"There" is a cubicle in the Bureau's Boston field office, which, typical of the agency, is not *actually* in Boston. It's in Chelsea. Maybe twenty minutes by car, depending on how miserable traffic is, from downtown Beantown. What they saved on land, they spent on the building. It's a modern glass and concrete edifice to the American taxpayer's dollars. Thanks, everyone. It's a really nice building. Brand new, it's a nice step up from the old digs at Center Plaza in downtown Boston.

Unfortunately, when we moved to the new offices in November last year, my boss was moved along with us.

My group, collectively, hates our boss. He is newer to the agency than most of us—he was not around in those crazy, high-pressure days in 2013 during and after the Boston Marathon bombing. Truth be told, I think (though we don't admit it) that we resent that. That event was a crucible. We bonded, took great pride in what we were doing and in our city. "Boston Strong." It's the real deal. And yet, even though he'll try to talk the talk like he's a local, pretending that he's into the Red Sox and the Patriots, we know it's a veneer. Bradford Macallister is *not* one of us. He's from New Jersey. And he was a Giants fan.

Don't get me wrong, I've got nothing against New Jersey. Against the Giants, maybe. Though, technically, they're the "New York" Giants, even though their home stadium is in Jersey. Still, not an indictment of an entire state. In fact, New Jersey has at least one thing going for it—many things, I'm sure, but this is the one thing I can absolutely, definitively state—and that is that New Jersey no longer has Bradford Macallister.

As a boss, he's mercurial. Sometimes he plays nice and pretends to be part of the group. But then, sometimes, oftentimes, his head is figuratively spinning in circles as he froths at the mouth, yelling and fuming and making all sorts of unintelligible noise. Frankly, we all wonder how he has stayed at the FBI for so long; it's been almost three years. Rumor has it that he's connected; a wealthy family with political influence someplace either got him the job, or protects him in the job.

Let me offer a visual clue, aside from his prep-school fashion sense on his fair-skinned, five-foot-eleven, gym-toned body, to help describe the type of guy Bradford Macallister is. His car—sure, you're not supposed to judge someone by their wheels—I get it and, normally, I don't judge. Except in this case. You see, Bradford Macallister drives a Range Rover Evoque.

Once you get past the fact that a US government employee is driving a British car whose interior was allegedly designed by Posh Spice, you can't really fault the car itself; the so-called "baby" Range Rover is certainly striking with its concept car looks. Black with black rims and black badging, this one, in particular, is really pretty cool. Nothing wrong with that, you'd say.

Except that license plate—still New Jersey tags, by the way—is MACQUE.

Get it? A portmanteau of Macallister and Evoque. *Ugh.* It's just so wrong, on so many levels. I guess if you were trying to be charitable, you'd say that Macallister does not have confidence issues. I call it blatant arrogance. And he acts that way for no good reason. Maybe I should just leave it at that.

He stays in his office, we stay in our cubes, we do our jobs, he pushes paper including dealing with one of his responsibilities which is oversight over our group. He's what we call a "desk agent," but he's still an agent, and per Bureau regulations, he carries his weapon with him at all times. His title sounds way better than mine; he's a Supervisory Special Agent (two capital S's, naturally).

Most of the time, Macallister is ignored or merely humored.

But this week has been different.

CHAPTER
2

BACK ON JANUARY 13, 2016, General Electric announced that it was moving its headquarters from Connecticut to Boston.

Unsurprisingly, that announcement set off a free-for-all of Massachusetts politicians scrambling to get in front of microphones and TV cameras to take credit. If the health of the economy was measured by some metric of self-congratulatory sound bites, we'd be all set for a while.

The back-patting has continued since then, with evening news announcers breathlessly panting the latest tidbits of info, from the company big shots moving into temporary offices, to the grand reveal of the new GE headquarters building. The official groundbreaking, accompanied by the usual politicos and local A-listers, happened earlier this year on May 8.

Unwilling to rest on that publicity, the big wigs dreamed up another stunt sure to lure votes in the next election. Or, quite possibly, the company itself came up with the plan in response to its tanking stock price, which, since late December 2016, had been in free-fall. Either way, on Friday, June 30th, perhaps after seeing that the groundbreaking ceremony did nothing to reverse their stock slide, they announced that, "tentatively on July 12th" (that's tomorrow, just in case you lost track), the president of the United States would be visiting with company executives, local business leaders and politicians to "celebrate the accomplishments of this storied company in this storied town."

That part in quotes I made up. I mean, it went something like that. You've read this kind of public-relations drivel before. After a while, it all sounds the same.

In case you were wondering, the talking heads on the TV financial shows said that GE's stock got a one-day boost from the announcement, only to resume its slide the next trading day, while the overall market went sort of sideways. "Pressure from short sellers and profit-taking held back overall market gains," the commentators commented. My portfolio is strategically positioned to hover between zero and nothing, so I can't say I paid it much attention.

Anyway, the announcement just eleven days ago triggered an orgy of planning at our offices. Liaisons with the Secret Service, with the local Boston PD, and, of course, the MBTA, otherwise known as the Massachusetts Bay Transit Authority. The latter is known more for the awesome excuse generator at *MBTAexcuses.com* than for its actual efficiency, and it's doubtful that POTUS will take a ride on the T, so I'm not quite sure why they are involved.

I joke around, but we have really been hard at work since the announcement on the thirtieth. There is a lot to do to prepare for a presidential visit, even if it's a quick in-and-out like this one. Security at Logan Airport, logistics and security for the transit to downtown, perimeter and crowd control at the event itself, and then the return trip to Logan . . . the list goes on and on.

The president's schedule is tightly controlled, usually weeks and months in advance. The short notice for this visit has compounded the difficulty of preparing for a public appearance like this one. On one level, it made some sense. President Trump had already been scheduled to visit President Macron of France on July 14 for Bastille Day, and this stop would be a touch-and-go for Air Force One after it departed from Washington and before it continued on to Europe.

Typically, the FBI does not get involved with the president's personal protection detail; that's the role of the Secret Service. But, here in

Boston, we vividly remember the Marathon bombing. With a projected route from Logan Airport into the heart of the city, and with numerous places to stage an ambush or a protest, the Secret Service would have their work cut out for them. And, with their ranks also anticipating planning and protection during the European visit, they would be stretched thin. Therefore, the FBI would partner with the Service to provide additional security and oversight for this event.

Terming it a "tentative" visit did not change our preparation protocols nor make those preparations any less thorough. Even though, like many presidential appearances, this one would happen only if there were no other suddenly more pressing presidential duties to attend to, like golf, or brush clearing, or interns.

Regardless, because the appearance would be in a public place with advance notice, we know that the whackos will be coming out of the woodwork. And we take this very seriously. My team is somewhat on the sidelines. Our job is to manage the flow of information, not to plan or analyze or pontificate. That doesn't stop Macallister from thinking that he's in the center of it all, so he's made our lives miserable for the last week.

Typically, my team's function is records management. But, part of our job is also to maintain contact among FBI program staff and with external agencies like the Secret Service, so we are kind of the conduit through which information and records passes. With the sheer volume of work and the quantity of calls coming in due to the presidential visit, we've back-burnered the records management work until things settle down, instead focusing on liaison work. It's certainly more exciting than filing. And it makes us feel like we are a little closer to the front lines.

Though, truth be told, I think we all want to be on the front lines. For no matter what your politics, a presidential visit is still something to behold. Unfortunately for my team and me, the admin staff will be holding down the fort, so to speak, in Chelsea, while the field agents will have the front-row seats to the spectacle.

Like I said, it's all planned to go down tomorrow late afternoon. And like you might imagine, Supervisory Special Agent Bradford Macallister's head has been spinning in circles for the last week or so. It might pop off tomorrow. Let's hope so.

3

TUESDAY, 1:10 AM — THE ATLANTIC OCEAN

WALLOWING NORTHWARD AT seven knots, the darkened, rust-streaked trawler barely warranted a passing glance. Common in these cold waters some sixty-five miles west-southwest of Brazil Rock, Nova Scotia, Canada, with dim running lights, hoisted stabilizers and net gear, and an oily but not particularly dark plume of exhaust smoke, nothing on this particular vessel stood out as it plodded on a northerly course toward the Bay of Fundy.

The wheelhouse was dimly lit. On the engine control panel, perhaps only half of the dials and gauges had functioning backlights. The overhead lighting was off. The helmsman squinted at a yellowish compass light; with the faded numbers on the compass card, it was taxing to read.

Completely out of place on this dilapidated bridge, the unworldly glow of the twelve-inch touchscreen on a Raymarine a eS127 chartplotter was the only source of any real light. And its installation—or lack thereof—was equally incongruous. Designed for a bracket, or maybe for slick flush mounting on an expensive yacht, the unit was hand-held—a trail of three black cables snaked out of its back and disappeared into a cavity under the forward-facing bridge windows.

With a stubby cheroot drooping from a corner of his mouth, his greasy black hair, his pock-marked and sun-darkened skin, and his blackened teeth all but invisible in the night gloom, Mohomed Yilmaz cradled the chartplotter, staring intently at the screen and at an arrow-shaped icon labeled *Flying Lady*. He tapped the icon and a data box popped up: sailing vessel; speed over ground, 8.7 knots; course over ground 084 degrees magnetic; CPA 3.2 nautical miles.

CPA. Closest point of approach.

"Yeterince yakin," he muttered. *Close enough.*

"Vakit geldi," he said in a louder, commanding, but concise tone. *It is time.*

CHAPTER

4

"THIS SHIT IS amazing."

No response.

"No, *really*, how does it know all this stuff?"

Still no response. Of course not. Talking to yourself while alone on watch passed the time.

Miles Lockwood, owner and, for the moment, sole watchstander, sat at the navigation station on his thirty-six-foot racing sailboat, *Flying Lady*. In the darkness, his face was illuminated by a red overhead light and by the glow of the seventeen-inch computer monitor in front of him. Fair skinned, with medium-length, dark-ish blond hair, and two day's-worth of salt-and-pepper stubble on his chin, Miles didn't look boyish, but he was not old, either. His hazel-green eyes, reflecting only the light from the monitor, glinted brightly.

Those eyes carefully studied the seventeen-inch monitor. Running the latest version of Expedition Marine software, the computer screen showed an icon for the boat's location in the middle of an electronic chart, with range lines showing the boat's heading through the water. Elsewhere on the chart, fifteen or so arrow-shaped AIS icons formed a messy line, stretching west to east.

Introduced in 2002, AIS, or Automatic Identification System, was transformative technology at sea. Most commercial vessels were required to have an AIS transponder with the ability to send and receive AIS transmissions. And in growing numbers, recreational vessels had at least an AIS receiver. In the small world of offshore sailboat racing, AIS transponders were generally required by race regulations.

Piggybacking on the radio waves used for VHF radio transmissions, an AIS transponder, attached to its own GPS antenna, sent a short packet of data—vessel name, identification number, position, speed, and course. If a receiving vessel had an AIS compatible chartplotter, surrounding traffic was plotted in real time. The safety implications of the technology were both obvious and real.

In sailboat racing, the tactical gain of knowing where your competition was, how fast they were sailing and in what direction, changed the game. The little, arrow-shaped icons were Miles's competition, and as he studied his screen, he was happy with what he saw. *Flying Lady* was leading the pack, having reached the fair current twisting out of the Bay of Fundy which now helped to propel him faster toward the finish. The boats behind had not yet reached the current line and were slowly but inexorably lagging further behind Miles.

The biannual Marblehead-to-Halifax Ocean Race was billed as the longest-running ocean sailboat competition, first being contested in 1905. The 2017 edition of the race had commenced about thirty-six hours ago on Sunday, July 9, under sunny skies and with a fine southerly breeze. The seventy-five-boat fleet started with two short legs along the shores of Marblehead, Massachusetts, for the benefit of spectators, and then turned to head in an easterly direction for the 363-mile race to Halifax, Nova Scotia, Canada.

One of the ten classes in the race was the doublehanded division, for boats sailed by only two crewmembers. Unlike the remainder of the fleet, the doublehanded boats were allowed to use autopilots. Therefore, one crew member could sleep while the other stood watch, tended to sail trim, and navigated the boat, while the autopilot handled the helming.

On *Flying Lady*, Miles and crewmate George Lakeland had nick-named their French-made autopilot "François." Sometimes they called it "Frank." And occasionally, when François's circuits did something unusual and unexpected, or, as Miles and George liked to imagine, took a smoke break for a Galloiuse, they called it "What The Fuck."

Fortunately, those intermissions were less frequent as bugs had been worked out of the NKE electronics system on *Flying Lady*, and for the past two hours or so, François had driven the boat perfectly.

Feeling good about not only the boat's position, but also with her excellent boatspeed now that the sea breeze had filled in after a light wind and slow start to the race, Miles reached into the cooler on the floorboards just forward of the navigation station and grabbed a Red Bull, hoping for one last caffeine hit to get him through the last forty-five minutes or so of his watch. Before heading up the companionway to get back on deck, he took one last glance at the computer screen. On the bottom left corner of the chart, a new arrow icon had appeared. Quickly, Miles grabbed the mouse and hovered the cursor above the icon. Fishing vessel; speed over ground 6.9 knots; course over ground 008 degrees magnetic; CPA 3.2 nautical miles "Three miles and crossing my course well behind," Miles said out loud to himself. "No problem." And he bounded back up on deck.

Below, cocooned in a sleeping bag, George snored.

CHAPTER
5

"BAŞLATMAK." IN GUTTURAL, nicotine-laced Turkish, the word was concise. An order. No room for negotiation or interpretation.

Launch.

On the wide aft deck of the trawler, two men strained against the inertia of a thirteen-foot-five-inch Zodiac ERB 400. The military-spec, hard bottomed Rigid Inflatable Boat (RIB) weighed only 145 pounds without crew or engine. However, now the RIB topped some 2,300 pounds, resting on cylindrical rollers nested into the trawler's open aft deck, built into the ramp area formerly used to pull fishing nets aboard. The Zodiac was fully inflated but listing to one side, equipped with an outboard engine and loaded with four black, jerry-can type containers and one big duffel bag. Five men sat aboard, perched on the inflated tubes, with two long, matte-black boxes on the floor of the craft at their feet.

On the trawler's aft deck, two strong deckhands grunted as they pulled forward, gaining a two-to-one advantage by using a tackle that was designed to slide the Zodiac aft on the greased rollers.

As the trawler crested a small swell, the angle of the deck changed just enough to overcome the inertia of Zodiac. Aided by the tackle and the exertions of the two deckhands, the Zodiac started to move on the rollers and, accelerating, dropped smoothly over the low fantail of the trawler and into the sea.

For a moment, the Zodiac appeared to be linked to the trawler, the bow of the smaller craft kissing the steel transom of the lumbering fishing boat as it was towed along by only the drag of the wake. The deckhands had dropped their lines; dead-ended on the trawler, they would simply pull through the blocks on the Zodiac. Slowly at first, then quickly as the distance opened and the drag effect of the wake lessened, the Zodiac separated from the much larger ship and disappeared into the gloom.

Gazing at the spot where the Zodiac once was, the two deckhands listlessly coiled the tackle lines, staring at the wake of the trawler. Winded by the task of pulling a ton of deadweight, neither man noticed that Mohomed had come down on deck or that he was holding a raised Makarov pistol. Likewise, neither man felt the sensation as a bullet entered their heads, the quick *POP! POP!* of the unsilenced Makarov's two shots blending into the clanging noise of the hoisted stabilizers.

Mohomed tossed the pistol in the wake. Working quickly, he grabbed the tackle line nearest to him and efficiently tied both men's ankles, then wrists, together. One man groaned. Agony. Pain. He was not blessed with a clean shot. His eyes fluttered open and met Mohomed's.

Startled and momentarily spooked by the gaze of the not-yet-dead deckhand, Mohomed shook off the sensation and resumed his work. Death would come for the launch man soon enough.

With a few quick spins, he released the shackle on the dead-end of the tackle line, removing the shackle from the welded ring on the side of the trawler fantail. Grunting, Mohomed slid a 150-pound iron weight onto the roller—conveniently placed there weeks ago for this very purpose. Attaching the shackle to the ring on the weight, Mohomed gave the tackle line a quick tug. Pointless, really. Almost a reflex action, nothing more.

With a sustained push, Mohomed got the weight moving on the aft-most roller. Picking up speed, it followed the Zodiac's path, dropping over the fantail of the trawler. But, unlike the Zodiac, the weight did not linger in the wake—it dropped straight toward the bottom, some 50 fathoms, or 300 feet, below the surface of the water.

Predictably, the tackle line followed the weight while Mohomed watched impassively. The tackle line suddenly came taut—yanking the two tied-together deckhands unceremoniously off the back of the trawler. Mohomed kept his gaze purposely unfocused. He did not want to risk another look at a dead man's living eyes.

"Insha'Allah," Mohomed muttered.

He knew full well that the tackle line might eventually chafe through, or simply disintegrate altogether, but that would take many weeks. And the bloated bodies, if not eaten by sea critters, might then float to the surface. It would not matter.

"Üç hafta." *Three weeks.*

He smiled grimly as he made his way back to the bridge of the trawler, taking the rusty steps two at a time. In three weeks, he'd be back home in Europe, the mission completed. The United States would be in chaos and the Great Satan would be brought to its knees in terror.

CHAPTER
6

THE MAN WHO CALLED HIMSELF Omar watched impatiently as the bow of the Zodiac RIB kissed the steel transom of the lumbering fishing boat, towed along by only the drag of the bigger vessel's wake. Fidgeting with his round eyeglasses and absently stroking his full, gray beard, he waited out the several seconds as the larger ship finally separated from the little craft, the trawler continuing to wallow northward.

On his right wrist was a Casio digital watch set to stopwatch mode. As the trawler disappeared into the gloom, Omar clicked the top right button and the seconds began advancing.

With a quick glance around the Zodiac, confirming that the other four men were seated and that the two long black boxes were evenly placed on the floor of the craft, Omar reached back to the tiller handle of the Torqeedo outboard motor. He'd trained with it previously, and it never ceased to amaze him. A twist of the throttle handle and the motor purred to life. Instant torque and acceleration; no ignition; and, other than a whine, virtually no noise. Fully electric, with a heavy, lithium-ion battery pack integrated into the casing of the motor, it generated power equivalent to that of an 80-horsepower gasoline engine—which would not only have required a heavy starter battery, as well as gas and oil, but also would have been substantially louder.

The heavily-laden Zodiac reached full speed in seconds, touching 18 knots, overtaking, then passing, the trawler. The man seated directly in front of Omar held an iPad. The device, which had a compass app already running onscreen, was angled toward Omar's line of sight. The heading that Mohomed had given Omar before the "launch" command was 025 degrees—and the iPad screen showed, to Omar's pleasure, 025 degrees. The Zodiac barreled forward into the night, skimming over the shallow swells, the wake of the boat making no more noise than the whine of the electric engine.

In training, they had been drilled with the speed, time, and distance variables, testing the Zodiac over and over. At 20 knots, in one minute, about a third of a mile. With the swell, Omar knew they would run slightly slower. Three miles to go—about nine minutes.

Omar knew from their research than the sailboat's LED masthead navigation light had a visual range of two miles. At three minutes past launch, the spotter should see a green light. Worst case, the nav lights would be off, so at six minutes past launch, if he did not see the light, Omar could use the hand-held VHF radio clipped to his chest harness. Mohomed would be angry with him for breaking radio silence, but, frankly, Omar didn't care. He'd never see Mohomed again, never have to listen to the guttural Turkish, smell the man's disgusting cigarettes, or even smell the man himself. Omar smiled. For the first time in weeks, his nostrils were clear. The dank, salty ocean air was not desert air, but it was still refreshing.

With the compass app wobbling between 019 and 032, Omar was confident that his piloting was good and that his course was true. The little Zodiac sped along, not a word spoken on the boat. The first minute passed, then the second. The Torqeedo ran on with an annoying whine, but the men were used to it from their training runs. Another minute. The electric motor could run for almost thirty minutes at full throttle before the built-in battery pack depleted to a zero-charge state.

One more minute counted by on the face of the Casio watch, and for the men in the RIB, a new challenge—as a sense of vertigo started to set in. With no moon or any real frames of reference, except, perhaps, the angle of the swell, it could become very easy to lose track of direction. Omar focused on the dancing number on the iPad screen, fixated on keeping it within a degree or two, alternating his gaze between the waves and the screen, trying to anticipate the movements of the boat as it was worked by the swell. On training runs, Omar had disliked this sensation, but now, on the *real* mission, he began to enjoy it. A child of the desert sands, which moved and shifted very much like the water, he smiled to himself.

"Lumière!" His musings were interrupted by the spotter's voice calling out in French. *Light!* Omar glanced up. Five or ten degrees to the right of his course, a green light had appeared. A sliver of white stern light also showed.

It must be the one.

Annoyed by the spotter's outburst in his native tongue, Omar hissed "Seb, English only!" Kneeling between the junction of the forward ends of the tubes at the front of the Zodiac, Seb's shoulders sank as the curly, brown-haired man with an unruly beard steeled himself for his next task, one where he would not have the option to make such a petty mistake.

As he made a smooth course correction, Omar couldn't decide if he was more disappointed in the spotter's breach of training protocol, or the variance off course. *It should have been directly in front*, he thought to himself. Obviously, it was going a little faster than Mohomed anticipated when he gave Omar the heading.

He tapped the man in front of him on the shoulder; with a flick of a wrist, the iPad was tossed into the water—the device no longer needed. Omar focused on the navigation light at the top of the sailboat's mast, getting brighter and rising, slowly and almost imperceptibly, off the water as the distance closed between the two boats on the dark Atlantic waves.

CHAPTER

7

GEORGE LAKELAND PRIDED himself on always being on time to start his watch. His internal clock was tuned to the sea. After thousands of miles of ocean sailboat racing, his stocky body anticipated the watch change. And so, a half-hour before he was due to relieve Miles, he was wide awake, ready to get dressed in his gear and to grab a snack. Back home, he could distinguish between the noises each of his three children made during their sleep, and on the boat, his senses were equally tuned. By feeling the motion of the boat and listening to the sound of the water, he could almost instantly determine the sea state and the boat's speed.

He unzipped his sleeping bag, ran a hand through his short, salt-and-pepper hair, rubbed the sleep from his brown eyes, and slithered out of the confines of his bunk. As was his custom, he'd check conditions on deck—prairie dogging, as Miles referred to the habit. George would pop his head out of the companionway hatch and look around to get a sense of the temperature and the breeze. If the hatch was slid closed, it signaled rain.

Tonight, it was wide open.

Normally, George liked to make a comment, joke, or some sort of verbal joust to announce himself, but he immediately sensed something different. Miles was standing by the wheel, not staring upward at sail trim or forward at waves, but facing the back of the boat, intently looking over the right-side, starboard aft quarter. "What's up?" asked George.

Miles turned his shoulders slightly but did not turn his head. "Hey." He didn't even so much as glance at George. His focus remained out over the sea. *Flying Lady* was moving well. The breeze out of the south was gusting at about twelve knots, the sea state was a minor swell, and the boat was ripping along on an easterly route heading toward Halifax at almost nine knots—flying a full mainsail and a "code zero" headsail. Perfect conditions. She was made for this type of sailing.

"Are we in the fair current yet?" asked George. "What's wrong with you? What are you staring at?"

"Yeah, we got the current," Miles spoke absently, then his tone turned sharp. "You hear that?"

Given his crewmate's obvious concern, George stepped onto the deck, forgoing a layer of warm clothes and his safety gear. He stood in the cockpit slightly behind Miles, his hand on the starboard primary winch, his eyes angled to follow the direction of Miles's gaze. Cocking his head slightly, George heard it too. An eerie whine, too consistent to be anything but man-made, getting increasingly louder by the second.

With a swift motion, Miles spun and, almost cat-like, bounded around George to the companionway. Smoothly, he dropped below deck. After hours and hours of experience on this boat, he did not need to look around to find the handholds, even in the black of night. George figured that Miles would take a look at the computer screen; he'd study it for less than twenty seconds, assessing the data that flowed constantly on the monitor, looking for AIS targets, checking that *Flying Lady* was still on course, tracking straight, and listening to the interior noises of the boat. Then he would reach under the seat of the nav station and grab the Q-beam, a one-million-candlepower spotlight. Miles could discern meaning from just about any noise his own boat made, and he disliked noises that he could not understand.

Buried under the nav seat, the Q-beam was entangled in a mess of gear. With the boat having been on starboard tack for much of the past ten hours, the gear had settled. Miles reached into the cavity and, by feel, found the spotlight—just as he heard a new noise.

POP!

Then, a much louder noise and an echo inside the boat, as George's body thudded onto the fiberglass deck.

CHAPTER

8

THE SHADOWY SHAPE OF the sailboat materialized in front of the Zodiac. A white hull glinted in what little light there was, a black mainsail with bright green, glow-in-the-dark draft stripes, a grayish headsail, partially blocked from view by the main, and, low to the deck at the base of the mast, garishly red instrument displays. The masthead tri-color LED shone brightly—green, then white, as the Zodiac closed the distance at more than twice the speed of the silently-moving sailboat.

A single human shape stood on the starboard side of the sailboat, staring directly at the Zodiac as it crossed the sailboat's wake. At the bow of the Zodiac, Seb crouched, carefully balancing his body while cradling a Russian-made pistol and waiting a split-second for the Zodiac to bounce over the stern wave from the sailboat—and then he pulled the trigger firmly.

POP!

The Makarov spat a round and the human shape collapsed to the deck of the sailboat. Seb had practiced this shot over and over again, and while it may not have been a clean kill shot, it would buy them the precious seconds they needed.

Omar expertly guided the Zodiac along the left side of the much larger sailboat. He did not want to damage the hull of the sailboat—in fact, he needed it intact. Though they had trained repeatedly, there were several unpredictable variables to contend with: the weather on the night of the intercept, what angle the sailboat would be at when they made contact, what speed it would be going, or how much it would be heeling over. They were fortunate it was a relatively calm night, making Omar's task easier, as the perfectionist glided his little boat into position on the port side of *Flying Lady*.

Seb, at the front of the Zodiac, kept the sights of the Makarov on the prone man lying in the cockpit of the sailboat. As the two boats touched, he vaulted over the sailboat's lifelines and onto its deck. He had to be fast, making sure the crew of the sailboat had no time to make a radio call. That was why they picked their target from the doublehanded division. Only two men would be aboard, and one of them was already splayed out on the cockpit floor. He was alive, but clearly wounded.

They had counted on their middle-of-the-night timing to better the odds that only one sailor was on deck. With the Zodiac humming alongside, now throttled down to match the sailboat's speed, the highest-priority task was to find the other sailor. Miles unwittingly accomplished that mission for the man who was now aboard his boat—popping his head out of the companionway, Q-beam in hand, useless, as he gaped at the maw of Seb's Makarov.

"Don't move," said the voice behind the barrel, in French-accented English. Miles froze, and in the dim light, he could make out a brown-haired man with an unruly beard on the deck of his boat. Breaking the one-eyed stare of the Makarov, Miles cast his eyes downward, as he focused in panic at a rivulet of blood crossing the cockpit floor.

The wellspring of that rivulet groaned, and Miles belatedly realized that it was George, lying motionless.

Moments began to blur together. As he watched, incrementally moving his head, Miles could hear the quiet voices speaking to one another.

"Secure to board two more." Two men, similar in looks with close-cropped dark hair and weeks-old dark beards, and similar in stature with medium builds, climbed up from the humming Zodiac and clambered over the lifelines of the sailboat.

A fourth man, broad-shouldered, powerful, and blond-haired, moved to the bow of the Zodiac and passed a rope across to the men who had just boarded the sailboat.

"Make fast the boat."

"Done."

The Zodiac's electric engine went silent. The little boat was now being dragged along by the sailboat, whose boatspeed, according to the red digital numbers on the mast, had dropped to below five knots due to the parasite now secured to her port side.

In the Zodiac, Omar looked at his stopwatch.

Eleven minutes. Very good.

"Transmissions?" he asked.

"Not likely," was the accented response from behind the Makarov.

"The boxes."

From the Zodiac, Omar and the big, blond-haired man, the two remaining men aboard, carefully hefted one of the long, matte-black boxes up to the lifelines of the sailboat, straining under the weight and struggling to maintain their balance in the tippy little RIB.

Above, on the sailboat, Seb didn't move, his gunsight still fixed on Miles's face. The two other boarders received the long chest and placed it gingerly on the deck of *Flying Lady*. The task was repeated for the second box. Less than two minutes per box, and they were both aboard the sailboat on the port side.

"Pass up the cans," said one of the men.

A moment later, and with much less precision than the two big boxes, the four black jerry cans were passed onto the boat.

"Gear bag."

Omar hefted the big, waterproof duffel bag over the lifelines and then climbed aboard the sailboat. Four of the five men were now aboard the sailboat.

Omar looked at George, then to Miles, then back at George. "This one," he said pointing to George.

Miles watched in terror, heart racing but afraid to move his head in the slightest. Seb didn't flinch a muscle—the barrel never wavered off Miles's face—as the two almost-identical men hoisted George off the cockpit floor. Weak and in intense pain, George still tried to twist away from the strong hands, to no avail. Dispassionately, the two men swung

George over the lifelines and dropped him into the Zodiac, where he landed on his back, spread-eagled, facing up to the inky sky.

Still aboard the Zodiac, the blond-haired man pulled a wad of zip-ties from his chest harness. He tightly bound George's legs and wrists to the handholds on the Zodiac's tubes. Powerless, fatigued, and overwhelmed, George could do nothing but watch, helplessly.

Using George's gut as a step stool, the blond man climbed out of the Zodiac and onto the sailboat, leaving George behind, alone and strapped to the little craft.

Once aboard, the blond drew his own Makorov pistol from his chest harness and trained its sights on Miles. Now relieved of this task, Seb lowered his weapon and awkwardly made his way to the back of the sailboat, where he crouched on the low, left side of the slowly-moving *Flying Lady*.

Seb had not practiced this task during their training. Eagerly and almost joyfully, he peppered the tubes of the Zodiac with bullets. Air hissed from the tubes as he changed magazines and, taking care to miss George's splayed-out body, Seb shot holes into the bottom of the boat. Water began to bubble into the RIB as it deflated and flooded. The craft began to sink stern down under the weight of the Torqeedo motor.

Omar looked forward at the mast; the boatspeed indicator was dropping as the drag from the sinking Zodiac increased. Five knots . . . then four . . . three. The Zodiac's stern was completely underwater, its bow held up by the taut line that secured it to *Flying Lady*, and George's body, strapped immobile to the bottom of the craft, was also half-submerged. Omar and Seb made their way to the very stern of the sailboat, making it possible for them to see into the now-precariously tilted Zodiac RIB.

Omar addressed George in perfect English, "You are the first casualty of this war. Perhaps you will be remembered in the history books." Seb looked at Omar, who nodded and then locked eyes with Miles with a menacing glare. Turning his attention back to the body in the Zodiac, Seb took careful aim at George's forehead, then squeezed the trigger one last time.

"Cut it," commanded Omar, and the Zodiac's tether was severed with a sharp blade. The last bit of remaining air hissed from the bow tubes as the boat sank in the wake of *Flying Lady*. Not a trace of the little craft remained.

Omar glanced to where the Zodiac had disappeared and turned back to face Miles. "I want you to remember that I spared your friend from a painful death by drowning as that boat went to the bottom. I will grant you the same courtesy when your time comes, but only if you cooperate. Do we understand each other, Mr. Lockwood?"

Miles stared, taken aback. This man knew his name. This was bad. *Very* bad. His fate was clearly written. All he could do was nod dejectedly.

Without the parasitic drag of the Zodiac, *Flying Lady* had accelerated to almost nine knots of boatspeed. "Drop the forward sail," demanded Omar.

Miles looked at the barrel of the Makarov, still pointed at him, then at Omar. The barrel dropped, but the weapon was not holstered. "I'm gonna furl the sail, instead of drop it. Okay?" Miles said to Omar, who tilted his head in question.

Fuck it, thought Miles. *I'll do it my way.* He stood and, with practiced motions, grabbed the furling line of the code zero in one hand and the sheet in the other hand. Easing the sheet, he pulled the furling line. The sail twisted around itself as Miles rolled it into a tight, vertical cylinder—still hoisted, but powerless. Boatspeed dropped to six knots.

Impressed by the sailor's skills, Omar nodded and, peering up at the black mainsail, stated, "Now, this one."

"I gotta turn the boat into the wind first," said Miles. Omar once again tilted his head. He was comfortable enough on the Zodiac, but he had much less confidence on the sailboat until the motor was engaged. Miles reached to his chest and showed the pirate the NKE remote fob that dangled around his neck, secured with a neon yellow line—an ugly, ungainly necklace. Without waiting for a signal of consent, Miles pressed the *10>* button seven times in quick succession, initiating a seventy-degree course change to the right, almost into the wind. The autopilot reacted instantly. The boat spun to starboard, almost throwing four of the five boarders off their balance. Omar, calm and collected, did not react to the sudden movement.

As the boat turned, without so much as a glance at his captor, Miles opened the clutch that held the mainsail halyard. The sail dropped fast, gathering on the deck on top of the long boxes in an untidy pile to port, and the boat, now without the magic of the wind powering it, slowed. Ungainly without her sails, *Flying Lady* squatted, began to roll uncomfortably in the swell, and stopped.

CHAPTER
9

THE TRAWLER HAD STARTED TO rock back and forth on the ocean swell that ran almost perpendicular to the trawler's course of 075 degrees magnetic. On the Raymarine screen, Mohomed had been watching the arrow icon depicting the target, which had been maintaining a steady course but now appeared almost stationary. As he'd been doing repeatedly for the last half hour, he tapped the icon and a data box popped up. Sailing vessel; speed over ground, 0.3 knots; course over ground 135 degrees magnetic. Mohomed knew from data that the target was close to, if not completely, stopped in the water—and its movement on AIS reflected the current flowing out of the Bay of Fundy, taking the boat along with it.

With a slightly northerly bias to her eastward course, the trawler was slowly closing the distance to the sailboat, which was still over two miles away.

Mohomed glanced up at the overhead, where a VHF radio was mounted on brackets, its faint orange digital display showing channel 16. In front of him, on the ledge below the bridge windows, were three handheld VHF radios—one on channel 9, one on 13, and the last one on 72. He picked up the radio monitoring 72 and twisted the volume knob clockwise to the maximum.

Any moment now . . .

Seconds passed as Mohomed clutched the radio, staring at it. Nothing.

Then, suddenly, a sharp burst of static, followed by four more bursts one second apart, crackled through the radio speaker. Mohomed knew that Omar, with precision as usual, had clicked the transmit button on his handheld VHF radio five times. He smiled. The signal confirmed that Omar was in command of the sailboat. No signal would have meant trouble, and though there was, of course, a contingency plan for that, it was better that the boarding had gone successfully.

Mohomed settled back to wait to see if the second signal would be transmitted.

CHAPTER
10

MILES LOCKWOOD HAD JUST finished folding the mainsail into a tidy, flaked pile, secured by ribbon-like sail ties, onto the boom of his boat when an alarm started to sound—a persistent, high-pitched *BEEP, BEEP, BEEP*—continuing without pause. The boarders looked at each other, then at Miles.

"What is that noise? What is beeping?" demanded Omar of Miles, who shrugged. Omar looked around, wildly. His crew, too, was unnerved. The beeping was incessant.

"Boat stopped. The autopilot can't keep a course. It doesn't like that." Miles reached to his neck lanyard fob and pressed the *STOP* button. The *Flying Lady* continued to wallow in the swell, but the beeping noise ceased. Miles was pleased with his little victory.

"Show me the controls," Omar demanded, "and start the engine." Gesturing toward the companionway hatch, Miles replied, "Batteries first." Omar looked around, confused. Clearly, the batteries were on, as evidenced by the navigation lights and the dancing red numbers on the mast displays.

"No, start the motor. *Now!*" exclaimed Omar.

Miles shrugged and pointed to the recessed box on the starboard cockpit side, behind the steering wheel. A chromed throttle control was mounted just behind a small engine control panel. Seb, who had remained standing toward the back of the boat after murdering George, clambered around the wheel, knelt in front of the controls and, after a brief inspection, pushed the throttle control to a vertical position and turned a key.

Below deck, the three-cylinder Yanmar diesel coughed, turned over, groaned listlessly, then went silent. The red displays had dimmed on the mast. Omar glared at Miles, who smiled ever so slightly. Emboldened by his second token victory, Miles spoke clearly and authoritatively. "I told you, batteries first. Gotta switch 'em over."

Omar, annoyed at these gestures of resistance, continued staring at Miles. With exaggerated movements, the powerful blond-haired man refocused the aim of his Makarov on Miles. At a subtle wave of Omar's hand, the Makarov was lowered slightly. *This Lockwood man might be difficult*, Omar thought, but he'd faced worse.

"Very well. You have taught me a little lesson, no? You are still in command of your little ship. Forgive my lack of comprehension." Omar bowed his head slightly. "Please, show me."

Surprised, and suspicious of the change in tone and the elaborate language, Miles nevertheless led Omar to the companionway. Below deck, Miles pointed to the side of the base of the seat at the navigation station. He reached for a circular red housing with a black, triangle-shaped switch, explaining, "It's on the house battery now. The autopilot uses a lot of juice. Needs to be on the 'both' setting to parallel the start battery in." Miles rotated the switch one click clockwise. "She'll start now."

Omar called up, "Again, Seb." Back at the helm, the shooter twisted the key again, and the Yanmar started instantly, idling smoothly.

With the motor on the sailboat running, Omar began to bark his commands.

"Seb, idle speed, course—due south. Bruce, John—boxes below deck. Hans, you're on Mr. Lockwood. Don't let him touch anything."

Miles, visibly stunned, processed the commands. He was expecting no names, and certainly not Anglo and European names. "Well . . . you know my name." Imitating Omar's flowery language, he asked, "What, pray tell, shall I call you?"

Still standing in the companionway, Omar did not appear amused. Straightening, he looked down at Miles, and from his heightened position of authority, spat, "They call me Omar." Two of the men on deck laughed.

Omar smiled. "I'm beginning to like it. You may call me Omar."

CHAPTER

11

ALL THE DOCUMENTS pertaining to the Marblehead-to-Halifax Ocean Race were online on one website—a list of boat entries, crew lists, tips for logistics, ads for sponsors, photos and results from past races, and instructions for the current year's race.

The race instructions were complex and comprehensive. They set out, naturally, the basics—dates, times, course, scoring, and so forth. And they included requirements for safety, among which was a requirement that each competitor carry enough fuel to run the boat under power for eight hours.

Always eager for even the most minuscule advantage, sailboat racers stripped as much unnecessary weight off their boats; less weight generally equated to more speed. At the slow speeds of sailboats, where boat speeds are measured in hundredths and a "fast" boat is still slower than an average weekend runner out for a morning jog, weight, and the resulting hundredths of boatspeed to potentially be gained, was important to these competitors—and, therefore, a quantity of fuel above the minimum requirement would be unnecessary weight.

Thanks to the wealth of information online, it had been easy for Omar to prepare. *Flying Lady* was a 2012 J/111. The online technical specifications on the J/boats website showed that the J/111 sailboat had an eighteen-gallon fuel tank and a twenty-one-horsepower Yanmar 3YM20 diesel engine. The Yanmar website included performance and consumption charts for its various engines. At 3,000 RPM, the little diesel engine drank about three-quarters of a gallon per hour and would push the boat at about seven knots of boatspeed. Therefore, thanks to the race regulations, Omar estimated that the boat would have at least six gallons of fuel on board.

The mission parameters estimated that they would need as much as thirty hours of range, or a more than a full tank of fuel. To give himself a reserve, Omar had brought the four five-gallon jerry cans of diesel, giving him twenty gallons, plus whatever amount of diesel was in the boat's fuel tank. With his usual precision, he would not leave this item to chance. And worst case, if he needed to conserve fuel, he would force Miles Lockwood to sail the boat for him.

Omar had studied the race entry list exhaustively to pick his target. A boat in the doublehanded class was a must. One that was an unknown was a plus. One that was captained by a first-timer to the race was also an advantage. And after that process of elimination, Miles Lockwood's *Flying Lady* emerged as the diamond in the rough.

Aboard his hijacked boat, Miles was forced forward—ostensibly to stay out of the way, but mostly, he surmised, so that he did not attempt to reach the radio. He briefly contemplated grabbing the EPIRB, the stand-alone "Emergency Position-Indicating Radio Beacon" safety device that was mounted below on his boat that, if triggered, would notify the US and Canadian Coast Guards of a vessel in distress, but he surmised that it would be quickly deactivated or destroyed by Omar's team before getting a position fix and transmitting a distress message.

He had no choice but to comply.

Meanwhile, the strange, long boxes were brought below deck. The big blond man joined Omar in the cabin as two other men on deck manhandled one box into position at the mouth of the companionway hatch. Clearly heavy, it was slowly passed below, with grunts. The men placed it on the port side "settee," a cushioned bench on one side of the cabin that could also serve as a bunk. Miles had slept there many times and his six-foot-one frame fit comfortably on the bench. The box looked to be about the same size as Miles, perhaps a smidge over six-feet long, and maybe two-feet wide and two-feet tall.

The practice from the first box facilitated the move of the second box, as the men gingerly passed it below and set it down on the opposite, starboard side bench.

Based on the sounds made by the men as they lowered their cargo into place, Miles guessed that they were not only heavy, but also perhaps fragile. The boxes appeared to be fiberglass, painted or perhaps molded in a matte black color, devoid of any markings. A seam ran horizontally along the sides of each box, perhaps three inches down from the top itself. Below the seam was a series of screwheads. No hinges were visible.

They look a lot like very plain coffins, thought Miles.

Whatever they were, Miles's instincts told him that they were bad.

CHAPTER

12

ABOARD THE TRAWLER, Mohomed fidgeted with the Raymarine, zooming in to the *Flying* Lady icon on the chart displayed on the sleek device's screen. With the trawler now angled north of east, Mohomed had closed the distance between the two vessels to just over one mile. In fact, through the dirty port side windows of the bridge, he could see the masthead navigation light on the sailboat, which showed both red and green lights. The sailboat was aimed directly at the trawler.

At 2:00 AM precisely, his attention was focused on the array of VHF radios, as he waited for a second signal. The radios remained silent which meant that further action on his part was not required. With a slight, relieved smile, Mohomed tapped at the compass and the helmsman complied immediately, turning the trawler to the right until the trawler's course showed 120 degrees magnetic.

Mohomed sighed. He'd watched the screen of the Raymarine plotter as the AIS icon of *Flying Lady* had slowed and wobbled around a bit. This device was truly magical, he thought. It was far superior to his ancient Trimble GPS that only showed latitude and longitude, and required him to manually plot his position on a paper chart. He'd started the journey doing just that, for sake of appearance if boarded, so that a paper chart would be up to date with the trawler's current position marked in pencil. After two weeks at sea, though, the willpower to make it look like he was navigating on paper had diminished, especially since he had this wonderful plotter. He should probably update the paper chart, he thought, but he reconsidered. His course would take him further and further from the coastline of Nova Scotia, back out to open sea.

He was tired. He'd never been this far from home. His trawler had been modified to make the long trip, its fish hold converted with giant plastic bladders into fuel tanks. The 2,700-nautical-mile journey back across the Atlantic would take another two weeks, the trawler getting progressively faster as it burned diesel and lightened itself. He looked forward to passing through the Straits of Gibraltar in fourteen days where he could take on fuel for the final 1,700 miles to his home port in Bodrum, Turkey, and where he would regain service for his mobile phone and would be able to search the internet for stories the destruction that he had helped to make.

And while the trawler transited the last leg of its trip, through the Mediterranean Sea to his home port of Bodrum, he'd be able to confirm that the rest of the money was in his account. Omar had shown him the wire instructions and assured him that the transfer was irreversible. It would make the long trip and the training worthwhile, he thought pleasantly. He'd pay his four crewmen and sell the trawler, not that he'd need the paltry sum fetched by the dilapidated little ship, not with the two-hundred-thousand American dollars in cash that Omar had given him, and certainly not with the one million euros that would be deposited in his bank account seven days from now.

He felt something, a tinge of remorse perhaps, for killing the two deckhands. He never even knew their names, they were just two men that the man Omar had brought with him, who had taken turns guarding the two long boxes until yesterday, when it was their task to inflate the Zodiac and to mount the heavy gray outboard motor. Mohomed was glad to finally have all of these strangers off his ship, and he sat back, content.

Below him, in the fish-hold bowels of his trawler, adjacent to one of the massive, temporary fuel bladders, a digital clock continued a countdown, displaying 45:50:32 . . . 45:50:31 . . . 45:50:30 . . .

CHAPTER

13

WITH THE BOXES SAFELY below in the cabin of the sailboat, Omar relaxed slightly. "On deck, now, please," he said to his broad-shouldered, blond-haired coffin-helper. "You, too," he added, looking at Miles.

On the Expedition screen, Omar noted the icon of the trawler, now over one mile away to his south and opening distance by the minute on a course of 120 degrees. The trawler was headed home, no longer needed, and it was time for Omar to make his course correction.

Once on deck, Omar pointed to the furled, but still hoisted, "code zero" headsail, commanding Miles, "Remove that sail."

With practiced motions, Miles arranged a halyard around a winch, opened a clutch on the cabin top, and went forward on his boat, taking the halyard tail with him. With one hand he eased the halyard, and with the other arm, he reached for the sausage-shaped furled sail as it dropped toward him on the foredeck of *Flying Lady*. Faster and faster he dropped the halyard as the sail plopped on deck around him. He opened the forward hatch and started to stuff the sail inside, glancing up to see his broad-shouldered, powerful, blond-haired guard, Hans, watching his every move.

Miles considered dropping a line from the sail overboard, fouling the propeller and stopping the boat, but he quickly rethought that idea. *What would they do? They'd just dive the prop and cut the line free, then kill me. And then do whatever they are planning.* No, he figured, better to wait and see, and he carefully unfastened the lines from the sail and stowed everything away properly.

Toward the back of the boat, Omar watched carefully, scanning the deck and cockpit of the slowly-idling sailboat. The boxes had been stowed, the gear bag had been passed below, and the four jerry cans of diesel had been lined up in the cockpit. All was in order.

"Seb. Speed seven knots, course two-seven-six," Omar said. "And you, Mr. Lockwood, you and Hans come with me. We have a message to send."

Omar backed down the companionway ladder, his eyes on Miles. With a forlorn look at Seb behind the wheel of his boat, and with Hans's hand prodding him on a shoulder, Miles followed.

On deck, Seb advanced the throttle and spun the wheel to the right. As the sleek white boat gained speed, a bow wave splitting from her sides as she cleaved the water, leaving Nova Scotia behind, *Flying Lady* carved toward the west, headed back toward the direction she had come from.

The Massachusetts coastline.

CHAPTER
14

BELOW DECK, MILES, STILL BEING watched by Hans's unwavering eyes, was shoved into the seat at the navigation table. He looked passively at Omar, who leaned toward him, instructing, "Send a message to your race organizers. You are retiring from the race with unrepairable mainsail damage. You are returning to Marblehead, using the motor."

At the nav table, Miles took the Iridium satellite telephone from its bracket and powered it on. "I need the information from in there," he said, pointing to the navigation table. Omar nodded and Miles raised the hinged cover of the table to reveal a cavity stuffed with papers, charts, and a binder. Flipping through the pages of the binder, Miles found a page within the printed race instructions that included a list of phone numbers and email addresses.

"No phone call. You can email them," stated Omar. Not a question, a demand.

"No. Not on this boat. Some boats have better set-ups. I can only get weather data and make calls through the sat phone. And send texts."

"Very well. You will text them," Omar agreed.

Miles looked at the phone which had completed its boot routine. He entered the phone number, then started tapping out the body of a text message, three key-pushes at a time. Slowly, methodically, he corrected several errors. He was not accustomed to this style of texting. Omar watched every input.

MHOR RC. FLYING LADY. WE ARE RETIRING FROM THE RACE WITH A TORN, UNREPAIRABLE MAINSAIL. RETURNING TO MARBLEHEAD UNDER POWER. MILES LOCKWOOD.

Miles replaced the phone in its bracket. "Wait," Omar said. "You haven't sent it. Send it."

Sighing, Miles replied, "It has to go in the bracket which is wired to the antenna on deck. It won't send from down in here." The satellite phone needed a clear view of the sky; Miles had equipped his boat with an external antenna, mounted on the stern rail, connected to the bracket with a thick coaxial cable. He pressed the green button and the characters disappeared, replaced with *MESSAGE SENT.*

"Will they respond?" asked Omar.

"I dunno. I've never done this race before. I've never quit before. In fact, I've never sent a text before with this thing. Only to myself, to test it. I have no idea if it even works out here." Miles shrugged. He hoped the message would not transmit. But he would be wrong.

Several minutes passed in silence. Miles stared at the computer screen. The Expedition software showed *Flying Lady's* westerly course as well as displaying the ragged line of arrow-shaped icons parading east, toward Novia Scotia. His competition. His *former* competition.

Would anyone on those boats be watching, and wondering, why one racer was now headed west? Miles looked at the VHF radio mounted on the bulkhead aside the navigation station and hoped that it would suddenly squawk with chatter from a concerned competitor.

The radio remained silent but, instead, to Miles's dismay, the Iridium phone chimed. Omar reached over to scroll through the words on the tiny screen.

FLYING LADY, MESSAGE RECEIVED. BAD NEWS. DO YOU NEED ASSISTANCE? MHOR RACE CHAIR

Omar, a quick study, pulled the satphone from the bracket and began to tap out a reply.

MHOR RC. NO ASSISTANCE REQUIRED.

"How would you sign off?" Omar asked Miles.

"Prolly say something like 'Over and out' like I was talking on the radio." Omar thought a moment and pecked out:

FLYING LADY OVER AND OUT. END TRANSMISSION

Omar replaced the phone in its bracket as Miles had done, and pressed *SEND*. On the screen: *MESSAGE SENT*. Omar waited a minute, staring at the phone. Miles, too, watched the device. No response. Omar yanked the phone from its bracket, stepped up in the companionway hatch, and hurled the satphone over the rail of the sailboat. "Nice toss, boss!" laughed Seb from the helm as the phone curved a perfect arc over the lifelines and dropped into the sea with a small splash. Seb's voice had a slight accent to it; French perhaps.

A real melting pot, Miles thought, as his only form of communication off this boat sank to the bottom of the Atlantic Ocean.

Life on the *Flying Lady* became considerably less exciting after the message transmission. With Hans guarding him from the main cabin, Miles was sent forward and he arranged himself on his sail pile with a view of the companionway. Omar stayed seated at the nav station, toying with the computer mouse and staring at the screen, while Seb and one man remained on deck. The fifth boarder racked out in one of the aft sleeping berths, wrapping himself in George's sleeping bag.

As the hours ticked by, the hijackers rotated positions, taking turns sleeping, monitoring the computer screen, and watching over Miles. Occasionally, one of them would come below to raid the food provisions in the galley locker or to take a water bottle or Red Bull from the cooler.

In his makeshift prison at the front of his boat, Miles began to work out their watch system, trying to fathom if there was a pattern. It helped to distract him. Because, otherwise, he could do nothing but stare at nothing, with his heart beating fast, and his throat dry, petrified . . . as he waited for a fate that he was certain to be death.

PART TWO
WEDNESDAY, JULY 12, 2017

CHAPTER

15

WEDNESDAY, 1:30 AM — THE ATLANTIC OCEAN

IN THE TWENTY-FOUR HOURS since Miles Lockwood's boat had been taken from him, the wind had dropped when the sun crept up from the eastern horizon in the wake of *Flying Lady*.

As the day had warmed, lulled by the still air of the cabin and perhaps a little dizzy from the awkward motion of a boat meant to sail with the wind, but, instead, had been laboring under the steady drone of the Yanmar, Miles had nodded off. Any sleep he gotten was fitful, at best. As dusk had drawn and with the cabin darkened, he had dozed off again.

Now, just past midnight, he was wide awake. He illuminated the time on his wristwatch with the touch of a button. 1:30 AM.

His resolve had strengthened with the passage of the day. And, now, he waited for his opportunity.

During the past twenty-four hours, Miles had carefully observed his captors. While they were obviously unfamiliar with the idea of sailing, they had appeared proficient enough with the boat under power, and they had kept to a reasonably structured schedule.

Two of the men had been consistently stationed on deck. From his distant view from the bow area of his boat, Miles could see that they occasionally traded places: one drove the boat, the other was a lookout. Though he could not hear voices from that distance, Miles had not seen the men conversing; they had sat separately, apart.

Below deck, two men would sleep in each of the two aft quarterberths.

And one man would sit at the navigation table, keeping watch on both Miles and on the Expedition display on the computer screen.

The basics of Expedition, Miles knew, were easy to deduce. Rolling the scroll wheel on the mouse zoomed in or out on the on-screen chart. A press and hold of the mouse button allowed the chart to be "dragged" so that it would keep pace with the boat's movement west. Manipulating the mouse to hover the cursor arrow over an arrow-shaped AIS icon would call up a data box on the AIS target.

Watching the screen was almost hypnotic. It gave the watchkeeper something to do. And most importantly, from Miles's perspective, it kept the watch-keeper's eye off the bow area.

The bow area, or forepeak, on a J/111 sailboat is a barren place, a stripped-out area forward of the mast in the bow: on the left side, hidden from view from the doorway to the space, a toilet and small sink, and on the opposite right side, a storage bin that Miles used for several pieces of safety gear. The remainder of the space was empty and would remain that way during a race.

When the long boxes had been loaded into the cabin, bags holding sails that had been on the berths and on the main cabin floor had been tossed into the bow area, creating a pile of bagged sails. This had been Miles's quarters for the past day.

He had not been allowed on deck or into the main area of the boat's cabin. He had been passed a water bottle and a nutrition bar occasionally, but otherwise, he'd had no contact with the five men aboard.

Except when one came forward to use the toilet. Perhaps it was discretion or some innate instinct that one man does not watch another use the toilet—but whatever it was, Miles had noticed that the watchkeeper always averted their gaze from the bow area of the boat and focused intently on the Expedition screen while their comrade went forward.

And that had given him an idea.

Get busy living or get busy dying.

It was a trite saying. He was sure it was a quote from *The Shawshank Redemption*, a movie he'd seen frequently screened on any of the high-numbered, no-name cable TV channels.

Miles, of course, had no idea what Omar had planned for him, but he knew that the time was fast approaching for whatever it was.

He remembered that he had been checking the computer just prior to the hijacking and that *Flying Lady* was about sixty miles from of Brazil Rock. He'd sailed about 185 miles of the three-hundred-odd miles to Halifax. Miles figured they'd wallowed around for less than an hour, between the intercept, dropping the sails, lowering the boxes below deck . . .

And killing George.

Miles grimaced as he remembered.

George.

If anything, he was going to do this for George. So that some-one could tell the story of the terrible thing that happened to George Lakeland, off the coast of Canada. Well, and for himself, too. He would not go down without a fight.

But Miles Lockwood was not that kind of man. He was no hero. He was privileged. Sure, he worked hard. He'd been successful enough in his residential real estate sales career to buy a nice house, a nice car, this nice boat. He'd never married, preferring instead to use his looks and his laid-back rich attitude to play the field and enjoy dating without commitment.

It was an easy life. He'd show houses, flirt with the ladies, close deals. He'd go sailing, racing his sleek boat where he could—Block Island, Annapolis, one trip to Bermuda. He'd drink rum and beer, tell sea stories, go back to land, and sell some more houses. Danger, risk, death . . . those weren't things that Miles faced. Ever.

Until now.

CHAPTER

16

AS THE YANMAR DRONED ON and Miles sat in solitude on his pile of sails in the forepeak of his boat, he did the math over and over in his head. Omar had said seven knots. They'd stopped the boat twice, for about five minutes each time, clearly dumping the contents of the cans into the boat's fuel tank. Each time, Miles had watched Omar carefully check the fuel gauge at the navigation table.

Those two, five-minute stops would be inconsequential in Miles's math—and he'd spent much of the last afternoon and evening double-checking the numbers in his head by tracing out figures on his palm. In twenty-three hours, at seven knots, the boat would have traveled 161 miles, give or take a little for current and wind. Miles knew that the course leg from the Massachusetts coast to Nova Scotia's Brazil Rock was 241 miles, and that last he had checked, he had about sixty miles to go to get to Brazil Rock and had ticked off a few, say five, miles between checking the computer and the hijacking. Therefore, the boat was currently about 25 miles from the race start area off Marblehead, and, if that was correct, maybe less than 15 miles from Cape Ann. If that was true, they would see lights on shore shortly.

He needed to make his move soon, or he'd lose his opportunity.

Miles stood. He leaned his head into the main cabin. Hans was posted as his guard, seated at the nav station, and appeared to be struggling to stay awake as he lazily looked at the computer screen. As usual, two men lay in each of the aft quarterberths, both asleep. Miles was pretty sure one of them was Omar.

"I gotta use the head," Miles whispered, loudly enough so that Hans could hear him, but not so loud that his voice would carry over the drone of the engine. Hans signaled his consent with a nod and turned his gaze back to the monitor.

Miles made a production of stripping off his gear. To ward off the chill, he had put on his foul-weather jacket and bib trousers at dusk. He tossed the gear onto the open storage bin opposite the toilet. Under the foul-weather gear, he was wearing shorts over Under Armour leggings, with a lightweight, long-sleeve T-shirt, a heavier quarter-zip shirt, and a fleece jacket. He kicked off his sea boots, stealing a glance at Hans, who was not watching.

Excellent, thought Miles.

He didn't really need to use the toilet, but to make his performance convincing, he opened the valves on the toilet and pumped the bowl dry. Then he let himself fall toward the starboard side of the boat, collapsing onto his pile of gear and the storage locker. As he hoped, Hans immediately looked up at the commotion and started to rise from the nav seat.

"I slipped," said Miles. "Weird wave action." Hans sat back down. "You mind if I crack the forward hatch to get some air up here?" Hans nodded.

Using the pile of foul-weather gear as cover, Miles rummaged in the safety gear bin, finding the two items he wanted by feel—a ziplock bag, and a small pouch with a metal cylindrical object inside about the size of a can of hairspray or shaving cream. Hanging above the locker were several spare sail ties. He grabbed four of them. Hiding his loot under his gear, Miles dropped the pile toward the port side of the bow area where it would be invisible to Hans, seated at the nav table. Now empty-handed, he turned his back to Hans, undogged the two latches on the forward hatch, and tilted it open a couple of inches. Its friction hinges would hold it in place. Cold night air dribbled into the forepeak.

Moving to the port side so that he would be hidden from Hans's view, and working silently, Miles retrieved his inflatable life vest—a Spinlock DeckVest, low-profile "personal flotation device" with an integrated safety harness that he had worn throughout the race but had taken off when he was sent to the forepeak. The life vest was normally automatically inflated upon immersion in water. Miles removed a small black dummy cap from the ziplock bag he had retrieved from his storage bin, and he swapped the automatic firing mechanism with the dummy cap. With that procedure complete, the life vest could only be inflated if he pulled on the inflation handle and would no longer inflate upon immersion.

Dropping the vest over his head, Miles secured the single front buckle and then looped the two crotch straps around his legs, snapping them into place on the harness.

He unwound his foul-weather gear to expose the cylinder pouch, the second item he had furtively removed from the bin. Bright yellow, it almost glowed in the forepeak. He attached the cylinder pouch with its two clips onto the right-side bladder of the DeckVest, wrapping one of the sail ties around it to double-secure it in place. He then tied two of the remaining sail ties together, securing one end to the harness ring on his chest and tying the loose end with a slip knot to the left-side bladder. He tucked the excess behind the bladder and shoved the fourth sail tie into the left pocket on his shorts. The discarded foul-weather gear and sea boots lay in an untidy pile in front of him.

Time for a quick inventory, he thought. Watch: time now 1:45 AM. Knife in place, strapped to his belt. Inflation on the Spinlock life vest set to manual. He checked the yellow pouch, making sure the flap that secured it closed was tight. He allowed himself one practice run—sliding the sail tie down on the pouch flap, pulling out the flap that was secured by Velcro, and making sure that he could slip the black cylinder within from the pouch. The black tube—which read "Spare Air" in yellow markings on its side—slid out smoothly.

He remembered buying the little unit at a local dive shop, thinking that it would be perfect for a quick trip overboard, to clear a line off the propeller or to check for damage in case the boat hit something large, like a log or even an uncharted rock. According to the Spare Air brochure, the bottle would allow fifty-seven breaths before being depleted. He'd played with it and inhaled a few times. The air tasted stale and dry, but it worked. Now, instead of being a frivolous toy, he hoped it would spare his life. Miles slid the tube back into the pouch and resecured it carefully.

He was ready.

Rearranging the pile of sail bags, Miles made a small mound, piling up the bags so that he could lean against them and have a view aft, toward the companionway. He laid back on the bags in an almost sitting position, carefully draping his foul-weather jacket across his life vest, mostly to cover the bright yellow Spare Air holster. With the slightly open hatch above his head, Miles settled back to wait, figuring that the men would change positions at some point, and hoped that he would not have to sit too long. He could feel the adrenaline. He could also feel panic.

This has to work, he thought to himself. *Otherwise, I'm a dead man.*

CHAPTER

17

MILES HAD BEEN WAITING patiently, fully alert though pretending to sleep on his sail bag. He consulted his watch again—2:32 AM. After his diversion, he had spent a solid half-hour preparing his escape, and then reworking the math in his head, checking and double-checking. He was running out of time as the boat moved inexorably toward the coast.

He could just see the side of Hans's head and noted that the man was still not paying attention. He knew it was the time of night when the body is the most tired and the mind is the least aware. He could see, through the open companionway, a human shape moving, silhouetted by the red instrument lights against a dark night sky. Miles did a quick crew count—one man driving the boat, two men still off watch and asleep in the quarterberths, Hans at the nav table, and the guy moving on deck. *That's all of them,* he thought.

This is it. His hands started to shake, and he forced them to stop. He clutched the edges of his foul-weather jacket as he stood up.

The shadowy shape began to descend the companionway steps. Sensing the motion, Hans instinctively reacted, turning his gaze to his left, toward the companionway, away from the front of the boat and Miles.

Now!

Miles dropped the jacket on the floor and, with one arm, pushed the forward hatch all the way up and open. As he had done so many times before, he grabbed the perimeter of the hatch opening with both hands and levered his upper body through the opening in a single, fluid motion.

Without so much as a glance aft, he rolled his body onto the deck and sprang to his feet. With confident, bounding steps, he ran to the bow, willing himself to move as fast as possible. Legs churning, Miles launched himself clear over the bow rail and executed a perfect knife dive off the front of his boat. Arms outstretched in front of him, his hands cleaved the water, his body slicing into the waves just in front of *Flying Lady*.

On deck at the helm, John saw their captive's head rise from the forward hatch, and he stood transfixed by the sight of Miles popping onto the deck and sprinting forward. A split-second after watching Miles leap over the bow pulpit, John yelled "Hey!" at the top of his lungs, while simultaneously snatching the throttle with his right hand and pulling it back to a vertical, neutral position.

Ten thousand pounds of sailboat does not stop instantly, and the boat continued to coast forward as Bruce, who had been descending the ladder into the boat's interior, awkwardly reversed direction and rejoined John on deck, open-mouthed and stunned into inaction. Below deck, awakened by the sharp change in engine noise when John chopped the throttle back to neutral, Omar sprang out of the quarterberth and lunged himself up the companionway and onto the deck. Hans ran to the front of the cabin, unbelieving that Miles had escaped out of the forward hatch. In the opposite quarterberth, Seb was slower to react, but woke with the commotion.

Omar joined Bruce and John on deck. John had pulled a flashlight out and was sweeping the beam across the lazy swells. The narrow beam did little to illuminate the area. "What the fuck just happened?" yelled Omar.

"He jumped. He popped out of that hatch and dove off the bow!" replied John. "He's not a fish. He's gotta surface!"

"Hans, get that big spotlight and get your ass up here!" commanded Omar. The three men on deck frantically searched the water around the boat as Seb came on deck, pulling his Makarov pistol from his chest harness. Aiming at nothing, Seb fired eight quick shots into the abyss, emptying the magazine. Most of the spent shells pinged off the deck and dropped harmlessly over the side.

Omar spun toward Seb. "What the—" He stopped, midphrase. "Yeah, wait, good idea. He's out there. Scare him." Seb had snapped a fresh magazine in the weapon, just as Hans appeared on deck, squeezing the trigger on the handheld, one-million-candlepower spotlight. Unfortunately for Seb, Hans had the light aimed directly at him, and the searing blue-white light temporarily blinded the short-tempered Seb.

Hans twisted the light's beam off the side of the boat and started scanning the waves, oblivious to his amateurish error.

"This is bullshit. Act like a fucking team. Slow down." Omar was annoyed as he glared at his men. "John, take the wheel and turn this thing around. Go back. Slow speed. Hans, on the bow with that light. Slow sweeps. Bruce, up on the bow, too—you're the spotter. Seb, sit the fuck down and tell me when you can see again."

John advanced the throttle to idle speed and turned the boat. With her tight turning radius, it took less than fifteen seconds for John to spin the boat around as the other two men went forward with the big spotlight. Omar ducked below to look at the computer monitor and to make sure John retraced their course.

Now familiar with the boat's navigation system, he glanced at their position and saw that they were just over ten miles from his harbor waypoint. Grabbing two more flashlights, he returned to the cockpit, handing one light to John and flicking on the other, sweeping the beam across the dark water and the unbroken waves.

Nothing.

The inky, rolling swells showed nothing. For two long minutes, the boat idled along, rolling in the waves, the beams of the puny flashlights dwarfed by the super-bright spotlight. "Reverse course again," Omar commanded, and John turned the wheel.

Another minute-and-a-half of silence as the boat, now aimed west again, slid over the swell, lights playing but not illuminating a single thing.

"You know, Omar, he dove right in front of the boat. Maybe we ran him over. Knocked him out." Omar cocked his head and listened to John's theory.

"Hmmm . . . maybe. Make another slow circle. A three-sixty. One last pass." Omar stared at the water. Omar wondered, *Did meek Miles jump to his death, trying to get run over by his own boat? Plausible, maybe.* Lockwood had showed some sparks of resistance. But he was a playboy. A dilettante. No way he could have fought them off. Omar grunted as the boat spun in a lazy, slow circle.

"Boss, do you see anything? I'm good now," Seb said, as he rose to join the men scanning the ocean.

Omar growled. "Not a fucking thing."

"Boss, I got nothing," Bruce called from the bow.

Omar looked forward at the pair up front, then at John on the wheel, and finally at Seb. Extending an open palm to the Frenchman, Omar pointed, with his other hand, at Seb's Makarov. Warily, Seb passed the pistol to Omar. Stepping up to the side deck, he aimed the weapon at Seb, glaring at him, but then spun toward the water. Venting his frustration, Omar fired into the depths, emptying the magazine.

Twisting his arm, Omar eyed his Casio wristwatch, saying, "Sunrise is at 5:16. We've got just over ten miles to go. It's better to get there before the sun comes up. Get this thing going." Omar stormed below.

CHAPTER

18

PETRIFIED, MILES SILENTLY BROKE the surface, allowing only his head to peek above the slow swell. He saw nothing, but he could hear the soft gurgle of the boat's exhaust and wake. He cautiously turned, realizing just how disoriented he'd become in his struggle to get away from the boat.

Then he spotted it.

From the water's surface, the thirty-six-foot boat looked tiny, and it was clearly motoring away from him. The white stern light showed brightly at the top of the mast—and he could just make out the red instrument displays at the base of the mast. A spotlight played listlessly ahead of the boat, and then was extinguished.

Miles brought his right arm out of the water and, with his left hand, pressed the "light" button on his watch. 2:39 AM. He waited, the time passing slowly, his arms and legs tiring as he treaded water. The white hull of the boat was barely visible now, the masthead light getting closer to the water as the boat receded against the horizon.

As he watched the masthead light, his heart rate slowed. He had done it.

He had sliced into the waves almost dead ahead of the boat. In the clear Atlantic water, Miles had twisted his body around and had seen the white-painted shape of his boat arrowing at him. The bow had cleared his head and Miles had his arms spread wide. The keel had slammed into his chest, knocking what little air was left in his lungs out with a great gasp.

Frantic and out of breath, Miles had clutched both sides of the keel, his eyes now wide open. He had forced his mind to slow down, to process one thought at a time:

The boat is slowing.

The engine noise is much less.

The weight of the water on my back is getting less.

The boat is slowing more.

I can hold my breath for at least thirty seconds.

It's only been ten or fifteen seconds.

With an unusual clarity of thought, probably from a combination of adrenaline and naked fear, Miles had been able to pull himself together. The propeller behind the keel was well away from him, and he figured the transmission had been shifted into neutral. The prop would be freewheeling with the leftover forward momentum of the boat.

As the seconds passed, Miles had found that it was getting easier and easier to hang onto the leading edge of the keel. In fact, he had felt himself floating upward some, as the boat slowed. With his left hand, he had pulled the sail tie slip knot, and with his right hand, yanked the length of sail tie so that it streamed along the left side of the keel. The boat had almost stopped, and he could hear footsteps pounding above his head, the water amplifying the noises of the men above.

With his right hand, Miles had clutched the leading edge of the keel, allowing his body to slowly be pulled along the right side of the keel fin. Because the root of the keel fin was only about three feet long where it intersected the canoe-shaped hull of the boat, with his left hand, he could easily reach the back trailing edge, where, on the opposite side, he had found his sail tie. Yanking it toward him, Miles had looped it through his DeckVest harness, tying a fast slip knot. He hadn't cared where he was, fore or aft on the root of the keel, as long as that simple knot held him under the boat, alongside the keel, directly under the body of the boat's hull.

His brain had been screaming for oxygen, Miles had repeated his practice in the forepeak, freeing the Spare Air bottle from its pouch.

The design of the unit was "always on," so there were no valves to turn or caps to open. He had brought the mouthpiece to his lips, sucked it tightly to his teeth, and inhaled. It had worked—and he finally had air his body so badly craved. *One,* he had counted to himself, figuring he'd allow nine more breaths to regain his energy and focus, then he'd conserve. *Two. Three . . .*

By the time he reached ten, he was beginning to panic, still perilously strapped to the keel. To calm himself, he focused on the movements of the boat.

He'd felt the boat turn. He could see the propeller spinning as the engine was put back into gear. The tone of the motor, clearly heard underwater, had barely changed. Idle speed. He had desperately wanted air—a great gulp of air—but the boat had idled on.

He had felt the boat turn two more times, his grip on the keel fin getting weaker and his resolve lessening with each pass.

Forty-eight.

He had taken forty-eight breaths from the Spare Air bottle. After his first ten breaths, he'd gone to one every ten seconds. They were shallow inhales, barely enough.

Less than ten theoretical snatches of air from the bottle, and it would be out.

Two minutes, three tops.

His thoughts and his count had been interrupted by the whistle of bullets in the water on the port side of the boat. Stomping noises. Then silence.

I gotta go for it, Miles had thought. With his left hand, he had yanked the slip knot on the sail tie on his harness. The pressure on his right hand, on the leading edge of the keel, had immediately increased. He had let go as he levered his knees against the keel, pushing his body away from the keel and using his hands to push against the hull, driving himself deeper. He had to clear the propeller and the rudder.

Suddenly, the engine noise had changed dramatically. With a whoosh of cavitation bubbles, the propeller blades became a blur. With one hand clutching the Spare Air bottle and the other hand flailing against the water, Miles had attempted to descend deeper into the Atlantic water.

It had been no use. The human body floats—and the air in his lungs and throughout his frame, together with his awful swimming technique, fought his efforts to dive. He had felt himself getting closer to the surface and he had taken one last, long gasp from the Spare Air bottle, and let it go, freeing both his hands to act in unison, propelling himself, willing himself, deeper.

Already very weakened from the minutes underwater and the exertion to hold himself against the keel, he didn't make it very far. He had been perhaps four feet under the surface when he gave up, allowing himself to float up, which is when he had surfaced and seen the boat slowly receding against the distant horizon.

Another look at the watch. 2:47 AM.

Exhausted, Miles reached across his submerged chest. He untied, unhooked, and discarded the Spare Air holster. With his right arm, he felt down to the left inside bottom of his Spinlock DeckVest harness. With trepidation, his fingers found the handle . . . and he yanked it. With a pop and a quick hiss, the compressed CO_2 in the inflation module filled the air bladders on the DeckVest. Instantly, he felt better, the life vest now supporting his body.

But then, without warning, a bright flash of light illuminated the space around him.

Fuck!

He had forgotten the integrated strobe light on the DeckVest, which was activated by water. He grabbed it, shielding the light with his hand. It flashed again, turning his hand momentarily translucent, and fighting the rising panic within him, he realized he had no idea how to turn it off.

Thankfully, the masthead light on *Flying Lady* never wavered in direction. He exhaled a sigh of relief as the boat continued to move away. *Land is that way,* Miles noted. *To the west.*

The shielded strobe continued its incessant blink.

As his adrenaline rush subsided, Miles collected his thoughts, breathing evenly, pulling his legs up into a huddle position to conserve his body heat. He knew the water temperatures in July off the Massachusetts coast would be in the sixties, and he recalled from his extensive safety training that he would have at least two hours before hypothermia would set in. If he was careful, and especially since the DeckVest life jacket would bear his weight in the water, he could stretch that to possibly six hours. He watched as the masthead light vanished below the horizon.

He was alone. He was alive. And he was free of his captors.

But he was running out of time.

CHAPTER
19

AT 4:30 AM, IN THE SILENT, peaceful twilight just before sunrise, a solitary sailboat had casually motored into Gloucester Harbor. Had anyone cared to be observant at this hour, they would have seen nothing out of the ordinary. The white sailboat's running lights were on and her AIS transmitter was broadcasting her name, *Flying Lady*, and her speed and course. At her transom, an American flag drooped listlessly, occasionally lazily fluttering with the momentum of the boat through the still, windless water. The tidy vessel passed between the outer channel markers and, just before reaching the US Coast Guard Station Gloucester, she turned to her left, into Harbor Cove.

The sailboat docked at an open slip at the charter fishing boat dock in front of the Harbor Cove Brewing Company brewpub. It was not a perfect landing, and there were some quiet cursing and mumbling as her crew secured docklines, but there was no one in the red-brick-paved parking lot that overlooked the docks to watch and critique.

Omar had arranged the scene carefully. They had docked the boat bow-in, so that the companionway hatch would face away from the docks.

Her masthead tri-color running lights remained lit. When the charter fishing boat crews arrived to prep their vessels for the day's outing, they'd see those masthead running lights from the parking lot. They'd be suspicious of this interloper, this lone sailboat among sport-fishers, but they might assume that it was a boat that came in overnight, seeking safety from the sea, her crew too tired to switch off the lights. In their quiet New England way, they'd grumble, but they'd leave the boat alone. For now.

Omar figured it would likely take them a couple of hours to realize that the boat was unoccupied, that its crew who arrived sometime in the overnight hours was not asleep below decks, and then possibly another hour for the Gloucester Harbor Master to amble over. Finding the boat empty, perhaps he'd leave a note on it with his phone number. He'd be mad but a clean, presentable racing sailboat on these docks was not a crisis. An inconvenience to the daily routine maybe, but certainly not alarming.

Eventually, Omar predicted, the Harbor Master would call the US Coast Guard Station Gloucester, located less than a quarter-mile away, and they would search their records for a boat named *Flying Lady*, which would turn up in a number of places including on the entry list for the Marblehead-Halifax Race. Then they'd contact the race organizers, who would inform the Coast Guard that the vessel withdrew from the race roughly two days previously, with mainsail damage, and intended to return to Marblehead.

With the Gloucester Harbor some ten miles closer on the boat's return track than the Marblehead harbor, the Coast Guard would logically conclude that the boat put into the nearest port, perhaps to make repairs, possibly low on food or fuel, or maybe just with a tired and worn-out crew.

And, with no crew onboard, the Harbor Master and the Coast Guard might assume that the crew Ubered their way to a hotel or to a friend's house for a shower and a meal. Obviously, someone docked the boat, closed its hatches, and coiled its lines neatly.

Omar estimated that it would be at least a day—maybe even two days—before any alarm was raised. And what alarm would that be? That a pristine white sailboat was found docked in Gloucester? They'd attempt to reach the owner, but, of course, Miles Lockwood would be unreachable. They'd scratch their heads and, needing action, they'd tow the boat from the docks, secure it to a mooring, and there it would sit.

And by then, it would be all over.

Omar turned his back to the sailboat, no longer needed, as he walked up the ramp off the floating docks.

His four men, working in pairs, had lugged the two heavy boxes, now wrapped in loose disguises, up the ramp from the dock. Omar carried the large, waterproof, duffel bag which he set down at the top of the ramp. Opening the bag revealed three smaller backpacks inside—one for each pair of men, one for Omar. He extracted the two smaller packs for each pair and his own.

They opened the three backpacks. In an OtterBox case, at the top of each bag, was a Google Pixel phone. Powering them on, they selected the OnStar app that had been preloaded on each device. At the top right of each screen, the men each tapped the Unlock icon, and in front of them, in the sparsely populated brick-paved lot, the parking lights flashed on three vehicles: a white Chevrolet Express cargo van, a silver GMC Savana cargo van, and a tan Buick Regal.

As planned, the five men split up toward the vehicles. No words were needed. Seb and John hefted one box and one backpack, and headed toward the silver GMC, while Bruce and Hans, with an identical load, aimed toward the Chevy van. The pairs slid the boxes into the cargo areas of the vans that had magically been unlocked by the OnStar system. Quietly latching the cargo doors shut, the pairs climbed into their respective vans—John and Bruce each taking a driver's side.

Meanwhile, Omar tossed his backpack and the now-empty duffel bag onto the backseat of the Regal and seated himself in the sedan.

Ignition keys had been placed in the cupholders of each vehicle. These particular vehicles had been selected partially because they were not equipped with the then-fashionable, start-stop ignition button, which requires a wireless fob. And, typically, a fob cannot be locked within the vehicle.

Engines were switched on and, inside each vehicle, the OnStar app was closed and the Pixel phones were powered off. Shifting the vehicles into gear, the trio exited the parking lot. The Regal turned right, onto Rogers Street, and disappeared into the Gloucester waterfront district. The two vans convoyed together for only a few hundred feet up Angle Street, where the Chevrolet turned left onto Western Avenue and the

GMC continued on Washington Street. All three vehicles would eventually make their way to the Yankee Division Highway, but not as a group, hence the reason for taking separate paths away from the harbor.

Less than five minutes had elapsed since the five men had gathered at the top of the ramp.

Behind the wheel of the Buick, passing Harbor Loop to his right, Omar allowed himself a grin. Moments ago, his crew had brazenly brought two highly radioactive weapons onto US soil, quite literally a stone's throw away from the sentinels of US Coast Guard Station Gloucester.

And not a single person had noticed.

CHAPTER

20

WEDNESDAY, 10:37 AM — FBI BOSTON FIELD OFFICE, CHELSEA, MASSACHUSETTS

AT 201 MAPLE STREET, in Chelsea, Massachusetts, the usually-humming Boston Field Office of the Federal Bureau of Investigation was a bit of a ghost town. It had been a quiet morning. Everything we could have done, was done. The phones were ringing more sporadically, and we listlessly looked at the backlog of work that had piled up in the past week or so, reluctant to get to it. Without saying it, we had reached a consensus; we would coast through the day, let the excitement die down, and get back at it tomorrow.

The actual agents were not at their desks, they were downtown or staked along either the inbound or outbound presidential travel routes, partnering with both local police and with the Secret Service. The honchos also wanted to be a part of the action, so they had parked themselves downtown, too, mingling and talking on their phones and accomplishing nothing except for looking important. A skeleton staff manned the usual office functions, including us. And my boss, Macallister, was grouchy. Naturally, he wanted to be downtown too.

To this day, I'm still not exactly sure how the call got routed to Macallister. After the fact, I did a bit of quiet research, and I'm pretty sure that, with agents massing in the field, the ranking desk agent in the office was Bradford Macallister. Therefore, whoever answered the "interagency" phone line had transferred the call to Macallister.

All I know for sure was that, at 10:37 AM, he was standing in front of me, glaring.

"Porker."

I fucking hated that. He would fake-pretend that it was his accent left over from his Jersey days, and he would roll the T in my last name, make it a K, and toss that insult every single time he addressed me. And he knew there was not a thing I could do about it. I could complain to HR—but, one, he's protected, and two, I could not prove malice. So, typically, I take it. But I could play my own game, too, so I pretended I was deep in concentration, looking at my screen, so that he had to say it again.

"Porker. You wid me?" Really? *You wid me?* You can take the boy out of Jersey and put him in a Range Rover, but he's still from Jersey. I pushed my luck.

Let's go for three.

"PORTER!" He more-or-less screamed, but at least he pronounced it correctly. Chalk a win for me. I looked up.

"My office. Now!" Macallister spun on his heels and strutted toward his office. I knew I'd probably pushed it too far, so without comment or hesitation, I followed. We wove our way through the cube farm to his office. Not a corner office. But at least an office with a door, and a window. He sat behind his government-issue desk, in his government-issue imitation Aeron chair, and pompously waved me to a government-issue side chair. I sat.

"I got a call ten minutes ago. Some police sergeant in Gloucester." He shuffled papers on his desk. "Ensign. Or maybe Hanson." More shuffling. Setting a bad example for proper phone log procedure, for certain.

"Okay, here it is. Hensen. Frank Hensen. Gets a 9-1-1 dispatch at about 7:30 this morning. Fisherman calls in. Heading out for some fishing and sees a guy in the water. They pick him up. He's hypnotic. They give him some coffee, or rum, or some ting, and bring him in. An ambulance and cop meet them at the dock. Medics take the vic to the hospital in the bus. He's barely conscious and making no sense. Wid me so far?"

I nodded, but I was not with him so far. Some ting? Ah, translation: *something*. He had me on hypnotic, though. I quickly calculated the odds of pissing him off versus asking a question. I went with both at once. "Yeah, I think I follow. Mostly. Not sure about the hypnotic part. The guy was hypnotized?"

"No, no, no," Macallister stuttered. "I dunno the fucking word. Hyp-*something*. Cold. Hypoxic."

I nodded again. Typical Macallister. I went with the cold part. Guy in water. Cold. Starts to make more sense. I inferred he meant hypothermic. Not hypoxic. Certainly not hypnotic. I didn't correct him.

He continued, "Anyway, the bus takes the vic to the hospital. Hospital in Gloucester, Eddie Gilmore or some ting. They check him out and the cop tries to get a statement. Which is difficult, because the vic is barely conscious. What the cop says that the vic says makes no sense. The vic claims his boat was hijacked a couple of days ago during the middle of the night, and that the hijackers were aiming toward Marblehead, and he jumped off. Fucking delusional. Cop says the vic has zero credibility. Like, none. Can't take him seriously.

"Cop gets a name from the guy, so he runs it. Name belongs to some real estate hotshot in Cohasset. The cop, whatshisname? Hanson. Hanson called him a playboy. Tells me he thinks this is some sort of insurance scam or something. Playboy sailor boy smacked his precious yacht into something, and it sank. Or playboy bought a boat and sank it because he's an idiot. Which is probably what really happened."

Macallister toyed at the sheet of paper once more, before concluding, "The story is bullshit. *Delusional*."

I nodded. Third time. My boss plowed on, continuing the one-way conversation.

"Anyway, Handsome calls his chief, who also thinks it is bullshit, but because of the hijacking part, he says to call it into the FBI. Wants to punt this nightmare to us. And now it's our problem." Pause. Macallister stared at me. "*My* problem. Well, *was* my problem. Now it's *your* problem."

Bobbleheaded, I nodded again. But, I was not quite sure what he wanted from me. Therefore, I asked, "I'm not quite sure what you want from me."

"We are required to check out any threat, no matter how unreliable it may seem. You need to go check it out because, well, someone has to. I got no one else at the moment. I think you can do it."

I considered this. I am, after all, an information management specialist. I am not an agent. This is absolutely, totally unprecedented, and way outside the normal procedures. But the boss has told me to go run a lead? *Um, okay, sure!*

"Ah . . . yes, sir. I'll go to Gloucester, run it down, and report back. You're assigning me field work? Just want to confirm that, sir."

Macallister grunted affirmatively. I guessed that he hated this, but he had no one else. They're all in the city. And he can't let a threat, as bogus as it might be, go unanswered. This could be a so-called "crime on the high seas," which, contrary to what you might think, is within the FBI's jurisdiction. Therefore, sending me to check it out would be his way of covering his ass. He's actually very clever—wasting his time pursuing a dead end won't look good, but wasting *my* time is good middle-management delegation. "Yes," he said. "Write up an Ops Order before you leave. Basic details, time, location, what-not. Email me the case number, and I'll sign off on it."

I stood. "Yes, sir. May I take the call log and your notes?" Macallister handed me a piece of paper, which was neither a proper complaint form, nor a call log form, and whatever it was, it was not completely legible. With his other hand, he picked up his desk phone handset. I knew, and he knew that I knew, that it was a gesture—he had no one to call. But neither of us wanted to continue this conversation or charade any longer. He put the dead handset to his ear, and I walked back to my cube.

I'd never started an Operations Order or case file before, but I've seen countless files. I could do this. Logging onto my computer, I quickly clicked the appropriate buttons. A new file opened. I started to fill it in. I have seen so many of these that I am comfortable with both the jargon and the shorthand.

Within ten minutes, maybe seven, I was done. My name as the case opener. Macallister as supervisory agent. The few details we had so far. A quick Google search and I got the correct name for the hospital in Gloucester—the Addison Gilbert Hospital—and confirmed the sergeant's name, Frank Henson. A quick narrative of my conversation with Macallister, written in such a way that it made him look good for authorizing me to run the lead. A side note highlighting the day and the circumstances that made me a logical, or inevitable, choice to do the field work. A spot for Macallister to sign off.

I saved the file, drafted and sent an email to Macallister with nothing in it but the case number, logged off, grabbed my backpack, laptop, and phone, and returned to Macallister's office. He was no longer pretending to be on his desk phone—but instead, he was occupied swiping away at his personal cell phone. Important government work to be sure, as he quickly clicked off the screen when he saw me at his door.

"You set that up already?"

"Yessir."

"I don't see an email."

No, of course you didn't. Because you were surfing something on your phone, dipshit, not looking at your work computer. It was difficult to keep a straight face when I said, "Sir, it's probably just arriving. I sent it moments ago. Maybe it takes a sec."

He shook the mouse on this desk and his screen woke up. I pretended to turn so I could pretend to not see him enter his password as he pecked out M – A – C – Q – U E 1 – 2 – 3. Now, I couldn't help but to stare, flabbergasted. Seriously? Top level government security and his fucking password was his fucking license plate? Yeah, because the added numerals, in sequence no less, will foil the most sophisticated hacking software. Right. I couldn't stand this guy.

He murmured, importantly, like he was sifting through several important emails. I could see there was only one new email. From me. He finally clicked on it and wrote the case number on a piece of paper. Ever heard of right-click copy-and-paste, moron? Laboriously, he clicked over to the case management program, logged on—with the same fucking password!—and entered the case number. He mouthed the words silently as he read my entries.

It occurred to me that I had never spent this much time, alone, with him, "working." I truly could not believe what I saw. How he kept this job was beyond me. I rocked a little on my feet, then caught myself. Stay cool, have him sign off, and leave. Finally, he reached the end of the file and grunted, clearly liking that I made him look good in the narrative.

"Right. Yeah. Okay. This works." He began to peck the keys to digitally sign the file. The computer would enter the date and timestamp. "Go."

I was elated. "Yessir." I turned and walked out. Wait. I poked my head back in.

"Sir. Can I take a pool car?"

Macallister's face immediately started to turn red as his eyes narrowed to slits. Oops, I thought. Too far, this guy is unhinged. I shouldn't have pressed it. Before he could react, I decided to let him save face. "Oh, wait, sorry, sir. Probably a bad idea. They'll need all the cars on reserve for this afternoon. I'll use my personal vehicle."

Funny, but I thought he was relieved that I had given him an out. His eyes widened and the stare softened. "Yeah. You can expense it though. I'll sign the expense report." Pause. "Thanks."

I'm shocked. We had . . . a moment. "Yes. Sir." I nodded one last time, spun on my heels, and fled.

CHAPTER
21

AS I WALKED TO THE parking lot, I considered my tactics. Because I cannot arrive in Gloucester, with any shred of credibility, in my car, without setting the stage beforehand.

A pool car would have been infinitely better. It might have given me stature.

I was nervous. There's a bit of a myth that there's a silly game of cat and mouse—FBI versus local cops. They can't stand our starched shirts and our "Federal Government" introduction. We can't stand their turf battles and small-town self-importance. For the most part, though, that's a made-for-TV conflict. The FBI partners regularly with the local police, for they know their towns and they know, mostly, their actors. Sure, there are some bad cops, jealous cops, or downright misguided cops, but I hoped Frank Henson is one of the good guys. He better be, or the moment he sees me, I could possibly be screwed. Because of my car.

I reached it. My 2009 Cinnamon Brown Metallic Ford Taurus four-door sedan.

It was in decent shape; I took care of it. But it was the possibly the least impressive, least imposing vehicle out there.

I had bought it off-lease in 2013. It was not my first choice, or second, or third . . . Well, you get the point. Really, it was a little humiliating; what self-respecting (then) twenty-three-year-old dude wants to be seen in that car? But what it lacked in looks and style, it more than made up for in price, especially after sitting in a dealer's lot for a long time, unsold. Because, really, who chooses a brown Ford Taurus? Except for the chick who originally leased it.

But wait, you ask, how do you know the lessee was a woman? The papers and the CARFAX® would only have the name of the leasing company.

Ah, but I'm with the FBI. I analyze everything. Constantly. It's kind of a blessing. And a curse. At the same time. It's a *blurse*.

Anyway, I digress.

First, there's a scratch on the passenger side door which has been patched not with paint, but with glittery brown nail polish. No guy would ever think to do that.

Second, the driver's seat creaks on every bump. But if it's slid back, the creak stops. The previous driver was shorter than me. Nail polish and shorter. Had to have been a girl.

I'd like to think that she was wicked smart too. Because who buys a brown car, except, as we've already established, someone who wants a cheap car. Really, can you see someone, who has eagerly traveled to the shiny showroom, who has voluntarily subjected themselves to the stereotypically shady sales tactics of an automobile salesperson, and survived, and who is primed and ready to pick out their brand-new ride . . . then pointing at the Cinnamon Brown Metallic Taurus while squealing, "That's the one! That's my favorite shade of shit! I'll take it!"

No, that does *not* happen. What happens is that my smart lady car buyer says, what is the best deal you can give me on that one—the one that is quite possibly the ugliest color on the plainest, most boring car, ever, so much that it looks like a government car.

I considered that. I'd come full circle. That never occurred to me. My car looked exactly like a pool car.

I backed the car out of the parking space, shifted into Drive, and paused. Plugging in my hands-free headset, I keyed in the number that Sergeant Henson left with Macallister. Pressing both the gas pedal and *SEND* simultaneously, I set off for Gloucester as I waited for the sergeant to pick up the call.

I have no badge, just my identification card, which has my picture on it but which does not proclaim "Special Agent" in big black capital letters. And while I have my boss's authority, I can't bullshit the sergeant into him thinking that I'm an agent. Instead, my plan is to come clean with him and explain the situation.

"Henson."

"Sergeant Henson, this is Ben Porter with FBI Boston. Good morning."

"Yeah, morning. You guys finally got around to calling me back."

"Yes, sir. In fact, I am on my way to see you. You spoke earlier to my boss, Supervisory Special Agent Macallister. He requested that I meet with you."

"Waste of time. Hang on." I heard muffling sounds. Henson had probably put a hand over the phone. I waited. A moment passed, and he was back on the line. "Well, I dunno. This guy is looney. A real pissah. Macallister give you the background?"

"Yes, sir. A boat, a hijacking. It does sound crazy. But we do need to check it out. It's probably a waste of time, but it's also what we do." I paused.

"Right-o." Henson's turn to pause. "Listen, I appreciate that. You're being real polite, though. I've dealt with your type before." He let that hang.

My type. I got it. And I thought, *This is the time to get Henson on my side.* "Sergeant, I'm not an agent. I'm a specialist. My colleagues are pretty busy downtown now, with, you know, the event tonight and the VIP. Still, we gotta check this out, especially given the circumstances in Boston being prepared for at this very moment. So, I'll meet you and your vic, we'll establish a timeline and some facts, and get back to real work."

Henson grunted and replied, "Yeah, okay. I appreciate your candor. I'm waiting at the hospital. Vic is due to get discharged in about an hour. Processing paperwork, that sort of nonsense. I'm not sure what to do with him. How far are you?"

"Forty minutes, sir. Give or take."

"Ask for me at the desk. They'll page me and I will come find you. No weapons inside so leave your piece in your vehicle."

I laughed at that one to myself. I don't carry. Unless you count my laptop—government issue and heavy enough to probably stop a bullet, certainly heavy enough to whack someone pretty hard with, though useless in a gunfight. "You got it, sergeant. See you shortly. Thanks."

The connection ended. Sergeant Henson was not one for good-byes, apparently.

CHAPTER

22

AT 11:45 AM, I PARKED MY Taurus at the Addison Gilbert Hospital in Gloucester, a mostly red brick building that looked more like a school than a hospital. Finding the main entrance around the back of the building, I passed under a columned portico and found the front reception desk. Inside, standing near the desk, was a uniformed, white-haired, square-chinned police officer.

I approached the officer and realized, thanks to his nametag, that this was my Sergeant Henson. Pulling my FBI ID card from my left pants pocket and offering my right hand, I introduced myself: "I'm Ben Porter. FBI Boston."

Henson stared at my card through square eyeglasses. Clearly, he expected proper creds: a badge folio, not an employee ID card. I decided to intervene: "As I said on the phone, I'm not an agent, I am a specialist. Trying to fill in and help out, sir."

Henson apprised me. Mildly overweight guy in a cheap, off-the-rack suit was probably not what he was expecting. But, to his credit, he seamlessly recovered and concluded a firm handshake saying, "Welcome to Gloucester. I appreciate you making the trip. Follow me."

We walked side-by-side toward an elevator bank, and, reading from his notebook, he dove right into a monologue which continued on the elevator as we rode, alone, to the third floor. "Okay. We got a call from 9-1-1 dispatch at 7:40 this morning. Fisherman calling in from a cell phone. He and his buddies found a guy in the water. The guy on the phone tells the dispatcher that they are inbound to the T-Wharf in Rockport Harbor at full throttle and will be there in a half-hour. 9-1-1 op can barely make out the words, wind noise or something.

"The 9-1-1 operator decides to dispatch PD and EMTs. I get the call to go to the wharf, and I head over there.

"I get there, and the ambulance is there, and nothing is happening. I'm thinking we got pranked. I'm talking to the EMTs about filing a false-call report when we see this boat ripping between the breakwaters at the harbor entrance, heading directly at the wharf. The EMTs grab the gurney and we meet the boat down at the docks.

"EMTs load up the bus with the vic and I told them I'd meet them here, but I wanted to get a statement from the guys in the fishing boat first. You want the names?" he asked, as he waved his notebook in front of me.

"Yeah, of course, but I can get them later. What did they say?" I asked as the elevator doors opened.

As we stepped off the elevator, Henson continued reading. "Nice guys. Clearly fired up. They were talking a mile a minute. They said they had left Rockport just before 7:00 AM for a fishing and whale-watching day trip out to Stellwagen Bank. At about 7:30, they spot the guy in the water. They almost ran him over, otherwise would never have seen him. They pulled him aboard and the guy is freezing, visibly blue. Teeth chattering. Can't understand a word he is saying. They got some coffee on their boat and they tried to get some in him, but he barfed it up. They had some extra clothes and wrapped him up. They wedged him in a corner on the boat, make the call to 9-1-1, and take off. Thirty minutes from pick-up to the wharf, running at almost full throttle, doing twenty knots or something. Those guys saved his life. But wait till you hear the story. It's gotten more ludicrous since the first time this guy told it."

I stopped walking and interrupted, "Wait. What? What do you mean, since the first time?"

Henson replied, "I tried to get a statement from him right after catching up to the ambulance here at the hospital. He was not very lucid, and I could barely understand him. Could barely get a name from him.

The punch line was that someone hijacked his boat. That's when I called your boss. While you were driving here, I talked with him again. He's warmer and more coherent. The story has gotten stranger. It's bullshit, if you ask me."

"Like, how strange?"

"I don't buy it," said Henson, sharply. "The name he gave me—this I told your boss—matches a real estate agent in Cohasset. Playboy type, from his web page. Not some hero who's gonna risk his life.

"Second time around on the story, he adds some detail. Now he claims that when the boat was hijacked, the hijackers loaded some sort of contraband on board and then headed back to Massachusetts. Then he risked his life and jumped off."

Pausing for a beat, Henson concluded, scratching his head above his left ear, "When I called your boss, I said this sounded like some sort of insurance scam. Guy sank his boat and makes up this story. Maybe he intentionally sank the boat but underestimated how cold the water was. It's suspicious, you know, that all of a sudden, he comes up with this so-called contraband. So where is it? Where's the boat? No one has seen it? No one noticed? 'Cuz there's no way all these pieces add up. You follow?"

"Yeah," I answered. "Still, I'm here. Might as well talk to him."

We walked a short distance from the elevator bank and arrived at a room on the third floor; more of an open corral with beds encircled by curtains. It was quiet. One curtain was closed. Henson dropped his voice. "Meet our playboy." He slid the curtain open.

CHAPTER

23

PROPPED UP IN THE HOSPITAL BED was a tired-looking, middle-aged, stubbled guy with bright hazel eyes. He stared at me. "You're the FBI? I'm Miles Lockwood." He spoke clearly, carefully. Not what I had expected. Though, what had I expected?

Not sure of that at all, I focused on those eyes and introduced myself. "Yes. Good morning. I'm Ben Porter. FBI Boston. Sergeant Henson tells me you've had an interesting morning." I conveniently omitted my job description and left my identification card in my pocket. Lockwood didn't seem to notice, or care.

He nodded, "Yeah, you could say that. Understatement of the year. It's been an interesting two days. I'm afraid Officer Henson does not believe me."

I looked at Henson, who was wearing his poker face. Completely expressionless. I guessed that meant he would be Bad Cop. I decided to play the role of Good Cop, thinking, *I am way out of my depth here.*

"Well, Mr. Lockwood, my job is to gather information." At least that part was true. I swallowed and continued, "Let's start at the end, the present moment, and work our way backward. Sergeant Henson called my office, something about a hijacker. That got our attention. Let's start there."

"Right." Lockwood paused, looking at Henson. "Start at the part he doesn't believe. And you can blow me off, too."

I noticed something. Lockwood was pissed off. Typically, I think, someone lying tries to gain your trust, ingratiating themselves with you. Lockwood seemed mad that he was not being taken seriously. He did not strike me as a playboy, nor did he appear delusional. I looked at Henson. His arms were crossed tightly on his chest and his chin was down. "Sergeant, it was a long drive. There any coffee around here somewhere?"

He looked at me for a moment like I had two heads, initially annoyed that the fake agent was sending him on a coffee run, till, clearly, it dawned on him. He's a smart cop. He knew I had to establish a rapport with Lockwood and having him there would impede that. He caught my eye and said, "Nope. Not on this floor. Gotta be some in the cafeteria. I'll grab you a cup. Regular?"

"Sure," I replied, wondering what regular was in Gloucester. Heavy cream, tons of sugar, probably. No wonder I couldn't lose weight.

Henson disappeared, sliding the privacy curtain closed. He did not offer coffee to Lockwood, who said, "Slick. Thanks. I can't stand him. He's been hovering. Probably wants to cite me for having no identification."

I was impressed that Lockwood figured out that I dismissed Henson, so I decided it was time to conspire. I leaned in. "Look, we don't have a lot of time. Sell me your story. Big facts. We will fill in the details later. What do you got, and how do I trust you? Start there."

Miles Lockwood stared at me, eyes narrowing. He took a deep breath. And started. "My name is Miles Lockwood. I live in Cohasset. I sell real estate. High end. I own a thirty-six-foot racing sailboat. I was racing the Marblehead-Halifax Race, doublehanded. That means two of us on the boat, not a full crew like most of the other boats. Fifty, sixty other boats. All racing.

"We started the race on Sunday. The breeze died out after the start and it was slow going. It's unpredictable, you know. Don't know how much wind you are going to have or where it's going to come from. Anyway, the wind filled in during the day on Monday."

I frantically scribbled in my notebook while cursing myself that I didn't think to pull out my laptop and transpose notes directly into the case file. Then again, this was a first for me. Lockwood continued his monologue, "Middle of the night, Monday night going into Tuesday, I was on deck and my partner George was off watch, asleep down below deck. We were about sixty miles from Canada. About halfway through the race. Open water, boat was cruising along. I heard a noise in the distance, a whine. I was trying to figure it out when George popped up on deck; he was on watch next but woke up early. He heard it too. I went below to grab a light, and I heard a bang. George was lying on the cockpit floor, bleeding, and a RIB was alongside with guys with guns getting onto my boat."

Lockwood stopped for an instant, eyes clouding, before continuing in a slightly slower tempo, "They had a gun pointed at me. I didn't dare move. I couldn't help George. All I could do was watch. They loaded two long, black boxes on the boat. Then they threw George into their boat and tied him down. They shot holes in the boat *and* in George. They cut 'em loose and they sank.

"They put me up forward, down below. We went west all next day, toward Marblehead. Middle of the next night, early this morning, I figured we were about ten or fifteen miles from the coast. I waited for a diversion and dove off the boat. They didn't find me. I froze my ass off in the water. Thought I was done. I vaguely remember being on a big center console fishing boat and then in an ambulance. And here I am."

He took a breath, collected his thoughts, and drilled into me with those hazel eyes. "Agent Porter, who are those men? And what's in those boxes? No one makes that kind of effort for nothing. What's in those boxes?"

He stopped and I looked back at him. This was quite a story. It did not sound delusional to me. And, *if* it's true . . .

I thought for a second. Lockwood remained silent. I respected him for letting me think.

"What's a rib?" I asked.

"What?" replied Lockwood, with a blank stare.

I repeated, "What's a rib? Who's rib? Your buddy George is bleeding and you're talking about ribs."

Lockwood cracked a smile, the first I had seen. "No, no, no. Not ribs. *A* RIB. Capital R, capital I, capital B. RIB. Rigid inflatable boat."

"Like a Navy Seal thing?" I guessed.

"Yeah, yeah, something like that. It had a Torqeedo," replied Lockwood.

I shook my head again and asked, "Huh? A torpedo?"

Lockwood grinned again. "Tor. Key. Dough." He said it slowly, dragging out the syllables. "Tor-key-doh. Torqeedo. It's a fancy, electric outboard engine. Barely makes noise. Super quiet."

I was starting to understand why Henson didn't take this guy seriously. The little bit I've heard was crazy enough, but have that story told by a hypothermic guy just pulled from the ocean, who was clearly a fast-talker—has to be, he's in real estate sales—and you'd hear garbled lingo about torpedoes and ribs. I considered my next question.

"How many of them?"

"Five."

"They use any names? What language? Accents?"

Lockwood paused. "Seb was driving the boat. Spoke perfect English with a French accent. The head guy introduced himself as Omar. But he was definitely not an Omar. Not Middle Eastern. Also spoke English, maybe a bit of a British accent? Hard to say, because he talked very formally. The accent was, um, I dunno. Maybe it wasn't an accent. Maybe he was just really precise. Or trying to sound like he had an accent. Anyway, he—"

I interrupted, processing this. "Wait, you said he introduced himself?"

"Yeah. He threatened me with a gun. Told me to behave or I'd end up like George."

"You catch any other names?" I asked.

"Got 'em all. Omar. Bruce. John. Seb. Hans."

As I scribbled the names in my notebook, I muttered, "How the hell you remember all those names?"

Lockwood snorted. "I'm in sales. I remember faces, and I remember names."

The curtain slid open. I was expecting Henson but got scrubs. A short, petite Asian doctor, who chirped, "Mr. Lockwood? Discharge papers. Sign here. Who are you?" she said, looking at me.

"Porter. FBI Boston. He can go?"

"Yes," she replied. Looking at Lockwood, she said, "We have clothes, donated, for indigents. Nurses will bring you something. This is all highly unusual, but you're fine, and we don't have the resources." She spun and left. Lockwood and I stared at each other, both of us clearly confused, just as Henson reappeared, having caught the tail end of the conversation.

"Problem is, no ID, no insurance, no nothing." He handed me a coffee cup. "They don't know what to do with him. Frankly, neither do I."

I made a snap decision, one that would literally change my life, forever. Of course, I had no idea about that, then, when I said to Henson. "I'll sign for him. Discharge him to my custody. Then he's not your problem. Not your PD's problem. He's my problem now."

Henson brightened considerably. "Done. Sorry I didn't get you a coffee, Mr. Lockwood. Good luck." He, too, spun and fled the room, almost as fast as the doctor. Clearly, no one at Addison Gilbert wanted anything to do with an unidentified dude telling sea stories. There would be no checkbox on the paperwork for that case.

A nurse appeared, carrying a plastic bag, which she handed to Lockwood. "These should fit. You should consider a donation, you know, when you find your wallet," she said sarcastically before she fled. There was a pattern here.

"Well, get dressed," I said to Lockwood, stepping outside the perimeter and closing the curtain. "You're coming to Chelsea with me."

I heard rustling as Lockwood got organized. He asked, "Chelsea? You said you were from Boston."

"Yeah, that's the way government works. Our office is in Chelsea. Saying 'FBI Chelsea' just doesn't have the same ring to it."

The curtain slid open and Lockwood emerged, wearing a baggy pair of chinos and a wrinkled button-down shirt, untucked. Clean and reasonably presentable, I thought. He was carrying a plastic bag with what I presumed were whatever wet clothes he arrived in; there was a rip in the bag and it was dripping. We walked to the hall, toward the elevator, leaving a drip-drip-drip trail behind us on the scuffed linoleum.

What am I doing?

CHAPTER
24

MILES LOCKWOOD WAS NOT impressed by my Cinnamon Brown Metallic Taurus. "My tax dollars at work?" he commented sarcastically, as we rolled out of the parking lot and toward the Yankee Division Highway, heading back to Chelsea. I didn't admit that it was actually my car.

"Yeah, something like that. Let's go back to your story. I gotta call this in first. My boss is not going to like this." I dialed Macallister. Voice mail. I left a message. "Agent Macallister. Porter. I have interviewed the victim and, um, while there are pieces of the story that do not seem credible at this, ah, juncture, I think this deserves further investigation. I am transporting him to our office. I'll be there in less than an hour." I paused. How does one terminate that message . . . Goodbye? Have a nice day? Over and out? I waffled for a moment and then just jammed my thumb down on the *END* icon. Problem solved.

"Let's talk about the boxes," I said.

"Am I under arrest?" replied Lockwood.

"No." I thought it best not to divulge that I didn't have the authority to arrest him, or anyone, for that matter. "But . . ." I paused, trying to weave this train of thought while weaving through typical midday Mass traffic, "you are, ah, sort of obligated to help me out. I could have, no, *should* have, left you with Sergeant Henson, who doesn't believe you—and with a hospital bill but without any identification. How d'ya think that would have worked out?"

"Mmm . . . prolly not so good," muttered Lockwood.

I continued, "Besides, if your story is true, you gotta report this, help us fill in the holes. Your story, to be frank, sounds like bullshit. But somehow, I believe you. I don't even know why. So, if you want to unwind this, I am your only ally at the moment. I'd like to talk about the boxes, Mr. Lockwood."

"Miles," he said.

"Yes, I know."

"No, I mean call me Miles. If you want."

I looked sideways at him, and he was looking at me with those hazel eyes. Trying to make eye contact, to show sincerity, as best as one could do at sixty miles per hour. I appreciated the gesture.

"Okay, Miles. The boxes."

"Right. Just over six-feet long. I touched one quickly. Plastic. Hard, smooth, matte-finished black plastic—"

"Wait," I interrupted. "How do you know the length?"

"They brought them below and put them on the settees—the, um, benches—in the cabin on my boat. Those are six-foot-three. I've slept on them a million times. I'm five-eleven. The boxes barely fit. It was almost as if they were made to go there." Miles paused and looked out the window. I waited and after a moment, he continued. "They were pretty wide—maybe two feet. The settees are about twenty inches deep. They overhung the sides a bit. And two feet high. They stuck a little over the backrests, but they fit nicely down the hatch. It's like they were made to go there. *Literally*."

"That's an interesting conclusion," I commented, "but how would they know that?"

"Easy. The entry list for the race is online and it shows boat types. Look up my boat on the builder's website and all those dimensions are there. Layout, general sizing, everything. They pick a doublehanded boat 'cuz there's only two of us. Plenty of room on the boat, only two guys to get rid of." He paused again, and then turned to look at me. "George. They shot George. They killed him! They sank him in their RIB . . .

"What do I do about George? I gotta call his wife. He has kids . . . He—"

"No," I held up a hand and interrupted him. I had actually forgotten about George. Shit. If this story doesn't check out, am I bringing a murderer back to my office? Wait. Double-shit. If there was a murder on board this boat, the FBI will go ballistic. Piracy with a hijacking *and* a murder *and* these box things?

The FBI is risk-adverse. That kind of news would ramp this immediately up to the highest levels. And the reaction would be instant. We're talking roadblocks and helicopters and news conferences.

"Hang on. I'm coming back to George," I lied, to cover my error and my lapse in judgment. I pretended to be focused on the traffic, checking my mirrors and scanning the road, as I tried to figure out what the hell to do next. *I've got a witness who is not entirely credible. That's it. No proof. No evidence. I'm going to look just as incredible—no, that would be un-credible—when we get to Chelsea.*

My anxiety was getting the better of me. *Focus on the facts, Ben!*

"Stay on the boxes," I stated, glancing over at Miles to resume the interview. *That's it! This is an interview. Establish the facts!*

"Yeah, okay." Miles paused again. "Right. Boxes. They were heavy. Two, three guys to pass them below. Lots of grunting. Swearing. 'Don't tip them,' they kept saying. Like they were delicate. Like they held—"

My phone blared its ring, interrupting him, and he stopped. I looked at the display. Macallister. I looked over at Miles and put my index finger to my lips in the universal shh sign. Then I reached down to swipe the phone to accept the call using, of course, my middle finger.

"Porter."

"What the fuck, Porker? You have no authority to transport this guy, whoever he is. You fucking turn around and put him back where you found him. Or you turn in your creds and get a new job. You are way out of line. You—"

Yeah, *what the fuck,* indeed. And nice way to start a call, asshole. I didn't let him get any further and interrupted him with an emphatic, loud "SIR!" He stopped talking.

"Sir, we have a situation. I made a decision. You sent me to interview this guy, who is sitting next to me listening because you're on speaker while I'm driving. So please listen to me and let me brief you." There was nothing on the other side of the call; Macallister was mute. I looked at the display—five bars and the call log time counter was ticking up, so it was not like the call was dropped. Taking his silence as tacit approval to continue, I did just that.

"The situation is, we have a potential terror infiltration. I have not had time to hear the entire story, nor have I had time to analyze the credibility of the story or of any threat. However, that being said, if part of this story checks out, we have six potential—" Miles poked my arm and held up five fingers. Right. "Sorry, five potential unknown subjects who have covertly entered the Continental United States, and we have a potential threat of something smuggled into CONUS. Two *somethings*. Two hard plastic canisters. Approximately six-feet in length and two-feet wide and two-feet high. Contents unknown." I paused for a millisecond, looking for the words. "Taken together, sir, these two items of information are extremely concerning. Especially in light of the event this evening."

Apparently, this got Macallister's attention, and he asked, in a normal tone of voice, "And this is being reported by who?"

"By our vic, sir. The guy with me. Name of Miles Lockwood, from Cohasset. It was his boat. He's the guy who was pulled from the water. Hy-po-ther-mic." I said the last word slowly, one syllable at a time. I definitely didn't need to get into the hypnosis confusion with Macallister again.

"You're saying this is the guy who jumped off his own boat and someone else took it from him?"

"Yessir."

"How'd those guys get on the boat?"

"It appears to have been a middle-of-the-night interception. A hijacking, if you will. The boat was in a sailboat race from Marblehead to Halifax, Canada. About halfway there, in open water. It was boarded in the middle of the night. Those canisters, those boxes, they were loaded with the boarders."

Macallister jumped in. "Lemme see if I got this straight. Boat going to Canada gets intercepted in the middle of the night by unknowns, who load something unknown on the boat, turn it around, and head for the United States coast?"

Didn't I just say that? "Yes, sir."

"We gotta run this down!" exclaimed Macallister. "Where the fuck are you?"

"Sir, I am maybe ten, twelve minutes out."

"Make it ten." Macallister hung up.

Miles looked at me. "That guy for real?" Miles was clearly a quick study. I was beginning to like him.

CHAPTER
25

NINE MINUTES LATER, just after 1:00 PM, we pulled into the Chelsea Field Office parking lot. I had focused on driving, hoping that the local police department and the Mass State PD were otherwise occupied preparing downtown and would not notice an older, shit-brown Ford weaving in and out of lanes on US-1 South. Miles and I had not talked as I contemplated what would be worse, held up in a roadside discussion with Massachusetts's Finest and being late back to the office, or just being late back to the office. I had played the odds and won. Fortunately.

Back on my floor, Macallister was in his office, on the phone. He jabbed his finger toward the hall in a left-ish sort of motion. Confused, I stared back at him. He cupped his hand over the phone mouthpiece and hissed, "conference room." Yeah, that was not obvious. Macallister held up a hand with his fingers splayed. I took that to mean five minutes. Accordingly, we rushed back here for . . . him to take a phone call?

Down the hall to the left-ish, Miles and I selected seats next to each other on one side of a ten-person table inside a glass-walled conference room. I pulled my laptop out and logged into the case file which I had started several hours earlier.

"Want some water? Coffee? I gotta take some notes." Miles merely shook his head back and forth. Inside, under the fluorescent glow of the office lighting, he looked pale and exhausted. He leaned back in the big chair, yawned, and closed his eyes. I settled into my work, first keying in a quick search on Miles Lockwood and finding nothing in our Guardian or other files. I continued furiously tapping keys and transcribing my notes from my trip to Gloucester. As the clock on the wall ticked away five minutes, then ten, I continued—working in details as best I can, adding tags along with time and location references as I went. It occurred to me that I probably write a better case file than an agent since, after reading so many of them, I know how to key in the data in a logical way that can both be searched later and can be descriptive.

I pulled a microphone out of my backpack, plugged it into my laptop, and said to Miles, "I'm gonna record this. I'll take notes, too, but it would be really helpful to have the recording to transcribe later. Are you cool with that? Do you agree?"

He nodded assent. I smiled, trying to build a rapport, but still said, "I gotta hear you say it. So your consent is recorded."

Miles spoke clearly and formally, "Yes, I consent to being recorded." He closed his eyes again.

"Thank you," I replied, and we lapsed back into silence. The audio file would be appended to my case file.

The glass door finally hissed open, as Macallister deigned to join us. At the noise of the door, Miles's eyes snapped open. Macallister looked down his nose at Miles's wrinkled, baggy outfit as he made his way to the head of the table, setting up an awkward arrangement: the boss at one end, and, down toward the far end, Miles and me. Not very congenial. Nor very professional, in my opinion. Macallister declined to offer a handshake or even a perfunctory introduction, and Miles looked over at me, an incredulous look on his face, and mouthed again, "this guy for real?" I grinned briefly, then, wiping the expression off my face, focused instead on my laptop. Miles took my cue and started to carefully examine the grain on the oak conference table. I wanted to point out to him that it's government issue so it's not real oak, just a veneer. The silence lingered for a few seconds longer.

"Okay." Without standing up, Macallister wriggled out of his suit jacket and made a production of rolling up his shirtsleeves. *Really? We're getting down to work, now?* I kept my jacket on.

"Right. Okay, I'm Supervisory Special Agent Macallister. Fill in some blanks for me. Quickly. Got it?" He didn't wait for an answer from Miles and barreled on. "First, when did this all go down, exactly?"

"Early yesterday morning. Tuesday morning. About 1:30 AM," Miles replied.

"You said someone hijacked your boat. How'd they get on it?"

"I heard a noise. I went below to grab a spotlight. When I came back on deck, George was lying in a pool of blood and a RIB was alongside with guys climbing out of it. Onto my boat."

Fuck. I had not told Macallister about George. I wanted to weave that in later, after getting to the boxes. I started to interrupt, to redirect the thread, but Macallister beat me to it. "Who's George?" It had to come out at some point, so I let Miles handle it, and I kept taking notes directly into the case file.

"He's my sailing partner. We sail doublehanded. Me and George. I own the boat, but he is really good . . . *Was* really good."

"What happened to George? He still on the boat?" Macallister asked.

"No. He's gone. They shot him when they sank their RIB that they used to board."

"Rigid Inflatable Boat. R-I-B," I quickly spelled out. Macallister glared at me.

"Yeah, of course, I know what a fucking RIB is." I was genuinely surprised. He looked back at Miles. "Now you're saying there's a murder, too?" he sneered.

Miles was unfazed. "Yeah. After they boarded, they threw George into their RIB. They tied him down. He was still alive. Seb shot George and sank the RIB. Then, after, Omar told me—"

Macallister jumped in again. "Wait a fucking minute, you're on a first-name basis with these guys?"

"Well, they used their names, so I fucking remembered them. I wasn't sitting around bullshitting with them. They took my fucking boat and murdered my friend. Don't believe me? Go fuck yourself!"

Ugh. This isn't going well, I thought. *Time to step in.*

"Hang on, Miles. We're just trying to put the pieces together. This whole thing is kinda far-fetched, from where we sit. So, take it one step at a time. We're on the same side." Miles nodded, appreciating my attempt to calm the room. Macallister was not quite as charmed.

"Shut up, Porter." On the bright side, at least he said my name correctly. Progress. Macallister turned to Miles. "Let's say I believe you. Tell me what happened next. Quickly."

Miles opened his mouth to speak but stopped as the glass door hissed open.

Oh. Shit.

It was her. The boss. I mean, the big boss. Jennifer Appleton. The Special Agent in Charge.

26

I HAD NEVER ACTUALLY MET the Special Agent in Charge, but she's renowned even beyond the Boston office. Super smart, never raises her voice or swears, a figure who literally glides through the halls of the building like a witch, constantly taking it all in. She knows everything. Speaking of witches, apparently, she even lives in Salem, and grew up there too.

Kind and gentle are not words used to describe the SAC. While her demeanor was placid, word had it not to cross her, or you'll find yourself dispatched to the worst assignment as the least senior employee in the least important office. Or even worse, get sent to the swamp in Washington, DC.

On the rare occasions when my group has gone out for drinks after work, talk invariably turned to the SAC—who she's destroyed, who better watch their step, and gossip like that. Both the men and the women in our group were in awe of her. Her lightly-tanned skin appeared unlined, perhaps because she seldomly exhibited stress, and her conservatively-styled, shoulder-length auburn hair never stranded out of place. She's always impeccably dressed, elegant without being stiff or frumpy, with what they called her "signature look," always a piece of custom, handmade jewelry, subtle but stunning. A simple tassel on a leather necklace accented by a silver clasp and ball, or a unique stone like an agate hanging from a beaded chain, or color-tone-matched bracelets on her wrist. Always silver accents, never gold. Gold might be gaudy, ostentatious, but silver could be cool, sophisticated. Like her.

"Mr. Lockwood, I'm Jennifer Appleton. Special Agent in Charge, FBI Boston Field Office." Her eyes never left Miles, who had straightened in his chair and was staring back at her, mouth slightly agape. She continued, flatly, "This is a very unusual story. I've been reading this case file." She gently lifted a tablet and waved it back and forth in front of us. I hadn't even noticed her carrying one. "Good idea, Mr. Porter, to be updating this in almost real-time. Very helpful. Therefore, I have the background. However, I have not the time."

The SAC casually raised her left wrist to look at her small, elegant watch. Silver, of course. "I have an appointment in the city this afternoon, and I do not do late."

Yeah, an "appointment." *The President of the United States is going to be in your city. On your watch.* And she calls it an "appointment?" This lady made ice look warm.

The SAC looked carefully at Miles and asked, "What I would like to know, Mr. Lockwood, is how you managed to escape these alleged hijackers."

Miles swallowed and spoke to the SAC for the first time. "I did the math on distance traveled, because I wanted to be close enough to the coast. And I wanted it to be dark. I got my opportunity and it was still the pitch black of night. I pretended to have to use the head. The toilet. So I could prepare. I have this air cartridge, the kind of thing divers use for a short time underwater. I have it if I have to check something out in an emergency under the boat. I set up the Spare Air with my harness, popped open the forward hatch, and when my guard was distracted, I dove off the front of the boat."

Miles took a deep breath as he looked from Macallister to Appleton to me. He would have seen poker faces. The SAC repeated, with a faint tone of incredulity in her soft, level voice, "You dove off the front of the boat? While it was moving?"

"Yeah. I actually wanted the boat to pretty much run over me so I could grab the keel as it went by, so that I'd get stuck under the boat. I wanted to hide under the boat. Lucky for me, I guess, the guy driving saw me dive off and chopped the throttle, so the boat stopped pretty quick. I tied myself onto the keel and breathed from the Spare Air. I counted my breaths.

"They circled the boat slowly and shot into the water. I was running out of air, so I dove down after they gave up looking, and they left without seeing me. Obviously."

Miles took another deep breath, which gave me the opportunity to catch up typing into the case file on my laptop. Miles picked up on this and waited another moment before he proceeded.

"Problem was, in those water temps, I had six hours, tops. I inflated my life vest and I caught my breath, waiting for the boat to disappear out of sight. After a while, I swam for a bit, toward the west, where the boat had gone, but I got tired. Then I just floated. They teach you a position where you curl up and try to conserve heat. I got lucky because I got picked up. Otherwise, I'd be dead."

A stillness fell over the room until the silence was broken by the SAC saying, delicately but dripping with precise politeness, "Thank you, Mr. Lockwood. Why don't you remain comfortable while I have a word with my colleagues. Special Agent Macallister, Mr. Porter, would you follow me, please."

She rose from her chair and glided from the conference room. Macalister and I followed.

CHAPTER
27

AT ROUGHLY THE MIDDLE of the length of each hall of conference rooms and offices, the architects of the building had designed "breakout spaces." Comfortable club chair seating, perhaps with a sofa here and there, around low coffee tables, always with exterior windows on one side and innocuous artwork on the walls. You know, government art—watercolor landscapes in pastel colors, bought as prints in some purchasing office bulk buy and spread out across the country in government offices. All part of the design story of the building. A place for impromptu meetings and collaborations, in a casual, congenial breakout space.

Which, of course, no one ever used. If you had something to discuss, you did it in a conference room, maybe with your sleeves rolled up to make it look like you were intent on an important task to the onlookers spying through the glass doors. You did not sit on the casual furnishings in the breakout space.

First, because there was no privacy.

Second, because it would look like you were taking a break.

And the FBI does *not* take breaks.

Macallister and I followed the SAC to one of these spaces, and we each selected a seat. In the nine months that I have been in this brand-new building, I have never, ever seen anyone sit in any of these breakout spaces. My ass is quite possibly the first ass in this club chair. I quickly realized that it was actually not that comfortable. Kind of stiff. I didn't sink in. Naturally, it was government issue. Which, I started to conclude, was a step below hotel room quality.

Macallister fidgeted in his seat, deferring to Appleton, who finally spoke. I, naturally, sat mute. This kind of confab was way above my pay grade.

"Mr. Porter. I'm aware that it is very unusual for you to do this type of field work."

She looked at me oddly before going on. "The case file you opened states that Lockwood's boat started a sailboat race in Marblehead with a finish in Canada. You go on to describe Lockwood's explanation of sailboat racing: that it is unpredictable. That you don't know how much wind there will be, or what direction it will blow. The boats don't go that fast."

I didn't dare interrupt but instead just nodded, to affirm, *yeah, that's what I wrote.*

Appleton continued, "With that type of imprecision, you couldn't possibly predict locations with accuracy or timing. Let's say this aggressor wants to intercept a boat, load whatever he has, get back to the US coastline, and then get into Boston in time for the event tonight. There are simply too many variables. With the weather, with the wind, with the erratic course that the sailboats take, how does one plan this all out to the hour? According to Lockwood, they took the boat, what, Monday night? Or more accurately, very early Tuesday morning? That's almost two days ago. *Two days!* Why not earlier? Why then?"

Slightly smirking, she went on, her tone almost imperceptibly rising. "And then this whole plot is foiled because Lockwood claims he dove off his boat—his moving boat! And he held onto the bottom of his moving boat? To avoid being shot at? That is an outrageously implausible story in itself."

Consulting the tablet screen, where I guessed she had the narrative portion of my case file open, she scowled, "Lockwood somehow survived being shot at, didn't freeze to death from hypothermia, got picked up just in time as he's turning blue, gets revived, calls the FBI . . . all in the nick of time? Oh, and *then* adds the part about these mysterious boxes being brought onto his boat?

"It doesn't add up."

Finishing her lecture, Appleton concluded, "And Mr. Porter, you fail to see that, because you have no training, and no authority, to do this work. You had no authority to transport this . . . this . . . witness, for lack of a better word. You are way out of line.

"This smells like a scam. The insurance theory seems very plausible. Mr. Lockwood sank his boat and was picked up by his accomplices. This is fraud. This is a police matter and should have remained a police matter."

The SAC had been glaring at me as she verbally cut my legs off at the knees. I felt like Monty Python's Black Knight. *Just a flesh wound!* But, even so, I could not contain myself. I was pissed off.

"Ma'am. With all due respect, of course. Special Agent Macallister assigned me to do this work. This is a terror threat. It is our duty to investigate. We have barely begun to do so."

I am in deep shit here. But I barreled on, gaining confidence. I've gone down the ole rabbit hole. There was no turning back now, and I continued, "And, if Lockwood's story turns out to be credible, we have five men and two unknown boxes of something inside the borders of the United States, who are not supposed to be here. This is a crime on the high seas turned terror threat. This demands our investigation."

I had locked eyes with Appleton during my tirade. I wondered, briefly, if her eyes got dried out. It remained so quiet that I could hear the faint hum of the air blowing through the air conditioning vent in the ceiling above the breakout space.

Without breaking my eye contact, she asked, "Mr. Porter, are you prepared to risk your career following this hunch of yours?"

I gulped. But I nodded, affirmatively. "Yes. To be honest, ma'am, I think it is a little harsh to tell me that I am risking my career by doing what I'm supposed to be doing. But all the same, there's something here and we need to find it."

Wait, what? Did I just fucking say all that to the SAC?

The SAC rose from her chair. Rather, she kind of levitated out of her chair

"Very well," she said. "You are wasting my time, Mr. Porter."

Turning to Macallister, who had, unhelpfully I thought, remained mute during this conversation, Appleton added, "So that we are clear, Special Agent Macallister, I do not condone this investigation. From where I stand at the moment, and from what Mr. Porter has already written in his case file, this is all an unsubstantiated story that is beyond belief, beyond verification, and is most likely a scam or a fraud. I expect better of you."

She sighted down her nose and lasered Macallister's eyes, whisper-snarling, "Clean this mess up and close it."

The SAC turned and glided away, vanishing down the hall.

CHAPTER
28

I GLUMLY WATCHED THE SAC float down the hall, thinking, *my career is over,* as I second-guessed myself, my initial confidence draining. Macallister, too, silently observed through hooded eyes as the SAC disappeared.

When she was gone from sight, Macallister broke my trance.

"Godmamitporterwhatwhereyouthinking?" The words blended into each other as Macallister fumed, a tiny bit of spittle forming on the right corner of his mouth. I prepared myself for another ass-chewing as I watched his eyes narrow to slits. I waited for what I expected next. Something along the lines of, *You're fired, Porker. Pack up your shit-brown Taurus and hit the road.*

I was way wrong. I couldn't have been more wrong.

Macallister casually leaned back in his chair, made himself comfortable as he crossed one leg over the other, and said evenly, professionally composed, "Holy shit, Porter, I've never seen anything like that. I can't believe you dared to cross the SAC. You're fucked, you know. *If* Lockwood is scamming us."

He chuckled, mirthlessly. I wasn't quite sure what to say, so I remained silent, wondering, against all odds, *What is happening? Is this for real? Is Macallister going to back me up?*

He was.

Looking at me, he said softly, at first slowly but then gaining pace, "She's fucking wrong. We have a fucking presidential visit in Boston, and we have this fucking looney sitting in our office building claiming that who-knows-what was brought into the country on his boat and we are sitting here chatting about it. We need action. We need to investigate this. With her or, it looks like, without her. What's next?"

I gulped. I couldn't quite believe what I had heard. *Macallister is on my side? We're doing this?*

"Sir," I said. "Thank you. But, the SAC basically told us to back off. Didn't she?"

"Yeah," he replied. "But I think she's wrong."

Macallister grinned, adding in a conspiratorial tone, "And she did tell me to close it. Let's close it. Like I said, what's next?"

I thought that over for a moment, examining the innocuous landscape print on the wall behind Macallister's head. It was a blurry, washed out watercolor, and I wanted it to be more in focus. Like the case. Like Lockwood's story.

That was exactly what was next, so I stood and said to Macallister, "What's next is we find some facts. Bring this thing into focus. Let's get the rest of Lockwood's story."

CHAPTER
29

WE RETURNED TO THE conference room where we found Miles leaning back in his chair, staring at the ceiling tiles, turning his gaze toward us as the glass door hissed closed. Miles eyed Macallister warily as my boss, forgoing his previous spot at the head of the long table, took a seat directly opposite of our witness. I sat next to Miles and flipped open my laptop screen.

Macallister looked at Miles, then me, then back at Miles. With his elbows planted on the oak veneer, Macallister restarted the interview. "Where were we? You told us about them taking the boat, and you told us about your escape, but we missed a part. What happened after they took the boat?"

I was shocked at Macallister's recall. That was exactly where we had left off.

Miles answered, "They loaded the boxes below into the cabin, I put the sails away with a gun to my head, we turned, and we started going west."

"How did you know what direction you were going?" Macallister asked.

"Uh, because the sun came up behind us, and later that day, set in front of us."

Macallister, unfazed by this little lesson, nodded. "Just checking. Continue."

"We motored all day and into the night. I tried to keep up with the math in my head. I know pretty much how fast the boat is going just listening to the engine revs. We stopped twice so they could pour more fuel into the tank from the cans they brought. When I jumped off, I figured we were maybe ten miles off the coast. I was hoping for fishing traffic. I got lucky, obviously."

Macallister leaned back in his chair and steepled his fingers. Previously, I would have thought he was trying to collect his thoughts before saying something stupid. But now, I figured he was actually considering all the angles. To his credit, he got through it. "If had you not jumped off, fair to say you expected that you would have ended up like George?"

"Yeah." Miles nodded. "They made that pretty clear. I was disposable. I think they kept me around in case something went wrong with the boat. Oh, and to call it in before getting rid of me."

"Wait, what?" I blurted. "Call in what?"

"After they took over the boat, they had me send a text to the race control. To the effect of," he held up both hands with his index and pointer fingers bent, and air-quoted, "my mainsail was torn, and I was heading back to Marblehead."

"You sent a text from the middle of the ocean?" I asked. I quickly typed that little gem into the case file.

"From a satphone. Iridium. Satellite phone. Not cell phone." Miles looked back and forth from Macallister back to me.

The reason for the text hit me at once, and I verbalized my theory. "Red herring. It was a decoy message. Such that the boat could return to the US. With a plausible reason, so it would be unlikely that anyone would take notice."

Macallister's eyes went wide as he added, "And with whatever the fuck's in those boxes."

CHAPTER

30

THE THREE OF US—Macallister, Miles, and me—stared at each other, until I broke the silence, saying, "A text message. From a satellite phone. Surely we can verify that!"

"Who'd you send the text to?" Macallister demanded.

Miles sat up straight in his chair, the look of exhaustion that had creased his face disappearing and with some brightness returning to his eyes. "Race control. The head of the race was a lady named . . . named . . . Shit, I don't remember. It's online, though. You can look it up."

"Where?" I asked.

"Race website," he answered. "Google the race and then look for documents, then sailing instructions. It's in there. I had a printed copy on the boat. I looked at it when I set up the Iridium to send the text."

Five years of tapping keys at the FBI made me a whiz at Google and web-based research, and in a matter of seconds, I found the page and the PDF that he was referring to, a document entitled "Sailing Instructions", which included, as Miles stated, the name of the chairwoman of the race, a Theresa Columbus in Sachem, Massachusetts, and a telephone number.

Jabbing at the speakerphone at the middle of the conference table, I dialed, hoping that the caller ID at the other end would read "FBI" and that would motivate the person at the other end to pick up that call.

"Hello, this is Theresa," said the speakerphone. Or, more accurately, said Theresa, through the speakerphone.

"Ms. Columbus, my name is Ben Porter, with the FBI Boston Field Office. You're the chair of the Marblehead-to-Halifax Ocean Race?"

"Yes," she replied. "What can I do for you, Agent Porter?"

Yup, like I said earlier, everyone assumes that anyone with the FBI is an agent. I didn't correct her, naturally, and dispensing with the pleasantries, I baritoned in my best I'm-not-an-agent-but-you-think-I-am deep voice, "I'm inquiring about a vessel in your race. *Flying Lady*. Captained by a Mr. Miles Lockwood. Can you tell me anything about that vessel?"

"Sure," she answered. "Definitely. Got notice from them that they retired. I would have thought they would have checked in again, but I haven't heard from them since."

Miles opened his mouth to speak but I beat him to it, simultaneously giving him the *Shh* sign with my finger and asking the speakerphone, "What do you mean, retired? Can you flesh this out for me, please?"

"Yes, of course," she replied nicely. "It was, um, Monday night. Really, Tuesday morning. Like two or three in the morning. This number, the number you called, is reserved for race participants. I have it on this stand-alone smartphone here. It pinged that night with a text from *Flying Lady*. The text read that they were retiring from the race with damage of some kind. Hang on, I can read it."

I visualized her doing what we all do, taking the phone from her ear and swiping away at it to find the correct screen and to put it on speaker. We heard some rustling and then she said, in a slightly more tinny voice, "It read, quote, *Flying Lady*. We are retiring from the race with a torn, unrepairable mainsail. Returning to Marblehead under power. Miles Lockwood. Unquote. That's it."

"And this didn't seem unusual to you?" I asked.

"Not really. I looked them up and saw it was a doublehanded boat. I remembered the entry and that this was their first race with us. And most, if not all boats, don't carry spare mainsails. So, yeah, it made sense."

Miles shrugged and nodded affirmatively. Macallister rolled his eyes. I got it, agreeing. Weird activity, this sailing thing.

Theresa Columbus added, "I texted back asking if they needed assistance, but they replied no. Then I marked them as retired in the race results and went back to bed."

"That's all?" I asked.

"Yup," she replied. "It's too bad, but it happens."

Macallister spoke up. "Ma'am, this has been helpful. I'm Supervisory Special Agent Macallister. We're going to need to see those texts, somehow. Don't erase them and don't do anything with that phone. Okay?"

"Sure," Columbus answered. "Just let me know what I can do. Is everything okay with them? Is there a problem?"

We looked at each other, trying to decide nonverbally who would come up with some line of bullshit to answer that loaded question. It was Macallister's turn to shrug, so I said, "No ma'am. No problem. Just a routine inquiry on a vessel returning to the States."

"Oh," she said. "I would have thought that was Coast Guard, not FBI. Which reminds me, yeah, I did think it was a little odd that they headed back to Marblehead. They were so much closer to Canada."

At that, Miles sat bolt upright in his chair, his eyes wide and his shoulders back. He opened his mouth and clenched his fists. He clearly had something to say but Macallister shot him a look, asking the speakerphone, "How'd you know that?"

"Easy. After I got the texts, I looked them up. On marine traffic. They couldn't have been more than fifty, tops seventy-five, miles to Canada."

Miles had risen from his seat and started to almost hop up and down. He slid his finger across his throat, signaling to us that he wanted us to end the conversation so he could speak. I wasn't quite sure what he had in mind, but I figured we were done with Theresa Columbus, so I said, "Gotcha. Thanks for your help. We may have some follow-up questions so please remain available. And like Agent Macallister said, we will need that phone."

"Right. No problem. Bye!"

The speakerphone and the helpful Theresa Columbus went silent. And Miles shouted, "*I am such an idiot! AIS!*"

CHAPTER
31

MILES LOCKWOOD PLOPPED BACK down in his seat, saying, "AIS. How could I forget? It was on the whole time. Transmitting the whole time. Why the fuck didn't I think of it before? It's so obvious!"

Both Macallister and I were confused. Miles, however, was on a mission, as he grabbed my laptop, where I still had the race website open, and started jabbing at the keys frantically.

"Gotta go to *Marinetraffic.com*," Miles narrated as he punched at my computer, repeating himself, "AIS. It was on the whole time. I never shut it off. It was on when they took the boat. It was on when I jumped off the boat. It was on the *whole* time. There. There. There," Miles was jabbing his finger toward the upper right of the screen where the *Marinetraffic.com* page had loaded, "search box. Searching Flying Lady." As he typed it in, Miles was agitated and excited.

"What the hell is AIS?" I asked.

"Automatic Identification System. Most boats have it. Almost all ships do. Commercial stuff. It's like a tracking thing. It links in with radio and GPS and broadcasts your position and speed and stuff. And receives, too, so you can see what the other boats are doing."

On the *Marinetraffic.com* screen, the search query had returned six vessels with the name *Flying Lady*. Miles clicked the first one of three with the description "Sailing Vessel (US)." "No," Miles said instantly when an image of a blue sailboat popped up. He clicked back, then on the next entry on the list. A white-hulled boat in the image. "Yes!"

He studied the screen for a split-second, looking at the data that appeared on the screen—a small map and a timestamp for "position received," then he bolted from his chair.

"The boat's in fucking Gloucester!" he yelled, then collapsed back into his seat.

The three of us stared at the screen in silence.

"And still transmitting. The last position received was . . . *is* . . . NOW!"

"We gotta go to back to Gloucester!" Miles hopped back out of his chair. *He's getting a good quad workout with all these chair calisthenics,* I thought.

"Not so fast," Macallister cautioned. "Let's take a closer look."

Macallister picked up the conference table phone handset and jabbed some numbers. Whoever was on the other end answered immediately. "Do we have an account for *Marinetraffic.com*?" he queried. Within seconds, he scribbled something on a pad of paper and passed it to me.

I pulled my laptop back in front of me, and, finding the sign-in box, I keyed in the hastily-transcribed credentials that Macallister had written down on the pad. Apparently, we do. Of course, we do. *Good call, boss,* I thought.

Logged into the site, I slid the laptop back to Miles, who brought up the history of the vessel's tracking. "Gold mine," I said, thinking, *this is unbelievable. Miles was right. Why didn't we think of this before?*

He clicked on "History" on the on-screen menu. "Looks like the boat stopped moving at about 4:30 this morning." The boat's track curved into Gloucester Harbor and back east, the track appearing to get longer as he zoomed out on the screen. "And here, check this out." He pointed at a blip in the track, otherwise mostly straight, at 2:32 AM.

"That's where I got off," Miles stated in a matter-of-fact tone. Like it's an everyday thing to dive off the bow of a moving boat.

"That fits. Not too far to Rockport from there," Macallister said, as Miles continued to zoom and drag the map. We quickly assembled the start of a timeline which I scrawled onto a pad of paper, reading it out loud as we worked backward in time:

"Today, July 12. 4:30 A M. The boat is stopped in Gloucester.

"Today, July 12. 2:32 A M. The boat circles. Lockwood claims this is where he dove off.

"Yesterday, July 11. 1:40 A M. The boat slows its eastward progress and then turns south and goes a short distance, then turns west and aims for Massachusetts, Cape Ann area."

I turned to Miles. "I'd say your story checks out." He nodded.

Macallister murmured his assent, still looking at the screen. I looked back and forth between the two of them, thinking to myself, *That's it? Follow the electronic breadcrumbs and the story is solid. This agent shit is easy-peasy.* But, fortunately for my credibility and possibly for my career, I kept that to myself, as a new thought jumped into my head. Jolting upright in my chair, I exclaimed, "So where the fuck are the boxes?"

With his finger tapping the location icon of the boat in Gloucester Harbor, Miles said softly, "Well, last we know, they are right here, but that was nine or ten hours ago." He traced an ever-widening circle on the screen as he manipulated the trackpad on my laptop with the other hand. The map zoomed out and New England came in, then out of focus, as the map grew in size to encompass New York State through Virginia.

Macallister stated, flatly, "Shit. Call it a ten-hour head start. At sixty miles per hour, six hundred miles, and counting. Those boxes could be anywhere in the northeast. They could be in New York City. They could be in Washington, D C by now."

He took a breath and continued, "Or they could easily be in downtown Boston and in position for tonight's event. Or at Logan Airport. Or *anywhere* in between."

32

WEDNESDAY, EARLY AFTERNOON — NEW MILFORD, CONNECTICUT

IN THEIR LOOSE FORMATION, the drive for the two vans and the single sedan had been uneventful, taking slightly longer than the predicted travel time due to morning traffic through the city of Hartford.

They traveled the Yankee Division Highway, then merged onto I-95 South, then took I-90 West in Newtown. Each vehicle was assigned a rest stop at separate service plazas on I-90 before exiting to I-84 West in Sturbridge and continuing into Connecticut.

Passing through the Connecticut State capital of Hartford, the three vehicles exited Interstate 84 before reaching the faded industrial city-town of Danbury, Connecticut. They followed Route 202 north several miles, the roadside peppered with an inconsistent blend of fast-food establishments, auto repair and sales enterprises, and tidy, unostentatious houses—a snapshot of small-town America, pleasant folks toiling in obscurity.

After making two turns in quick succession off Route 202, one-by-one the drivers found their assigned destination. Upon his arrival, last in line, Omar was exceptionally pleased by the selection of the layover location. Secluded from prying eyes by those two jogs off the main road, it was a cluster of three long, low, one-story industrial structures, with brown-asphalt shingled roofs and drab beige walls fenestrated by brown overhead doors. It was perfect in its nothingness.

The complex was not fully occupied, either, and both pedestrian and vehicular traffic was minimal. The only clue to their presence was, upon its arrival, the tan Buick Regal parked outside an overhead door among many other identical overhead doors—an ordinary automobile in an ordinary setting.

The two vans had been pulled into a cavernous work bay upon arrival, and the silver GMC was already, after only a couple of hours of effort, beginning to assume a new appearance. This was the more complicated project of the two, therefore it was commenced first.

Expediency was not a concern, though; there would have plenty of time for the work that lay ahead for the day. Accuracy and precision were important, though, and Omar was nothing if not precise. He scrutinized the work his men were doing, but he allowed his thoughts to wander.

After the sunrise, sitting alone at a plastic Formica table, Omar enjoyed a leisurely breakfast at the McDonald's at the Charlton-Mass Pike Service Plaza, the last service plaza before I-84. Sipping at a hot coffee, the man who called himself Omar thought, *hardly an Arabic bean, but acceptable.*

He contemplated his breakfast, though, as virtually unpalatable. It had been some time since Omar had been on American soil, and, trying to blend in at the counter, he had ordered two "Egg McMuffin" sandwiches. Forcing one of the concoctions down, Omar deliberated the irony of worrying about a potential radiation leak from the boxes against the wholly unnatural meal that he was consuming.

The combination of caffeine and protein, however unhealthy, began to take its restorative effect on his body and mind. With his spirits perking up, he watched the commuters coming and going. Would they act this casually tomorrow? Would they be so carefree, so nonchalant, as they went about their morning routines?

Slowing sipping his coffee, Omar considered that the plan had gone well. It was time to move forward.

Omar had chosen this stop for himself not only to ensure that he would not be in the vicinity of the vans, but also because it was approximately halfway on his planned drive for this morning. Powering up the Pixel device and joining the open Wi-Fi network at the service place, Omar pulled up his destination from a stored list. New Milford, Connecticut. One hour and forty-seven minutes.

After switching the Pixel to "Airplane Mode," he manually stepped through the on-screen directions, memorizing them. Powering off and pocketing the mobile, he stood, gathering and then disposing the waste of wrappers and napkins and coffee cup. Omar took leave of the McDonald's and returned to the Buick.

Shifting the Regal into "Drive" and carefully merging into the flowing traffic, he followed the signage to I-84 West. Seconds after merging back onto the Mass Pike, the sedan passed under one of the ubiquitous toll gantries, with a paraphernalia of equipment dangling off it and with its camera flashes blinking erratically. Fueled by caffeine and American fast-food, Omar laughed out loud.

I'm hiding in plain sight, he thought, driving under the unblinking electronic eye of the tolling gantry. That was the genius of the plan. Just as it was while on the boat: with the AIS tag, the boat was perfectly visible. And therefore, invisible in its anonymity.

That part of the plan—exploiting a very real deficiency in American security—had gone perfectly. The US-flagged vessel had blithely and innocently motored back into US waters, without even so much a glance by Customs, Immigration, TSA, or the Coast Guard—none of the agencies that comprised the Department of Homeland Security.

The boat was one of thousands on the Massachusetts coastline. The only people who care about sailboats are sailors, and in the crowded summertime harbors, one more boat was just that, a single vessel, unremarkable. No one would look for it. Because, of course, no one knew to look for it.

Immediately after arrival at the drab New Milford complex, Seb and John had parked the silver GMC van in the assigned garage bay. Leaving the long, black box inside the van, they unloaded the remaining contents of the van's cargo bay. A tidy arrangement of materials and tools were laid out carefully next to the vehicle: several cardboard boxes, approximately five feet long and nine inches square, an array of tools, several bottles of various solutions, and a pile of rags.

With the rags, they had thoroughly wiped the exterior and then polished the silver-painted surface with an alcohol agent. Slicing open the cardboard boxes, they removed rolls of white vinyl, and carefully began unspooling the vinyl onto the slab sides of the van, holding it in place with bits of tape and carefully positioned magnets.

Joined by Hans and Bruce upon their arrival in the white Chevrolet Express van, the team of four men, having practiced this procedure before, slowly but effectively changed the color of the GMC from its native silver to a bland white, peeling and sticking and cutting the vinyl wrap carefully onto the cargo van. By the time Omar arrived, somewhat delayed by the traffic that had built during his leisurely breakfast break at the Charlton service plaza, white vinyl was drooped over most of the van, cut into rough pieces and ready to be molded and adhered to the sheet metal.

The crew had made excellent progress, and the silver GMC was becoming white. Omar looked at his watch. It was now early afternoon. Plenty of time to finish the GMC later. It was time to move to the Chevrolet, and then to send it to Chicago.

CHAPTER
33

STARING AT THE MAP OF THE northeast of the United States on my laptop, Macallister, Miles, and I sat mute.

Macallister reclined in his seat, crossing his arms over his chest. I had gained a new-found respect for him, and I let him think.

Finally, he leaned forward, saying, "We need more evidence. We bring this to the SAC now, we got nothing. All we know is that the boat appears to be in Gloucester and that it really did turn around. Other than that, we got a text message, and anyone could fake a text message. What we have so far is inconclusive.

"And, Porter, I think it would be best if we have some semblance of a plan in place."

I was way out of my league. *A plan? By me?* I stared at the screen, hoping to find an answer there. All I saw was the map, zoomed out to show New England, New York, Virginia, Pennsylvania, Maryland, and the track of Miles's boat stretching almost to Canada and then turning back and—*the boat.* Start there. It was our last lead, *and* it was also our biggest clue. Duh.

"A plan. *The* plan. Here we go. Miles and I are going to Gloucester. You know anyone there? Gloucester PD or any agents we have nearby?

They gotta surround the boat, but subtly, and quietly. No one gets on or off till we get there. They don't touch it till we get there."

I sat up straight. "We need to find another thread. Two threads would be better. Hopefully, we can find something on the boat that leads us off it."

"Yeah," Macallister said softly. "You know, we're going off the reservation here. The SAC will be pissed. If asked, I'll tell her you are taking Lockwood home. I'll handle getting some help in Gloucester. I can do that from here."

He stood. "I'll be right back. Update that case file while I'm gone."

As he pulled open the glass door, he said, "And grab some coffee. You're gonna need it. I'm gonna see if I can get us some help from Anastasia. You're gonna need that, too."

"So," Miles said as the glass door closed behind me as I brought two sixteen-ounce coffee cups back into the conference room, "who's Anastasia?"

"Well, let me give you a bit of background." I paused, wondering how to phrase this. Should I just come out and say, *I'm obsessed with her, but I have never spoken with her*, or should I play it a little cooler? Probably the latter.

Definitely the latter.

"Anastasia is Anastasia Volkov. She's the de-facto head of our operations center. Computer whiz. She's like thirty, thirty-one, so she's not our most senior Intelligence Analyst, but she's the best. She's legendary, even beyond Boston. Whenever there is a problem to be solved, she is always in the mix."

"In other words, she's a nerd," stated Miles.

"Not exactly," I chuckled. "I've actually never met her in person. Maybe we both get to meet her, if Macallister can convince her to help us."

I pulled my laptop closer and began to type, updating the case file as we both sipped at our coffees. I wondered if the SAC still had her tablet and was reading it.

Probably not, I thought. *She's probably downtown by now.*

As I typed, initially rapidly but then more slowly, I began to second-guess myself again, replaying the mostly one-way conversation

Macallister and I had with the SAC, my confidence draining. *This is too much for me. She's right. I have no training to do this work.*

Self-confidence has always been a struggle for me. My weight, of course, didn't help. I'd attempt to use humor to, well, break the ice with people. But humor is subjective, right? I mean, am I funny? Or just weird?

What do I say to Anastasia if Macallister gets her to help? Do I admit that I am wading into waters way deeper than I can handle? Do I bluster? Do I play it cool? What do I say to *her*?

I'm single, I haven't dated since school and, truthfully, that was nothing serious. Anastasia is *way* out of my league, right?

Glancing at Miles, I wondered if he ever thought like that. *Nah.* He's got that manner, you know, of a salesman. The ingratiating grin and the clear eyes. He sells himself then he sells whatever it is that he wants you to buy. I need to do that.

My resolve strengthening some, with an inkling of some self-confidence, I clicked save on the case file as the glass door hissed open and Macallister barked, "Follow me."

CHAPTER

34

IN A MOSTLY WINDOWLESS area in the core of the building, we have our operations center. It hums twenty-four-seven. Staffed round the clock, year-round, the ops center ties us in with Homeland Security and all those other agencies with the acronym names. I don't know any of the people working here. But, like everyone else in the building, I'd know of Anastasia.

She was known to speak very little about her upbringing, preferring to concentrate on whatever work was at hand rather than dwell in her past. The story that I heard was that she was adopted by an American family at a young age and that she was a Ukrainian orphan by birth. Her adoptive family was wealthy, and she wanted for nothing, but had no interest in a privileged lifestyle. After graduating from the Massachusetts Institute of Technology, majoring in computer science, she joined the Bureau. Her hint of an accent, with her olive skin and flaxen, long, straight hair, makes her exotic, as does the small, silver Russian wristwatch on her left wrist that she was known to wear, with its Cyrillic markings. Unique. Stunning. And she was wicked smart. So smart that, even if you've never laid eyes on her, you'd respect her for her intelligence.

We reached Anastasia's space. Not an office, not a cube. Basically, just a corner with a giant workstation with maybe ten or fifteen screens. Big flat screens overhead, angled down, a bunch of big LED monitors, and a desk surface with a couple of keyboards and more screens. In a room with several of these behemoth workstations, these edifices to technology, Anastasia's was by far the largest. The electric bill for this place must be insane.

Anastasia spun her chair to face us and stood, extending her right hand toward Miles. "Mr. Lockwood, it's my pleasure."

Miles blushed and stuttered, "Yes, ah, ah, Miles is good." They shook hands, somewhat formally.

"Wonderful, I'm Anastasia. Hi, Ben." She sat back down, motioning at a couple of wheeled chairs nearby. We grabbed them and rolled them over. *Hi Ben?* Like we've met before? I'm, well, smitten. What a great word, *smitten*. It's—

Anastasia broke me out of my ridiculous thoughts. "Where do we start? Good case file, by the way. I skimmed it while Macallister was bringing you down here. I'll reread it after you leave. You've gotta get a move on."

As she was talking, Anastasia had been gathering some items on her desk—an iPhone, an earpiece, a charging cord, and a car ignition fob. She shoved the untidy pile in my direction. "Here. Phone."

She swiped the phone open and manipulated menus for a moment, then she held it, face up, toward me. "Thumb." I complied, pressing the ball of my thumb on the sensor at the bottom of the screen. She locked my thumbprint into the phone and continued.

"This earpiece and phone are a little special. If you pull the earpiece out, you can use the phone like normal or as a speakerphone. If you put the earpiece in your ear, it automatically senses that and connects to the phone."

"So, it's like those new Apple AirPods!" I exclaimed, referencing *the* must-have accessory that was released in December 2016.

"Other than being far more advanced and far more discreet, yes," she huffed. "Anyway . . . I can track you with the phone. A bit more high-tech than the usual 'find my phone' feature that is baked in. I can also talk to you directly without making a call, and if you are on a call, I can sort of conference in. Basically, you have zero privacy with this thing nearby, so keep that in mind. I can also send stuff to the screen and also see and hear what the camera and mic on the phone are picking up."

For some reason, I was instantly reassured by this gross invasion of my privacy. Anastasia would have my back. I nodded my understanding.

She handed me the ignition fob. "Car. You can't show up in Gloucester and run this down driving that brown piece of shit you have. Black Dodge Charger. Not a stock engine. Keep it under a hundred. Blue and reds behind the grill. Use 'em. Go."

Apparently, I didn't move fast enough, because Macallister reiterated, "Go. We'll get you some help in Gloucester."

I shoved the phone in my suit coat pocket, the fob in my pants pocket, and inserted the earpiece into my left ear. I was armed with some pretty cool FBI tech, but I was still unarmed with any sort of weapon. Other than, of course, my wits and my charm. *I got this*, I told myself. *Self-confidence, right, Ben?*

As Miles and I walked toward the parking garage, I straightened my posture and pushed back my shoulders. *I got this.*

35

IN THE UNDERGROUND GARAGE, we found our ride lurking in a corner, backed into a spot with the glint of the blue-and-red strobes just visible behind the grill work. With an air intake scoop sculpted on the hood, giant black wheels, and windows tinted way darker than would be allowed by the local cops, this thing screamed drug lord, or, possibly, FBI. Undercover it was not. I was stoked.

Behind the wheel, I jabbed the start button and quickly found the switches for the lights and siren. Flicking the strobes on and casting an alternating blue-and-red glow onto the garage walls and ceiling, we headed for the road and for Gloucester.

I ran through my options. First and foremost, as the crow flies, it's a shorter distance to take Route 1, but with this car, I'm taking the highway.

After I barreled onto the I-93 North ramp, I tried out my new phone by merely asking, "Anastasia? Can you hear me?"

She instantly replied through the earpiece, "Yes. What's up?"

So cool! I contained my glee at having this technology and said, "Can you connect a call for me? So I don't have to dial?"

"Of course. Who are we calling?"

"Sergeant Henson," I replied. "His number is in the case file. I want to see if the boat that picked up Miles had that AIS thing. Need a name from Henson. I didn't get it at the hospital."

I heard a click or two and then a ring. Henson picked up the call immediately.

"Henson."

"Sergeant Henson, sir, this is Ben Porter. We met earlier when I—"

"Yeah. I remember who you are. What's up?"

Gotta admire him getting to the point. I paused and said, "I'm working on my case file. Do you have a note of the name of the fishing boat?"

"Hang on." I heard some grunting and some rustling. "Yeah. Bite me."

I stared at the rapidly-moving highway through the windshield. "Sorry . . . um . . . did you get the boat's name?"

Henson laughed. I didn't know that was possible. "That probably doesn't come across well. What's with these stupid boat names, anyway? The name of the boat is, quote, *Bite Me*, unquote."

Unbelievable. So much so I said it out loud. "Unbelievable. Somebody named a boat *Bite Me*. I guess it fits. You got the owner's name, right?"

"Sure. Rodney Lailey. L-A-I-L-E-Y. Home address in Newburyport. Need it?"

"I don't think so," I replied. "Many thanks. I'll call back if I need it. And thanks again." Before Henson could respond, and potentially ask questions of his own, I jabbed the *END* icon.

Almost instantly, Anastasia's voice chirped in my ear. "Got it. Good call. Hang on, let's see if it's got AIS."

"Got it," Anastasia said again. "I must figure out how to export the track and overlay it on the other one. But to my eye, it matches up. The *Bite Me* intersected but did not cross paths, more or less, with *Flying Lady*. Hard to tell but we're assuming they're not at the same time, and the *Bite Me* track shows a blip about where Miles said he was picked up, and then a straight shot back into Rockport."

"But," I interjected, "this doesn't tell us anything new, it just further corroborates the story."

"Exactly," Anastasia responded. "I'll still pass this on to Macallister."

"Okay," I replied. How does one end a conversation when there's no end button? It's like she's always there. Apparently, Anastasia agreed.

"I'm going to a different phone to help Macallister get some assets moving in place in Gloucester. Ben, you drive like an old lady. Get a move on!"

I looked at the dash. The speedometer showed eighty-eight. "Old ladies who drive a DeLorean?" I asked. No one laughed. Maybe they didn't get it. I stabbed the gas and the Dodge surged faster.

CHAPTER

36

IN FRONT OF ME, CARS WERE scattering at the sight of the blue-and-reds in their rearview mirrors. I glanced at the dash. Ninety-five miles per hour on the speedometer. Time to check out the fluorocarbon output as the Dodge flew, effortlessly, down the left lane. *This thing is so sweet.*

I realized that Miles had not said a single word since we had gotten in the car. "You okay, man?" I asked, inclining my head in his direction.

He nodded, but barely. "Yeah. A lot happening. I'm thinking that . . . never mind."

Miles looked tired and distracted, so I tried to engage him. "Dumb question, but do you know where we are going?"

He started to speak, "Not really. Never been to Gloucester before. Except this morning, obviously, but I, um, didn't drive." He smiled. I laughed.

Miles began to jab at the Dodge's in-dash touchscreen display, saying, "I can program this. What's our destina—" but stopped midsentence as the iPhone screen flicked on, showing a map with a driving icon on it.

Anastasia, in my ear, said, "Of course I know where you are going. No need to use the car's GPS. I've sent directions on your phone."

This is a little creepy. I pointed at the earpiece and said, to anybody who might have been listening, "Actually, Anastasia, I was talking to Miles. But thanks. Do you mind if I have a conversation with him? Or can you put us all on speaker?"

"Of course, I can. Pull the earpiece out. And plug the phone in. It's going to use up the battery."

I handed the charging cord to Miles, who found a USB receptacle and connected the phone. Meanwhile, I extracted the little gadget from my ear. This was much more convivial. And my ear was beginning to hurt.

"Hey, I got a question," Miles said. "Anastasia, see if you can find vessels around me, using the AIS records, around the time of the intercept. You should be able to see on my track when we stopped going east. That Zodiac with an electric motor has limited range. The little boat had to have been launched from another vessel. Can you see if you can find another vessel with AIS that transited nearby?"

I stole a glance away from the road and looked at Miles. His eyes were brighter, and he was alert. He had reengaged. *This guy is sharp*, I thought.

"That's brilliant, Miles!" I exclaimed.

"Yes, very interesting idea, Miles," Anastasia added softly, almost sweetly.

I took my eyes off the road for another second, glancing over at Miles. He was staring at the phone, his mouth slightly agape. I thought, *He's beginning to like her too.*

The mood of the awkward little love-fest triangle (if you could even call it that) was shattered by Macallister's voice over the speaker, who barked, "Update from my end. I've dispatched local PD, and I have a couple of assets moving into the area. They are going to surround the boat and clear the area around it, then wait for you."

The phone went silent as I wondered what he meant by "a couple of assets." Before I got the chance to ask, he reminded us of just how precarious this little operation was.

"This is sure to call some attention. You better find something there, and fast, or we are all going to be in deep shit with the SAC. And if you don't find something, and whatever went down is targeted at Boston this afternoon, we're in deeper shit.

"'Bout time you picked up the pace. You'll be there shortly."

CHAPTER
37

I'M FAIRLY CERTAIN THAT I still, to this day, hold the land-speed record from Chelsea to Gloucester. Forty-two-point-four miles in thirty-three minutes.

I had turned to Miles, pointing at the phone, and asked, "You good to help navigate? I have no idea where we are going."

"Yep," Miles said as he angled the iPhone screen toward him. "Phone says we're coming up on a rotary. Stay right."

The Yankee Division Highway sports a couple of roundabouts, those traffic management circles popular in eastern Massachusetts. You don't see them much elsewhere. Except Europe, I guess. Never been there. Actually, come to think of it, I'm not very well traveled.

We carved off the divided highway, entering Gloucester proper, as our blue-and-red strobes cleared a path for us. "Follow Washington Street to the waterfront. Couple more turns," Miles said.

After a quick right-left, we could see the water ahead—and a sea of flashing blue-and-reds. "Looks like Macallister got it done," I muttered, as I piloted the Charger into a brick-paved parking lot on the waterfront. I aimed for a spot where there were a lot of uniforms and no other cars, figuring that I'd let the black Dodge make my entrance impression for me. I popped the earpiece back in my ear and unplugged the phone, saying into the air, "Anastasia, if you're still with me, we're here."

I stopped the car just shy of a group of easily a half-dozen cops, all of who were staring at the Dodge. Gathering the phone but leaving the car running and lights flashing, I stepped out, carefully but slowly buttoning my suit coat as I stood erect. *Play it cool, Ben, play it cool.*

"Agent Porter."

You have gotta be kidding me.

"Sergeant Henson," I smiled, as I wondered why he now addressed me as "Agent." Macallister, I bet, set that up. "It's nice to see you again," I added politely.

He shook his head to agree, but his body language said that he was confused as he took a step backward. "Yes, sir, Agent Porter. Small world, right? Anyway, we've evacuated the docks. Fishermen none too pleased. Lost their charters for the day. Also, we evac'd the restaurant," as he pointed to the building to my left, where a sign by the street proclaimed "Harbor Cove Brewing" in giant letters. "We established a perimeter on the other side, and on this here side, to keep the lookers back a ways."

I looked around the area, thinking, *Shit! This is a far more involved scene than I expected. Macallister was right. This is gonna attract attention.*

However, I managed to keep my demeanor placid as I said, "Good. Carry on. We're going to the boat. Miles had materialized beside me and I added, "You remember Mr. Lockwood."

Henson grunted a curt, "Yeah. That your boat, Mr. Lockwood? The *Flying Lady?*" Miles barely nodded a yes as Henson continued, "We've already been down there, when we cleared the docks. Doesn't look like anyone is on it. We didn't go aboard."

Henson's tone had seemed a little more deferential. I think the sergeant had realized he had fucked it up. I bet he'd been fascinated to know that we had no authority, other than Macallister's, to be here. Naturally, I declined to share that with him.

Together, Henson, Miles, and I walked to the top of the ramp that led to the docks. There were maybe four sportfishing-type boats at the docks, all backed in, and one lone, white-hulled sailboat with a black mast, tied bow-in among the big sportfishers.

Showtime, I thought to myself. *And I'm in the field and I have no idea what the fuck I am supposed to be doing.*

"Let's take a look," I said. "I need some gloves and shoe covers, and I need two men."

Henson nodded, glancing over at a cop standing nearby, who trotted off to a squad car. He quickly returned with the requested gloves and covers. "Let's go," ordered Henson. Apparently, he was to be one of my two men, and he and glove cop led Miles and me toward *Flying Lady*.

At the junction of the dock and the finger pier, Miles stopped and pointed up toward the top of the boat's mast. "Running lights still on. We already know AIS is still on. They left in a hurry."

"Or," I countered, "they left it on so it wouldn't look abandoned."

Frankly, I had no idea what I was looking for, but Miles clearly did. "Tied up correctly, looks tidy, and I don't see any damage. I think you're right. They wanted it to look normal."

The four of us gloved and covered. I happily deferred to Henson and his partner; they were armed and had their service weapons drawn. I had a phone. Not much good in a gunfight. Though, realistically, I thought it would be doubtful that there was anyone on the boat.

The two policemen clambered onto the boat. Miles and I waited on the finger pier, watching, as Henson took, to his credit, the center position in front of the cabin opening, with his piece aimed at the black plexiglass hatch. His partner stood slightly to the side. They both looked at me and I nodded to Henson.

With one hand steadily holding his unsafetied weapon, Henson used his other hand to slide the hatch open. Almost in unison, the two cops tilted their heads to look inside.

"Looks clear," Henson said loudly. He stuck his head deeper into the hatchway. *This guy has some balls*, I thought, as he carefully descended the ladder to the interior, with his partner attempting to awkwardly cover him from the hatchway.

After a moment, Henson reappeared through the hatchway and stated, "It's clear. No one here."

I looked at Miles and said, "Let's go." He lightly swung himself over the lifelines of the boat. I followed in a much more ungainly fashion.

With the policemen standing off to the side, Miles and I peered into the dimly-lit interior of the boat.

"They're gone." Miles looked me in the eye. I knew exactly what he meant. The boxes.

Not quite up to speed, Henson, of course, was confused. "You gonna search the boat? How many were you excepting? This doesn't make any sense. This ain't protocol."

"No, it's not," I replied. "No need to search the boat. Frankly, we didn't expect anyone. And we are not going to contaminate the boat any further. I gotta call this in. Can you clear the boat and go back to the ramp. Please."

Henson clearly did not like this, but complied, climbing off the boat with his partner, name withheld. As they shuffled off toward the ramp and back to their compatriots, slowly, too slowly for my impatience, I said to, well, my earpiece, "Anastasia? You getting this?"

"Yup," came her voice, loud and clear in my ear. "Me and Macallister."

The voice in my ear became Macallister's. "Sitrep," he said, asking for a situation report.

I spoke clearly, carefully. "Sir. We've boarded the boat. No one here. The perps are gone. And the boxes that Miles said were brought on board are gone."

CHAPTER

38

I CONSIDERED THE SITUATION, the shit-show that I was now standing knee-deep in. This boat, the cops, and the flashing blues-and-reds in the parking lot above me, and the now very real possibility that something really bad had gone down here earlier this morning. *We have to escalate this. The SAC is gonna go ballistic, though.*

I never found out for sure, but I think at the same moment Macallister was having similar thoughts. He broke the silence on our electronic connection first, almost reading my mind, saying, "Porter. Sit tight. I'm calling the SAC and then conferencing her in. Come up with a report for her. Sell the story."

In my earpiece, Anastasia's voice chimed, "I'm connecting us to the SAC now."

There was a brief pause, and Appleton's voice came through the earpiece. "SAC Appleton."

I pointed at my ear and mouthed-whispered to Miles, "Appleton." He shrugged.

Macallister immediately began, speaking very formally. I was relieved he was going to break the ice. If that was even possible with the SAC. "Ma'am. Agent Macallister. After we spoke this morning, new evidence came to light on this matter. We confirmed several pieces of Lockwood's story. Porter will brief you."

"*WHAT!*" exclaimed the SAC. "Macallister, were my instructions unclear? Did I not make it obvious to you not to waste resources on this? I have POTUS in Boston shortly and you are wasting my time. This is beyond unacceptable!"

My turn. I appreciated Macallister going first, and I was going to back him up. We would die on the same hill on this one.

"With all due respect, ma'am," I started, "you said that you did not condone this investigation. You did not specifically direct us to cease the investigation."

Oh boy. Here I go again. I am so fucked if I can't convince her.

Before she could say anything, I barreled on, gaining confidence as I spoke. "I will summarize this quickly, but I assure you, we have the evidence to back this up. We were able to locate Lockwood's boat electronically. The track of the boat, and its movements over the last forty-eight hours or so, are consistent with Lockwood's timeline. The positions and the story match exactly. We also confirmed that a text message had been sent from Lockwood's boat that would give the boat cover, so to speak, to return to Massachusetts.

"Lockwood and I are standing on the boat as I speak. It is in Gloucester. And the persons who took it from Lockwood are no longer with it. Nor are the boxes that Lockwood said were brought aboard."

I took a breath. To my surprise, she did not respond, and I wrapped up. "Of most concern is that the boat got to Gloucester before sunrise this morning. So that means that whatever and whoever was on the boat could be anywhere in New England by now. Could even be in New York. Could be to DC. Could be in Boston. On that, we have essentially nothing. All we know is that, according to Lockwood, they loaded two six-foot long boxes onto the boat. We don't have a clue what's in 'em, and now they could be anywhere." I stopped talking.

After a second or two, Appleton said, quietly, "One moment. Let me consider that."

I imagined a giant supercomputer in her cranium, lights flashing and fans whirring and processors processing, and I said nothing.

The SAC asked, "You said you had Lockwood with you? Mr. Lockwood is a material witness, and he is with you? I am not sure I like that."

Wow. I was expecting another ass-chewing, not a question like that. "I understand, ma'am. But we thought having his eyes on the boat were going to be more productive that just having my own on it." I astounded myself. I contradicted the SAC. Again.

"Hmmm . . ." Another quiet pause from Appleton. "Alright. At least for now.

"While I am deeply disturbed by the fact that you and Agent Macallister continued to pursue this, I will admit that this information is concerning. Very concerning, if it is true.

"However, your story is still largely dependent on Lockwood. Who's to say that he didn't just turn the boat around and bring it to Gloucester, and then arrange for an accomplice to stage his rescue later?"

I looked over at Miles, who was sitting near the steering wheel of his boat. I knew he wasn't lying. But she was right. The evidence we had so far was circumstantial.

"I totally understand, ma'am. I don't see it that way, though. He was picked up and was hypothermic. You can't fake that. You'd have to go to an extreme to do that, and for what gain? His boat would have been safe in Gloucester, so why would he do that?"

"Mr. Porter, it's not my job to figure that out. It's yours," she replied. *Oh, that's fair,* I thought.

I suspect Appleton realized the same thing, and she quickly added, "I take that back. Alright, I'll give you some leeway. You've proven that you are onto something, but I am not totally convinced. Macallister, you still on the line?"

"Yes, ma'am," he replied immediately.

"This is all highly unusual. But I am leaning toward Mr. Porter's assessment. And I will authorize you and Porter to continue this line of investigation on a limited basis. I need more data. More proof.

"Macallister, who's the agent on duty this afternoon at the office?"

There was a brief pause before Macallister replied. "Frenkle. Gene Frenkle. On the noon to eight shift."

"Very well," she said. "I will notify Special Agent Frenkle about Mr. Porter's role in this. Do you need any more assets?"

"Yes, ma'am. I've arranged for two forensics teams to go to Gloucester."

"Without my knowledge?" she demanded.

"Yes, ma'am. I saw time as of the essence."

Wow. Well done, Macallister. The SAC was clearly even more annoyed when she said, "Special Agent Macallister, Mr. Porter. I am appalled that you've gotten this far without telling me. I'll concede that if you are right, you made the correct call. But I need cold, hard evidence, and I need it fast.

"I'm going to go brief the Secret Service. We may need to lock it down. Do not fail to keep me posted."

CHAPTER
39

I MISS THE OLD DAYS WHEN a call ended with a "click." Now a call just ends. And many times, it's just a bad cell connection dropping, ending the conversation prematurely, and you're talking to thin air. Or wondering if the other side "hung up" on you. I wanted to ponder this some more, but I guess I had more pressing things to think about.

Without a plan, I climbed off the boat, saying to Miles, again, "Don't touch anything and don't go in the cabin." He didn't respond, he just remained sitting on the deck of his boat, back by the big round steering wheel, looking more tired than I'd seen him yet.

Standing at the junction of the finger pier and the dock, I stopped, pulling the phone from my pocket with one hand and pulling the earpiece out with the other hand. I figured I better hold the phone—otherwise, the penetrating eyes of the assembled Gloucester police department, currently staring me down, would assume I was talking to myself. I considered taking my shoe off and talking into it, *Get Smart* style, but discarded that terrible idea.

"Anastasia? Macallister?" I said, the phone now to my ear.

"Here," they chorused in unison.

"Well, that went well," I sarcastically and completely unnecessarily snorted, before setting up my question. "Macallister, what'd you mean, you have two forensics teams en route?"

"Porter, seriously?" he laughed. "I'm way ahead of you. I got a team en route a while ago. And," he paused, I heard clicking. "Give them maybe five minutes. See what you can get off the boat. We need prints, we need photos, we need anything to prove that someone or something was on that boat."

He broke off for a couple of seconds, then said, "Listen, I gotta go. Appleton is calling again. I'll hold her off for now. See what you can find." He disconnected without waiting for my response.

I decided to go talk to Henson, and I figured I better meet the team, so I walked back up the ramp, putting the earpiece back in my ear, mostly for show. I thought it made me look important.

"Sergeant Henson." He looked over and we started to walk toward each other. I thought it was time to loop him in, and I continued in a lower voice, "Let me loop you in. You already know Lockwood's story, which we all thought was bullshit a few hours ago. Looks like we were wrong. The situation is that we believe this boat was used to smuggle people and items into the country. It was offshore, near Canada, in a sailboat race before heading here. We are confident of the timeline, but we have no data on motive. We know the boat got here this morning, just before sunrise. What can you find out to help fill in the blanks, after sunrise?"

Henson looked at his feet, shuffling a little, stalling for time. "Ummmm . . . ." Drawn out. Not good. He started to talk and then stopped. This was going to take a while. "Um, we got nothing. First we knew of it is when your people called and told us to evac the docks and make sure nobody was near the boat. We cleared the restaurant too. The fishing boats at the dock had already come back from their morning charters or hadn't had charters. Maybe we should talk to the captains, see if they saw anything. They're usually here before first light."

"Good," I said. "Round 'em up and interview them on the deck of the restaurant. Anything odd they saw, or if—and when—they saw the boat." Henson shuffled off. I looked around, just really becoming aware of the growing crowd of curious people, tourists and locals alike, that had started to mill around the perimeter that Henson's crew had set up previously. This would be on social media in a matter of minutes, if it was not already. I paused, looking for Henson's sidekick who had come down to the boat, and I found him leaning against a squad car.

"Officer," I said as I walked to him. "I didn't catch your name. Thanks for your help on the boat."

Surprised at my thanks, he brightened and straightened up. "Wilson. Ken."

"Gotcha, Officer Wilson. Anyway, I am getting a little concerned about the crowds. Let's kill the lights and strobes, but don't close down the perimeter. Widen it out a little if you can. Give us some breathing room and some privacy. I got a forensics team coming and we don't need this trending on the Twitterverse, if you know what I mean."

"Yeah, no problem. We can move some of the squad cars and back these folks up. I'm on it, sir." Wilson spun smartly, waving to a couple of other police officers to join him.

I walked back to my Dodge and plugged my phone back in to boost its charge. I'd like to say that I had some revelations, but truly, I just sat there for a few minutes, staring at the unmoving dials on the dash. I wondered what Macallister was up to. Probably wishing he was playing Solitaire on his computer, but more likely, getting yelled at by the SAC. Better him than me, for now.

CHAPTER
40

A FLASH OF LIGHT IN THE rearview mirror caught my eye, and I saw a black, unmarked Chevrolet Suburban followed by a black, unmarked Ford Transit van pulling into the red-brick-paved lot with their blues-and-reds flashing at the inside top edges of their windshields.

My forensics team.

I pressed the start/stop button in the Dodge, finally turning off its idling engine, and stepped outside, again carefully buttoning my suit coat. *I better put on a good show, or this is going to go south quickly.*

A mix of men—all men—disembarked from the two trucks, two from the Transit and four from the Suburban. Different heights, different colors, different hairstyles, different clothes, and there was no way I would remember all the names. So, I looked for the alpha.

These teams function a little bit like a pack of dogs. Dogs quickly establish a pecking order in their groups, with the alpha dog taking control. And the alpha is not necessarily the biggest, the smartest, or even the best leader. I needed to make myself the alpha to their alpha, and fast.

Alpha's don't drive—they're too important because they are texting and emailing and calling and reestablishing their authority. When I saw a close-cropped, tall, lanky guy dressed in a suit and tie climb out of the front passenger seat of the Suburban, scan the area, and single out me, I figured I had my guy. We walked toward each other and he pulled his cred pack out of his jacket pocket, flashing it with a practiced gesture and saying or, more accurately, stating, "Agent Porter, I'm Special Agent Russo. Lead of this ERT team, and of the HERT team with me." He nodded his head toward the two men dressed in khaki cargo pants and black T-shirts standing in front of the Transit van and stuck his right hand out at me.

We shook hands, firmly. The fact that he called me "Agent" gets us off to a good start—thanks to Macallister, I presume—and I don't correct him. Wisely, nor do I correct his redundancies. Thanks to my job, I'm a master of all acronyms FBI, and you know how much we love our acronyms. An ERT is an Evidence Response Team and a HERT is a Hazardous Evidence Response Team. Adding the word "team" after saying ERT is like saying "ATM machine".

Wait.

An ERT *and* a HERT?

This had not occurred to me, but, obviously, it occurred to Macallister. Whatever was in those boxes was probably hazardous. I mean, no one went to this trouble to pack them full of chocolate. Although that amount of chocolate would probably be hazardous.

So, I nodded in agreement with Special Agent Russo, as if I was well informed, and said, "Welcome to Gloucester." Profound, right? I knew I had to take control and after a short, awkward pause, I continued. "Right. You've been briefed?"

"Yes. A sailboat, possibly transporting something illicit, several suspects. We're going to—"

I cut him off. "Right, here's the *full* summary. Two boxes, six-feet long by about two-feet square, which may be dangerous, and which are no longer accounted for. Five hijackers. Two original crewmembers on the boat. One allegedly killed during the hijacking. The other one escaped. We need to establish, first, who was on that boat. Whether there were more than the original two crewmembers.

"And, just as critically, we need to establish whether there were really boxes of something brought aboard, and if so, what is in those boxes. Let's go."

I started walking toward the ramp and Russo fell in step beside me, with his three-man team from the Suburban in tow. Two suits and three guys in standard-issue FBI windbreakers. We made quite a parade.

One of the two HERT squadmembers, standing in front of the Ford van, asked to our backs, "You want us too?"

Russo turned slightly and started to open his mouth, so I decided to cut him off again. I was the alpha. "Yeah, get a lay of the land," I said, waving him on. "Follow me." We reached the top of the ramp in formation, Russo and me side-by-side with the five men single-file behind us. This would look great on Instagram.

Clearly, Russo was pretty sharp. I guess that goes with the territory of collecting evidence, though, as you better be observant to do that job. As we walked down the ramp, he very pointedly asked, "Who the fuck is sitting on the boat?" He had zeroed in on the sole sailboat at the docks, and the sole figure on said boat. Observant for sure.

"That is Miles Lockwood, owner of the boat, and the guy who managed to escape. He is our material witness."

"He's contaminating the scene."

"Maybe, probably not. I've kept an eye on him and he has not gone below since we got here. He's obviously going to have his prints and whatnot all over that boat already. So, I left him there. Needed a good place for him to wait. Where he couldn't talk to anyone."

"I don't like it," Russo replied. "It's going to taint the timeline."

"Understood. Why don't you get what you need from him and then we will find a place to stash him. That work for you?" I figured some conciliation might be helpful, and fortunately, Russo seemed to agree.

"Okay, I can live with that. Is he a flight risk?"

I chuckled. "I've spent the better part of the day with him. He's cool."

Russo grunted an "okay" and turned to one of the windbreaker guys, saying, "Take that dude back to the truck and print him. And don't let him move from the truck."

"Miles," I called. Miles had been watching us approach, and, at my call, he stood and deftly leapt off the boat and onto the dock. "Would you go with this gentleman and get printed? We gotta get your info so we can start culling whatever is left from the bad guys."

"Yeah, of course," Miles replied. "Whatever you guys need. Obviously, my personal stuff is down below. And George's stuff. Maybe you can get something off his gear."

"Who's George?" Russo asked.

Miles and I both started to reply but I barged on, alpha style. "George is the other legit crewmember on the boat. He was killed during the hijacking."

Russo groaned. "This thing is going to be a fucking mess. Too many people. We're going to be lucky to get a few clean prints and some DNA samples. Who else has been on this boat?"

I hesitated, a little embarrassed that my crime scene protection measures were, well, pathetic and nonexistent. "Me, and two officers from Gloucester PD. Henson and, ah, Wilson. They're up there in the parking lot—"

"Why the fuck have you been climbing all over this thing?" Russo demanded.

I felt like I was losing my alpha status, so I did the only thing I could do. I name-dropped and bluffed, all at the same time. "Because my SAC, who is probably also your SAC, told me to find out whether the boxes were still here. Want me to call her?" I pulled the special phone from my pocket for emphasis.

"Not to interrupt your little argument, but has it occurred to you to test whether the boat is even safe to be on?"

Russo and I both turned to the voice, which was from a black T-shirt van guy, who had been standing well back from the boat. I had kinda wondered why he and his partner had hung back, and now it made perfect sense. *Oh shit*. We all started to back away from the docked boat, almost crowding each other off the finger pier.

Black T-shirt guy smiled, not nicely, though. "We're going to suit up. Maybe you guys better clear the area. And you," he said, pointing at Miles, "come with me."

En-masse, we all, now eight men, retreated from the boat, reforming our procession back up the ramp, back toward the watching eyes of the growing crowd, the Gloucester PD and, now, to my dismay, a van plastered in the "Channel 7 News Boston" logos.

"Get me those two cops you mentioned," Russo demanded to me as we crested the top of the ramp.

"One's already right here," I replied. "Officer Wilson, join us, please."

Wilson, who had been standing near the top of the ramp, walked over.

Russo took on a nicer tone, almost conspiratorial, and said in a low voice, "Officer, I hate to do this, but I think you'll agree it's necessary. I gotta print you. Sample you too. I can request the records from the portals, but this is faster. We gotta eliminate your data from whatever else we find on that boat. Can I get your cooperation?"

Wilson replied politely, "Sure, but I don't think it will matter. We gloved up."

Shit. I had forgotten that. "Right," I blustered. "Before we got on the boat. Shoe covers too. And we didn't go below. Just looked down the opening hatch thing. We could see what we needed from there, then we got off. Except Miles."

"Hmm," Russo hummed. "Alright, for now. Don't go anywhere, please." Turning to me, he asked, "Where's the other one?"

Wilson took a step backward as I answered, "Rounding up witnesses. Other folks who might have been on the other boats this morning." I paused and then continued with my account of our initial inspection of the boat. "So, our initial inspection of the boat was fast. On and off. I reported to the SAC from the boat, then I got off. Told Henson to talk to the charter boat captains and Wilson helped out with perimeter management." I looked around. "Where's Miles?"

"Probably in the van," Russo replied. "Let's go."

Russo was wrong, he wasn't in the van. We found Miles and the talkative, black T-shirt guy standing behind the van's cargo doors. Before we could say anything, black T-shirt said, "I wanded him. He's clean, but he can't stay here. Put him in one of yours."

"I can do that. Miles, you mind waiting in the car? And where's your partner?" I asked.

"Suiting up. I'm next. We work in a pair."

"I'm suiting up too," Russo stated.

"Not a chance. Sir, we will do a recon and report back. That's our job," black T-shirt replied. Russo took a microstep backward. Not as alpha as I had expected.

I stole an important-sounding phrase from Macallister. "Time is of the essence, as I am sure you know." I nodded at black T-shirt as the cargo door opened to reveal an ungainly creature clad in a head-to-toe hazmat suit. Great. More fantastic images for the crowd to post to their social media. And we would have two of them.

I retreated with Miles to the Dodge. "Probably better here than their Suburban. You okay?" I asked.

Miles nodded a yes. "Tired, I guess. Can't stop thinking about George. We should be sitting on the patio in Halifax, having a beer or two, enjoying some nice Canadian hospitality. This sucks."

Miles plopped down into the passenger seat of the Dodge. I didn't know what to say, so I kind of grunted and walked over to Wilson. "Keep an eye on my witness, please. He should stay with the car."

"Roger that," Wilson said, "I'll make sure—" he stopped, mid-sentence, gaping at the two men in the hazmat gear who were plodding to the ramp, both carrying large, black cases. I looked around the parking area. There wasn't a single person there who was not looking at the HERT guys. *Oh boy.* I hoped Appleton wasn't watching the local news on TV.

"Porter, you look good on TV. Sitrep?" Macallister's voice blasted in my earpiece. I had forgotten that thing was there. And, of course, *he's* watching the local news on TV.

"Hey," I replied, talking to air but knowing he could hear me. "The HERT guys are going to sweep the boat. I have to agree, though I know the optics don't look good."

"Yeah, it's not ideal. People are going to start to talk, make shit up, you know, the usual public response. So far, it's benign. The TV news is saying stuff about drug smuggling, intercepts, stuff like that. We're not going to contradict at this time. But in-house, they're going nuts. Appleton is demanding an update. I'm holding her off. I need something, concrete, now. Or, like, ten minutes ago."

"Understood," I replied to Macallister as I followed the HERT men down the ramp.

"I'm out, but call me if you need anything. Thanks, Porter. I know this is tough, but you got it."

I appreciated that comment from Macallister. I was way out of my comfort zone, out here in the field, following a Hazardous Evidence Response Team to a potential crime scene. Except, apparently, they did not want to be followed, since one of them turned around and said, in a voice muffled by the mask, "Agent, get the fuck outta here. You can't be here."

I shook my head no, emphatically. "Whatever I've already been exposed to, I've already been exposed to. I need a report, as fast as you can get me one. Whatever you got. Whatever you get. Anything you find." Kind of repetitive, I guess, but it seemed to work since the guys continued to the boat without further questions to me. In the suits, it was difficult for them to climb over the lifelines, and even more difficult to pass the black cases onto the boat but, eventually, they made it, and they disappeared into the cabin of *Flying Lady*.

CHAPTER
41

WEDNESDAY, SAME TIME — NANTUCKET ISLAND, MASSACHUSETTS

THE VIEW THROUGH THE thick glass windows was stunning—a perfectly charming tableau of the quaint, yet busy harbor at the posh and fashionable Nantucket Island. A summer retreat for the one-percent, the island carried an air of indifferent exclusivity, where wealth was never discussed, even though it was on constant display.

Moored at the end pier of the Nantucket Boat Basin was an imposing 235-foot, expedition style motor yacht. More of a compact ship, her high bow towered over the pressure-treated planking of the docks, with her polished topsides capped by a bulky superstructure that was bristling with antennas and domes. The rear section of the vessel was configured with a teak-decked helipad, on which rested a Eurocopter EC155, painted to match the colors of the yacht and dwarfed by the massive bulk of the vessel.

Oblivious to the picturesque scene outside, the yacht's oligarch owner sat at his desk in a plush, overstuffed, high-pile carpeted, sound-attenuated office on the top level of the vessel and rubbed a plump hand absently across his flabby jowls. Surrounded by original works of art, bathed by the soft glow of discreet, indirect lighting, he had his own oasis and no need to leave or to be distracted by the world immediately outside. And, at the moment, he was intently focused on a large, flat-panel LED television screen, tuned to the signal of Channel 7 News Boston that was being picked up by one of the several satellite receivers atop the superstructure.

On-screen, a perfectly-coiffed, but breathless reporter ad-libbed a report: "I'm standing near a dock in Gloucester, where it appears that the FBI has intercepted and apprehended some sort of criminal activity." The image cut from the close-up shot of the reporter to a wider image, showing a trio of black vehicles with tinted windows arranged on a red-brick parking area at the head of a ramp to the docks, as the reporter continued her voice-over: "There has been no information from the Bureau yet, and the Gloucester Police Department has refused to comment. We do know that the Harbor Cove Brewing Company restaurant was evacuated earlier."

The reporter paused her narrative for a moment, and the image changed again to a view of a docked, white sailboat, now with the word *LIVE* displayed at the bottom left corner of the screen. The camera panned from the sailboat and zoomed on a solitary man, somewhat portly, wearing a navy blue suit with coattails flapping in the gentle breeze. The man's face, brow furrowed in concentration and eyes clearly fixated on the sailboat in front of him, remained on-screen as the reporter's voice-over concluded, "The FBI's attention is focused on the sailboat at the docks. Sources say this could be related to drug smuggling."

The picture cut back to the reporter, now stabbing her microphone at a casually-dressed tourist, or townie, or someone unimportant, and, uninterested in the blather, the oligarch jabbed at the mute button on the remote, muttering to himself, "Drug smuggling? Hmmmph."

Rearranging his bulk in the executive-style swivel chair, he growled, "But how the fuck was the boat discovered so soon?" The office remained silent; there would be no answer to his question.

He turned his attention to a computer screen, searching for news on the presidential visit scheduled for later in the day in Boston. There was nothing new. He glanced at the scrolling numbers showing the various market indexes; they were flat.

Reclining in his richly-appointed leather swivel chair, the oligarch considered his options and realized that he had none. Adjacent to his office, the wheelhouse choked full of electronic wizardry, where he had tracked the sailboat on AIS the night before, was useless. A phone call was a possibility, but potentially dangerous.

He decided he could do nothing but wait, and as he watched the silent screens, he reflected on how this had all come together.

Since arriving in the United States as an inquisitive, resourceful eight-year-old, the only child of an immigrant mother who had taught him to hustle, to blend, and to survive, Anatoly Petrikov had grown into wealth ruthlessly, mercilessly destroying the lives and livelihoods of those who dared to oppose his wishes or who blithely stumbled into his path. Starting at age thirteen with the proceeds of a stolen diamond, he initially traded precious stones, parlaying his successes into a growing empire of commodities, metals, and currency. Preferring schemes that did not involve companies or investments that relied on many employees, he was able to cull his opponents—oftentimes taking their assets and making them his own—without attracting unwanted attention, all while carefully cultivating a public image of a philanthropic gentleman.

With the trappings of success, he had anglicized his first name to Tony, figuring it felt friendly and casual, and with his outrageously loud, yet captivating belly laugh, and his charismatic manner, he operated in two worlds. On the surface, he played the part of an approachable and outgoing vodka-tipping, magnetic tycoon, who donated at charity balls and who enjoyed a good party. But, in private, he never hesitated to lash out at anyone who crossed him, preferring to silence them permanently rather than spending the time to convince them to cooperate. He was unafraid to do his own wet work. In fact, he enjoyed it.

Enjoyed it too much, perhaps.

Petrikov's magnetism masked his inner evil. Upon an introduction, he would talk about how he made his initial stake: "It was my grandmother's stone, brought to New York from the homeland by my mother. My mother, on her deathbed, gave it to me. I realized its value and sold it, parlaying the proceeds to my ultimate success trading in precious gems." He'd allow his head to droop and his shoulders to sag, as if the emotion was too much, and he'd conclude, "I owe it all to her." He'd wipe an invisible tear from his cheek, pretend to regain his composure, and then chuckle, "I owe it to her, and to some luck, and to a good eye!"

It was all a lie.

CHAPTER
42

1965 — NEW YORK CITY

ANATOLY PETRIKOV'S TALE OF rags-to-riches may have been partially true. What made it an outright lie, however, was his omission of two crucial details.

His grandmother's gem from the Motherland? No. He swiped that first diamond from a merchant on the street, who had taken pity on his mother and who was reaching into his wallet for a bit of cash to give to the poor lady with a young boy in tow, shyly hiding behind her. Hiding, indeed, as that boy surreptitiously heisted a black velvet box from the merchant's satchel.

Petrikov was equally adept at hiding that night, first when he hid in the common bathroom in their tenement building in Hamilton Heights, an immigrant neighborhood in northwest Manhattan. His mother, as was her custom, would leave their tiny, two-room walk-up flat after dinner to use the facilities and wash up before bed. She would be in good spirits that evening, thanks to the bounty of the merchant's generosity which had put fresh food on the table, a welcome departure from their usual spare fare.

Realizing, as he ate that feast, that he much preferred not to share, and tired of the tedium of making ends meet one meal at a time, the boy decided to go it alone. His mother whistled a toneless tune as she knocked on the bathroom door. Hearing no response, she pushed the door open and entered the room. As she locked the door behind her, her son bludgeoned her with a block of wood.

Dragging the not-yet-dead body back to the flat, Petrikov hid until late at night, when he tied his mother's tiny body into a canvas sack and pulled it thumping down the stairs to the tenement's basement. He shoved the sack into the fiery maelstrom behind a heavy, cast-iron furnace door.

Wiping his sooty hands on his trousers, he returned to the flat. He packed his meager belongings—some clothing, his mother's pitiful, but nevertheless useful "rainy day" stash of cash, and, of course, his newly-acquired velvet box—and without a backward glance, quit the Hamilton Heights tenement and disappeared into the night.

Days later, clean and clad in a dapper outfit courtesy of a withdrawal from his deceased mother's stash, Petrikov introduced himself to the New York City Diamond District. The correct, expected appearance is the most effective disguise, and Petrikov masked, even ignored, his youth as he marketed that first stone. Nothing appeared amiss; the gem was cradled in an appropriate, black velvet box, and the silver-tongued young man who sought the best value for his diamond impressed the jewelers with his polite, charming magnetism. He made his first trade calmly and captivated his audience.

With the proceeds, he made his way to the burgeoning Brighton Beach area of Brooklyn, which was swelling with an influx of Russians and would soon be nicknamed the "Little Odessa." He would buy the immigrants' gems for a song and sell them at a tidy profit in the District.

Back in Brighton Beach, his profile soon rose, and his charisma and polished looks attracted the attention of the *vor v zakone*. The *"vory"* was *the* crime boss of the *Bratva*—the New York arm of the Russian mafia—and Petrikov was hooked. He would become the dealer of the *Bratva* to the Diamond District. His fortunes soared.

CHAPTER
43

1996 — NEW YORK CITY

BY THE EVE OF THE TURN OF the century, some thirty years after his first diamond sale, Petrikov was in his groove. In Brighton Beach, he was feared and anyone who dared oppose him might find themselves at the bottom of the aptly-named Gravesend Bay, spending their eternity rotting against the massive concrete pylons on the Verrazano Narrows Bridge. In Manhattan, he enjoyed the trappings of his ever-increasing personal wealth, the power that he wielded, and the dual life that he lived. He was a regular at the museum balls and on the fashion show runways.

Along the journey of his rags-to-riches story, he had picked up a fashionable accessory for himself: a wife. Married in 1984 at a lavish, exclusive ceremony at the New York Aquarium, which Petrikov rented for a weekend at great expense, the stunning Irina Borisyuk gave the rising oligarch an added layer of credibility. The birth of a daughter two years later offered Petrikov a moment of humanity and truth in a life that had been launched with a theft and a murder.

But, on a foundation that precarious, that moment was bound not to last, and Petrikov quickly resumed his trajectory deeper into crime. In 1992, when feared Russian criminal Vyacheslav Ivankov appeared in Brighton Beach, Petrikov willingly ceded his power to Ivankov. By pretending to be obsequious to the brutal reputation of the newcomer, Petrikov's brilliant strategic ploy placed Ivankov, not Petrikov, in the crosshairs of an FBI investigation. Ivankov didn't last long and was arrested three years later, charged with extortion.

Petrikov was elated. The FBI was elated. They assumed that they had found the boss; they had no idea Petrikov existed. To protect their ten-year-old daughter, Irina arranged to spirit her away from the confines of the insular Brighton Beach *Bratva* community to boarding schools, and she disappeared from her father's life of crime. His feet, too, disappeared from his view, as the once-dapper Anatoly ballooned into obesely giant Tony, fueled by an endless supply of vodka, caviar, and properly-saucer-sized *blini*.

And as Petrikov's girth grew, Irina's interest in her once-fashionable husband waned. Dripping in jewels, some illicit and some legitimate, in Petrikov's opinion, Irina had become a botoxed, platinum-blonde-dyed society lady, devoid of personality and most likely sleeping with whomever she cared to bed. Yet, she was still useful to Petrikov as arm candy at the charity events where he liked to be photographed; a first-wife unicorn who was age-appropriate and unmockable, unlike those girl-toys his peers liked to flaunt while being ridiculed behind their backs.

Until it was Petrikov's moment to be ridiculed. And not for his choice of a woman.

CHAPTER
44

2005 — NEW YORK CITY

AFTER BEING DEPORTED TO Russia in 2004, Vyacheslav Ivankov, the former Brighton Beach *vory* who Petrikov had framed for extortion, stood trial for a murder charge. The crime boss was acquitted, no doubt due to some clever behind-the-scenes witness manipulation. And, once free of the confines of arrest where he had languished for the past decade, Ivankov swiftly took his revenge on Petrikov.

Recruiting a diamond merchant named Victor Wolford as an unsuspecting ally, Ivankov treated Petrikov with the same medicine by which Petrikov had served him: he framed him.

Wolford had gotten his start in the jewelry trade on historic Jeweler's Row, an architecturally-significant part of the Loop community in downtown Chicago, Illinois. Well-traveled, erudite yet unassuming, the prematurely gray-haired diamond dealer was known for his somewhat irritating habit of removing and twirling his eyeglasses as he transacted. *Unnecessarily distracting*, one might think as they sat across from the dealer as he scratched his chin and contemplated an offer for the gem on the black velvet mat in front of him.

Mannerisms matter. Wolford discarded the glasses in favor of contact lenses as he rose to prominence on Wabash Avenue. And, while Chicago gave him his start, it was New York City that proved lucrative; maintaining his original shop as a toehold in the midwest, he expanded to the

New York City Diamond District, a move that not only added a layer of credibility, but also offered extensive access to connections and clients as he became known as one of the most respected men on West 47th Street.

Offices aside, Wolford was unafraid to leave the canyons of New York or Chicago for the depths of a mine in South Africa or for the open pit of the Argyle trench in remote Western Australia. Wolford relished those adventures; a break from the smog and stagnant urban air reminded him of a youth under the open skies of sandy Nevada. He cultivated a reputation as the Indiana Jones of the diamond trade.

Thus, with a well-known background and a well-stamped passport, he was unsurprised when a Russian-accented voice on the telephone to his office in the Diamond District asked him to appraise and then represent a stone recently mined near the Lower Lena River in Russia.

What surprised him was the caller's description of the stone: "It is very large. It is estimated at almost 300 carats."

Wolford had chuckled. Such a stone was almost unimaginable. Thirty carats would be an outstandingly rare stone. Three carats would fit nicely on a rig. Three hundred carats would be comparable to the Cullinan Stone held by the British Royal family: indeed, fit for a king, no less. "There must be some mistake, perhaps in translation?" Wolford had replied to his caller.

"No. It is so. It was found last year. In 2004. I am a representative for the Russian government."

"What do you intend to do with this stone?"

"We will sell it. To the highest bidder. Quietly, of course. It will fetch a considerable sum."

Wolford chuckled to himself. *Quietly* would be an understatement. Such a transaction could be afforded by only a select few. This was the opportunity of a lifetime. Still, he considered, he would be careful. "And what do you intend me to do?"

Without pause, the Russian-accented voice answered, "You shall appraise the stone and you shall conduct the offer. You come highly referred as a resource."

"By whom?" Wolford asked.

"Our representative in your country. Anatoly Petrikov," the caller replied, rolling the consonants in his thick accent.

Since establishing himself in New York, Wolford had dealt many a stone for Petrikov, who often commissioned the merchant to travel overseas in the hunt for a buyer for one of the gems he managed to rustle up through his Brighton Beach connections. Indeed, Wolford may have surmised that Petrikov's stones came by illicit manner, but business with the man paid well and evidence against him was scarce. Intrigued by the size of the diamond and by the lure of the potentially lucrative commission, Victor Wolford eagerly agreed to participate in the transaction.

Wolford immediately began to work his connections in New York and Chicago. A consortium could buy the stone, and perhaps cut it to smaller, more palatable stones, or perhaps he would find an individual investor who wanted this singular gem. A billionaire to be sure, but they were easy for Wolford to come by with his international contact list. He was enthralled by the prospect of reaching into this exalted market; it would be the capstone to his career.

Within a year, it all turned out to be a hoax, a giant fabrication orchestrated by Ivankov, which positioned Petrikov as a greedy shyster attempting to sell Russian state property, and Wolford as the rube who thought he could broker The Creator, as the stone came to be called. The stone was real, for certain, an uncut gem which was the third-largest diamond ever discovered in the vast and resource-rich country of Russia, but it was never intended to leave the Russian Diamond Fund in the Kremlin.

Wolford became the laughingstock of the both the Chicago Jeweler's Row and the New York Diamond District, a place where honor was held in the highest regard, and transactions are finalized with a handshake. He had no choice but to close his offices, both in New York and in Chicago. His credibility had instantly vanished and, with it, his business. His inventory of stones was also under suspicion and he was forced to liquidate his holdings at a massive loss. Dejected, disgraced, and in default of loans, he disappeared.

Petrikov, too, was forced from the District. He would no longer be trustworthy to his compatriot Russians, for who would dare transact with a man who tried to sell one of the Kremlin's jewels?

Outwardly, he attempted to cover his embarrassment by denying that any of it had ever really happened, and that he was a victim of forces beyond his control. For this, he had one advantage: in Little Odessa, he was still feared, for few things are more frightful than a Russian seeking revenge. But in the City proper, he had lost any stature he once had.

To distract himself, he focused his attention elsewhere, attempting to build on his already considerable wealth by pursuing legitimate business opportunities. Petrikov pretended that his business life was prosperous, and with his wife at his side at the charity balls, he would turn a cold shoulder to those who dared question his right to be there.

And all the while, his humiliation fueled a hidden rage, which simmered until it was triggered.

CHAPTER
45

2015 — NEW YORK CITY

On a cold, early winter evening, flush with vodka and fat with *blinis,* Tony Petrikov stumbled through the foyer of his sumptuous Manhattan penthouse. The late-day western sunset smoldered orange, tinting the interior of the space with a reddish glow, matching his mood. Another day of mindless negotiating and legitimate work. The oligarch missed the Brighton Beach days, the conviviality of the *Bratva* and the finality of knowing that if a deal went wrong, a life would be ended—not usually true in the boardrooms where Petrikov operated now.

The reddish glow transformed into the red mist of that old, familiar rage, as Petrikov heard the sound of a man's voice from his own bedroom. Snaring a long carving knife from the kitchen that adjoined the foyer, Petrikov, with an unusual, animal-like grace, slipped toward the bedroom. With a snarl, he launched himself through the doorway at the stranger who was buttoning his shirt.

Decades ago, Petrikov might have been a threatening figure, but now, he was a flaccidly large caricature of the imposing *vory* he once was, and the stranger merely laughed before darting from Petrikov's range and fleeing the penthouse. The Russian turned to his naked wife, cowering among the rumpled bedsheets, and stabbed. He knew this stranger was not the first, but it was the first one he had caught, and he took no pause before slaughtering Irina Borisyuk Petrikov.

The sun had long since set and darkness had descended over Manhattan by the time Petrikov completed wrapping a lovely Persian carpet around his lifeless bride's dismembered body parts, carefully encased in plastic garbage bags. Irina's precious, matching, flawlessly white Shih Tzu dogs sniffed at the rolled-up rug as Petrikov laughed a mirthless laugh and thought, *Now what?*

He could chase down his wife's lover, but why? That man would be just the most recent of his wife's dalliances. Frankly, he didn't care; her affairs had kept her quiet, and hunting down one man would bring little satisfaction.

He wanted more. He was tired of this charade of his life.

Fear. Power. Money.

Not good enough, he thought.

Evil.

What combines all of those things? What can I do that transcends belief?

Another moment passed until, now, a real belly laugh. *That's it!*

Standing, he crossed to the windows, looking down on Manhattan. *Would I miss this view? No. Would I miss the underlings, the overhead, the sycophants who preened for my attention? The* Bratva *who turned their back on me? Definitely not. Dump this place, terminate the people, move what business I needed to conduct to the yacht. Let this fucking fickle city go up in flames. And restore my reputation as someone who you dare not fuck with.*

Grinning, he settled at his mahogany desk, flopping into the burgundy swivel chair with the satisfying creak of expensive leather under his prodigious bulk. Selecting a smartphone from the several in front of him, he swiped through contacts, eventually tapping on one that he had not used in many years.

He needed someone with talents similar to his own. Someone who had creativity and aptitude for connection and convincing. Someone who had traveled. Someone who he had once trusted.

After a few seconds, the connection was completed and he spoke into the device: "Victor, it's Tony."

For a beat or two, the luxurious penthouse remained silent except for the sniffing of the two dogs, the thick glass silencing the outside world, and the insulated walls and high-pile carpets muffling any ambient noise from the city streets below. Petrikov spoke again.

"It has, indeed, been a difficult time. But I have an idea. And you could be useful to me. Your, shall we say, special talents are well suited."

Absently, Petrikov rubbed his jowls as he listened to the response, eventually chuckling and saying, quite kindly, "Wonderful. This will make back that lost decade, and then some. There will be no promises, no failsafes, no security. Yet if we succeed, you'll be paid exceptionally well, and while we're at it, we're going to make so many people miserable. Especially those who turned their backs to us. Here's what you are going to do."

CHAPTER

46

WEDNESDAY, 3:25 PM — GLOUCESTER, MASSACHUSETTS

I STOOD, UNMOVING, planted to that finger pier, for what seemed like an eternity. According to Macallister, who at first had watched on TV and had then checked my location with the superphone that Anastasia had given me, it was nine minutes.

It was a *really* long nine minutes.

A hazmat-clad figure emerged from the cabin, looking at a device held in a gloved hand. Standing in the boat's cockpit, he set the device down and slowly removed his helmet and face mask. It was talkative, black T-shirt guy, and his hair was soaked from sweat and matted down on his forehead, which was ruddy-red from the heat inside the suit. "Agent," he said quietly, beckoning me closer. "I got good news and I got bad news. Good news is you're not going to die. Bad news is that this boat is contaminated with radiation."

"What kind of radiation?" I interrupted. I was running through reports and analyses that I had worked on and remembered that there are many types of radiation. Most radiation is benign. Some radiation is, well, anything but.

"Can't tell yet. The portable detector is not sophisticated enough. We will take samples and run tests in the lab and—"

I interrupted again. "Is it localized in a specific part of the boat, or is it throughout the entire boat?"

"Hard to say. We gotta complete testing and document locations, but it seems to me that it is concentrated in the middle section. I guess you'd call it the living room, or something? I'm not much of a boater. It's not as—"

My manners suck. I interrupted him again. "Levels?"

"Point-zero-five up here on deck. That's normal." He waved the device in front of himself, and added, "But two-point-zero-eight below, in the cabin.

"That means nothing to me. Help me out."

He smiled, grimly but smugly. "Two-point-zero-eight is not dangerous for a short time, but high enough so that no one is getting on this thing without protective gear. It's also high enough to cause real concern. We're running some other tests and—"

"Got it. What else are you testing?"

"We're going to rescan and redocument on an area-by-area basis, to see if we can localize higher levels. We'll do a blacklight test, a chem test, a bio—"

"Carry on, thank you." I stepped away from the boat. I know the HERT has a standard operational protocol and that they would run through a gamut of tests to make sure their evidence collection was complete and not based on a preconceived bias, but none of that mattered to me. I collected my thoughts for a few moments and then I pulled the phone from my pocket while removing the earpiece. For the first time, I noticed a speed-dial icon on the home screen that read "HQ" below it. I tapped it.

Anastasia's response was almost instantaneous. "Ben, what do you have?"

"They detected radiation on the boat."

Her reply was less than instantaneous, and almost blasé. "Oh."

"I want to brief the SAC. Can you connect her?"

"Yeah, stand by one," Anastasia said flatly.

There was a brief pause, but less than fifteen seconds later, Appleton's voice said, "SAC Appleton."

"This is Ben Porter. Ma'am, the HERT detected elevated radiation levels inside the boat."

"And?" she replied.

"Uh . . . um," I stammered. *What else does she want? Hijacked boat, brought in covertly, with a radiation signature? This is bad, right?*

I could think it, but I couldn't verbalize it. She repeated, "And? That's all you have?"

"Yes, ma'am. The HERT will continue testing. But that seemed to be crucial information that you needed to have. That the boat had a radiation signature. Enough that they are not letting anyone else on the boat without protective gear. Obviously, we need more data and figures and so forth. I think we can assume that there was something bad onboard that boat."

I heard her take a deep breath, probably one of exasperation, before she spoke again. "Mr. Porter, I don't operate on assumptions. Anything else? Factual?"

"Not at this time, ma'am."

"Not good enough. I need data. Evidence. Or at least a hypothesis. The president is due to be in the air to Boston in less than an hour. You're on the scene. Call me back if you get anything new. Otherwise don't interrupt me with assumptions."

The phone went silent.

CHAPTER

47

NOT GOOD ENOUGH? I SEETHED. I'm the guy on the scene, there's radiation on the boat, there are missing boxes *and* missing hijackers.

Dejected and pissed, I dropped the phone to my side. I didn't reinsert the earpiece. Naturally, the phone immediately started to vibrate, and I scanned the screen. HQ. Anastasia or Macallister. I slipped the phone in my pocket.

They could wait a few minutes. I needed time to think. I turned back to look at the boat. Talkative, now sweaty, black T-shirt-encased-in-a-hazmat-suit guy had disappeared back into the cabin. I looked toward the parking area. Lots of eyes stared at me, standing solo on the dock, my suit coat tails flapping in the gentle breeze. I wondered if the television cameras were focused on me.

The phone buzzed again. Fuckit. I jammed the earpiece in and snapped, "What?"

Macallister laughed. The guy actually laughed. "Porter. Relax. We're on your side. And you may have jumped the gun with a call to the SAC. I listened in. Let's talk this thing through."

I inhaled the salty Gloucester air, belatedly acknowledging that Macallister was correct. I should have come up with something more. *Okay. I can do this.*

"Right," I replied. "Talk it out. What facts do we have?"

"We have the boat. We have its location history. It was clearly turned around midway to Canada and returned to the United States," Macallister summarized.

"And we have Miles's account that his sailing partner George was murdered. But you cannot corroborate that, can you? Maybe Miles is complicit in this thing," added Anastasia.

That hadn't occurred to me. Shit.

But, wait—the corroboration is right in front of me. The boat.

I trotted over to the boat and tapped on the fiberglass hull, which rang out with a hollow sound. Addressing the masked head that popped out of the hatch, I asked, "You said levels were low on deck. Are they low enough and safe enough that I can bring ERT down to look for prints and stuff on the deck only?"

The head nodded affirmatively.

"Good. Thanks. Macallister, you getting this? HERT says we can have ERT on the top of the boat. Outside the cabin. They can gather prints or other data off the deck. Miles said George had been shot when the hijackers boarded. Let's see if there is any blood residue."

"Got it. I'll send a message to Russo," Macallister responded. "Keep talking. What else?"

"Radiation. There's zero basis for any radiation readings on that boat. Conventional weapons, drugs, that sort of contraband, those don't have that signature either.

"Also, the boxes were heavy but not too heavy. Lockwood said that it took two men to lift them. That they looked like some sort of plastic material. So, I think we can reasonably conclude that if radiation is present on the boat, they were either not lead-lined, or they were thinly lined. They were too light to be lead boxes. You wouldn't be able to lift something that big. I don't think so, anyway."

"Where does that leave us?" Macallister queried. "Plastic box with a radiation signature. Do we assume it is a weapon? And if not a conventional weapon, or a bio weapon, a nuclear weapon? Some sort of suitcase nuke?"

"Plausible," I mused. "Let's go worst-case scenario. Let's say they were nukes. Some sort of weapon of mass destruction. Two of them."

The connection went silent as we considered that threat. I had watched as Russo's evidence collection squad mobilized and now began to clamber onto the boat. Showtime for the social media folks watching from the parking area above.

If only they knew what had possibly been inside that boat . . .

"Wait a minute!" I blurted. "We gotta put two-and-two together. We're forgetting the delivery method."

"Whaddya mean?"

I paused before I answered Macallister's question, putting my thoughts in order as I started in slowly. "First, remember the size of the two boxes. Two men to carry each. You're not going to hike through the woods from Canada to Maine lugging those things. You can't put them in a vehicle and drive through a border crossing, because the border crossings all have radiation detectors. Therefore, you bring them in by boat. And, as we've already established, they brazenly called it in and gave themselves the cover story that they are quitting a sailboat race and returning to land."

I swallowed and concluded my theory, "The boat docked in the dark hours in the morning. No one would notice, and even if they had, they had their cover story already established. You could bring *absolutely anything* into the United States that way!"

CHAPTER

48

"YOU'RE RIGHT. IT COULD BE absolutely anything," Macallister repeated. "But, in this case, what we have is something with a radiation signature. And whatever it was, it was taken off the boat something like eleven or twelve hours ago."

"Sure, but we still don't know if Miles, or George, was involved," Anastasia interjected, finally breaking her silence.

"I don't think that matters, at the moment," Macallister retorted. "Working on the theory that Miles is telling the truth, which I tend to believe at this point because the rest of his story has checked out, there are five unknown subjects cavorting around within our borders with something radioactive. We're calling the SAC. Anastasia, connect us. Porter, you ready?"

"No," I answered, as a helmeted head emerged from the boat. "Lemme get a report from the team on the boat first."

Talkative black-T-shirt-guy had pulled off his face mask and was beckoning me over. "Agent. We got a lot more to do but I wanted you to know we isolated the location. Highest readings on the benches on the left and right of the cabin. Nothing in the way back, very low readings in the front. Also, the bench cushion indentations show an outline of something heavy placed on them. Roughly six feet long and overhanging the edge, which puts them wider than twenty inches. At that location is the highest reading. Two-point-two-one. Both sides. Whatever was on those benches was hot. And it was hotter whenever it was there. It has definitely had some time to dissipate."

"Got a blood stain here, too," added the evidence collection agent squatting in the cockpit area of the boat. "It was washed, but poorly. We'll be able to ID it."

"And I'm getting multiple prints off the steering wheel and this here throttle control," called out a second evidence response squadmember from the back end of the boat, adding, "Definitely more than two people on this boat recently."

"Thanks," I answered. Turning slightly, and sort of awkwardly, not really sure how to carry on a conversation with Macallister and Anastasia without appearing to talk to the evidence team, I yanked the earpiece out and, bringing the phone to my ear, said quietly, "Macallister, did you hear all that?"

"Yeah."

"Good timing, huh? I'm ready for the SAC, now."

Well over a minute passed, and I watched the Evidence Response Team picking away at the deck of *Flying Lady*; the Hazardous Response teammember had disappeared back into the cabin. Then, the cool, even voice of Jennifer Appleton, through my earpiece: "SAC Appleton. This better be useful."

"Ma'am, Macallister. We have discussed a plausible theory. Porter will brief you."

Thanks, boss. Shit. Here we go. "Ma'am. Ben Porter. I'll take this sequentially and will summarize. Facts established are, one, we know the boat's past course and early morning arrival in Gloucester, which was not its announced return port. Two, we currently have an Evidence Response Team on the deck of the boat looking for further corroboration of the presence of, and hopefully the identification of, the hijackers. They have confirmed the presence of more than two individuals on the boat recently, and they have discovered the presence of a blood stain. Therefore, our material witness's story has checked out in all regards, to the points that we've been able to verify. Three, the HERT confirms dangerous radiation levels at the two locations in the boat that our witness describes the boxes as being placed."

I paused to catch my breath and the SAC, apparently not one for breathing, immediately asked, "What conclusions, if any, do you reach by that, Mr. Porter?"

"Ma'am, if you wanted to transport two heavy and large boxes, by the witness's description, into this country, you'd bring them in by vehicle. You would probably not carry them through a forest or across a desert. But, at vehicular border crossings, we have radiation detectors. Therefore, you'd be intercepted.

"What it appears happened here is that they hijacked a recreational boat and used that boat to transport their radioactive boxes. And, of course, to transport themselves. At present, neither the boxes nor their carriers are accounted for."

"But—" the SAC interrupted.

I ignored her and parroted her word as I continued. "But, those carriers and their cargo disappeared some twelve hours ago. The radiation levels have dissipated since then. We can logically assume—no, conclude—that the cargo was highly and dangerously radioactive. A cargo that was brought into this country bypassing normal border security. And that we have five potential suspects cavorting around within our borders with their dangerous cargo."

I heard Macallister quietly snort when I used his "cavorting" word, but other than that, there was no response at the other end of the call. I hoped I still looked good on TV. Appleton's voice broke my reverie. "That's . . . *disturbing*. But also adds up. Someone smuggled a radioactive device into the country by boat, evading border security and the radiation detectors at the border crossings. Clever. Those devices could be in Boston right now."

I could actually hear her swallow through the call. *Eating crow, huh? How's it taste?*

I waited and Appleton continued, "Porter, I know you're not an agent. But you picked up the thread and have followed it. You've been right all along. I owe you an apology. That can wait. Hang on a minute."

I could hear Appleton's muffled voice as she spoke to someone else and then, more clearly but not meant for me, "We're done. Cancel POTUS."

Holy shit. My words just changed the presidential schedule.

"Porter, you still there?"

"Yes, of course, ma'am."

"I can't take the chance that those boxes are intended for POTUS. I am covering my ass at this end. But regardless, those boxes are intended for something. And you said they've got a twelve-hour headstart, so they could be a distance from Boston. Let Anastasia know what you need. What's next?" she barked.

I quickly gathered my thoughts before spouting, stream-of-consciousness style, "We have a lot of work to do here. Both evidence teams are already working on the boat. I've got Gloucester PD rounding up witnesses who may have seen the boat come in this morning. And Anastasia, have you backtracked the boat's AIS signal? Can you ID the intercept?"

"Not yet. We will get to it immediately," Anastasia quickly replied.

"Okay. Proceed." Appleton said. "Problem is, now what? Ben, how are you going to find the perps?"

Huh? Now I'm *Ben*? And now this is *my* problem?

I looked around again, reminding myself that this *is* my problem. This is *my* case.

"We have to find clues as to where the five suspects have gone. Obviously, we have to chase this down."

Great. *We have to chase this down?* I'm not an agent, I'm hanging out with a civilian who is wearing borrowed clothes and who is part of the case, and I'm briefing the SAC. With whom, apparently, I'm suddenly on a first-name basis. This gets better by the minute.

"Ben. Good work. Carry on." That was high praise from the SAC as the connection terminated. I looked at the phone's display. Back to the icon screen. The call was over. I put the earpiece back in and stuck the phone in my pocket.

I allowed myself to bask in my new-found awesomeness of being a nonagent who is pretending to be one, now with the blessing of the SAC. But then I regrouped and got back to work.

WELL OVER AN HOUR had passed. The ERT guys continued crawling around on the deck of *Flying Lady*. The HERT men remained cocooned, probably very hot, inside the cabin. Russo was pacing on the finger pier, alternating between chatting on his phone and barking at his team. I had returned to the Dodge to check in with Miles—who, not helpfully, was fast asleep in the passenger seat.

I went to look for Henson, who I found on the deck of the restaurant, holding court at a big round table with four men and two women. They looked like they all knew each other. Gloucester is a small town, so they probably did.

"Sergeant Henson."

"Agent Porter."

"Got anything for me?"

"Sure," he said. "That's quite a show you got going on down there, on the boat. Find anything?"

I was annoyed. *I'm* the one asking the questions. "Plenty. Like I asked, what do you have? Folks," I said, sitting down at an open seat at the table and cutting Henson out of the conversation, "I'm Ben Porter. FBI Boston. Let's talk about that sailboat. What did you see and when did you see it?"

The gazes in the group were mostly downcast, examining the black-wire-mesh table, except for one of the women, who made eye contact. I held her stare for a beat and asked, "What's your name?"

"Agnes."

"Hi, Agnes. Can you help me out?"

"Maybe. I saw the boat come in."

"Great. You catch the time?"

"Yeah. Well, not exactly. Before sunrise. It was between 4:00 and 5:00." She raised her arms above the table and looked at her wrists—she wasn't wearing a watch. I liked Agnes. Smart. Told me a key fact without speaking, that she couldn't give me an exact time, without a watch. I wondered what else she saw. She continued.

"I work on *Timeless*. With Markie here." She glanced to her right. Markie was a heavyset guy, bent and faded Red Sox cap pulled tight over his forehead, staring at the table. "We had a charter, supposed to leave at five, so we was already on the boat, jus waitin' for them in the cabin. They was no shows. We get to keep the deposit. We was sittin' in the cabin, waitin', and I saw the lights of the sailboat come in and take the slip three down from us. Couldn't really see the boat, on account of Johnnie's boat *Cayo Loco* being between us. But we saw them get off and walk off the dock. Left the boat lights on. I figured they'd be back."

"That's great. Really helpful," I said. "You notice how many people? Or where they went after they got off?"

"Nah, couldn't really see much. I didn't really pay attention. Sailboats at these docks are unusual. Figured they'd had some weather or something. But I didn't really care. Pissed that we lost our charter. Maybe four or five people. Didn't see where they went. Up the docks."

"So, then what? Did you stay on your boat? Leave? Follow them?" I could only hope.

"Nah. We hung out for a while. See if the charter showed. Left at around six or maybe six-thirty. I went back home to bed. Markie called me. Said there was police and a big show here, so I came back."

She jabbed Markie in the ribs. He looked up, squinting. His eyes were bloodshot. "And you were where, Markie?" I asked.

"Had a drink. Or two. Took a nap on the boat." His head bobbed back down. He was either still drunk, or really hungover. In other words, totally useless as a witness.

"Thanks, Agnes. Sorry 'bout the charter. You mentioned a Johnnie owning the boat next to you? Which one of you is Johnnie?" I cast around the table. Gloucester fishermen might be really good at what they do, but they are not known for being chatty. No response.

Markie mumbled, "Not here. Johnnie's not here."

Fortunately for me, as this was painful, Agnes added, "No charter today. He's home."

"Okay, well, thanks. Sergeant Henson, would you please collect the contact info from all these folks? In case we have an opportunity to ask more direct questions." Henson nodded. I stood up. Except for loosely corroborating *Flying Lady's* arrival time in the harbor, which we already knew from the AIS signal, I did not expect to get more from these potential witnesses.

I walked away from the table and leaned on the deck railing, taking in the Gloucester waterfront. It's a beautiful harbor. The sportfishing docks, where the ERT men were crawling over *Flying Lady*, were at the end of a little cove—an outshoot of the main harbor, and the restaurant sat at the head of the cove. It was a bit of a narrow view with some warehouse-type structures to the left, the cove in front, and the red-brick parking lot to the right. The mass of people pushed up against Officer Wilson's barricades had grown in that parking lot. I groaned, growling to myself that this interview with the locals was another dead end. Forensic analysis of the boat would take many, many more hours—if not days. I needed a lead. I looked up to the bluebird afternoon skies above the Gloucester harborfront and, at that precise moment, I got the lead I needed.

Up high, nestled in the eave of the restaurant building, was a shiny black dome. I recognized it instantly. A *security camera.*

I turned some more and, sure enough, there was another one on the opposite side of the building. Clearly, the cameras were meant to monitor the deck area. *Man, I hope that they are real and that they are wide-angle,* I thought, chastising myself for not thinking to look for these things earlier.

I walked back toward the parking lot, slamming my hip into one of the wire-mesh tables as I reached the end of the deck area, but not caring, as I yanked out the earpiece with one hand and pulled the phone from my pocket with the other hand. I was getting pretty good at that move. I jabbed the HQ speed-dial icon, and Anastasia's voice immediately said, "Yeah?"

I stopped in my tracks, now far enough from the crowd of Gloucester PD in the lot and from Gloucester fishermen on the deck for some privacy. "Okay, the pub. It's called that on the sign but—"

"It's called the Harbor Cove Brewing Company. I can see it on my map. You're right next to it. Why?"

"Cameras. At least two of them. On the deck facing the water."

She whistled. It was a long, slow, almost sexy whistle, and then she drew out an equally slow, "How did I forget to think about that earlier?"

"Yeah, me too. But, what now?"

"Perhaps you can find anyone in charge of that place. And see if they've got tapes, cloud storage, whatever."

"Gotcha." I swiped the call off and trotted back toward the building, past the fisherman and Sergeant Henson gathered on the deck, and into the pub.

CHAPTER
50

IT TOOK A MOMENT FOR my eyes to adjust to the dim light inside. In contrast to the open, sunny deck outside, the interior of the pub was dark. With heavy woodwork and large, brownish beams, it vaguely resembled the inside of a ship. Marine artwork cluttered the walls, and nautical-looking objects hung from the ceiling.

And, it was a mess—tables littered with half-eaten meals and half-full pints of beer. I searched and found a door marked "Office" toward the rear. It was partially open, and I could see light inside the room. I knocked.

"Yeah?" The voice was gruff, tired, and not friendly.

"Ben Porter. FBI Boston. May I come in?"

"Yeah."

I pushed open the door. The office was tidy, small, and barely housed a large desk. Crammed behind that desk sat a large, red-cheeked and black-haired gentleman with a carefully trimmed full beard. He was clad in a green-checked shirt. He looked like Paul Bunyan. Not the kind of restaurant proprietor who you'd dare to engage in a game of dine and ditch.

"Good afternoon," I said as pleasantly as I could, then repeating, "I'm Ben Porter. FBI."

"FBI, huh? You got more of a clue than the cops? They shut down my lunch business. Got no happy hour business, either. No way am I cleaning this up and getting prepped for the dinner crowd. Your people kicked everyone out. No explanation. You here to pay off all those tabs?"

"Mind if I ask your name?"

"Jebediah Baker. I own this place. And I got pissed-off customers, pissed-off staff and cooks, and a ton of food going to waste on the tables. Not to mention some pretty good beer, if I do say so myself, going flat. Disgraceful to waste beer like that," he scoffed.

"Couldn't agree more, Mr. Baker," I said. "Listen, I've got people on-site already, and more coming. We will get you back in business as fast as we can. What I want is access to your security cameras. The ones outside, on the deck. I hope they are real."

"Yeah, of course, they're real. I got 'em all over. I can even watch from home if I need to."

"What do you mean, from home?" I asked.

Baker pointed past me and I turned slightly. There was a small monitor in the corner on a shelf with some black boxes below it. He continued, "I can use my phone or my computer at home to log in and see what's happening. If I take a night off, I can watch the back bar. The kitchen. Everything. They record twenty-four-seven. Footage cycles once a week."

I exhaled. *Brilliant.* Way to go, me, spotting those cameras. "Great, Mr. Baker. Sounds like you got online access. Can you set me up? Or better yet, set up my partner?"

He hesitated. "Don't you need a, um, whats-it-called, the order from the judge?"

"A warrant? Technically, yes."

My turn to hesitate. *I don't even know how to go about getting a warrant. Fuck.* I decided to bluff, to put on my big-boy agent voice and bluster. "I can call my office and within a couple of hours, we'll have our warrant. And this place will be crawling with agents, and you'll be closed indefinitely. Or, you might consider we have a crisis outside, and the faster we get access, the faster we get you back in business. Your call."

Baker took only a split-second to make his counteroffer. "Well . . ." drawing it out, "how 'bout those tabs?"

Tough negotiator. I didn't dare waffle or tell him I had to call my boss. Hmm, how would that go? *Yeah, Mr. Baker, I'm not an actual FBI agent, and my boss is with POTUS' Secret Service team doing damage control on a now-canceled visit to Boston, I'm sure she'll be glad to stop whatever she's doing to pay for lunch.*

Making a spot decision that I hoped would not backfire on me, I yanked out my wallet and tossed my American Express card on the desk. "Tell you what. You give me that access right this second, I'll expense it. Uncle Sam will pick up the tabs. How 'bout that?"

With a giant paw, Baker scooped up my Amex and made it disappear while saying, "Alright." He paused and picked up an iPhone from the desk. "So, what you need to do is—"

"Hang on. Mind if I get my office on the phone?"

For the first time, he smiled, probably because he was still holding my card, no doubt thinking that it was government-issue with an unlimited line of credit. "No problem."

No problem for you, maybe. I was having second thoughts, but this was too far gone now. *Better play along,* so I pulled my phone out, tapped the HQ icon and then the speaker icon. Now knowing the routine, before Anastasia could say anything, I started right in. "Anastasia, I'm with Mr. Baker, proprietor of the pub. He has kindly offered remote access to his camera system. Mr. Baker, could you talk us through access?"

Within moments, Baker quickly explained how to access his DigiSummit surveillance system via the cloud. I could hear Anastasia's slow whistle as she clicked through a website. "This is good. I can manipulate this," she said. "Ben, give me some time. I'll call you back as soon as I can." And she ended the call.

Baker stood up, palming his phone while still holding my Amex card. "Let's go settle up," he said, happily. Together, we left the office and headed to the bar area. "Can I pour you a beer? This one would be on the house. Finest local brew around," he said charmingly.

I shook my head ruefully. "Sorry, but I'm on the clock. Next time," I replied, as cheerfully I could, but thinking, hoping, *maybe my card will be declined*.

It wasn't.

CHAPTER
51

I WAS GETTING ANTSY. It had been about a half-hour since I had taken my leave of Mr. Baker. I had returned to the deck where I sat down, by myself, at one of the wire-mesh tables, taking in the view and trying to think of my next steps. While watching one of the ERT guys taking notes and measuring something on the ramp to the dock, and wondering why that was relevant, I heard a voice over my shoulder say slowly, in a thick Gloucester accent, "mind if we john you?"

John me? Oh, wait, *join me!* I nodded my assent as I looked to see who my visitors were.

A couple, who I recognized from the confab with Sergeant Henson earlier, carefully sat down. Both were older with graying hair, tanned faces etched with deep lines from years on the water and looking pleasant enough—they had not said a word during the discussion a bit more than an hour ago. The voice belonged to the man, who continued, "I'm Thomas Riggs, and this is my wife and co-skipper, Helen." Helen smiled pleasantly as her husband added, "We own *Dreamcatcher*."

Yes! I thought. That was the big sportfisher parked at the dock next to *Flying Lady*. "It looks like a beautiful yacht," I said.

"She sure is," Thomas replied. "You know, mostly all boats are called *she*, not *it* or *him*. Goes back a long way, that tradition, to talk about boats as ladies. Why, you know, back in aught-two Lloyd's of London decided to ignore centuries of tradition and began to refer to boats as 'it.' Disgraceful, we think. Centuries of maritime tradition . . ."

I tuned him out as he droned on. I'm sure there's some interesting history there, but I was a little preoccupied with the whereabouts of two radioactive boxes, so I waited for a pause in Thomas's monologue, finally interjecting, "That's fascinating. Always wondered. Say, did you notice anything about that sailboat when she pulled into the dock this morning?"

Helen spoke for the first time. "No, 'fraid not. We had the day off. Only came down here to see what all the kerfuffle was about."

Inwardly I groaned as Thomas eagerly jumped in. "Now, dear, that's an interesting word. You know, the origins of—"

"Not now, dear," Helen said to her spouse. "He wants to know about the sailboat."

"Right-o," replied Thomas. "Sorry, young man, we don't know much."

Thanking them for their time, I stood, beating a quick retreat before the etymology lesson turned from kerfuffle to catawampus. Don't get me wrong, Mr. and Mrs. Riggs were lovely folks, and spending a couple of hours bullshitting about words would normally be a fine way to pass the afternoon, provided there was a beer, or three, involved. I couldn't stand to wait any longer, so I pulled out the phone and jabbed at the HQ icon.

"Hey, Ben," Anastasia answered, "I was about to call you. This video is helpful, but the rez sucks."

"The rez?" I asked.

"Yeah, resolution. It's not great quality video, and we're zeroing in on predawn and postdawn hours. Unfortunately, the cameras skew east, so brighter sky to the east has overexposed parts and underexposed other areas. I've sent the footage to my team to enhance."

"Hang on. Macallister is upstairs, working on building a squad. I'm conferencing him in."

After a short pause, Macallister's voice, short in tone, said, "What do we have?"

"Here's what we got so far, without video enhancement. Tough to see the boat docking, but we can see the lights on the boat and the vague shape of it. We can see people getting off the boat, quickly and orderly. Five people. All appear to be men. This matches Lockwood's story. Then it gets interesting.

"We see two men each, carrying two big bags. Not boxes. Bags. We can enhance those, easy—and I got the guys on-site taking some measurements for reference. We just have to scale against something known in the video frames. We can also estimate weight by how they lean into the load and by how big the men are who are carrying each load. So, we'll have a pretty good physical description too.

"Obviously, we are trying to enhance the faces, see if we can get facial recognition. It's too dark in the source video, which is low resolution already, and they keep their heads down. Maybe they knew there were cameras."

"Hang on," I jumped in. "You said two pairs of men, carrying two bags. That's four. What's the fifth guy doing?"

"Number five was last up the ramp. Carrying a duffel bag."

"And then what?" Macallister exclaimed.

"I'm getting there," Anastasia responded, snappily, perhaps annoyed by the interruptions. "We got one camera overlooking the deck from the right, and that one has picked all this up. Its field of view includes the docks and the ramp up from the docks. But the focus is obviously on the restaurant deck, so all this happens on the periphery. Again, like I said, we're gonna enhance it, and I think we have a shot, but I'm not sure we'll have enough to get facial.

"That was the primary camera that we looked at first, and it's going to be helpful, for sure. But the other camera on the deck, the one on the left, is going to take more time. That field of view is also the restaurant deck, so with the other camera, you can see the whole deck. Follow me?"

I got it. The fields of view crossed and overlapped. Anastasia didn't wait for any confirmation of understanding and barreled on.

"In the background of that view, we can see a sliver of parking lot. And just at the edge of the frame, I can see two pairs of parking lights blink on, then off. Like when you use your key fob to unlock your car. And—I think I can see the plates. It's an oblique angle and it's at the very edge of the screen. Can't make them out, because they are a distance away and, of course, the camera is focused on the closer deck, but I can see them. We are focusing our enhancing efforts on those two license plates. Because who else is getting into cars at that time?"

Anastasia paused, audibly taking a breath, and Macallister started right in, asking, "So how long? How much—"

"Still not done. There's more, too," Anastasia responded. "There's another camera at the front of the building, over the front door. It picks up the street. Again, out of the focus area. But we ran the timestamp around the cars getting unlocked, out a few minutes to account for loading, and we got only one vehicle passing the camera. The timing lines up, but that one could be anybody." She stopped for an instant, then said, "Now, I'll take your questions."

"You didn't answer my first question," Macallister said. "How long to enhance?"

"Dunno . . . obviously we are going as fast as we can."

"Anastasia," I said, looking out over the parking lot, "you told us that a camera picked up the top of the ramp. What did the men *do* at the top of the ramp?"

"Hmm, good question, Ben," she answered. "Hadn't really thought about that. They paused for a short while, and I'll go back over that section of video to double check, but then the lights flashed."

"Did they stay together?" I asked as I walked to the top of the ramp, glancing backward at the restaurant deck and, now that I knew they were there, easily picking out the black domes of the security cameras.

"Hard to say," she answered. "I'm playing it now. So, they get to the top of the ramp, two pairs with two big bags first, followed by number five with the duffel bag. Number five puts down the duffel bag, he's opening it, he's pulling out smaller bags and giving them to the other guys. They're doing something with the little bags. Okay, lights flash and . . . yes! They split up. Two pairs and number five, solo."

I started to say, "Are there three cars? Are we missing one? Is that the one you saw drive by the—"

Macallister, talking over me as I spoke, interrupted. "Porter, get back to Chelsea. You've seen enough there. You've had eyes on the place. The ERT can continue looking for stuff. You can help with this analysis, assuming you're done there."

"Yeah," I answered. "I interviewed the fishermen, got nothing. I did learn why a boat is a *she,* though. Not real helpful, but interesting."

Macallister snorted. "Fucking useless. I'll keep in touch with Russo and see what they've got, if anything. Anastasia, get those enhancements done!" Then he was gone.

CHAPTER
52

BEFORE LEAVING GLOUCESTER, I had fueled up, physically, thanks to my new friend Mr. Baker. I had ducked back inside to his office, asking for two things, which he graciously provided with a genuine smile.

After deciding not to say farewell to Special Agent Russo, I had slipped into the driver's seat of the Dodge, carefully placing the two tall to-go cups that I had gotten from Mr. Baker into the Dodge's oversized, American-sized cupholders. Miles woke up when I had slammed my driver-side door closed and started the motor of the Dodge. "Where to?" he had asked, drowsily, glancing at the two cups. "Is that coffee?"

"Back to the office. And, yeah, I got myself some coffee. Figured you could have a treat."

Miles had taken a careful pull from the to-go cup. "Ahhh, no shit? You're the best!" he had exclaimed.

"Yup. Like I said, I got coffee. You got Harbor Cove Brewing's finest. You said earlier that you should be sitting in Halifax, sipping a beer. So, this is the least I can do for you. Enjoy. I'm a lot jealous."

Miles had grinned happily, murmured a sincere "thank you," and then sipped his ale slowly, almost reverently, as we drove south.

Juiced on Mr. Baker's excellent coffee, I was fully wired some forty-five minutes later when we walked into the Chelsea office's operations center, which was now humming with activity. Apparently, this investigation was gaining momentum.

Miles and I pulled up two chairs. "Anything?" I asked Anastasia.

"Oh, yeah. Lots. First off, Miles, I could use your help. You claimed they brought boxes onto your boat. I don't see any boxes. Watch."

On her biggest screen, the footage from the deck-facing security camera at the Harbor Cove Brewing Company began to play. Even though Anastasia had narrated this sequence to me just an hour ago, it still seemed like watching a blockbuster movie for the first time. I was spellbound.

As Anastasia had mentioned earlier, the videos were very low resolution. And, even though I knew what was going to happen, it was still a surprise, especially to Miles, watching his ghost boat pull into the dock among the big sport-fishers. Together, we watched in silence as the boat's lines were secured and neatly coiled. We continued watching as the five men unloaded the sailboat and carried the long bags up the sloped ramp.

"Hang on," Miles said sharply. "Those have gotta be the boxes. They wrapped them in something. Can you pause and zoom in?"

Anastasia answered, "Sure, but it will just get blurrier."

On screen, the image grew slightly. Miles stood, leaning closer to the big screen, and repeated, "Yeah. They wrapped the boxes in something. Like a sail bag. See, this here," he said, pointing at the screen to what appeared to be a marking of some type on one of the bags, "that's like my sailmaker's logo. Those look like sail bags. We call 'em turtles. They're long and wide with a long zipper down one side. They're to hold a rolled or flaked sail."

He plunked down. "Those kinda look like my sail bags. You didn't let me go below and check the cabin. I bet my bags are missing."

"So, you're saying they disguised the boxes?" I asked.

"Yup. Those are definitely the size of the boxes. Even the way they are carrying them. It was like that when they loaded them on the boat and then brought them into the cabin. See how they are carrying them level? Looks like they're being real careful not to tip them. Definitely the boxes, but now in sail bags. I don't get it."

"It's brilliant." Collectively, we all jumped at the sound of a new voice, which I instantly recognized as belonging to SAC Jennifer Appleton—who had returned from Boston and silently, without warning, glided into the room. She allowed her presence to sufficiently awe us before continuing. "They casually dock a sailboat. They casually saunter down the dock, carrying what, sail bags? And they casually load their sails into their vehicles."

She paused, shaking her head side-to-side, before adding, "They could have done this in broad daylight and nine out of ten people would never have noticed. Maybe even ninety-nine out of a hundred. They're not acting furtively. They're not scary. They're hiding in plain sight."

On the screen, Anastasia had restarted the video, and our group watched as what Appleton had said sunk in. She was correct, of course. As we watched, the men disappeared off-screen, innocently carrying their disguised cargo.

Miles snorted a short laugh. "Right, and now they've got what looks like a sail bag in the back of a car or something. They've been at sea for a while. If anyone stops them, not only do they smell bad, but they've got a smelly sail bag in their car. Who would care?"

No one had an answer. We sat in silence. The deception was so simple.

Appleton concluded. "Okay, so you've just confirmed what Porter has been reporting. Those missing boxes *are* missing. Right. But they're not that clever. We've got them on video."

She fixed her stare on Anastasia and demanded, "When will the enhancements be done?"

"THE VIDEO ENHANCEMENTS will be completed shortly," said a new voice from an opposite workstation.

We turned to look at Vanessa Raiden, who I knew to be Anastasia's longtime associate, but had never laid eyes on. In fact, given the positioning of her workstation, I hadn't even seen her earlier this afternoon, before I headed out on my second trip to Gloucester with Miles.

Raiden was not quite the legendary Intelligence Analyst that Anastasia was, but with her lithe, five-foot-ten frame, mocha skin and straight, swooping black hair, she was certainly no less striking. And it quickly become apparent that she was just as smart.

"And, in the meantime, as the tech team is working on the videos, I've got something. I heard the conversation about trying to track a boat that may have been in the vicinity of the *Flying Lady*. I've been working on that. Check this out."

On the giant monitor, a map of the North Atlantic replaced the security camera images on-screen. "I created an animation from the AIS data. This is coordinated from various sources but sped up in time to make it watchable. Okay, now, look here," she said, pointing to the waters off Marblehead and at an arrow-shaped icon, "that's *Flying Lady*. And look here," she pointed to a position well southwest and offshore of Nova Scotia, "that is a fishing vessel, broadcasting no name, just an MMSI number."

"MM what?" I asked.

"That's the AIS identification number. Stands for Maritime Mobile Service Identity. Nine digits. Unique to each AIS transmitter. Naturally, I looked at the data transmitted along with the GPS data. There's nothing there. No name, no call sign, *nothing*. Which is suspicious in of itself."

"Hang on, though," said Miles. "It's not really all that suspicious, and nothing we would ever look at on the water. I mean, really, some of the commercial boats don't squawk a name, especially the fishing boats. Again, not unusual. So why are we looking at *that* one?"

"Watch," replied Raiden. As the animation continued, the fishing vessel moved in slow circles, remaining southwest of Nova Scotia, appearing to, well, fish. The *Flying Lady* icon slowly departed Marblehead and then sort of meandered toward the western tip of Nova Scotia. "What I can't figure out is what you were doing for, like, the first twenty-four hours, Mr. Lockwood."

He laughed. "Call me Miles. And that's sailboat racing. There wasn't much wind, so you sail angles, looking for a breeze, trying to go as fast as you can, which is really not that fast. Five, six knots, rarely pointed exactly where you want to go."

"Doesn't sound like much fun," Raiden said. "Okay, here we go. It's late afternoon on Monday. Your boat is starting to move more consistently."

"Yeah, the breeze filled in. Good angle," Miles commented.

"And watch the fishing vessel. Now it is midnight on Monday." The fishing vessel and the sailboat icons had converged, and Anastasia zoomed in on the map. The fishing vessel was now moving more northwards, but it looked like it would pass behind the sailboat, which was now sailing a straight course slightly north of east.

"Mmm-k, now it's about one in the morning. Tuesday morning." As we watched the animation, the fishing vessel took a sharp turn to the right and started traveling east, while the sailboat slowed, then stopped, then started moving again—this time very slowly due south, then sped up in a westward direction.

"Rewind, please," said Miles as he stood, pointing at the screen. Raiden reversed the animation. "Here." The sailboat icon had slowed, almost to a stop. The timestamp showed 1:41 AM. "That's when they killed George." He sat back down as the animation restarted again. As the icon moved again, then turned slowly south, Miles muttered, "That's when they loaded the boxes below." He slumped down in his chair, and the animation continued, with the sailboat heading west and the fishing vessel heading south of east.

We watched in silence, with Raiden slowly zooming out as the two vessels diverged. The timestamp showed a day go by, changing from Tuesday to Wednesday. The sailboat maintained a steady course toward the Massachusetts coastline while the fishing vessel headed east, deeper into the Atlantic Ocean. "Okay," Raiden narrated, "we're going to watch the sailboat first, then the fishing vessel. Check this out. The animation is now showing early Wednesday, just after two in the morning today."

The screen zoomed in on the sailboat's track. Just off the tip of Cape Ann, the moving icon stopped, then circled several times, before resuming its westerly course. We all turned and looked at Miles—who sat and watched, totally emotionless. This had been the moment he jumped off his boat. I started to realize the magnitude of what he'd done and with the decision that he'd been faced with.

I held onto that thought as the animation continued, and we watched, silently, as the *Flying Lady* icon carved a course into Gloucester Harbor, finally stopping at the docks where we found her. Raiden manipulated her mouse and the screen zoomed out slightly, saying, "Okay, now keep watching. See that marker I placed on the screen where the boat circled? That's Miles. And the new track you see drawing—that's the fishing boat that picked up Miles, owned by Mr. Lailley from Newburyport. *Bite Me*."

I loved how she phrased that, saving the boat name for last. She said it so matter-of-factly, with no emotion, and no humor. All business, but I was still amused, as I watched the new track angle out of Rockport Harbor—curve east, then south—and finally stop a short distance from the marker that represented Miles's location.

Appleton spoke for the first time in a while, verbalizing what we were all probably thinking. "You realize how lucky you are? You jumped off your boat some seven miles from Cape Ann, and you treaded water for, how long? And this fishing boat just *happened* to take a course that would find you? How did you not die from the cold?"

Interesting, I thought. He told us that when the SAC first met him, when she thought he was pulling a fast one. Now she's intrigued. I, for once, kept my mouth shut.

Miles laughed. "Yeah, lucky for sure, but it was a calculated risk. Water temps are in the sixties this time of year. Figured I had four, maybe five hours. Maybe even six. Watching this, I'm actually surprised, a little, at how far I made it swimming. I swam a bit, toward the coast, before getting tired. That's why the track and the marker don't meet up. And come to think of it, had I not swum, I would have missed those guys heading out fishing."

"Chance in a million," Appleton stated.

"Keep watching. I'm going to rewind back a day," Raiden said. On-screen, the animation had showed *Bite Me* returning to Rockport, and as Anastasia back-stepped the time, the tracks erased from the screen while she zoomed back out. "Watch the fishing vessel."

She restarted the animation and we watched, again, as the fishing vessel and the sailboat diverged. This time, Raiden kept the focus on the fishing vessel, and the *Flying Lady* icon moved off the left side of the screen. We watched in silence as the track plodded slightly south of east, tracking away from the Nova Scotia coastline and aiming well south of the desolate Sable Island.

"So, it's still out there?" I asked, finally breaking the silence.

"That will be up to me to find out," Appleton answered. "I'll liaise with our friends who have the imaging capability. But I am not convinced. All this particular vessel did is get relatively close to Mr. Lockwood's boat. How can you be certain you are tracking the correct vessel?"

Heads bobbed in agreement; she was correct. The fact that both vessel courses got near each other was hardly conclusive. Raiden smiled, "Yes, of course. Before creating the animation, I did some research work on the fishing vessel. First, a little background. There are three types, basically, of AIS devices. Class A is for big ships and is required if the vessel is over three hundred tons. Class B is lower cost but does pretty much the same thing as Class A. Except, it doesn't transmit voyage data. And then there's a receiver only, which can receive from either Class A or Class B—but doesn't transmit. The unit on the fishing vessel is Class B."

"Yeah, and my boat is a Class B also," Miles said.

"But what does this tell us?" Appleton asked.

"Getting there," Raiden replied. "When you get an AIS, it has to be programmed by the retailer. And then that data is used to register that device, with that unique MMSI number, to an international database. Remember what Miles said earlier? That you don't necessarily have to program stuff like the vessel name into the AIS device? A friendly retailer could be convinced not to, and maybe they could be convinced not to register the MMSI number in the database, though that would be risky. If anyone searched the number that you are broadcasting and came up empty in the registration database, that would be a red flag.

"In short, that registration database is public."

Wow, this Vanessa Raiden is sharp and really dug into this, I thought, as she continued, "Unfortunately, with respect to our fishing vessel, the details are not hugely helpful. But, here's the smoking gun—it's AIS track started in Turkey.

"The vessel's track was recorded by AIS as it transited the Mediterranean Sea. Then the signal disappeared, just outside the Straits of Gibraltar. It came back on south of Novia Scotia two weeks later. But, of course, unless you searched for that exact MMSI and examine the data, you wouldn't know that. Once the signal appears, it looks like any fishing boat, working the sea."

Raiden paused and surveyed the group, making sure we were all paying attention, before asking, "Now, why would a fishing boat from Turkey be off Nova Scotia, Canada?"

"That is certainly not coincidental," concluded Appleton. "Owner? What else do we know?"

Raiden replied, "It's from a port city called Bodrum. In the Med. But the MMSI registration has no vessel name, and the owner's name is listed as Mohomed Yilmaz. No doubt a fake name. That's the most common Turkish surname. Probably with a false address too. We could put boots on the ground in Bodrum but, realistically, that would take days or even weeks for usable intel to surface. See the problem?" Raiden asked the group, rhetorically.

We nodded our understanding just as Raiden's computer beeped and at virtually the same time, the desk phone started to ring. "Yes!" yelled Raiden as she spun toward her monitor.

The enhancement team had finished their work. On the screen, with the group of us huddled together, shoulder-to-shoulder, Raiden scrolled through two grainy images extracted from the Harbor Cove Brewing Company's surveillance camera videos.

We had two license plates.

"Run those plates!" Appleton shouted.

CHAPTER
54

WITH THE RESOURCES OF an FBI operations center, running a license plate is child's play. Within seconds, we had two hits.

Our targets were identified as a silver 2016 Chevrolet Impala with New Hampshire plates, registered to a rental car agency, and a white 2007 Chevrolet Express van with Massachusetts tags, owned by Jonathon Bardsman of Newtown, Massachusetts.

The rental car agency was located just outside the Portsmouth International Airport at Pease. The Bureau operated a small satellite office in Portsmouth, and within minutes, Macallister had agents in a vehicle to make the ten-minute drive.

Appleton instructed our duty agent to immediately dispatch one of our agents to Newtown; in the meantime, the Newtown police were contacted and were requested to go to Mr. Bardsman's address.

Raiden posted the information on the license plates and vehicle descriptions onto the FBI's Information Technology systems.

And within twenty minutes, our lead evaporated.

In New Hampshire, our agents burst through the door of the rental car agency with the registration information attached to our target license plate. Two minutes later, a computer check showed that the car in question was in the airport lot, where our agents found it, unrented and untagged. The plates had obviously been removed from the vehicle.

In Newtown, four police officers surrounded the white Chevrolet van at Mr. Bardsman's address. The old vehicle was sitting off to the side of the driveway in dismal condition; it appeared to lean to the left on a sagging suspension and was so dirty that it took the police a moment to realize it had no license plates. Knocking at the door, the officer found the Mr. Bardsman—a cantankerous, heavyset, balding, sixty-something-year-old carpenter with a bad attitude and no work—inside. He hadn't been outside in days. Hearing the police officer relay that description on Raiden's speakerphone, I wondered if it occurred to the carpenter that he might consider a smile, some sit-ups, or maybe retirement.

Appleton was as much annoyed as Macallister was unfazed. "Of course they're stolen plates," he spat. "But they got plates. We gotta track 'em."

"We need a warrant for that," Anastasia cautioned.

Macallister's eyes narrowed. I knew that look. "We don't have time. Track 'em, and we'll sort it out later."

As Macallister stalked out of the operations center, to my surprise, Appleton didn't hesitate. "Agreed," she purred. "Track the plates. Now, please."

It appeared to me that the SAC was fully engaged in the case.

CHAPTER
55

HIGHWAY ENTHUSIASTS (yes, all three of you reading this) know that Interstate 90 is the longest highway in the United States, stretching from Seattle to Boston. Here in Massachusetts, we call our 138-mile section of that 3,020-mile road the "Mass Pike," depicted on road signs with a logo of a Pilgrim's hat, probably because we want to remind drivers that the Pilgrims settled Massachusetts to avoid religious persecution and to build a toll road.

Horizontally splitting the state, for us, the Mass Pike starts on the New York and Massachusetts border in West Stockbridge. Thanks to the notorious Big Dig, which is allegedly the most expensive highway construction project in the States, the Mass Pike and I-90 ends at its easternmost-point at Boston's Logan Airport.

More relevantly, less than a year ago, in October 2016, the Massachusetts Department of Transportation activated its state-of-the-art tolling system on the Mass Pike.

Previously, almost every entry and exit point on the Mass Pike had a tollbooth, and drivers would pay by the distance traveled between booths. Now, with tolling gantries spanning the roadway constructed between almost every exit, there's no need to stop; the high-tech equipment mounted on the gantries captures the signal from an E-Z-Pass transponder or, in the absence of a transponder, a camera snaps a photo of a license plate. Oh, and the gantry captures your speed too.

Not to worry, you're told, your speed data is not used to issue speeding tickets. Just the toll data, so either your E Z-Pass account gets dinged for the toll, or you get a bill in the mail for the camera-capture of your license plate. When the system launched, one news story after another raised the possibility of the authorities using the cameras to track individuals, which MassDOT vehemently denied. *We're the government, you can trust us.*

Naturally, that was the first database that Vanessa Raiden checked and, sure enough, within minutes we had hits from the Mass Pike toll cameras.

"Got one. Toll number 620. Weston. Going west." On a second monitor, Raiden brought up a map of the Mass Pike, jabbing her finger at the screen just west of where I-95 intersects the Pike, between Newtown and Weston.

One of her assistants, a geeky-looking guy with short, spiky, silvery-blond hair and purple eyeglasses on the far side of the workroom, was looking for the other plate, and he, too, exclaimed, "Same here! Weston toll. What's your timestamp?"

"5:53 AM," said Raiden.

"I'm two minutes behind you," the assistant said, tapping at his keyboard.

With my index finger, I leaned in and traced an imaginary route from Gloucester, catching I-95 South and then turning west onto the Mass Pike. My finger followed the Pike west to the New York line.

"Got mine again. 583, that's . . ." Raiden's fingers worked the keyboard, "Charlton. Lewis, where the hell is Charlton?" she yelled at her assistant.

"Near Sturbridge," said Miles.

Of course, the realtor knows his geography, I thought, again wisely not opening my mouth, congratulating myself for my discretion. *I'm learning . . .*

"And then nothing. No more hits. Where'd it go? What do you have?" Raiden asked Lewis.

"Same here. 583. Forty-three minutes later."

"They probably took 84 West. Which is really south, there, toward Hartford. Very convenient route to Hartford and then to New York City," Miles said pleasantly, in what had to be his realtor sales voice.

The room went silent. New York City? Raiden had zoomed out the map screen and, sure enough, Miles was spot on. Mass Pike to 84 to . . . *somewhere* in Connecticut.

"No tolls there," Anastasia stated flatly, as she looked at the screen.

"Yeah, but there are tolls everywhere in New York. Bridges, tunnels, New Jersey Turnpike. Fucking place has fucking tolls all over the place." We all turned as Macallister rejoined us. Of course, he'd know if there are tolls on the New Jersey Turnpike.

Raiden sighed. "All over the place, indeed. We got lucky with these hits because we have access. This is a local system. Probably not totally legit for me to be in the DOT database, but whatever.

"But now we gotta get into the E-Z-Pass systems in New York, New Jersey, Pennsylvania . . ." Raiden's voice dropped as she spoke. "Macallister, for that, you're gonna have to get us warrants, judge's orders, the works. We can do it, but it will take some time." She groaned, clearly thinking about the magnitude of the task.

"Hang on," I said. "You got the toll data. Can we get the camera images? Get a visual on the vehicles? Let's work with what we have first."

"Nice thinking, Porter. Go with what we have," repeated Macallister.

"And isolate faces from the videos and run them through our facial recognition routines," Raiden added. "The SAC said she could work on seeing if we can locate that fishing vessel with satellite assets."

I added, "Miles. You said you remember faces and names. Let's get you with one of our composite sketch guys. We can flesh out any imperfections from the video stills. I'll update the case file and see if anything else pops out."

"Gonna be a long night. I'll get you guys some coffee and order in some dinner." We collectively gaped at Macallister, shocked that he'd offer coffee, much less dinner, as he walked out of the room.

I looked around, realizing, for the first time since returning from Gloucester, that a day which had started with the office as a ghost town was now buzzing, and that evidence was mounting that something potentially very big was going down. The wheels of the FBI were really beginning to spin into motion.

It was, indeed, going to be a long night.

On this warm, early evening in July, it would not be unusual to see a person hovering outside the side employee entrance of 201 Maple Street, perhaps enjoying a moment in the fresh air, making a personal phone call, or sneaking a quick fix of nicotine.

The parking lot afforded no visual privacy, but the outside world was kept at bay by a high, reinforced, black iron fence which surrounds the ten-story building. The arrow-shaped spikes atop each black iron baluster were both decorative and threatening; their purpose obvious but disguised by their apparent delicacy.

To one side of the employee entrance canopy, a small, three-car-width-wide planting area softened the expanse of blacktopped lot against the drab, whiteish-gray concrete façade of the building. Somewhat blending into the shapes of the trees and bushes sprouting from a well-tended mulch bed, a sole figure thumb-typed intuitively on the ten-key pad of a charcoal-gray flip phone. After the briefest pause to reexamine the characters on the tiny screen, and without even so much as a glance around after a final button was pressed, fingers clapped the clamshell device closed and snapped the rear battery free from the case. Dropping the now two-part device in a pocket, a sliver of a silver wristwatch just barely glinted in the low rays from the early-evening setting sun as the figure vanished into the structure.

CHAPTER
56

WEDNESDAY, 6:56 PM — NEW MILFORD, CONNECTICUT

THERE WAS ONE FINAL TASK to complete. Hans pulled out the Pixel phone that he had used to unlock the van and handed the device to Omar. For the first time since that morning, the phone was powered on.

Reaching into his pocket, Omar withdrew his own Pixel and powered on that phone. The boot procedure took several long seconds and Omar waited impassively—then jolted upright as the Pixel vibrated, signaling an incoming message. This phone number for this device was known to only one person and usage of that number was reserved for an absolute emergency. Indeed, the plan was that the device made only outgoing calls. An incoming message was a real problem.

Omar's eyebrows raised as an icon showed the receipt of a new text message. He placed his right index finger on the rear fingerprint sensor of the device, and with his left hand, tapped the message icon.

The sender field indicated a blocked number, and the message was a succinct two words: *CHANGE PLATES*.

Omar's mind raced through the possibilities, and he concluded that the lack of supporting verbiage was a good sign. One of their three stolen license plates had probably been reported. That was a possibility they had considered. And the solution was simple.

Omar angled the device's screen toward Bruce, who glanced at the words and nodded his understanding. Returning his attention to his

Pixel and swiping to the telephone icon on the glass face of the device, Omar located the contact list. Only two numbers were stored in the list, and he selected the one saved as "C." Within a split-second, the other device lit with an incoming call. Omar had then swiped the calls off, that last test complete.

Manipulating the menu on Hans's Pixel phone, Omar set the phone to do-not-disturb mode, with a single exception: the number from the most recent incoming call.

With care, the men slid the long, matte-black plastic box from the carrying bag used to disguise it as it was brought off the boat. Carefully opening the box, Omar had located the detonation device within, and he connected a short cord to Hans's Pixel phone.

After carefully nesting the wired Pixel device inside the box, Omar had slowly, with trepidation, powered on the detonation device with a simple, shiny-metal toggle switch. The next call to that Pixel from Omar's phone would detonate the weapon within the black plastic box.

He had resealed the box and exited the van, slamming the rear cargo doors closed. No words had been needed and no good-byes were said.

With a thirteen or fourteen hour drive to Chicago in front of them, the Chevrolet Express van had pulled out of the work bay with Hans driving and Bruce in the passenger seat. Outside, one would be required to be extra-vigilant to notice that the red-lettered Massachusetts license plate with its white background had been changed to a blueish-white background Connecticut registration plate. But it was difficult not to notice that the plain white cargo van was also now sporting the ubiquitous purple and orange FedEx logo on its flanks. The two-color, block letters in a sans-serif font were straightforward to duplicate; the graphics supplier had done its job perfectly. The logo had been pulled from FedEx's home page and enlarged to scale to the side of the van after a brief pass by a real FedEx van with a tape measure to get the letter height. The company's white vans were almost everywhere, and their use of normal cargo vans, as opposed to UPS's larger, brown box trucks, had made FedEx Omar's chosen company to impersonate.

In the warehouse, Seb and John continued wrapping the GMC in white vinyl. This vehicle had a much shorter drive in the morning; New

York lay only ninety minutes away, a quick drive, as long as the van left early enough to time the morning traffic correctly.

As the two men fiddled with the sticky vinyl, working out air bubbles to ensure a perfectly smooth, white surface, Omar pulled out a Samsung phone, powered it on, selected the only contact number stored in the phone, and sent a brief text: *July 13 9:33 EST.* Turning the device off, he snapped the back cover off and removed the battery.

Stepping outside, he tossed the parts into the backseat of the Regal, turned the ignition key, and headed south on Route 202.

Stopping at a pizza place less than a half-mile south, Omar ordered two pies, three salads, and sodas, looking no different than any father grabbing a family meal on his way home from work. Except, of course, this meal was for three men who had just smuggled themselves into the United States.

Back at the work bay, they ate in silence, their first meal since the fast-food, rest-stop breakfasts earlier in the day. There was little to talk about; they had spent the last two-and-a-half months together and wanted to be done with each other's company.

CHAPTER
57

FEBRUARY 2017 — ASPROVALTA, GREECE

USING THE SAMSUNG DEVICE while on a public Wi-Fi network at a café in Asprovalta, Greece, Omar logged into Gmail through the phone's browser and checked the drafts folder; it was empty. He composed a new message:

Greece is a dead end. Nothing big enough and/or available here. Why bother? Easier to assemble our pieces at home than to go to this trouble.

Omar saved the draft, finished his coffee, and waited. New York is seven hours behind Greece, so for the last month, his duty was to check the drafts folder each day at three in the afternoon, or eight in the morning in New York. Omar had learned to blend in nicely with the locals, loudly sipping a cup of excellent Greek coffee, *metrios* style, midafternoon. Most days, there was nothing in the folder. Today, there was a response right away, added below Omar's words:

And risk what? Too many eyes locally. Need to dispatch where you are. And bring in. Too many sensors and cameras here.

Omar glared at the little screen. It was easy to contradict the reality in Greece. He had scoured the docks in the large port city of Pireaus, Greece, for a suitable vessel with a desperate owner and captain. Now, in the smaller port of Asprovalta, he faced the same failure. Omar still needed to locate and prepare a suitable vessel, and he needed it to depart in early June. He would need about ten days to transit the Mediterranean

Sea, plus roughly twenty days to cross the Atlantic Ocean. He felt that he was running short on time.

Omar thumb-typed his objections into the unsent, draft email: *Need a month just to get there. A month prior to prepare. A month prior to that to acquire all the parts and materials, and assemble a team. I can do this in the States in a third of the time. It's unnecessarily complicated.*

He slurped his coffee. No one gave him even a glance. Swiping at the device again, he saw an appended reply.

Fine. Renege on our deal. Don't come back. And watch your back. Or try Turkey. You have got plenty of time. Your choice.

Omar's glare at the tiny screen morphed into sad resignation. He had, indeed, a little more time, and Turkey was a good option. If he could get this mission completed, he would once again be a man of means, and he typed:

Turkey it is. Will report in a week.

Omar savored the last sips of coffee, making sure he did not inadvertently suck up the harsh grounds at the bottom of the ceramic cup. Looking back down at the screen, he saw that the draft had been deleted. Omar switched apps on the device and plotted a journey to Turkey.

CHAPTER
58

MAY 2017 — BODRUM, TURKEY

THE SUGGESTION—OR WAS IT a directive?—of Turkey had proved fruitful and Omar had quickly identified Mohomed Yilmaz and his rusty, but serviceable, long-range trawler as the vessel and for his transport.

The pieces fell into place nicely. Omar assembled a four-man team of soulless men and sourced weapons and the Zodiac for the hijack of the sailboat. As the departure day neared, the team would take the RIB out into the Mediterranean waters, ostensibly to go night fishing, but really to rehearse the timing for the rendezvous with the sailboat.

While still in Greece, Omar had researched the odd pastime of offshore yacht racing and selected his final target as entries had trickled in for the 2017 Marblehead-to-Halifax Ocean Race. Miles Lockwood was a compelling choice. He was a first-timer in the race. He was a realtor, and his personal website included his photograph, useful for identifying him once the target was intercepted. And his boat, pictured on both his website and in various places online, was perfect: an unassuming, bland, mass-produced sailboat.

Omar had scoured online for specifications, photos, and dimensions of Miles Lockwood's J/111. Doing more research, he even found a sistership for sale in Port Grimaud, France, and, armed with a tape measure and a smartphone camera, he indulged in a journey to Saint-Tropez, meeting a yacht broker to review the boat in person. Confirming the dimensions on the sistership and taking hundreds of photos to show the team, Omar familiarized himself with the little yacht. Based on the depth of his interest, the yacht broker was brokenhearted when Omar, trying to come up with a suitable excuse to end the tour in a subtle way, opined that the lack of privacy in the toilet area was problematic.

Measurements in hand and posing as a trade show representative needing carrying cases for a specialized product, Omar had purchased, through the wonderful anonymity of the internet, the custom-made, molded boxes to his exact specifications of dimension and design. His employer had assured him that the complicated and rare innards for the boxes would be provided for him in Bodrum.

He had also ordered carrying sacks for the boxes, fashioned painstakingly to resemble the baggy blue sail bags he had seen stuffed in the forepeak of the sistership he had toured in France. The bags would be too slippery to use in the Zodiac transfer, but they rolled up tightly and were easy to stuff in the waterproof duffel bag. They'd slide the boxes into the bags before disembarking from the boat, and, carrying their bagged sails, they would look like ordinary sailors returning to land from a day on the water.

Omar's boundless creativity in deception used bait crates as a disguise as the team loaded the components for the mission onto the trawler, using the trawler's own small crane to lift the crates from the beds of cargo trucks on the pier onto the fantail of the trawler itself. They would meet the cargo at a vacant warehouse that they had rented and repackage it into crates. Fuel bladders for the trawler, food stuffs and supplies, and, of course, the boxes themselves were transported, in broad daylight, from the warehouse to the docks.

It was Omar's revelation that two identical, or closely-similar white vans, sitting overnight in the red-brick Gloucester parking area, may catch unwanted attention, and the solution that he proposed was to arrange for one silver and one white van. Only a van connoisseur would have discerned that the silver van and the white van were, for all intents, identical except for their paintwork; differed only by the brand badging and by the arrangement of the front grill and headlights.

Just prior to departure, Omar had arranged for vinyl automotive wrap to be delivered; for practice, the team wrapped Mohomed's aging Toyota HiLux in trendy matte black, much to his delight.

And with his affinity for a swindle, Omar would assemble the devices that would eventually detonate in the bowels of the trawler and erase its existence, all while seated at the trawler's galley table during the Atlantic crossing, with Mohomed watching but wrongly assuming that they were for the undisclosed mission in the United States. Omar hid his subterfuge in plain sight, as usual.

CHAPTER

59

WEDNESDAY, 9:48 PM — FBI BOSTON FIELD OFFICE, CHELSEA, MASSACHUSETTS

THE BRIGHT SIDE, if there was one, was that Macallister's dinner had been top-notch. Over-the-top, top-notch. Either he was trying to curry favor, or he was trying to show off.

My opinion of my boss had changed significantly over the past day, and I saw him in a new light. He wasn't a total asshole, after all. He had become a colleague who I now respected. I hoped the feeling was mutual, that I had also earned his respect. That, I would appreciate.

And I really appreciated the grub.

He had brought in a spread of take-out from a local, high-end, popular restaurant that was housed in a converted firehouse. Fast food, this was not. This was proper gourmet take-out, an artfully prepared and carefully packaged spread with a charcuterie platter, surf-and-turf tacos, a variety of burgers and toppings, and several salads. Macallister himself had set up one of the big conference rooms with the feast. The only thing missing was the party atmosphere, and maybe a nice glass of wine or a beer. But, all the same, it was a tremendous pick-me-up after a long day.

Unfortunately, it was mostly downhill from there.

Macallister had sent agents to Gloucester to begin canvassing the neighborhood for cameras and witnesses. The search for cameras would take time, a laborious, door-to-door process. And, due to the early hour that the boat had docked, and due to the late hour that the investigation finally kicked into high gear, we had yet to find any new witnesses or any new cameras.

As the hours had ticked toward midnight, our collective moods had become darker and darker with the night. The warmth of the food buzz had long since worn off, and tempers were short as lead after lead had hit the proverbial brick wall.

We had a glint of forward motion at about 10:00 PM. Appleton had whisked back into the operations center with a faint smile on her face. The SAC had looked fresh. Her clothes were unwrinkled, her hair was perfect, and she showed not the slightest hint of exhaustion. Her energy was briefly contagious as she announced, "Our liaison system worked. Turns out, the CIA has a guy in Bodrum, Turkey. They woke him up. He's going to check out the Mohomed Yilmaz lead. We're getting some boots on the ground," she had concluded triumphantly.

Tapping at her keyboard, Anastasia had snorted, "When? That's, ah, seven hours ahead of us. It's just after five in the morning there."

The SAC's face had drooped ever so slightly. "I understand it's a long shot, but we should know more in several hours. At least it's *something*," she snapped.

"I got something," I said. Macallister had also authorized me to send Special Agent Don Simmons to the US Coast Guard Station Gloucester, as I had wondered how a boat could simply dock, unannounced, in the harbor. The agent interviewed the chubby, homely, farm-girl-seeking-high-seas-adventure Petty Officer Third Class Michelle Kayes, who had the ten-to-six "radio watch" that spanned late Tuesday night into Wednesday morning, and who was just arriving for her Wednesday night to Thursday morning shift.

On the phone earlier, and half-listening to the SAC's update, I had learned from Agent Simmons that the incoming shipping lanes to the port of Boston were managed by US Coast Guard Sector Boston, and typically USCG Station Gloucester was not to be concerned with vessel traffic. But, a duty of the radio watch, an anachronism in this age of digital communication and radar, was to monitor local traffic. In summer months, daytime was busy, with pleasure craft mixing with working fishermen, but night traffic was typically limited to commercial activities.

I manipulated the controls on the desk phone to select speakerphone mode while narrating, "On the phone, I've got US Coast Guard Petty Officer Kayes and Special Agent Simmons. Officer Kayes, can you run this down again for the benefit of my team?"

Petty Officer Kayes, in her lilting, midwest twang, recounted her story. "Before dawn Wednesday morning, I saw an AIS contact bearing a pleasure craft icon entering the Gloucester AOR—that means Area of Responsibility. AIS icons had begun to show, like normal, in Gloucester and Rockport Harbors, as the fishing fleets powered on and prepared to head to sea, but that vessel was the only westbound traffic. I was curious and so I clicked on the vessel icon and brought up the vessel's data—*Flying Lady,* homeport Cohasset, Massachusetts, sailing vessel, and the vessel's past track. It had departed from Marblehead three days prior, took a jagged course east toward Nova Scotia, and then, before reaching Nova Scotia, turned back toward the Massachusetts coastline. That Marblehead departure point seemed familiar, and so I had pulled out the most recent LMN."

"What's an LMN?" Macallister interrupted.

Agent Simmons butted in to answer Macallister's question. "It's a Local Notice to Mariners. A weekly publication used to report on missing or out-of-place navigational aids, maintenance items, and items of interest to seafarers. I'm texting you a link."

Our interview with the Petty Officer paused as Raiden brought up the link to the online publication, and, in the Chelsea office, we discovered that in the LNM District 1, Week 27/17, page 32, it read: "Location: Marblehead; Chart: 13276; Date: 09-July-17; Day(s): Sunday; Time: 1155-1430; Event / Sponsor: Marblehead to Halifax Ocean Race / Boston Yacht Club."

"Did you read it?" Petty Officer Kayes asked us, over the phone. Without waiting for an answer, she continued her story. "I used my personal phone to google the race and found a website with links to race entries, which included a vessel named *Flying Lady* with a Cohasset homeport that was listed in Class 7."

In Chelsea, Raiden duplicated Kayes's Google search in real time. We watched as Raiden's screen displayed what the Petty Officer narrated: "A few clicks later, I found a 'Race Results' link, and followed that to a page listing a series of boat names and finish times. In the Class 7 section, at the bottom: '*Flying Lady*—J/111—Miles Lockwood—RET'.

"I didn't know what RET stood for, so I googled that, too. Sailing race abbreviations RET. It's short for 'Retired'."

"Are you still with me?" The Coast Guard officer paused for a moment but, again, she did not wait for a response, defensively declaring, "I checked it all out. It was obvious that they were a US-flagged vessel that had to quit their race. I entered the contact in the log. And that's it."

Appleton leaned toward the phone with an incredulous look on her face. "I'm not sure I follow. Because it was a US-flagged vessel, it can come and go as it pleases?"

"Sure," replied the Petty Officer. "Happens all the time, every day, every port. Vessels go out, they come back in. Now, if they dock at a foreign port, we have procedures they need to follow, of course. Not our procedures, but with Customs and Immigration. But obviously this one didn't go to a foreign port. It went out, it came back. What's the problem?"

No one in Chelsea wanted to answer that question, and I hit the mute button on our end as Simmons thanked Petty Officer Kayes. Our group looked at each other in disbelief until Macallister, his mouth pursed into a grimace, grumbled what we all thought, "*Fuck*. The Coast Guard watched it happen."

Appleton added, "Do I conclude that this AIS system is the perfect cover for anything nefarious, because it gives a false assurance that what is tracked is what is meant to be?"

I nodded, wisely, for once, not correcting her redundancy in saying "AIS system." And, having done work with Raiden on this earlier, I was able to elaborate and concur with her, "It would appear that *any* US-flagged vessel departing from a US port can return to any port in the US, regardless of the departure point, regardless of distance traveled offshore, as long as that vessel does not stop in a foreign port. And this doesn't just apply to boats like Miles's doing a recreational sailboat race. It's *all* vessels: sportfishers, cruisers, coastal freight, ferries, and commercial fishing."

Pausing to make sure that Appleton was still paying attention, I locked eyes with her as I gamed out my own analysis. "Imagine the bad guys hijack a large commercial fishing boat well offshore. They could load whatever or whomever on it. And then that fishing boat can casually return to the States, and Customs and Coast Guard won't even look at it. The cargo could be weapons, drugs, any sort of contraband.

"Or, it could be people. Imagine a foreign government—the Chinese, or the Russians—wants to send spies into the United States with no record at a border crossing or no record of immigration at an airport, even under a false identity. A maritime infiltration for a spy would be absolutely undetectable!"

Shoulders dropping even as she scribbled notes on a pad in front of her, Appleton sighed before responding, "Unbelievable. Those missing people and boxes are a very real threat and canceling POTUS's visit earlier does not diminish that threat. They're up to something. I'm going to brief the director!"

The SAC swept from the room.

CHAPTER
60

WEDNESDAY, 11:00 PM — NEW MILFORD, CONNECTICUT

OMAR ALLOWED HIMSELF A smile, recalling first meeting Mohomed Yilmaz and introducing himself, *I am the man they call Omar.* He'd chosen his nickname carefully; in Arabic, Omar meant long-lived, and in Hebrew, it meant eloquent. The name had stuck firmly, to the point where even he had begun to think of himself as that name.

Glancing at his watch, he noted that the naïve Mohomed would not be long-lived. Certainly not long-lived enough to ascertain that the wire instructions Omar had assured him were "irreversible" were merely a figment of Omar's deceitful imagination.

In the work bay, the men lethargically cleaned up the remnants of dinner and vinyl, stuffing the trash into a large, black, plastic garbage bag. Stepping into the now-white GMC van, Omar repeated the task he done hours earlier inside the Chevrolet van, first testing, and then connecting the remaining Pixel phone to the detonation device.

After Omar completed that work, he assigned one of the men to affix stickers to the sides of the black box, while the other man pulled the New Hampshire license plate off the GMC's bumpers and attached a Connecticut plate. The New Hampshire tag was stuffed into the garbage bag, which was handed to Omar, along with a Connecticut plate for the Regal.

Accepting the plate and the trash bag, Omar grimaced. The two items were metaphors for what his life had become. A random string of letters and numbers, with no personal connection, and a stuffed bag of garbage, detritus from deception. Seb and John, paid pawns in the game, were too simpleminded to care; their thoughts were on their payday tomorrow after a successful delivery. They were faceless; their places could be taken by any number of men with no morals and an empty wallet. They lived in the shadows.

Conversely, Omar was ready for his life in the shadows to be over. He would have the means to be the creator of his own new life, with a new identity. He would prosper, and he would be comfortable. But he would be careful, this time.

And from a distance, shielded by his new identity, he would be able to watch what happened to those who abandoned him, who turned on him, and who would suffer, as he had been forced to do.

In Turkey, Omar had logged into the Gmail draft folder for the last time on June 10th, typing: *Departing tonight. Anticipating intercept July 10 or 11. Delivery a day or two later.* And then it would be over.

The exact date would ultimately depend on the pace of the sailboat race. It was the perfect cover; arbitrary and loose enough not to attract suspicion but defined enough to be actionable. Or, hidden in plain sight.

CHAPTER
61

WEDNESDAY, 11:55 PM — THE ATLANTIC OCEAN

THE ENGINEER'S HELPER appeared in the wheelhouse of the trawler, a few minutes early for the midnight watch change. There were only five of them remaining on the trawler—Mohomed, the helmsman, the engineer, the engineer's helper, and the cook. Aside from the cook, they had taken turns standing watch, monitoring the autopilot, a grainy radar screen, and the Raymarine display. It had been boring work. Mohomed had kept a wary eye on the engineer's helper, who seemed to be thrilled with the chance to stand a watch.

The next days across the Atlantic would be dull and unexciting, and Mohomed wondered how soon the novelty of watch standing would last. At the moment, though, he didn't really care. He slept on a bunk just aft of the wheelhouse, always within earshot. He'd get the boat across the ocean, now, thankfully, without Omar and his team aboard.

Mohomed waited patiently for a few minutes while the new watch stander reoriented himself, adjusting to the overcast night at sea, the monotony of the dark gray sky intermingling with the monotony of the dark gray swells. The two men did not speak to one another. Mohomed would wait out the five minutes till midnight, and he sat back in his chair.

✳ ✳ ✳

The momentary thrill at 7:58 PM, earlier that evening, had passed. But had been a notable time, nonetheless.

As anyone who has ever flown a long flight might understand, the shortest distance to a place far away is not the compass bearing to that point as drawn on a flat map. Instead, it is the geodesic, or as more commonly known, great circle route.

The math for this complicated projection was impossible for Mohomed, but with the sophisticated Raymarine GPS plotter, it was done by merely touching a finger on a soft key icon on the display.

At 2:00 AM on Tuesday morning, about forty-two hours ago, Mohomed had waited for the second signal, which would have meant disaster. Something would have gone terribly wrong, and it was an evacuation signal. Mohomed would have had to maneuver the unwieldy trawler alongside the small sailboat, so that Omar and the four other men could reboard the trawler. The mission would have failed.

Fortunately, the radios had remained silent, and Mohomed had turned the trawler to a compass course of 120 degrees magnetic, taking a course that would make distance between the ship and the Nova Scotia coastline, while also making progress to the east, back toward Europe.

Mohomed would maintain the 120 degree magnetic heading until reaching his waypoint, or turning point: a spot in the water exactly 100 miles south of Sable Island.

A sliver of land almost due south of the eastern tip of Novia Scotia, Sable Island is a protected Canadian nature reserve. The chances of anyone at the Federal Government outpost on the island monitoring a vessel that far south were slim to none. The fishing fleets would be much closer to the island, most likely in the fertile waters north of the island. Air traffic to the south of the crescent-shaped island was nonexistent. It was a lonely spot of nothingness on a vast ocean.

And still, for Mohomed, making that waypoint had been a momentous occasion. He had already entered the new course and future destination off the Straits of Gibraltar and had waited till the exact moment to press the button to calculate the great circle route. He had needed this finality, this moment of truth—this moment when he turned, finally on a course for home.

Home. He looked forward to retiring from the sea. He would take the money that Omar had left for him, find a place far from the water, and live out his days among green grass. He wouldn't miss the gray water, the fickle ocean weather, or the constant dampness.

Looking at the clock on the Raymarine plotter, still set to Eastern Standard Time, Mohomed had noted the time: 7:58 PM. It had been some forty-two hours since the intercept. Forty-two hours closer to home. Forty-two hours since ridding himself of the foreigners.

He didn't care about their mission, whatever it was. Omar had been careful to keep the Turk in the dark; all Omar wanted from Mohomed was the trawler and a crew to operate it for the long trans-Atlantic journey and then for the equally long trip back across the ocean.

During the voyage, he had overheard Omar talk of the "Great Satan" and of its destruction, so Mohomed had concluded that the ominous-looking, long, black boxes were weapons or bombs of some sort. The foreigners certainly treated them with care. But Mohomed thought otherwise, at least as far as the men were concerned. Omar might use the verbiage, but it did not come naturally. He was pretending.

And for what, Mohomed cared not at all. Not about any politics nor about any crusade. He cared for one thing only: the money, and the escape from the sea that the money would allow him to make.

At the precise moment that he had reached his waypoint, one hundred miles south of Sable Island, he had turned the dial on the antique, yet reliable, autopilot to 117 degrees—the first step in a slowly changing course that would drive his trawler across the globe, across the Atlantic Ocean, and away from this inhospitable place. Toward home. Toward a new future.

Once the course change was complete, Mohomed had manipulated the controls on the Raymarine plotter once more, switching the device's AIS settings to "receive only." The device would now only receive AIS signals. It would no longer broadcast location data. Once near the shipping lanes off Gibraltar, he planned to switch the transmit mode back on. However, for the long journey across the Atlantic, the trawler would be invisible.

✳ ✳ ✳

For the past four hours, the trawler had plodded through the inky swells, still maintaining a slow seven-knot pace, making only about thirty miles of eastward progress from the waypoint south of Sable Island.

Mohomed gave the tall chair behind the helm to the engineer's helper, who eagerly accepted the con, taking the Raymarine plotter. Turning his back to the wheelhouse windows, Mohomed walked off the bridge. He needed to take a piss, and he needed a nap.

Working his way belowdecks to the crew quarters, he glanced at the bunks. All three men were sound asleep. The oddities of a watch schedule, and the activity almost two days ago, not to mention the anticipation, had run them ragged.

In the filthy head compartment, Mohomed relieved himself, not bothering to wash up or to even flush the ancient marine toilet.

As he climbed the rusty stair back toward his bridge, he caught a view of the dark ocean through a porthole. The low overcast skies made the night preternaturally dark. In the faint reflection on the dirty porthole glass, he caught a glimpse of himself, yet the eyes were not his. He paused, a tremor of chill passing through him. They were the eyes of the deckhand. The deckhand he had shot, who had looked at him.

Who had locked eyes with him as he died.

Mohomed shivered. Then he caught himself, shaking his head as if to clear his eyes and muttering to himself, "önemli değil." *It's nothing.*

There was nothing there—only the charcoal ocean waves against a blackened sky. But it *was* something, and deep down, he knew it.

At that exact moment, there was another shudder—though this time, not of his body, but of the entire ship. Almost a gentle rock at first, like a brief premonition, and then a massive, jolting quake. Mohomed froze in place—*up to the bridge, or down to the engine room?*

Ultimately, in those few seconds, it didn't matter. The device that Omar had placed under the fuel bladders had been triggered by the timer, set more than two days ago. The charges ignited the diesel vapors that had been trapped for weeks in the converted fish hold, creating a concussive blast as the fumes exploded.

The massive blast concussion instantly killed the three sleeping men.

In the stair enclosure, Mohomed dropped to the deck. He remained conscious; however, his eardrums had blown out, and his eyeballs had been shaken so violently that his vision had blurred.

In the relatively small area of the converted fish hold, the bladders gave out and mixed liquid diesel with the exploding vapors. The lethal combination of searing high temperature, air in the hold, diesel vapor, and thousands of gallons of fuel, all in a confined space, took only seconds to create a super-heated inferno, in turn producing immense outward pressure. The old trawler didn't stand a chance. The ancient welds that tied the steel plates of her hull together were ripped apart below the waterline. To the ship's credit, the engine did not falter as it drove the vessel below the waves, its momentum quickly flooding the hull and superstructure, forcing the boat under.

In the stairwell, Mohomed lay on the floor, his senses overwhelmed, not realizing what was happening as the cold water covered him, smothering him.

On the bridge, the engineer's helper was the unluckiest. Spared the full concussive force of the initial blast, he nonetheless felt the massive shudder as the inferno in the hold blew out the bottom of the ship. He saw flames ripping from the sides and hatches of the trawler. And he watched, helplessly, as the bow drove under water. It never occurred to him to pull back the throttle as he stood, transfixed, rooted to the spot, watching the sequence of his own death. The ocean bashed in the bridge windows and he drowned, holding the Raymarine plotter in one hand.

Less than four minutes after the timer clicked to zero, the trawler was gone beneath the waves, the leaden overcast mixing and swirling with the remnants of the burning diesel smoke. A slick of oil and a few pieces of flotsam marked the grave, only to be dissipated by the relentless, never-ending swell under the cloak of night.

PART THREE
THURSDAY, JULY 13, 2017

CHAPTER
62

THURSDAY, 12:10 AM — FBI BOSTON FIELD OFFICE, CHELSEA, MASSACHUSETTS

JUST AFTER MIDNIGHT, our team was stymied.

One dead end after another. We were attempting to track three stolen license plates, somewhere in Massachusetts or Connecticut. Or New York State? Or Vermont? We had nothing on our targets since the last hit from the Mass Pike toll gantry outside of Sturbridge.

The town of Gloucester was all but asleep; agents could continue knocking on doors, looking for cameras and witnesses, but given the hour, progress was glacial.

With the benefit of hindsight, we were dismayed to learn that the Coast Guard had tracked the boat as it carved into Gloucester Harbor, though we couldn't fault the USCG, for why would that one particular boat have attracted suspicion?

Appleton floated back into the operations center, announcing, "I have an update. We have communicated data to our man in Turkey. He will be starting his recon shortly. It is morning there. Additionally, I have been assured that we will have the satellite image data within three hours, and that we might even get eyes on the fishing vessel. Soon, we will have something *new*."

That was not the break we needed. That was a tease.

We needed a break, but we were about to get a shock.

Macallister's phone blared its notification tone, with perfect timing as a punctuation mark to her "new," and she glared at him. I wondered if perhaps her energy was false, and if the stress of canceling the POTUS visit and then briefing the director about our stalled investigation was getting to her.

Macallister ignored her stare as he swiped at his phone. His face dropped and he swiped again, this time squinting at the device.

"That ain't good," he muttered to himself, before raising his eyes to us in the room. "Message from Agent Russo in Gloucester. The HERT squad sent their preliminary, uh, data to TEDAC. Lemme see if I can understand this."

TEDAC, yet another government acronym, referenced the Huntsville, Alabama Terrorist Explosive Device Analytical Center. TEDAC works interagency, meaning that they served not only the FBI, but also the Department of Defense, Department of Justice, the Bureau of Alcohol, Tobacco, Firearms, and Explosives, to name a few, and TEDAC was the absolute authority when it came to analysis of bombs, weapons, and the so-called "improvised explosive devices," or IEDs, that terrorists conjured.

Macallister spoke slowly, "Russo says TEDAC adjusted the readings they got on the boat for decay time, which is, um, the amount of time since the boat got there this morning to when the samples were taken."

He stopped, looking up and then back down at the screen, "The results are conclusive. The levels are convincing enough. The levels are weapons-grade. Those things are most likely a weapon."

He gulped. "TEDAC says we're potentially dealing with a nuclear weapon of some kind."

"No," Appleton yelped, bolting from her seat and, uncharacteristically gracelessly, dashing to the exit. Over her shoulder she growled, "Not *a* weapon. *Two* of them!"

CHAPTER
63

IN BOSTON, WE KNEW THAT the discovery that radiation levels detected on *Flying Lady* pointed to a nuclear device would be setting off alarm bells throughout the Bureau's network, yet it would be like yelling "shark!" at a crowded beach. The panic would be palpable, but the threat would be invisible. And our job was to find that threat.

The message from TEDAC had scattered our team from the operations center, first Appleton to brief the director, then Macallister to conference with the evidence teams still in Gloucester.

Less than a half-hour later, Appleton strode back into the operations center, pausing and scanning the room, asked, "Where is Mr. Lockwood?"

Miles was my guy, so I replied, "With a composite artist. So far, he's done three sketches. He did the head guy first, then the two others. There was a total of five guys on the boat according to Miles, and that matches up with what we see getting off the boat in the security camera footage."

"Do we have the sketches?" she asked.

"Here." I pushed them across the table.

Anastasia jumped in, saying, "We isolated a few head-on shots of faces from the videos. I printed them." She passed a small stack of grainy photos to me and continued, "We are enhancing them. Should have them shortly. Unfortunately, they will still be very blurry and low-resolution. In addition, they're back-lit, with the brighter, presunrise sky in the background. We'll still run them through facial recognition, and use them to fine-tune Miles's sketches so we can do a full-color image and map the faces . . . see if that gets any hits."

Appleton perched on one of the imitation-Aeron chairs at the table, sliding the three sketches toward herself and carefully arranging them in front of her. "Who's in charge?"

"This one," I said, pointing at the sketch in the center, titled *OMAR*. She intently studied the bearded face, his eyes masked by unassuming owl-shaped glasses. "Miles said that guy was in charge. Spoke in a very formal tone. Perfect English. Educated. Eloquent. Polished. He dictated the message Miles texted to the race official. We talked to her earlier yesterday, by the way. The race official, I mean."

I looked at my laptop case file screen, consulting my notes. "Theresa Columbus. She lives in Sachem. She said the smartphone that she used exclusively for the race had pinged at about 2:30 in the morning, on Tuesday the 11th. She exchanged texts with *Flying Lady*, and she updated the results page on the race website, then she went back to sleep. We sent an agent out to Sachem to look at her phone. Here are the transcripts of the texts."

I passed a sheet of paper to Appleton, who skimmed the brief text messages. "This seemed totally normal to her?" the SAC asked.

"Apparently," I replied. "I asked the same thing. She said that one—she knew this was a doublehanded boat, and that having only two sailors on the boat would make it more difficult and, two—that most boats don't carry a spare, um, what'd she call it, a *mainsail?* So quitting because of a torn mainsail and turning around would be logical."

Appleton considered that explanation for a moment and, pointing at the picture to the left, said, "Who is Hans?"

"Miles said that Hans was the last guy he saw on the boat," I told her, looking at my notes. "Hans was supposed to be guarding him down below. Before, you know, Miles dove off the boat. Spoke with maybe a hint of an accent. German, maybe."

"And this one? Seb?" Her fingers grazed across the sketch of a man with curly brown hair and an unruly beard.

"The man that shot George Lakeland. French accent. Though, none of them said much. Miles said they were not chummy with each other. Not conversational."

Macallister had come back into the room. He looked as tired as the rest of us felt. The lack of significant progress had a real demoralizing effect on the investigation, even as asset after asset had been assigned to the case.

Standing behind me and looking over my shoulder at the scattered images on the table, Macallister said. "Hired guns. Thugs. Goons. Goombahs."

"The profile, little as we know, does fit," agreed Appleton.

A printer near Anastasia's workstation whirred and she removed the single sheet of paper in the output tray. "Another sketch for you," she said, lifting and sliding the paper onto the table. *JOHN*. Dark hair, medium-length, a hint of a beard, big ears. Like the others, fair-skinned.

"John, Hans, and Seb—all single syllables. What're the other names?" Macallister asked. I thought that *syllable* was a pretty complex word for him.

"Bruce. Bruce was the other heavy. We don't have his picture yet," I replied.

Macallister shook his head, saying, "Nah, the names gotta be fake. We can run 'em down, but those four names? Like something out of a script. One word, easy to say, easy to communicate." Well, yeah, I thought, most names are one word. But he had a point, even though I think he meant one syllable.

"But what about the head guy, Omar? That's two syllables," Anastasia noted.

"Dat guy look like an Omar to you?" Macallister retorted. "I know I'm not supposed to profile, you know, but that guy is no Omar. You know what I mean. It's like me. My name says Princeton, but I'm still from Jersey."

I couldn't help but laugh. Macallister even grinned, too. He had made his point in a nice, self-deprecating way, and, he was right. Our Omar looked like a businessman. Wavy, thinning hair atop those owl-shaped eyeglasses, perched on a bland face with a full beard.

Appleton shook her head, ruefully. "You're right, you know. We've got bits of clues. It's like this picture of this Omar." She slid a grainy still shot from the video file and placed it next to the composite sketch. "It's the worst possible combination for facial recognition. A low-resolution, back-lit profile image of a bearded guy wearing glasses. We can't see the eyes, we can't see the chin or the shape of the mouth, we can't see the cheekbones. The nose is partially masked by the glasses and is in shadow.

"It's like the license plates. We have a clue, but beyond that, we don't have a description. We don't know what to look for. We need something more!"

CHAPTER
64

THE SPECIAL AGENT IN CHARGE wanted more, and with the timing that made her career legendary, we got more.

Raiden's computer chimed with an incoming message. She had received the camera stills from the Mass Pike tolling gantries.

The east-looking cameras showed two nondescript vans with two figures visible through the windshield, but with the rising sun back-lighting the vehicles, the images were of no use to make out the features of the individuals behind the glass windshields. The west-looking cameras got perfectly illuminated shots of rear cargo doors with black-tinted rear windows, and of the stolen license plates.

With the images from the gantry cameras, Raiden was able identify the year, make, and model of the two vehicles. Both were model year 2015—one a silver GMC Savana cargo van with the rental car agency's New Hampshire plate, and the other a white Chevrolet Express cargo van with the Newtown carpenter's Massachusetts tag.

We now knew what to look for.

Unfortunately, the vehicles were ridiculously common and trying to match them up through the network of cameras after their exit from the Mass Pike would be pain-staking and slow. Nevertheless, Raiden assigned two techs to start that difficult and time-consuming project. She also assigned a tech to research stolen vehicle databases for anything that matched those makes and model years.

And I had a strange sense of déjà vu. Something resonated with me when I leaned back in my chair at the table to examine the images of the generic vans, now printed and posted on our whiteboard.

Vans. Generic. *That's it!*

I swiveled in my imitation Aeron and hunched over my laptop, clicking through internet searches and finding images from the marketing websites of the vehicles. One Chevrolet, one GMC. I clicked frantically, trying to confirm what I suspected.

Across the big worktable, Macallister and Appleton watched, silently, allowing me to chase my train of thought without distraction.

Attempting to articulate the jumbled thoughts in my head, I spluttered, "Here, look. Chevy Express van. Marketing site. See, it has no side windows. Just the ones up front, where the driver and a passenger can sit. Back is cargo, no windows on the side. Same with the GMC. The vans are identical, absolutely identical. The only difference is this," I pointed at the screen, where I had two search windows side-by-side. "Front grill, headlights, they're the same. And look here. Pictures from the toll gantries. Same vans. They're both cargo vans!"

Dead silence.

As that silence persisted, I had bent back to my screen, leaning close in and staring at the GMC and Chevrolet websites, clicking through the interior photographs, confirming, again, my suspicion. Appleton broke the silence and commented, in a patronizing tone dripping with sarcasm, "Mr. Porter. Yes, cargo vans. That's the correct conclusion. I'd expect nothing less from an information management specialist. Excellent conclusion. But I am not sure how that gets us any further with the investigation."

I burst out laughing. It didn't bother me. I replied, still laughing, "I'll take that as a *complisult.*"

More silence. Until Macallister blurted, "What the fuck is a *complisult?*"

I laughed again. "It's a combination of a compliment and an insult. A *complisult!*" I looked at Appleton. "No worries, though. I get that you don't get it. I didn't really explain it right. Let me try again. We saw this earlier when we watched the security camera videos, and we totally missed the significance of it because we focused on the two vehicles, the two sets of parking lights that flashed in the lot. We couldn't make out the vehicles. But now we know. They're *both* cargo vans. Each one has only *two* seats. Driver and passenger. That's *four* people. *Five* got off that boat. We've got to be missing a vehicle!"

Silence. Again. I counted in my head. *One hippopotamus, two hippopotamus. Or is it hippopotami? Or hippopotamuses? Whatever.*

Macallister broke the silence and said, succinctly, "Holy. Shit."

Slowly, Anastasia wheeled back to her station, sort of forcefully elbowing me out of the way. Jabbing at her keys, she brought up the files downloaded from Mr. Baker's DigiSummit site, scrolling through the cameras at the Harbor Cove Brewing Company. "We did see this before, we just missed the connection. The front camera, where is it . . . ?"

We watched as she spooled through footage, stopping it, reading the timestamp, starting it again, alternating between the videos from the two cameras mounted on the street-side of the building. Finally, she stopped and pointed at the screen, where we could now make out the hazy image of a sedan. She repeated, "Like I said, we did see this before. There was one other vehicle that passed the front of the building just after we saw the vehicles reversing out of the frame from the camera at the back corner of the building."

The image was so blurry, it was virtually useless. Maybe it could be enhanced, maybe not. Either way, we finally had another thread to follow.

CHAPTER
65

WHILE WE HAD WAITED FOR the video enhancement in hopes of getting a better look at the sedan, Miles had finished his work with the composite artist. I had set Miles up in a vacant office and he had quickly fallen asleep on a shapeless, firm, government-issued sofa.

The final sketch—Bruce—had been placed on the table, and Macallister had taken the sketches and taped them to a whiteboard with Omar's face at the top of a shallow pyramid. Macallister arranged the pictures of the other four men in alphabetical order on a second row.

I poured another cup of coffee, having already lost track of how many cups I'd had that day. I'd driven to Gloucester twice, run the case, and gotten on a first-name basis with the SAC. Who, by the way, had materialized next to me at the coffee counter.

"Ben."

"Can I pour you one?" I asked, motioning to the stack of cups and the black nectar in the clear glass carafe.

"Thank you, but no. No caffeine for me." She smiled kindly, the usually cold and stoic demeanor gone from her face. "I want to apologize about earlier. You were right, it was an insult, and grossly unjustified at that. You have far exceeded my expectations today. I cannot express that enough. Your instincts have been spot-on. I am very impressed. So, thank you. And I am sorry. It won't happen again."

I straightened my posture, grinning from ear to ear. "Thank you. And no worries, like I said. I was not really articulating very clearly. Or, articulating clearly. You know what I mean," I grinned.

She laughed softly. "I do, and thank you." She gracefully turned and glided away.

I stood stock-still, enjoying the compliment and the feeling that came with it, for a moment. Then I tightened my tie at my neck and walked back to the operations center to rejoin the team.

The techs working tonight had worked their magic on the blurry security camera footage. Raiden grinned kindly at me as I leaned over her shoulder, looking at an image of a sedan on the screen, frozen in motion. "It's a Buick Regal. Model year somewhere between 2008 and now. We'll analyze the exterior details and narrow it down. Mass plates. One occupant."

"Fantastic!" I exclaimed. "Can you track the plates? Mass Pike too?"

"Already done. Just like the last two. Entered the Pike in Newtown a few minutes behind the vans. Also exited after the Charlton toll gantry, presumably in Sturbridge, but . . . hang on." She tapped at her keyboard and jotted something down on a pad, looking up and down and back up at the screen. "Interesting. Took much longer to transit the same distance than the other two vehicles."

"Stopped for gas?" I wondered.

"Nah," Macallister jumped in. "Betcha he got breakfast." He walked over to Raiden's desk, peering at her notes. "Those are the times for the vans? From entry to exit?"

"Yup," she confirmed.

Macallister straightened up. "They all stopped. Shows, what, forty, forty-five minutes between exits for the vans? Those exits are closer. No traffic at that hour. They *all* stopped. Buick guy just stopped longer."

I turned toward Macallister. "How do you know that?"

"I drive the Pike all the time. Thirty-five minutes between those tolls. Tops. And not hoofing it. Just driving normal." He paused, looking around the room. Anastasia, Raiden and I stared at him. "What? Makes perfect sense. Those guys got off the boat in Gloucester and were hungry. There's, like, three service areas in between those tolls. You don't get scanned going in and out of the service stops."

Macallister strode over to Raiden's station and, pointing his index finger at the unmoving image of the Buick Regal on her screen, said, "This guy took a longer stop, had a leisurely breakfast, then continued—getting off at the same exit, following the vans. That's Omar, guarantee it."

Wow. I was impressed. I could see that Raiden was impressed too. We had all underestimated Macallister. He wasn't done yet, either. Carefully studying Raiden's screen, he stated, "That's a 2014 or newer. Sparkling silver metallic. Probably bought at a big discount. They got a new body style coming out this year."

He's like the Rain Man of Regals, I thought. *I better not say that out loud.*

"Sparking what?" Raiden quizzically asked.

"Dats the color. Sparkling Silver. Metallic." Macallister backed away from the screen and nonchalantly folded his arms in front of his chest.

"How the hell do you know that?" I blurted out.

"I know cars, and I gotta say, I love the names they come up with for colors. Just call it fucking beige. Or better, tan. Cuz that ain't no silver," Macallister snorted.

I couldn't help myself and I burst out laughing at the absurdity of it all. We're tracking a potential terror threat and we're getting a lesson on automotive color naming by Bradford Macallister. I think even Macallister saw the ridiculousness in it, and he chuckled as well. That mirth died off quickly, though, when we collectively realized that we were still no closer to our objective. We suspected that finding a Buick Regal, though much less popular on the roads than the two ubiquitous cargo vans, would be a real challenge. In reality, this new lead was as tenuous as the other leads had been.

CHAPTER
66

THURSDAY, 3:30 AM — NEWPORT, RHODE ISLAND

AT 3:30 AM, THE 235-FOOT, expedition-style motoryacht dropped her anchor at just offshore of Goat Island. The inner anchorage of Newport Harbor was too constricted for the large vessel, and her oligarch owner did not intend to stay long enough to have his crew dock the yacht at the Goat Island Newport Shipyard.

Only a few interior lights glowed from the yacht: the bridge, a smattering of portholes forward and low to the water, where the crew resided, and the dim walkway courtesy lights on the perimeter of the miniship. From atop her radio mast, a single, white anchor light showed, almost an afterthought: for no passing vessel could see the tiny light against the dazzling up-lit EC155 helicopter on the motoryacht's aft deck.

The pristine vessel had slipped her lines at the Nantucket Boat Basin just after sunset the night before. Departing Nantucket, the vessel transited the 75-some-odd miles to Newport, looping north of the island of Martha's Vineyard before running southwest down Vineyard Sound, turning northwest around the Buzzards Bay Tower and finally arcing north, into the mouth of Narragansett Bay. A nighttime transit would not be unusual for such a vessel; crews commonly repositioned these types of yachts while their owners slept soundly on finely-woven Egyptian cotton sheets.

But not this owner.

Anatoly Petrikov had turned into his luxurious, main-deck master stateroom early. The shades on the massive, forward-facing windows had been drawn by a faceless crewmember, and a small carafe of vodka chilled in an ice bucket beside a thawing shot glass, dripping condensation onto an ebony-lacquered bedside table.

A midnight nip or two had not helped the vindictive Russian settle. He was too close to his objective. An objective that might be handsomely profitable, to be sure, but profit was not his motivation. Instead, he was driven by his rage, and by the promise of revenge.

For revenge, a dish best served cold, can be supremely satisfying.

Over two years ago, on that dark, early-winter's night in Manhattan, and much like a similar night in 1965, Petrikov had waited for most of the city to slumber.

There were no tenement stairs to navigate this time, though; Petrikov summoned the private express elevator car to his penthouse. Yanking at the identical Shih Tzus, with their matching collars and leashes, and dragging the rolled Persian rug, now clumsily wrapped in brown paper and clear packing tape, into the elevator, he had pressed the lowermost button.

This time, instead of shoving his bundle into a furnace, he had manhandled it up and over the chrome-accented rear bumper of a black Cadillac Escalade SUV. Settling his bulk into the driver's seat and arranging his protruding gut under the bottom rim of the custom burgundy leather and polished burled walnut steering wheel, he had started the vehicle with a satisfied sigh. After a decade of pretending to live a legitimate life of a businessman, he was finally taking matters into his own hands.

In the dark of night, traffic was light, and he had made good time as he departed the island of Manhattan across the Brooklyn Bridge, picking up Interstate 278 South and then merging onto the Belt Parkway. With the lights of New Jersey twinkling across the mouth of the Hudson River, he had sped south toward Brighton Beach, and to his ultimate destination: a small marina on the north side of Sheepshead Bay where he maintained a vessel for this very purpose. He had used it on occasion for pleasure over the past decade, but not for this. And he was pleased to be returning it, and himself, to what he liked best.

He had parked the Cadillac in the lot adjacent to a small bar and lounge that overlooked the marina docks. The Escalade was a familiar sight here; even though he was not as feared as he once was, he knew no one would touch the car or give it a second glance, even at this hour. Leaving the Shih Tzus in the rear passenger area, he had opened the tailgate and shouldered his carpet bundle, carrying it to a thirty-four-foot, center-console Regulator fishing boat. It was one of the few vessels in the marina but was not alone; early-winter, off-season fishing in the waters off New York Harbor was common enough for hardcore anglers.

After dropping the bundle into the Regulator, he had returned to the SUV and retrieved the Shih Tzus, who, though unaccustomed to being out and about at this time of night and at this time of year, remained reasonably silent. The trio had boarded the Regulator and Petrikov started the two Yamaha outboard motors, then cast off the lines and aimed the Regulator toward open water.

Instead of hugging the shoreline and heading northeast to his usual Gravesend Bay nocturnal destination, Petrikov had headed southwest, the Regulator carving a path through the waves at thirty knots. The Russian had inhaled the cold, salty air; he was not chilled in the slightest as the Regulator had sliced through the waves for twenty or twenty-five minutes; Petrikov hummed to himself as the Yamahas purred behind him. At his feet, the Shih Tzus had shivered and cowered.

Pulling back the throttles and glancing at the console-mounted GPS receiver screen, Petrikov had estimated he was at least ten miles from either the south shore of Long Island or the east shore of the New Jersey Highlands. As the boat rocked, engines ticking over at idle, he had wrapped the boat's anchor and chain around the carpet bundle, and he had dropped the mess, and his dead bride within, over the side. As it bubbled into the depths, he had made a note to himself to buy a new anchor for the Regulator.

With a glance at the Shih Tzus, he had rummaged in the boat's console drawers that were lined with diving and fishing gear: leaders, lures, lines, weights, knives, swivels, the lot. Figuring the dogs were about twelve pounds each, he had selected a five-pound dive weight and threaded the dog's leashes through the slits precut in the weight.

Standing, Petrikov had hefted one of the tiny dogs, its once brilliantly bright white fur now dirty and matted with salt and grime from the cockpit floor of the fishing boat, and he tossed the dog over the side. Splashing into the cold Atlantic, the dog had naturally floated, paddling frantically with its stubbly legs but making no progress against the taut leash. The dog's oversized round eyes bulged, widened in terror. Petrikov had belly-laughed as he pitched the second Shih Tzu into the swell.

And finally, the big Russian had dropped the dive weight, lashed to the ends of both leashes, between the two dogs. The weight had sunk the length of one leash, pulling one dog under water as the second animal flailed against the pull against its neck. Spluttering, the first dog had resurfaced, and the tension of the weight transferred to the other dog. A dismal ballet had begun as the waterlogged animals labored to remain afloat.

Petrikov had fished a cigar from the center console and lit it, settling back to watch the show. The dive weight was just enough mass to counter each dog's natural buoyancy, and it was only a matter of time. Puffing at his cigar, Petrikov had leaned against the center console tower, chuckling as he enjoyed the moment, occasionally flicking a hot cigar ash toward the struggling, frantic Shih Tzus. Once the dogs succumbed to the cold water and yielded their small bodies to the Atlantic, he advanced the throttles and aimed the Regulator back to Sheepshead Bay.

Now, off Newport, Petrikov grinned as he recalled his private, petty show of violence to rid himself of his wife and her ridiculous tiny dogs. It had felt good.

This time around, it would be anything but private—it would be a cataclysm that would destroy the lives of everyone who had slighted him, who had turned their backs on him, all for a misunderstanding. The *vory* would be silent no longer.

With his yacht stilled at anchor, the megalomaniacal Russian drifted into a short sleep. He would wake before the sun and see this thing through.

CHAPTER
67

THURSDAY, SAME TIME — FBI BOSTON FIELD OFFICE, CHELSEA, MASSACHUSETTS

AT 3:30 AM, THE MOOD WAS SOUR, and the investigation was going nowhere. Appleton had disappeared. I assumed she was updating the honchos in Washington, DC. *She's getting crucified*, I thought. Thanks to the hour, at least the din and hue from the politicians bitching about the visit from POTUS being canceled had died off. However, the FBI Boston Field Office was not looking good and I think we were all wary of the morning, when the second-guessing would begin in earnest and we in Chelsea would be hung out to dry, chasing phantom hijackers and their mysterious, but presumed dangerous, boxes.

"We got anything from facial recognition?" Macallister asked Raiden, who was tapping away at her keys, shaking her head *no*.

"Images are way too blurry to be useful," Raiden answered. "I mean, we can enhance to read letters and numbers like off those license plates, but we just don't have the kind of clarity and definition that we need to map a face. Especially a face that is partially masked, like our Omar guy. Still trying to join the artist sketches to the video stills, but we don't have anything usable on the UNSUBs yet."

Frustrated, I walked over to the whiteboard where Macallister had built his pyramid of suspects, otherwise known as "unknown subjects," or UNSUBS, in FBI and law enforcement parlance.

On the whiteboard, either Macallister or someone else had also taped up the grainy still photos extracted from the videos, so we now had ten pictures on display. Atop the board were the two images of Omar, one from the video and one from the sketch created by our composite artist and Miles. Below, in a row of eight pictures, were two images each of the alphabetically-arranged, single-syllable-named bag men: Bruce, Hans, John, and Seb.

I was staring, helplessly, cluelessly, at the board when Appleton re-entered the operations center, announcing, "I just spoke with our liaison in Turkey before coming in here. We now have a name. Have a seat."

The group assembled back at the conference table and Appleton, standing over the end of the table, began relaying the new intelligence from Europe. "First. Our liaison in Turkey. It's, what, sometime well after ten in the morning there? This represents only an hour or two of legwork. He was tasked to look for leads on the fishing vessel based on what little data was registered to it via the AIS system. Therefore, he knew where to start, physically, and he had a name to start with.

"His first stop was at the fishing vessel docks in Bodrum, and he immediately struck gold. This Mohomed Yilmaz is a real person. A real name. Well known on the docks, with a story to match.

"Mr. Yilmaz owns a large, offshore-fishing trawler. Though it was in poor condition, it was still a long-range trawler. Mr. Yilmaz was barely making ends meet and could not keep up on the maintenance needs of his vessel or his equipment, therefore he could not attract qualified crew. In other words, he was trapped in the downward spiral of a vicious cycle.

"However," Appleton continued, "several months ago, Mr. Yilmaz was ready to bury himself at sea, but something changed. There was activity on the trawler, maintenance items being addressed, and a new inflatable tender. A Zodiac. The trawler made several trips out into the Med and back to its dock, with no catch, but with several added new crewmembers, perhaps in training. Our liaison's source said the new crew was led by a man with a graying beard and eyeglasses."

"Omar," I said.

"Possibly," Appleton agreed, "probably. The new men were all foreigners, assumed to be English, German, or French. Anglo-Saxon, basically. That, of course, lines up with the five guys on our whiteboard over there. All could pass as English, French, or German."

We all nodded, and Anastasia was the first to speak up. "So, you're thinking our group is European?"

"Maybe," Appleton answered. "I think it's too soon to reach any conclusions, really. Putting an identifiable name to the Turk is a huge help. We'll get that face and name on Interpol and into our systems. We will have a dossier in no time. Maybe we can link him with someone else. What good that does us in the short-term, in search of the missing boxes, though, is probably limited. And while it's helpful that we have a real touch-point, which is the origin of the fishing vessel that staged this invasion, we really don't have anything new on the UNSUBs in play.

"And speaking of the fishing vessel, more bad news. It seems to have disappeared."

We looked at each other, confused. "Disappeared?" asked Raiden. "Like, it's no longer transmitting an AIS signal?"

"Correct. The AIS signal stopped transmitting at around 8:00 PM last night, at almost precisely one hundred miles south of Sable Island. And, I received nothing useful from the satellite imagery," Appleton said, glumly. "They scanned the entire area for me both before and after the AIS signal from the fishing vessel disappeared. We found the vessel in the images taken that morning and again that afternoon, right where it should be. The vessel was going only about seven knots per both our imagery and the tracking data, so using that as our baseline, we can establish a relatively tight search radius. We might be able to find it visually again when we get this morning's pass later." With the report of her findings concluded, the SAC seated herself in one of the rolling chairs.

I looked at her carefully. The frustration of one dead end after another continued to take its toll.

"I don't get it," Macallister muttered. "You're saying the satellite doesn't see anything?"

"Not exactly. It verifies that a ship was transiting the area where the trawler's AIS signal was. But our target stopped transmitting, meaning one of two things. Either our target turned off its AIS system, and it will reappear somewhere in the world—when is anyone's guess. Or, our target managed to disappear like our vans disappeared off the Mass Pike. Either way, it is another dead-end at the moment."

The room went quiet, to the point I could hear the cooling fans whirring in the many computers. Shoulders slumped and once again, our little team looked completely demoralized.

"Let's take a break. Get some fresh air. Go for a walk outside. Clear your heads. We'll reconvene in twenty minutes or so, and make a list of our knowns and our unknowns." Appleton stood and approached the whiteboard. "We'll start with this gentleman." She lightly pressed her index finger on the top sketch.

"Who are you, Mr. Omar? And what are you up to?"

CHAPTER
68

THURSDAY, 4:30 AM — NEW MILFORD, CONNECTICUT

LIKE THEIR ARRIVAL IN THE STILL, predawn hours into the Gloucester harbor just a day before, they used the tranquility of the morning to depart their hide in the low-slung industrial park. Engine ticking over softly, the GMC Savana reversed out of the overhead door, its glinting, now-white body emblazoned with the purple-and-orange FedEx brandmark. Red brake lights flashed, the reverse lights clicked off, and the van slowly pulled from the lot, rejoining Route 202 South, ready to take its circuitous route to Wall Street.

Omar watched it leave, then he tossed the black garbage bag into the Regal and stole a glance around the lot. With no one in sight, and not caring about security cameras which might, or might not, have him in their unblinking stares, Omar bent over the rear of the sedan, swiftly unscrewing the two slot-headed fasteners which secured the false Massachusetts plates to the rear of the vehicle and then attaching an equally false, light bluish-white Connecticut plate. After Omar had showed him the two-word text message the afternoon before, Bruce had done well, finding and liberating three Connecticut plates from various vehicles scattered around the low-slung complex. Fortunately, the state required a front and rear plate, and removing the front plates from a vehicle pulled nose-in to the side of the building was quick and stealthy, and would likely not be noticed by the vehicle's owner come dawn, since the rear plate would still be properly in place.

Starting the Buick, Omar made his way to Route 202, in no particular hurry, eventually joining a smattering of nondescript vehicles in the equally nondescript tan Regal.

Pulling to the right of the road, the Buick slid into the empty parking area of the darkened pizza place, stopping in front of a blue dumpster toward the rear of the lot. Quietly and quickly, Omar exited the car, carrying the garbage bag, and gently placed it inside the trash container. He positioned it carefully, ensuring that as it rested, the bag was slightly open with a cardboard pizza box bearing the name of the joint just peeking from the black plastic bag.

With the New York target lying only ninety miles away, but wanting the predawn hours to mask their departure, and to give them a cushion of time to account for the unpredictability of traffic, the scheduled departure was far earlier than it needed to be. Both the van and sedan would take a meandering route toward Manhattan.

Settling back into the sedan and activating the turn signal, Omar merged back onto 202 and then onto Interstate 84 West, headed toward New York State. The rising sun began to paint the sky out his rear window. In about five hours, the man who called himself Omar would make his two phone calls.

CHAPTER
69

THURSDAY, 5:04 AM — FBI BOSTON FIELD OFFICE, CHELSEA, MASSACHUSETTS

I CONFESS. I DID NOT DO as the SAC requested. Instead of going outside for fresh air, I found an open office with a sofa and lay down, balling my now miserably wrinkled suit jacket into a pathetic excuse for a pillow. The sofa felt like it was covered in a fabric woven from porcupine quills. Chenille, this was not. It hardly mattered, though. I dozed off in seconds, my last conscious thought not on the case, but on wondering what Macallister would name the sofa's color. *Fawn? Buff? Sand? Oatmeal? Who gives a shit?*

I woke with a start. I had gotten no closer to describing the color of the sofa, but my mind had gone elsewhere. There was something in my head. I couldn't quite reach it—it had been there, but I had lost it.

Looking at my watch, I saw it was 5:04 AM. I leapt up, grabbed my jacket and hurried back toward our workspace. I ran my tongue across my teeth; they felt furry. *What I wouldn't give for a toothbrush. How 'bout for a shower and a change of clothes?*

Passing by a window and looking down into the still-empty parking lot, I felt the thought again, pinging around my subconsciousness, but still out of grasp. I slowed my pace and stopped, gazing for a moment out the window. I marveled at the majesty of the imminent sunrise, just minutes away; taking deep, regular breaths, and allowing my mind to appreciate

the beauty through the plate-glass window. The eastern sky was painted at the horizon with bands of brilliant reds and oranges, which faded into a light gray and then, higher into the sky, into an inky black-blue. Piercing the urban metro Boston haze, a lone star shone bright white.

A lone star. *That's it!* That was my thought. Without intending to, I stopped breathing, my eyes wide, staring at the star.

After taking a moment to collect myself, I dashed down the hallway, entering the operations center at a full run. The team, everyone—Appleton, Macallister, Anastasia, Raiden, and a few more heads that I didn't recognize—were huddled around the table. In unison, they turned at my abrupt entrance.

"OnStar!!" I yelled.

Grabbing an empty imitation Aeron, I didn't sit, instead standing behind it and grasping the backrest and rolling the chair back and forth, using it as my podium. "OnStar," I exclaimed again, catching my breath. "It's been right in front of us this whole time!"

The group stared at me, and Macallister, as usual, succinctly asked, "What the fuck are you talking about, Porter?"

This time, I would articulate clearly. I turned to Anastasia.

"Okay, Anastasia, pull up the video feed of the men walking up from the boat up the ramp. Put that on the big screen. Then put the other video, from the camera with the parking lot in the background, on the big screen next to it, to the right."

With a flurry of keystrokes, she made the videos appear on the screens, and then turned to me, looking for further instruction.

"Great. Now, can you play them simultaneously? So that they're synced in time for playback?"

"Sure. Of course," she replied. "Ready and . . . go."

The videos began to play. The right screen showed a static view of the empty restaurant deck with the parking area barely visible in the background. On the left screen, we watched the now-familiar silent movie of two pairs of men climbing the pitched ramp from the dock to the parking lot, as they strained against the weight of the long bags with, presumably, the boxes disguised within. The lone man carrying the duffel bag, who we now knew to be named Omar, followed. At the top of the ramp, the men set down their loads, and Omar placed his bag on the ground. He pulled items from the duffel and distributed them to two of the men.

"Watch carefully," I commanded.

On the left screen, five men grouped at the top of that ramp. Three of them cradled something in their hands. On the right screen, a pair of vehicle parking lights flashed, then, a second later, another pair of vehicle lights flashed.

"That!" I shouted. "Did you see that?"

They looked at me like I was insane, except for Appleton, who wore an odd expression. I assumed it was because of her error in dismissing my earlier revelation on the third vehicle. Macallister continued to stare at me as Anastasia broke eye contact, looking away.

"Okay, you don't see it. It's subtle. It's so subtle we all missed it before. Anastasia, rewind a few seconds, to where they take the stuff out of the bag and hand it around."

She did as I requested, and the silent movies started playing again. This time, however, when the left screen showed three men in the frame, cradling something in their hands, I yelped, "Pause!"

The images froze on both big screens.

I walked over to the left monitor and, reaching my left arm out, I gently touched the screen, pointing at the still image. "See that? No one, and I mean no one in the world, holds their car keys like that. And certainly not three people at the same time!"

I stopped for effect, enjoying the moment, letting the silence linger for a second, before disclosing my breakthrough.

"Chevy van. GMC van. Buick sedan. All General Motors brands . . . that they unlocked with phones, or, more accurately, with an app on those phones. With OnStar."

I paused again theatrically, still drawing out the moment, and, looking around slowly at the faces gaping at me, I cracked the case:

"We find the OnStar link, we find the vehicles."

The silence hung in the air for several seconds, until it was broken by Macallister. "Wait, I don't follow. OnStar covers millions of cars. How do you isolate these three?"

"Good question," I replied, taking a seat at the conference table, my moment of dramatic glory over. "I think it's pretty easy, though. We need OnStar to isolate an unlock event in that location. I mean, realistically, how many other cars were unlocked at that precise time, at that exact location? We know the make and models to look for, so they should be able to zero in on it. We just need to get into OnStar."

Anastasia, who had been silent and appeared distant, recomposed herself and spun her chair back to her workstation. "You're absolutely right, Ben." She pounded at her keyboard for a few minutes, pausing only to say quietly, "We're a little off the books here. We need authority from the top."

Turning to address the SAC, Anastasia asked hesitantly, "Ma'am? Are you good with this?"

Appleton nodded. "Yes, yes, of course. First, I'll have to make a phone call, but yes, proceed with getting set up and liaised in OnStar's system. Just don't pull the trigger on the search until I get back." She stood and quickly left the room.

Now I was the one who was confused. "Wait . . . *what?* What do you mean?"

Anastasia slowed her keyboarding and then stopped. "It's like this: typically, we need a warrant or a court order. Which we would get, of course, but that, as you know, that would take some time. The folks at OnStar understand this. They even have a disclaimer buried on their website. Check it out."

On another screen, she had pulled up the OnStar website and navigated to a help topic page. With the cursor arrow, she pointed at a line of text in a small font: "We do not monitor or otherwise track the location of OnStar-equipped cars, unless required to by a valid court order in criminal procedures or under exigent circumstances."

"See those last three words. I think this qualifies." Anastasia left the help topic page open as I reread the sentence, with Macallister's chin almost resting on my shoulder as he leaned in to examine the screen from behind me.

"Yeah. I'm getting the feeling that you've done this before. 'Under exigent circumstances,' of course," Macallister sneered in a sarcastic tone.

Anastasia grinned thinly. "Maybe." She paused for a beat and continued, "We have, shall we say, a convenient path into the OnStar system. But we do need authorization and a trail, so to speak. The SAC will make the call and establish the trail. Kind of a formality though, because, wait . . . *No!*"

That was not what I was expecting.

"Vanessa!" yelled Anastasia, bolting from her chair. "The server is down again. I can't open the port. Call that moron Lewis and get him in here to fix that thing once and for all. I'm going to go and reboot it."

I looked at Anastasia's primary screen and saw only gibberish. It was like trying to read the green cascading text in *The Matrix.*

Maybe it was the Matrix . . .

How would I know?

I pondered that existential thought as Anastasia ran from the room and Vanessa Raiden snatched up a telephone handset. Macallister and I looked at each other, dumbly. *Now what?*

He snickered, clearly also seeing that we were dead in the water without the techspertise. "Wanna grab a coffee, Ben?"

I smiled. "Sure. That's like, um, my eighteenth coffee in the last two days," which had basically blended together. As we left the room, I remember thinking, trying to remember if he had ever—in all the time that I'd worked there—used my first name before.

I think this is a first.

CHAPTER
70

THURSDAY, SAME TIME — NEWPORT, RHODE ISLAND

THE RISING SUN PAINTED the pseudo-industrial Newport harbor front a pinkish tone, accentuating the colors of the red-brick and pastel-painted, clapboard-sided buildings in the soft light.

Leaning casually against the glossy superstructure, Anatoly Petrikov enjoyed the silence of the sunrise. One hand rested on a bright-varnished teak caprail, and the other hand cradled a mug of a Russian coffee drink nicknamed the Raf: a shot of espresso steamed with cream and sugar. Tendrils of light steam lifted from the mug and they, too, turned pink in the diffused morning light.

He idly considered the Clairborne Pell Bridge, the largest suspension bridge in New England that linked the Newport mainland with Jamestown Island. The Newport Bridge dominated the skyline, its iconic profile a centerpiece in photos and on tourist tchotchkes, and Petrikov wondered how much explosive it would take to sever one of the suspension cables and tumble the bridge into the waters of Narragansett Bay. At rush hour, naturally.

His moment of dark fantasy was broken by the almost-unheard buzz of a vibrating smartphone. Petrikov's excellent sense of hearing dispensed with annoyingly loud ring tones; he could hear the haptic motor in the phone without issue, especially in the stillness of the morning.

Noting the blocked and restricted number on the caller ID read-out, he swiped at the phone and raised it to an ear. "Da?" he asked, reverting, as always, to his native language to answer a call. *Yes?* He had been told it seemed charming. Old-worldly.

The caller spoke. A woman's voice. "It is the wolf."

Not one for pleasantries, Petrikov barked, "Where the fuck have you been? They already found the fucking boat. It was on the fucking news, for fuck's sake!"

"It's worse than that," the caller replied evenly. "Now they're going to find the vehicles. They've figured out how to track them."

"Impossible!" Petrikov roared. "How? License plates?"

"No. I couldn't prevent that. But I dealt with that independently. Yesterday."

"Dealt with? Meaning what?"

The woman sniffed. "Really? I texted him and told him to change the plates. This is not the problem. The problem is that they discovered they could locate the vehicles with OnStar," the woman replied.

"OnStar? How? How was this not anticipated?"

"It was considered but as highly unlikely. They would have to know where to look, and we estimated the boat would not be discovered so quickly. And—"

"And I know they found the fucking boat. I just said so," snarled Petrikov. "How did they find the fucking boat so quickly?"

"Because of an event that we could not have been foreseen. Lockwood dove off the boat. He somehow survived and he was rescued. He was brought to shore. He was interviewed by an administrative staffer, not an agent. This staffer had no experience, no credibility. But somehow he triggered an investigation."

"What is his name?"

The was an ever-so-slight pause on the connection before the woman's voice responded, "Ben Porter."

Clenching his left fist so tightly that it began to redden, and almost crushing the coffee mug with his right hand, Petrikov snarled, "He can wait. What about our man? Was it our man that let this Lockwood escape?"

"I can't know that. But, yes, it would appear so."

Petrikov seethed, his anger escalating as he absently muttered phrase after phrase of Russian curses—always colorful, for the guttural language lends its sounds well to anger—while he stomped to his office on the top-most deck of the massive, expedition-style yacht. He reverted to silence, though, as he quickly consulted a computer screen, checking the overseas markets and domestic futures, then jabbing keys in a quick, almost frantic search. Finally, he growled, "How much time?"

"Not long. Minutes, possibly. Hours, probably, at most."

Petrikov flung his coffee mug at the computer screen on the desk, shattering only the mug and merely toppling the screen in a mess of brownish liquid that pooled on the polished wooden desk and dripped onto the pristine white carpet.

His fat-face reddened as he struggled to regain his composure and tried to decide what to do. Despite his flabbish bulk, he remained strong and he contemplated hurling more items, but ultimately decided the exertion was futile.

"So close. And a fucking disaster. Call him and call it off. If they catch him, he'll sing. I don't trust him."

"Agreed. But my hands are tied here. Eventually, probably soon, he will be caught."

"*Da.* Understood. He would rather be caught by them, than by me." The ruthless Russian exhaled, that familiar rage strengthening his resolve and, ironically, helping him to regain his composure. Inhaling deeply, he breathed into the phone, "Now wait."

Petrikov, somewhat calmer now that the decision had been made, righted the monitor and then sat at the desk. First consulting his watch and a chart, he cradled the smartphone to his ear as he worked the computer keys. He was no stranger to planning and contingency, and he quickly found what he was looking for and relayed a string of instructions to the caller before swiping off the call.

The oligarch surveyed the small disaster on his desk and the muddy stain on the white carpet as he picked up the desk phone and dialed the extension for his pilot's cabin on the yacht. Without so much as a "good morning" when the line was answered, he demanded, "Prepare the helicopter and file a flight plan for New York. We leave immediately."

Petrikov slammed the handset into the cradle on the phone with such force that not only the plastic handset cracked, but the cradle also dug a divot into the polished wooden desk. Without so much as a backward glance, the Russian strode toward the helipad on the aft-most deck.

CHAPTER
71

THURSDAY, 6:09 AM — FBI BOSTON FIELD OFFICE, CHELSEA, MASSACHUSETTS

IT ALL CAME TOGETHER very quickly, in under an hour. Shockingly fast, in fact, once we had that incredibly powerful lead to follow.

Bearing our fresh coffee cups, steaming merrily, Macallister and I had both returned to the room and positioned ourselves at the table, waiting for the technology experts to find our prey. Miles, too, wandered in, looking disheveled but rested and he, too, sat at the table. Macallister didn't bat an eye at the interloper, who, by all right, was really not authorized to be in the room, but who had established himself as part of our team.

As Raiden finished verbally beating up poor Mr. Lewis (or was Louis his first name? I didn't know, yet) for the server problem, Anastasia returned to the room and took her seat at her workstation. After a flurry of keypresses, she stated, "Vanessa, the port is open. Stand by."

As she spoke, Appleton charged into the operations center, declaring as she crested the door, "You are authorized to proceed with the OnStar link."

Raiden nodded and said, "I'm in, Anastasia. Here we go." She worked in silence, occasionally jotting notes on a pad of paper. The only noise in the room was the click-clack-patter of her fingers dancing across the keyboard. We all watched, entranced.

Finally, she broke the suspense, saying only, "Got 'em!"

As one, we all leaned forward, waiting.

She said it again, this time louder. "Got 'em!! Got the unlocks in Gloucester. Vehicle data coming up. Give that a second."

More tapping. She was clearly in a zone.

"Okay. Three vehicles. I'm getting location data. Hang on."

"Chevy van. It's . . . it's in . . . New York! North of New York City. Looks like Yonkers, or Bronxville. Moving south on I-87!"

"Holy shit. We gotta get assets there! I'm on it!" Macallister yelled, breaking the trance, as we all realized it was go-time. He grabbed a phone at a spare desk and started dialing.

Raiden's fingers blurred as she worked the keys. "The Buick. The Regal. It's . . . it's moving. Pretty fast. Somewhere in New York, maybe Connecticut. White Plains, maybe. Moving, must be on a highway or something. I'll come back to it."

Anastasia interrupted, "Find the other van. I'll see if I can work on the Buick."

Raiden grunted an affirmation and continued tapping at her keys, relaying her discoveries in phrases, "The other van. The GMC. Getting it in . . . wait . . . Illinois? Yes, Illinois. Near South Bend on I-90, I think, moving . . . west." She turned and looked around the room. "We need more people! Escalate this! I got this one—I'll call Chicago." Raiden yanked her desk phone out of the cradle as Appleton bolted from the room, not at all gracefully, to trigger the crisis mode of an FBI investigation.

Miles and I sat, stunned, as it unfolded. Frankly, I was way out of my league, now. Well, *still* way out of my league, just as I was when I set off to Gloucester to meet Miles the morning before.

I wanted to see this thing through, but I had no contacts, no direct access to other agents, or any connections to police departments. I felt useless.

Of course, Miles was equally useless. A nice, tidy, four-bedroom center-hall colonial in Cohasset with curb appeal was not what we needed right now.

As the pace and volume in the room began to escalate, Miles caught my eye and leaned in toward me, quietly intoning, "I've got a sense about these things. This is the calm before the storm. This is only the beginning."

CHAPTER
72

BY 6:30 AM, THE TECHS IN OUR operations center had linked us to the Strategic Information and Operations Center, the massive, forty-thousand-square-foot, high-tech data center in the FBI's national headquarters building at the J. Edgar Hoover Building in Washington, DC. We now had multiple, two-way "Secure Video Tele-Conference" (SVTC) feeds between our operations center and the SIOC crisis room, and we could mirror our computer screens to theirs. The activity in that place had picked up, perhaps keeping pace with my rising blood pressure.

I had learned enough in my five years in the Bureau to know that the field offices might be wary of getting the pencil pushers in Washington involved, so I had not been surprised when Macallister had grabbed a desk phone and barked, "We're keeping this in-house. We gotta move fast. I'm calling 26 Federal and then I'm calling CIRG."

Our case files are chock-full of acronym after acronym, but that one is little-used, at least in my work. It is an acronym that is probably little-known by the general public, either. Short for Critical Incident Response Group, it is a relatively small group of exceptionally-well-trained agents that are kept in a ready state to respond to any crisis—tactical, surveillance, behavioral analysis and negotiations, and, relevant this early morning, hazardous device interception and disruption. The Navy has its SEALs, the Army has its Delta Force, and we at the FBI have our CIRG.

In New York, we have one of our largest field offices at 26 Federal Plaza, which, probably also little-known to the general public, also happens to be the tallest of all the US-government owned buildings at forty-one stories.

I could hear Macallister talking to someone, probably the on-call duty officer, in short, staccato sentences, but I could not make out what he was saying, as Raiden was also snapping at her desk phone, calling our Chicago field office.

I looked at my watch. Chicago is an hour behind, so just after 5:30 in the morning there. The office would have a skeleton staff. Even the New York office would not be fully staffed at this hour.

"Porter!" Macallister yelled my name, spinning around in his chair. "Need your help. Get over—wait, never mind. Raiden?"

"I'm on the phone!" she shouted back. "What?"

"How the fuck do I transfer this call?" Right. Macallister was a little weak in the technology department.

"What's up?" I asked.

"I need you to narrate. Brief it. This thing got, like, a speakerphone?"

"I can do a briefing. Hey, um, Ms. Raiden? Can we conference both Chicago and New York so I do this once?"

"Yeah, good call, Ben. Stand by one. And call me Vanessa." Raiden returned to her station and started slapping at buttons, then saying to me while pointing, "Go stand there, Ben. Look at the camera. You've got an SVTC to New York and Chicago. And"—more keyboarding—"and to DC, too."

I looked where she was pointing and saw, for the first time, the eye of a camera. I looked at the monitors showing the interiors of what I guessed were New York and Chicago's crisis centers, and at a larger screen which I knew was SIOC. *Oh shit. Hold it together, Ben.*

I couldn't make out the faces on the screen, but the voices came through clearly. A male voice from the speaker said, "This Special Agent Peck, New York. Duty officer 'till 8:00 AM."

"Chicago here. My name is Special Agent Byrne," said a second voice, this one female.

Thankfully, Appleton came over to stand beside me, and she started the briefing, "This is Jennifer Appleton. Special Agent in Charge, Boston Division field office. This is a matter of national security. Yesterday, I briefed the director who, in turn, briefed POTUS, but at that juncture, we did not have the information that we have now. For now, I am taking authority and responsibility." She paused a beat and continued, "Porter, take it from here. Succinctly, please."

Showtime for me, I thought. *Here we go.*

"Good morning. I'm Ben Porter, Boston office. Since yesterday morning, we have been working on what appears to be a threat that was originally thought to be a hoax but is now considered very credible. It is our working theory that we have two potential cases, or boxes, which are highly radioactive, that have been covertly brought into the Continental United States, by five suspects.

"In the absence of other evidence, we consider that the two threats are a worst-case scenario and are nuclear weapons of mass destruction of some kind. The cases that these presumed weapons were transported in are rectangular in shape, approximately six-feet long and two-feet square. The casements are black in color but may be disguised. The vessel that was used to transport these devices into CONUS was located in Gloucester, Massachusetts, yesterday, after the devices had been removed by the five UNSUBS, who are still at large. Currently, we believe that the devices are being transported in two cargo vans. We have located both vans via the OnStar system, so we are able to track them in near real time. One of those vans is in Illinois, the other is in New York.

"We have zero intelligence as to the planned destination of each van, and we don't know if they are operating independently or together. We also know that another vehicle is involved, driven by the man we believe is acting as the leader of the group. Obviously, it is a priority to intercept all three vehicles, but we need to focus more on the vans. We need to intercept the vans and determine if they do, in fact, contain the boxes—and if they are weapons, then neutralize them as quickly as possible."

I took a deep breath. I had maybe jumped to a few conclusions, I thought, but it seemed to make sense, at least in my head.

The Chicago voice waited for only a second or two before starting in with her questions. "I think I understand. Do you have any of this in a file you can send?"

I added, "Yes, I will link you both to the case file. However, it is not up-to-date with this latest development and it includes the investigation history which, at this time, is probably more of a distraction than a help."

"I understand that the priority is finding these two vans . . . but what do we do when we find them?" New York asked.

I had no idea what they were supposed to do. I was helpless and I started to sweat. Fortunately, Macallister still had my back, and he responded, "We're mobilizing CIRG. The priority is getting eyes on the vans. The SAC here has the authority to engage until Washington decides to take over."

"Understood," the woman from Chicago responded.

"Yes, sir," said New York.

Macallister again replied for our Boston group. "You get your local people going and tell me when you have agents to deploy. I will let you know then CIRG is ready. Keep this call open and keep us updated."

Surrounded by the monitors and humming computers and the din of the noises transmitted over the SVTC with the three other offices, I couldn't help but wonder what Macallister meant when he said *until Washington decides to take over.* I was worried Boston would lose control. Because, at that moment, no one knew our UNSUBS better than this little group in Chelsea.

CHAPTER
73

HUNCHED AT HER WORKSTATION and hampered by the constraint of being able to track only one vehicle at a time through our link to the OnStar system, Vanessa Raiden alternated targets, focusing on the vans. Her position reports indicated that all three vehicles were moving consistently, and she not only verbalized her commentary for the benefit of the SVTC, but also rebroadcast the information on computer screens both here in Chelsea, and also in the SIOC in Washington and in the field offices in New York and Chicago: "The Illinois van is still moving west on I-90. Our New York van is crawling south on I-87, but it's slowed down. Must be morning traffic."

Anastasia added, "the Regal is also moving slowly on . . . 678. Either Jamaica or Queens."

With all three remaining in motion, the debate turned to the intercept. Now that the case had been picked up by the honchos in Washington, DC, it became a full-on crisis. Anastasia was also tasked with liaison, and she could barely keep up with the requests for information, while Appleton was taking call after call, her voice losing its normal even tone and becoming more frantic and stressed.

Only Macallister seemed unfazed by the escalating commotion and, within the past hour and with assistance from the SIOC, he had succeeded in connecting with two detachments of CIRG agents in both locations and had sent them all the pertinent details of what we had, including year, make, and model of the two vans, stock manufacturer images, and our photos sourced from the toll gantry cameras on the Mass Pike. Waving to get my attention, he asked, calmly, "Porter, what next? Whaddaya think? How do we stop them?"

I was both amused and horrified by his question. The morning before, I was a faceless cube dweller. Now, I was being asked for strategic terrorist intercept tactical advice. The world works in odd ways, I thought, trying to focus amid the distractions in the room.

I figured I might as well verbalize my train of thought, and as I spoke, one by one, the players in the room as well as those watching and listening in from the SIOC started to pay attention to my monologue.

"Since all the vehicles are currently moving, I think we can conclude that danger is not imminent, like, within the next few minutes. Unless, of course, their goal is to detonate a weapon while sitting in bumper-to-bumper morning traffic in Manhattan and Chicago," I said, thinking it through. "But we don't even know that those are the targets. It makes sense, as they easily could have made it to DC, for example, instead. So, I think we can reasonably conclude those are the general target areas. Likewise, I would guess the target time is sometime this morning. Otherwise, why wouldn't they avoid the morning traffic?"

I turned to Raiden. "How far from Manhattan is the New York van, accounting for traffic?"

She considered her screen for a moment, then said, "About an hour to midtown, give or take a few minutes."

"How 'bout the other van?" I said.

"To where?" she asked.

"I dunno, Midtown Chicago? The John Hancock Building. The really tall one."

"Hang on . . . Probably around ninety minutes. As the crow flies, that van is a little further from the center of Chicago as the other van is from the center of New York City. But in Chicago, it's an hour earlier, so maybe less traffic."

"What are you getting at, Ben?" Appleton interjected. I realized that the SVTC had gone silent, and that all eyes from all the offices linked in were on me. I crossed to the center of the space and looked directly at the camera.

"Frankly, I'm not sure yet. I'm trying to visualize what they're up to. Let's say they have a specific target in both cities. They're moving toward them. But the Buick—who we assume is Omar—is also heading toward New York. Why? If they're going to detonate a weapon in New York, why would he also be headed that direction? Wouldn't he want to be as far away from wherever a bomb is going to detonate?"

I stopped, considering my own question. And then it hit me. *S-I-O-C. The first word is Strategic. It's part of the ploy!*

"Wait," I blurted out, "We gotta consider what we think those boxes are. Let's say it's a WMD. If it's a suitcase nuke, the leader—Omar—is not going to be anywhere nearby.

"But what if it is something else? He still needs an exit strategy. Plenty of mass transit options out of the City.

"Maybe it's some sort of dirty bomb. What's the blast radius of a dirty bomb? Fairly minimal, right? The bomb itself will do some damage, but it's the radiation that does the real harm, and its largely psychological harm. It's panic. It's a weapon of panic, not destruction. It's useless for a suicide bomber, but perfect to cause *chaos*!"

"It's like the Marathon bombing," I concluded. "The casualties were limited to a very tight radius. Remember after? We thought it may have been a dirty bomb. We tested for radiation. Quietly, of course, so we didn't cause panic. But that's the goal of a dirty bomb—*panic*. The casualties are secondary, and the property damage is almost nil."

Macallister was nodding in agreement, and once again, he backed me up. "I think you're right, Porter. They could drop the devices somewhere in the hearts of those cities and move out. They can detonate them from a block away and they won't be harmed. The panic and confusion that follows gives them the cover to move out with everyone else."

"Exactly!" I replied. "And, if that's true—a big *if*—then we need to shadow them till we can stop them safely and quickly, and CIRG needs to have a way to neutralize them as soon as they do."

Momentary silence filled the room until a voice suddenly boomed from the speakerphone and a figure moved into view on the SIOC video relay. "This is the director."

Holy shit. I just briefed the Director of the Federal Bureau of Investigation.

"I've been brought up to date. I am horrified by the ease that these suspects and their cargo entered the country. We will return to that, later.

"In the meantime, your analysis seems plausible, and regardless of the actual composition of the weapon, one of the words you said is of paramount importance. That word is *panic*. We *cannot* cause mass panic in both of these cities at once. As soon as that hits the airwaves, every other major metro area and city in the country will follow suit, assuming that they are next. We cannot let that happen." The director let those words sink in before concluding, "What tools do we have at our disposal to neutralize whatever it is that we are dealing with?"

Macallister, without hesitation, answered the director's question. "We got three Total Containment Vessels in the New York area and one in Chicago metro. I've already confirmed this with CIRG."

"Are those ours, or NYPD?" Special Agent Peck asked over the SVTC, still on duty at the New York office.

"Those particular TCVs belong to the NYPD bomb squad, but we've already secured the cooperation to use them. We have our own, but these are better positioned. We have one of our own in Chicago."

"And how do you intend to use them?" the director asked via the SVTC from the SIOC.

"Like Porter said, we gotta intercept them and take 'em down quickly," Macallister responded.

There was a pause, followed by, "Who the hell is Porter?"

Macallister almost laughed out loud. I could see him stifle a snort before replying, "Sir, that would be Ben Porter—here in our Boston field office. He initially took the lead on this case and it was his insight that got us to this point. His instincts have been spot-on so far, sir."

Yeah, and you won't look so bad yourself, Macallister, being my boss and all that, I thought. *The boss who started off yesterday calling me Porker and is now singing my praises to the director.* Like I said, the world works in strange ways.

Interrupting my thoughts, the director boomed, "Very well. Not sure how you pull off trailing a vehicle down a city block with a TCV. Figure that one out and keep me posted. I'm standing by in the SIOC."

As the director moved off-screen, I realized he had a point. A Total Containment Vessel is not exactly incongruous. Mounted on a trailer, it is a giant sphere capable of retaining the pressure caused when a bomb detonates. But another thought gnawed at me. It suddenly occurred to me that visibility would be the least of our worries. I waded back into the conversation that had picked up on the video conference, saying, "Umm, a TCV might not be the answer."

"Why not?" someone on the call asked.

Macallister turned to look at me and scowled. Before he had a chance to ask the same question, I quickly replied, "Because it's not big enough. Physically. The boxes are estimated to be six feet long. Unless there is some sort of subassembly inside those boxes, I think we have to assume that is the length of the device. We need something bigger."

"No problem," a voice said. "This is Phil with CIRG. We have worked up a tactical profile. We have hardened bomb containment trucks. Like box trucks. We plan to roll four vehicles—two for the team of agents that are apprehending the drivers, a third for the bomb squad, and the fourth will be a containment truck. You get us in a pattern behind those vans and tell us when they stop, and we will be in position in under a minute."

I nodded. Macallister nodded. The room nodded. It seemed like it was coming together, gelling as a workable plan. Accordingly, I said so.

"That seems like a workable plan. How much time do you need to mobilize?"

"In process," the voice named Phil replied. "Question is, where do we fall into place behind your vans?"

The room nodded again. Group think is very powerful. And also, very intimidating, especially as the heads in my room turned to look at me and the heads visible in the SVTC turned to look at the video feed from Chelsea. Great, they're all looking at me, in my day-old suit and tie, unshowered and hardly emblematic of the stereotypical FBI agent. I have to get over myself and get on with it, I thought, pulling my thoughts back in sync with the case.

"The working hypothesis is that the targets are within the city centers. Position outside the city, ready to roll onto the highway which we think is most plausible." I looked at Raiden's screens; she had set up one to search the New York van and a second to search the Chicago van, updating on-screen maps to show the location data from OnStar as fast as she could. "Still on 87 South in New York and 90 West in Illinois. Vanessa, in a half hour, if they stay on those roads, where will they be?"

Raiden considered my question, scribbling notes on a pad then saying, "I'm guessing one near Yankee Stadium in New York, and the other merging from I-90 with I-94. Just south of Chicago proper."

"You get that?" I asked, to the maw of the camera. "Can you get there, then?"

CIRG Phil (or is it Phil CIRG?) replied, "We're on it. Relocating is going to be a problem so . . . I hope you're right and that's the spot."

"Yeah," I said, "me too."

CHAPTER

74

SPECIAL AGENT JACKSON ROBINSON'S phone had rung at 6:19 AM, shattering the stillness of his quiet home. His two preteen boys and his wife were still fast asleep, but Robinson had already been awake and savoring the calm before the storm, when enthusiastic footsteps would ring from the stairs as the boys bounded down, ready for another day of summer vacation and excited for a planned weekend fishing trip with their dad, a giant of a man with a dark-chocolate-colored polished scalp and tidy, meticulously trimmed chin goatee, who worked odd hours and who they rarely saw.

Robinson's schedule was unpredictable, for when he was on-call, he knew not to make plans. A CIRG agent slept with one eye open and was expected to be instantly ready when called into action. One of those calls had just come in, and a part of him selfishly hoped that, whatever it was, it would not drag into the weekend.

Robinson had been picked up by his partner, Special Agent Blake O'Donnell, the CIRG team leader on call in the Chicago metro area. Enroute to the rendezvous site in O'Donnell's duty vehicle, a black Chevrolet Suburban, they had listened to a briefing on the phone as they had sped through the early Midwest morning.

By 7:20 AM, the pair had met up with the remainder of the team in a parking lot at East 71st Street, in an area south of Chicago known as Greater Grand Crossing. The lot was seconds from the on-ramp to I-94 North that led to downtown Chicago. The men had dressed in their tactical gear and had been joined by the rest of their team, all kitted out for battle.

Also parked in the lot was another black Suburban, driven by Special Agent Tom Barry, and two vehicles from Special Agent Bomb Technician (SABT) Program: a black box truck with "FBI Bomb Technicals" emblazoned in gold on its sides, and an unmarked, white, bomb containment box truck. The four vehicles would certainly attract attention, and Robinson hoped they would not be parked here for long.

In each vehicle, radios were receiving constant chatter from the CIRG CMU (Crisis Management Unit) in the Washington, DC SIOC, where a mission controller directed an operation that included a CIRG team in New York City, code-named "NOVEMBER TEAM," and O'Donnell's Chicago team, code-named "CHARLIE TEAM." O'Donnell and Robinson's Suburban would be "Charlie One," Special Agent Barry in the second Suburban "Charlie Two," the bomb squad "Charlie Three," and the containment truck "Charlie Four." The vehicles planned to proceed from the lot in that order.

In O'Donnell's passenger seat, Robinson examined a large tablet screen which showed a road map of the area. On the map, there was a clump of four black dots at their location, and also a red dot which had been making steady progress north on I-90, moments from reaching the merge to I-94. That red dot, they knew, was their target, but they had also been advised by a woman named Vanessa Raiden, an Intelligence Analyst in the FBI Boston Field Office who was doing the tracking of the vehicle, that there was thirty-to-sixty-second latency delay in the location data for the target.

In both cities, local police had been sent descriptions of the vans and the plate numbers, but nothing had been reported yet as a positive match. Charlie Team waited, tensely, not knowing when or how, exactly, they were to intercept their target, described as white 2015 Chevrolet Express van with Massachusetts plates, number of occupants inside unknown but presumed to be two men, transporting a dangerous cargo that was currently assumed to be a radioactive weapon of some kind. The expression that the CIRG agents wore was serious and focused. The CIRG teams preferred to operate with a detailed strategy, with contingencies, in place, but given the short notice, there had been no time to put a proper plan together. All they had, really, were orders from the director himself: intercept the van and secure its cargo and passengers, as fast as possible.

Then, at 7:45 AM local time, CMU broadcast the order: "Charlie Team, go!"

O'Donnell's right hand yanked the gear lever into drive and the Suburban lurched forward, blasting onto I-94 with the three other vehicles closely behind.

On Special Agent Robinson's tablet map, the target's trail of breadcrumbs had proceeded on I-90, which would lead directly into the heart of Chicago. However, that red target dot was still well south of downtown proper and several miles south of the John Hancock Tower, which had been identified as a recognizable landmark in Chicago and therefore a potential target.

The mission control voice originating from the SIOC CMU droned on, like a train conductor, "New York. Still moving south on the FDR Drive. Chicago passing Fuller Park."

Though the tablet showed the two black dots representing the Suburbans a short distance from the red dot, with the position latency, Robinson figured they were just behind the target, but with the morning traffic building, O'Donnell could simply not catch up without letting the less-maneuverable and slower box trucks drop too far back.

For the first time since getting on the interstate, O'Donnell spoke to his partner while holding the mute button for his headset, "Man, you know they are broadcasting your helmet cam feed? Hold your head steady and look with your eyes, dude!"

Robinson's head had been swiveling left, right, center, up, down and all around—and the chagrined Robinson realized that the people overseeing the op in the SIOC would feel like they were watching a video taken by one of his preteens with a smartphone.

On the radio, the SIOC conductor droned, "New York, passing midtown. FDR Drive. Traffic moving slowly. Chicago target is moving faster than New York. Chicago has crossed I-55, passing Little Italy, next intersection is I-290."

The Charlie One Suburban's speed had picked up somewhat as the convoy approached the I-290 interchange, which meant that the target, ahead, would have accelerated earlier and gained distance. The mass of vehicles in front was not as tightly packed but there was still no visual of a white Chevrolet van.

As the convoy moved north, Robinson kept an eye on the breadcrumbs on the tablet as O'Donnell searched for the van visually. Then, the radio blared with a woman's voice, shouting, "This is Raiden in Boston! Chicago van just exited the highway, moving east on West Washington Boulevard!"

As Robinson prepared to take exit 51C, the tablet showed the van was on a surface street, turning right from West Washington to North Desplaines Street.

A voice over the radio asked, "Why is it turning? Where's it going?"

The train conductor voice from the SIOC immediately said, "Charlie One and Two, close the gap faster and establish a visual. Repeating: target is a white Chevrolet van. Believed to have Massachusetts plates. Charlie Three and Four, accelerate."

Robinson shook his head, thinking, *we're pushing this thing as fast as we dare. Easy for them to say from their computer screens.* In the morning traffic, the target dot on the tablet had slowly traveled south and appeared to halt for a moment at an intersection, perhaps waiting for a green light.

The mission controller continued his narration as the dot began to move again on the map. "Target has turned left on West Jackson Boulevard. Repeat, now traveling east on West Jackson. Charlie Team, it's a multilane, one-way street. You're a block behind."

O'Donnell replied, "Charlie One, copy that."

Behind, in the second Suburban, Special Agent Barry confirmed, "Two, Wilco."

Robinson, a lifelong Chicago native, spoke evenly, "It's headed into the heart of the city. It could be going anywhere—City Hall, the Mercantile Exchange, Jeweler's Row, the Hancock Building. There's fifty high-profile targets in that area."

FBI Boston Field Office

Toiling somewhat out of the main action, and perhaps hoping to redeem himself from the apparent server problem early that morning, Vanessa Raiden's purple-glasses, spiky-haired assistant Lewis announced, loudly, "I have more visuals." On one of the big screens, he had brought up the feed from the cab-top-mounted camera on the Charlie Three bomb squad truck. From the higher perspective, we could see in the distance, a block-and-a-half ahead, as the two black Suburbans ran a red light to make their left turn, almost causing traffic to come to a complete stop in a pile-up.

On-screen, we watched as the Suburbans made laborious progress struggling, trying to catch their targets, the camera feed showing snarled traffic as the convoy approached the bridge spanning the Chicago River. The dot representing the Chevy van was crossing the bridge.

For a moment, on its cab-top camera feed, we could see the bomb squad truck closing the distance to the snarled Suburbans. Finding a break in traffic, finally, the two black SUVs darted ahead and accelerated toward the bridge.

The bomb squad truck lagged behind as the SIOC mission controller stated, "Charlie One, the target is less than a block ahead of you. Stopped at South Wacker Drive intersection."

Chicago

"They got the green on Jackson! They're gonna cross South Wacker Drive!" Robinson yelled.

With a break in traffic, Special Agent O'Donnell slammed his right foot to the floor, and the throaty V-8 engine of the Suburban growled as the big SUV barreled across the intersection. In his mirrors, he could see the second black Suburban scant inches behind as Special Agent Barry matched his speed perfectly.

The radio barked, "Charlie One, you're almost on the target! Do you have a visual!"

Robinson shouted back, "No! No white vans!"

As the Charlie One Suburban crossed the Wacker Drive intersection, O'Donnell was forced to slow and swerve the big vehicle into the right-hand, buses-only lane, with a clump of vehicles—a black Ford Expedition, a FedEx van, and a yellow cab—blocking the center and left lanes.

Out his passenger side window, Robinson caught a glimpse of an empty grassy park, and then turned his head to examine the vehicles visible to his left that O'Donnell was trying to pass.

FBI Boston Field Office

I stared at the video screen that showed the helmet-cam feed from the Chicago CIRG agent in Charlie One.

It can't be.

At that second, the helmet-cam agent riding in Charlie One had turned to his left, literally staring into the passenger-side window of a FedEx van. After a night of studying our UNSUBs pictured at our whiteboard, those of us in Boston knew those faces. But no one knew them like the one person who had actually seen them, and from the conference table, where he'd been patiently and quietly watching for the past three or so hours, Miles shot to his feet and hollered: "That's Hans! That's the target!"

Macallister roared, backing up Miles's conclusion, "Agreed! Take the FedEx van!"

Chicago

Over the radio speaker, both O'Donnell and Robinson could hear the urgency in the voice yelling *"Take the FedEx van!"*

O'Donnell did not hesitate and swerved the big black SUV in front of the slow-moving van to block it, and Barry positioned the second Suburban to the right of the van. With the melee in the center lane of the three-lane road, the containment truck pulled abreast of the van using the left lane with the bomb squad truck behind. The van was boxed in.

Before the tires had screeched to a stop, Robinson had his passenger door open. Leaping from the Suburban with his weapon drawn, and dressed in his head-to-toe tactical gear, Robinson made an imposing figure as he raced around the front of the Suburban and yanked open the driver's side door of the van.

The figure inside, of medium build with close-cropped, dark hair and a weeks-old dark beard, gaped at the alien figure outside his door as he raised his hands off the steering wheel. Robinson reached a burly, powerful hand into the van, grabbing the man's shoulder and wrenching him from the vehicle. The specially-trained CIRG agent knew just how much force to use, and he pulled the man clear of the van without dropping him onto the pavement.

"What's the cargo?" Robinson bellowed as O'Donnell appeared at his side.

"Wha-wh-what?" the man mewed.

"The cargo. What is it? NOW!"

"It-it-it-it's a . . . it's a bomb," the man cowered. He had a minor role to play in this operation, and this was not what he was told to expect. With the giant, tactically-clad CIRG agent looming over him, flanked by a second imposing agent, the man's resolve had evaporated into the humid Chicago morning air.

"How does it detonate?" the CIRG agent thundered.

"B-b-by-by a phone. Remote. Not me. I can't do it!" The man was about to collapse onto the asphalt, held upright by only the strength of Robinson's grip on his upper arms.

With his target acquired and contained, Robinson calmly asked, "Control. You copy?"

Over the headsets, the SIOC CMU voice replied, "Copy. Target is a weapon. Bomb squad, go."

During this exchange, on the other side of the truck, Special Agent Barry had his weapon unholstered, trained on the big, blond-haired man seated on the passenger side. Stoically, the big blond stepped from the vehicle, his hands in clear view. Barry frisked him efficiently, pulling a small black pistol from a semiconcealed chest holster.

The two occupants of the van were unceremoniously frog-marched clear of the van, and they were shoved into the rear passenger doors of Barry's Suburban, to be covered by Agent Barry's partner.

The radios of Charlie Team crackled through their headsets, occasionally interrupted by the flat monotone of the SIOC mission controller, with the voices being relayed over the SVTC via SIOC to the Boston, New York, and Chicago Field Offices.

O'Donnell: "This is Charlie One. We have two UNSUBS in custody."

He paused. "My agents are clear. Bomb squad, you are clear to approach."

"This is Charlie Three bomb squad. Stand by." Two SABT men, wearing Explosive Ordinance Disposal (EOD) suits, advanced to the rear of the Chevrolet van, while the CIRG agents had fallen back slightly, perhaps unconsciously opening the distance between their bodies and the presumed weapon.

"Charlie Three. Opening cargo doors. Confirming cargo. Single black rectangular box. Five or six feet long. About eighteen to twenty-four inches wide and tall. Unsecured on cargo floor. Control, how do you want to proceed?"

"This is mission control. You say unsecured?"

"Charlie Three, yes, affirmative. The box does not appear to be linked to the vehicle. It appears to slide freely. Probably not going to detonate by moving it. It must have moved every time this van hit a pothole."

"This is control. Stand by."

The activity around the van slowed as the men waited for their orders from Washington. The decision whether to move the device or not, or to try and defuse it in place, would weigh heavily. The SIOC crisis response team made their decision and it was relayed to the men on the ground, "This is control. Remove box from van and get it into the containment truck."

"Charlie Three. Roger that. Hope this fucking thing doesn't arm."

Gingerly, the SABT two-man team cautiously slid the black box between the cargo doors. At the containment truck, another bomb squad member had opened the rear door, exposing the glint of something metal within the darkened interior. Time seemed to slow, as the squad moved with deliberate pacing, their movements almost slothful in the bulky EOD suits. They carefully, delicately slipped the rectangular box from the Chevy van and hefted it into the waiting maw of the metal containment vessel inside the rear of the box truck. Finally, the containment vessel was locked closed and the doors to the box truck were swung shut.

On the radio: "Charlie Three. The target is contained."

"This is control. Charlie Team, confirm suspects in custody."

"This Charlie Two. Affirmative, confirmed. Two suspects. In the Two vehicle."

"Control. Copy. Charlie Four, is your containment vehicle secure?"

"Charlie Four. Affirmative, secure. We are ready to roll."

A look of relief evident on his face, O'Donnell quickly directed his team to move out. "Robinson. You're driving the van. I'm going to lead. Fall in behind me. Two, fall in behind the van. Copy?"

Robinson nodded and swung himself into the driver's seat of the Chevrolet van, his headset still connecting him to the Charlie Team. Barry also grunted his approval; the second agent in his Suburban would continue to guard the suspects.

With drivers in place, O'Donnell shifted his Suburban into gear and pulled back into the middle lane on West Jackson Boulevard. The van and the second Suburban fell into place behind him, followed by the two box trucks. On the radios, they received their final orders from the SIOC: "This is control. Charlie Team, take your next right onto South Wells and loop back to Wacker to get out of the city on 290 West. Traffic is clear. Stand by for your destination; unless notified otherwise, assume you are going to Roosevelt."

As team leader, O'Donnell replied first, "Charlie One, moving out," as he led the convoy toward the FBI Chicago Field Office at 2111 Roosevelt Road. In the trailing vehicles, one by one the agents confirmed their understanding of the instructions.

"Charlie Three. Copy."

"Two. Copy."

"Four. Copy."

As the convoy began to move, the few startled pedestrians who had been watching in concern went back to their real worlds on their smartphone screens. The take-down had been executed flawlessly by the Chicago CIRG Charlie Team agents.

THURSDAY, 9:05 AM — FBI BOSTON FIELD OFFICE, CHELSEA, MASSACHUSETTS

WHILE MOST OF US in the Chelsea operations center and in the SIOC were absorbed on the intercept in Chicago, once that van had stopped, we realized that we faced a major problem.

Our Yankee Stadium intercept staging location was wrong, and the New York CIRG "November Team" had been playing catch-up.

Now, without the need to cycle between the two data streams from OnStar, Raiden had almost real-time tracking on the New York van with only a few seconds of latency. "They got off the FDR Drive!" she shouted. "Exit one! They didn't go through the Battery Park Underpass. They're on surface streets turning . . . hang on . . . turning right onto Broad Street."

Someone in the SIOC shouted, "That's the Financial District! What's there?"

"What the fuck's *not* there?" Macallister bellowed. "You got it all there—the 9/11 Memorial, Wall Street, New York Stock Exchange, Federal Reserve, One World Trade—it's a fucking cornucopia of high-profile targets!"

Once again, Macallister astounded me. Who says "cornucopia" in regular conversation?

The director's voice boomed from the speaker: "C'mon! You gotta close the distance faster. Take 'em down!"

I looked at Macallister as I racked my brain, verbalizing my thoughts. "Who uses silver trucks? No delivery companies I can think of. UPS is brown, DHL is yellow. What are we missing?"

"Doesn't have to be a delivery truck. Maybe they don't use the same ruse twice," Macallister observed.

"Yeah. Could be anything. Tradesman, contractor, cleaning company. You think they lettered it?"

"Not necessarily," Macallister replied. "But honestly, I don't have a fucking clue."

I grimaced. Correct again, Macallister, and succinctly well-put.

On the big screen relaying the helmet-cam feed from a CIRG agent in New York, the action picked up, and we watched as the long, creased, black hood of the "November Team" leading Suburban flew south on the FDR Drive, headed toward the heart of New York City's financial district.

New York

An hour earlier, sitting in the shotgun seat of the November One black Chevrolet Suburban, Special Agent Heather Rourke was pissed off. The firebrand, pale-freckled redhead, a tightly wound ball of spunk and sarcastic wit, was out for blood, thanks to her ex-husband, who had once again stiffed her on an alimony check and refused to take their kids this week, when she had been on call for her CIRG squad. And instead of getting into the chase, her Suburban, and the three other vehicles of November Team, had been idling just outside Yankee Stadium, in the Harlem River parking lot which offered immediate access to the entrance ramp for I-87, also known as the Major Deegan Expressway.

Two-and-a-half miles north of Yankee Stadium, their target had exited I-87 and crossed the Harlem River at the University Heights Bridge. A laptop computer was balanced on the center console of her Suburban, and as the Chicago take-down was broadcast over the open channel to the SIOC, a second receiver had been tuned to a dedicated CIRG channel.

Both Rourke and the ebony-rock of her partner behind the wheel, Special Agent Leroy Havens, had monitored the broadcast from their fellow CIRG agents in Chicago, while also listening as the strategists in DC watching the map tried to predict the target's destination. Uptown, Midtown, or . . . where?

As November Team had sat, uselessly, near the stadium, the target dot had worked its way south on surface streets and picked up the Harlem River Drive. The debate over the CIRG channel had been split. One option had the Team backtracking to the George Washington Bridge, which would have meant a substantial detour. A second option was to use one of the smaller bridges across the Harlem River and try to wind their way through the surface streets in Harlem. The final option was to wait and watch.

The minutes had ticked by as the target dot passed the team, separated only by the Harlem River and by only about seven hundred unpassable feet.

Finally, the CIRG tacticians in DC had given the "go" order— November Team was instructed to parallel the Harlem River Drive by using I-87 to I-278, and to cross over the river using the Robert F. Kennedy Bridge, thus remaining on the wider, multilane highways instead of risking the narrow surface streets.

From the perspective of Special Agents Havens and Rourke, this had quickly turned out to be a colossal mistake, as the traffic forced them to almost a halt, their sirens and flashing emergency lights all but useless as they forced their way across the jammed RFK Bridge. The target dot on the laptop screen map was gaining distance by the second as the Harlem River Drive became the FDR Drive.

As November One had finally merged onto the FDR Drive, with the East River to the left and the cityscape to the right, Special Agent Rourke had kept her head steady, repetitively scanning her eyes back and forth, searching the traffic ahead for a silver GMC Savana cargo van with New Hampshire tags, but knowing that they were too far behind, due to the delay at the RFK bridge, to see their target.

An identical Suburban, November Two, lagged at least a quarter-mile back, and well behind Two, an SABT squad truck and a containment truck valiantly but ineffectively tried to match the pace of the more agile Suburbans.

The formation of the four vehicles of November Team was sloppy but unavoidable. As the target dot continued south on the FDR Drive, in the leading Suburban, Rourke had muted her microphone, asking Havens, "Downtown or through the Battery Park Tunnel to the 9/11 Memorial?" Special Agent Havens merely shook his head. The Team was at the mercy of the dot.

With traffic clearing at the sight of the intimidating, blacked-out Suburban with emergency lights strobing, November One had started to close the distance to the target dot. When they were perhaps a quarter-mile behind, the radio linked to the SIOC mission controller blared, and their laptop screen map confirmed, "Target has taken Exit One and turned north on Broad Street. Target is a silver GMC van presumed to have New Hampshire plates. Engage! November Team, close the gap as fast as you can."

Havens slid the Suburban into the right lane, onto South Street, and turned right onto Broad Street. Rourke yelled, "Heading toward the exclusion area! They're gonna get stuck!"

With a slight nod of his head, but without losing his focus, Havens indicated his understanding—Broad Street was closed just north at Beaver Street due to the no-vehicle restricted area which had been imposed around the New York Stock Exchange in 1996, in the aftermath of the 1993 World Trade Center garage bombing. The exclusion area had since expanded to close several adjacent streets to vehicular traffic.

Accelerating up Broad Street toward the exclusion area, the big black truck swerved around a garbage truck, flashed by a delivery truck, and shot past Stone Street, toward Beaver. Rourke stared at the map, confused, as the dot that indicated their vehicle passed the red dot that indicated their target.

On the radio, the mission controller calmly stated, "November One. You have passed the target. Repeat, you have overshot the target."

A pause, and the controller said, "November One. Left on Beaver Street, one block and loop back to Broad."

Special Agent Havens replied for both him and Rourke. "This is November One. Copy that. We did not pass a silver van. Repeat, we did not pass a silver van."

"Roger that. November One, turn left on Beaver. November Two, what's your status?"

"This is November Two. Traveling North on Broad. Control, give me a distance to target."

After a split-second, mission control replied, "You're a block back."

"November Two, closing the distance. Stand by."

In November One, Rourke's head rotated left and right as she haplessly searched for their target. Havens put every bit of his extensive driving training to use, deftly maneuvering the eighteen-foot-long Suburban through the narrow streets. Horns blared and middle fingers were raised in that quintessentially New York City salute among drivers. Havens kept his eyes focused on the road and kept the Suburban unscathed.

As he squeezed through New Street, the mission controller's voice lost its calm monotone and screamed, "They turned! November Two, target has turned right onto South William Street. You've passed the turn. Stop and back up!"

"November Two, copy."

"Shit!" Rourke yelled as November One aimed back toward Broad Street. "You gotta turn right! But it's a one-way, going the wrong way!" Through the windshield, they could see November Two stopped at the intersection, attempting to back into the flow of vehicles. As Havens tried to turn right onto the sidewalk, the two Suburbans inadvertently created a bottleneck and halted.

The target dot continued to move smoothly, gaining distance.

FBI Boston Field Office

Raiden shook her head emphatically, the frustration and pressure evident in her voice. "The location data is as real-time as I can get it. And there's no way they swapped the OnStar brains in the van yesterday and are spoofing it in another vehicle. How the fuck did they miss them?"

The dots continued their out-of-sync parade on the screen. I didn't understand how November One had missed the van. Leaning over to Raiden's assistant, Lewis, I whispered, "Are you recording the feed from the helmet?"

"Yeah, of course," he replied.

"Play it back. From when they got on the surface streets."

He nodded and banged at the keys, bringing up the helmet-cam-feed on one of the smaller screens at his desk level.

Clicking a mouse, he said, "About here. Look, you can see the truck accelerating."

On-screen, it was obvious as the big SUV sped up. That section of Broad Street was anything but broad; a two-way street with a single line of traffic in each direction and curbside parked cars. We watched as the Suburban darted into the oncoming traffic lane, fortunately with a gap, sliding past a garbage truck with inches to spare, almost sideswiping a FedEx truck that was pushed into the curb as the Suburban forced its way through the narrow street.

Broad Street became a one-way as it passed Stone Street, and other than a box truck with an open cargo door pulled to the left curb, there were no other vehicles.

The camera view shook side-to-side as the agent looked around quickly, Lewis commenting, "That must have been when control told 'em they missed it."

I stood stock-still. They had missed it. But I didn't.

"Rewind, please."

"It's not there, Mr. Porter. They're not driving a garbage truck."

"Rewind, please," I repeated softly, insisting.

He looked at me strangely, but then bent back toward the computer, restarting the video. We watched again as the Suburban swerved around the garbage truck, and I calmly said, "Stop."

On the edge of the view, it was obvious. Pulled to the side to make room for the menacing, supersized, black Suburban was a white GMC van with FedEx markings.

I pointed at the screen, and yelled, as loud as I could, "It's another FedEx van! That's still the disguise! Somehow, it's now white! GMC van with the FedEx logos!"

Before the room could react, Raiden shouted, "It stopped! William Street and Wall Street!"

New York

At the intersection of William Street and Wall Street, a white GMC van with FedEx markings stopped at the sidewalk behind a larger truck, also parked and making some sort of delivery.

Dressed in black polo shirts with purple accents that were embroidered with the FedEx logo, purchased as a pair on eBay for forty-four dollars, John and Seb casually opened the rear cargo doors and slid out a large black plastic box. On both sides of the box, white letters spelled out "National Park Service."

Carrying the box, the pair of men proceeded to walk into the pedestrian-only zone on Wall Street and were immediately stopped by a uniformed New York Police Department officer, who confronted them, saying, "You can't just walk in here. What's up?"

One of the delivery men replied, "Yeah, sorry, we're running late. Should have gone around like usual but traffic is a bitch. Just got to drop this at Federal Hall."

The officer examined the two uniformed men, the lanyards around their necks with a plastic-encased, FedEx picture identity card, and their package, which was emblazoned with the National Park Service logo and name. He looked past the men to their parked delivery van, then gazed up the street, toward the Federal Hall National Memorial building, the ornate Greek Revival structure where George Washington took his oath as the first president of the United States that stood opposite the New York Stock Exchange, and back at the box. "Okay. Next time follow procedure."

"Thanks, mate," the delivery man replied. The pair set off again.

Walking the short block to the pedestrian-only intersection of Wall and Broad, they placed the package on the lowest step leading up to the

Federal Hall entrance, 174 feet from the steps of the New York Stock Exchange, and turned to return to their van.

FBI Boston Field Office

The camera image blurred when the New York CIRG agent scanned the area as the November One Suburban finally extricated itself from the mess it caused on Broad Street and shot up South William Street. The agent's head movements made it all but impossible to follow on-screen.

"Can't we get better visuals here?" Macallister demanded.

"Yessir. Hang on. November Three has a cab-top camera." Lewis clicked at his machine, and in seconds, we had a new feed on another screen: a high view from the cab of the bomb squad truck, who had caught up to the Suburbans as they were jammed together on the one-way street. The convoy was now barreling past pedestrians on William Street.

With that new, elevated stable perspective, we watched as November One and Two pulled up abreast of a white GMC FedEx van and smoked to a stop, the four agents inside the SUVs leaping out, only to surround an empty vehicle.

From the helmet-cam feed, we watched a bobbing image as the agent ran toward an NYPD officer at the corner of Wall and William.

New York

"Where's the driver?" Special Agent Rourke shouted at an NYPD officer who was posted at the vehicular roadblock at the corner of Wall Street and William Street.

The officer's eyebrows shot up and his mouth gaped open at the sight of four FBI agents, carrying weapons and dressed in black tactical uniforms, as the giant bomb squad truck and equally-big containment truck stopped at the intersection beyond, quickly snarling traffic. "They . . . they . . . there's two of them. They had a package for Federal Hall." The officer pointed up Wall Street, and Rourke took off at a sprint with Havens.

In seconds, Special Agent Rourke eyeballed the two delivery men walking in the direction of their van, their FedEx shirts making them stand out on the street that was otherwise lightly peppered with casually-dressed tourists. She bolted toward them with Havens on her right flank and the two agents from November Two behind her left heel. As she ran toward them, Rourke accosted the black-shirted delivery men, snarling, "Where's the package?"

One of the two men froze. The other, with curly brown hair and an unruly beard who was short-tempered himself, yanked a Makarov pistol from his waistband and, before either agent could react, he squeezed the trigger.

The shot was made from the hip and unaimed, yet at that short range, it didn't matter as it connected, piercing Rourke's left pelvis just below, and clear of, her body armor. She spun slightly from the impact and fell toward Havens to her right. Under three seconds later, the two agents from November Two had passed Rourke and tackled both delivery men, shoving them to the ground and roughly disarming them.

Two SABT agents ran past the melee, looking for the black box with the National Park Service markings that the NYPD officer had just told them about. The Chicago and New York SABT teams had communicated outside of the chaos of the connection with SIOC, and the New York squad traded speed for risk, not bothering with the bulky EOD suits.

Though it seemed to fit into its surroundings due to the lettering on its sides, the black box still was easy to spot on the granite steps of Federal Hall. Calmly, yet swiftly, the two SABT men hefted the box and carried it back to the waiting containment truck.

The November Two agents forcefully shoved the two delivery men into the backseat of their Suburban while Havens carry-walked the badly-injured Rourke to November One, carefully lifting her through the driver's side rear passenger door.

Thinking quickly, Havens pointed at the van, then at one of the SABT agents. Their training was exhaustive, and they knew how to improvise—the SABT agent knew what the team leader required and immediately hopped into the driver's seat of the white van.

Agents and squad members disappeared into their vehicles. Vehicle doors slammed shut. Radios squawked with the mission chatter:

"This is November Four. Target is secure to transport."

Serenading again with his usual monotone, mission control replied, "Copy. Clear the area. One agent takes the van. November Two, you have the UNSUBS in custody?"

"November Two. Affirmative."

"Two, go to 26 Federal. Van to follow. One, escort Three and Four to the NYPD disposal area at Rodman's Neck. Switch to channel Bravo for instructions and to coordinate with NYPD."

After getting Rourke settled, and finally able to speak, Havens spoke sharply, "This is One. Negative. Rourke is hit. Need priority clearance to medivac!"

The pitch of the monotone increased in tempo and tone, "Roger. Stand by, November One."

"This is November Three. We got my SABT partner in the van. We are ready to roll. No need for an escort."

"Control. Copy that, approved. November One, New York-Presbyterian Lower Manhattan Hospital. One-half mile north. We will coordinate for you there. Go!"

It was 9:32 AM.

CHAPTER

76

I HEARD THE SOUND OF scattered applause and backslaps over the secure video teleconference connection to the SIOC, but I didn't share their enthusiasm. In our Boston operations center, I watched with concern as the van dot remained stationary on the map screen. Looking at Raiden, I wondered what she was doing as she anxiously tapped at her keyboard.

"Vanessa? The van's not moving."

"Yeah," she replied tersely. "Not bothering to update anymore. Two down. We got one to go. And the Buick is no longer transmitting to OnStar."

"I know!" Anastasia blurted. She had taken over the tracking of the Buick from Raiden earlier on, and she had been working her computer with growing desperation as the chases progressed in Chicago and New York.

The ruckus at the SIOC died quickly as they, too, realized that we had an agent down and one more target to find.

Raiden was typing feverishly but did not appear to be making progress, and her frustration was evident in her voice when she mumbled, "Last time I updated that location, it was on 678 in Jamaica, New York. I can't think of any targets there. No big buildings, nothing prominent."

"Yeah, you're right, there's nothing there except a big, fucking ginormous airport," Macallister said bluntly. "That's the John F. Kennedy International Airport."

Raiden groaned. "Oh, shit. I can't get the data from OnStar. Anastasia, what happened?"

"The location data stopped streaming," Anastasia said. "I don't know why. I've been checking and rechecking the port. It's open but the data stream stopped. I can't figure it out."

Raiden replied, "I bet the ignition is off. You've got to be in another service. It's not on active transmit. OnStar keeps track of where the vehicle is, even when it's off. In case they need to do an ignition block for a stolen car, for example, but it's a different data service. Hang on, I can get it." She clacked at her keys for a moment or two, then said flatly, "I got it. It's at . . . yup, JFK. Terminal Four parking lot."

The director, now front and center on the SVTC feed from the SIOC, boomed, "Are you saying we have a bomb threat at JFK?"

In Boston, they all turned and looked at me. I was not so sure I enjoyed the scrutiny, but I gathered myself, stood up straight, and said, "No, sir. I think that is very unlikely. We know of two cases brought from the vessel. We think the ringleader is driving that vehicle, but we have no reason to believe that he is in possession of a third weapon."

"Well then, find him."

Yeah, easy enough. Some sixty million people pass through JFK every year. On average, that's in the neighborhood of seven thousand people per hour.

Macallister interrupted my math exercise, saying, "Let's get the Port Authority or NYPD cops to secure the vehicle until we can get a forensics team there. Raiden, we need access to the JFK cameras. In Terminal Four."

"I'm on it," Raiden responded. "It's going to take a little time, though."

Special Agent Peck, the now-on-overtime duty officer in New York, added, "I can coordinate the New York Police and with Port Authority, and I'll get an Evidence Response Team enroute out to JFK."

I sensed this was going to be a fruitless effort, and wearily, for the first time in quite some time, I sat in one of the now-familiar imitation

Aeron chairs at the conference table. I shook my head as Miles caught my eye, asking, "Our man Omar is gone, right?"

"'Fraid so," I replied. "I don't get it . . . we still have a lot of puzzle pieces to put together."

Macallister slumped into the chair next to me. "You're not kidding," he said. "What the fuck just happened?"

CHAPTER
77

THURSDAY, 9:43 AM — TERMINAL FOUR PARKING LOT, JOHN F. KENNEDY INTERNATIONAL AIRPORT

NYPD OFFICER JIMMY CHEN was the first cop to arrive at the Terminal Four parking lot at New York's John F. Kennedy International Airport. Already on patrol duty, Chen had gotten the call while doing a loop on the South Service Road that ran adjacent to the 678-Van Wyck Expressway, doing a boring routine patrol as he passed by the air cargo buildings, noticing nothing out of place as rush-hour traffic slowly dissipated.

The radio in his aging Ford Police Interceptor Sedan, a glorified Taurus, had crackled moments ago, with a dual-dispatch to both NYPD and Port Authority, "All units, advise location and proximity to Terminal Four lot, requesting a visual on a suspect vehicle." Excited to have something to do and to break the monotony of his morning, Chen had responded and gunned the engine, merging first onto the Van Wyck, then darting off to the access road to the lot, as the dispatcher read him the details of his target, "2015 Buick Regal, Mass tags, light brown or tan color."

The radio voice had directed him to a location in the lot, while Chen wondered why dispatch wanted a vehicle inspection when they already knew where it was parked. Guiding the Police Interceptor to the perimeter of the lot, he found a tan Buick sedan with Connecticut plates parked nose-in, partly shaded by one of the few trees that bounded the lot between it and the access road.

Clicking his vehicle into Park behind the Buick, and leaving his lights flashing but the siren off, Chen examined the sedan. He had been directed to this spot to locate a tan Buick with a Massachusetts license plate. But this car had a Connecticut plate.

Chen slowly exited his sedan, wondering if he should wait, per protocol, for a backup unit to arrive. Looking at the unassuming vehicle, he decided the situation was benign, especially since this was probably the wrong car, but he drew his service weapon nonetheless and approached the left side of the parked Regal.

One glance into the interior of the vehicle was all it took for him to realize that the situation was anything but benign.

Splayed across the front seat was a man's body, awkwardly twisted from a semisitting position in the driver's seat with the torso resting across the center console, and the head facing the sky from the passenger-side front seat. That head, or at least what remained of it, was a disfigured, bloody mess.

Chen wished he had waited for his backup.

As Omar had driven toward New York, south on Interstate 684, in the anonymous, tan Buick sedan among so many other morning commuters, the Pixel phone had blasted its ringtone at 5:40 AM.

Omar had not understood, at first. That phone was never supposed to ring. It had received a single text message yesterday, and that had been unnerving enough. But a call? What possible reason could there be for an incoming call.

The phone was tasked only to make two test calls, followed by two trigger calls.

The incoming ringtone continued to blare, and with a swallow and a dry mouth, Omar had reached for the phone, the caller ID screen on the glass facing showing only "RESTRICTED" and no number.

His thumb had automatically swiped to connect the call. After a short pause, Omar greeted the unknown caller with a single word: "Yes?"

After a brief second of silence, a woman's voice: "You have been compromised."

Another beat of silence, and then the voice had continued, "He instructs you not to make the calls to New York and to Chicago. Again, I repeat: do not make the calls. He has given you an out. He booked you on Virgin Atlantic twenty-six, departing at 8:15 AM to Heathrow. You must make the flight. Use your real passport. Leave the car unlocked at JFK short-term parking at Terminal Four and leave the keys in it. Someone will sanitize it. Turn this phone off now. You must discard the phone immediately. In a way it cannot be found. Do you understand?"

Omar's mind had raced but his voice had said, meekly, only one word, repeating the only word he had said thus far: "Yes."

The connection had gone silent. The display showed only, "CALL ENDED."

The fact that the caller had known that his "real" passport was unused had validated the call.

The fact that the caller had said that "he has given you an out" was a terrible sign. It was a sign of failure. The mission was somehow in peril.

Unconsciously, Omar's foot had pressed harder on the Buick's accelerator pedal. He wanted that "out."

Omar knew his way around the City. 684 South to the Hutch, cross the Whitestone Bridge and follow the signs for 678 to the John F. Kennedy International Airport. Virgin Atlantic would be in the giant Terminal 4, with a parking lot literally across the airport access road. Checking the dashboard clock in the Buick Regal, he realized he could make it to the airport in time to clear security and border control, and to get on the flight.

Shortly after merging onto the Hutchinson River Parkway, Omar had slid into the left travel lane in order to use a rare left exit from the parkway that led to a roadside Mobil service station in White Plains, which, with its center location on the divided parkway, was also utilized by the opposing traffic lanes. Getting out of the Regal, he had slung a small backpack over his shoulder, the only item remaining from the large duffel bag that had been used on the sailboat. That duffel bag was now buried among the debris in a dumpster behind a New Milford pizza restaurant.

Inside the station's common building, he had ducked into the restroom, locking the door behind him. He would have to be quick, or an extended visit to the restroom would not only cost him valuable seconds, time that he would need to make the flight, but also potentially raise the ire of a commuter who had one too many coffees.

The backpack contained a change of clothes, a clear plastic bag of toiletries that would pass TSA muster, an electric razor, and his real identification.

Omar had buzzed the razor across his face, trimming and then, with the razor guard removed, erasing his beard. It had taken some time as he carefully cleaned his face. With the beard finally gone, he had stabbed a contact lens into his right eye, then into the left. Stuffing the glasses and the razor back into the backpack, Omar had smoothed his hair and examined his reflection in the mirror. It would do.

Walking back to the Regal, he had subtly dropped the Pixel phone into a curbside storm water grate. And, despite his outwardly placid demeanor, his thoughts had been jumbled and blurred together, and as he merged back into the traffic, he had wondered what precipitated that phone call at 5:40 AM.

The plan had been so simple. He was to have placed the calls, sequentially, to the Chicago bomb and then to the New York bomb, at 9:33 AM. The exact time didn't really matter, as long as it was a few minutes past 9:30 when the boxes were to have been placed on the sidewalks. Omar had decided to make the calls from New York itself, at the West 79th Street Boat Basin, a place that he could get to early, and dawdle, unnoticed as he enjoyed the morning water view and waited for the clock to strike the detonation time. He liked the irony of sending the detonation signal from within one of the very cities that was a target.

Two phone calls, two bombs triggered. Omar would have popped the SIM card out of the phone and walked casually to the boat basin docks, and equally casually, would have tossed the Pixel into the murky, deep, and fast-flowing waters of the Hudson River. And, remaining nonchalant, the unremarkable man would have strolled to the east on West 79th Street, passing under the Henry Hudson Parkway overpass, and then perhaps to one of the walking paths—it didn't matter which one—to disappear into the melee of New York City on a Thursday morning in mid-July.

Wall Street would have been five miles south, and one would not have expected to hear sirens at first. His options were numerous and all equally unexciting. He could have wandered through the halls of the Museum of Natural History, just three blocks from the Boat Basin, or he could stroll in Central Park. Eventually, perhaps he might have caught a cab to 125th Street and hopped on a Metro-North train headed out of the city, just another New Yorker, feigning a blasé composure. No one would have been looking for him. And no one would have noticed him.

Omar would have vanished, until it was time to resurface under a different name to collect his pay and to be the creator of his new life.

But that did not happen.

Instead, as he drove toward JFK, he wondered what would happen to the mercenaries. Would they drop their packages? Those two overcomplicated, fake "dirty" bombs which Omar had assembled in Turkey with radioactive medical waste that his employer had provided. Those two overcomplicated devices which created the overcomplicated delivery method of transporting them by sea. Omar had shrugged; it was not his place to object. Back in Greece, he had tried to suggest to his employer that the ruse could have been easily accomplished from within the United States, but he had been rebuffed.

In any case, he still wondered what would happen to the men; he had no way to contact them once the mission was in motion. That was part of the plan. Except for the phones that would allow Omar to detonate the devices remotely, the men were on their own. There was no link back to Omar. Indeed, if the long boxes were still in the vans with the men at the prearranged time, they would almost certainly be killed. Motivation, Omar thought, for them to deliver the packages as planned.

Even though the devices were deadly at short range, Omar had been told the radioactive content was relatively benign. He began to second-guess the plan as he drove toward JFK. What would happen if the men dropped the boxes on the sidewalks at 9:30, and he didn't make the calls? Would the men escape in the vans? Would quarantines be set up around those suspicious packages in both Chicago and New York? Or, was it no stretch of his imagination to conclude that the unknown caller saying "compromised" had meant that the vans might be stopped prior to reaching their destinations?

He had no way of knowing.

Omar reached the Terminal Four parking lot at JFK with plenty of time to make his flight. As he switched off the ignition of the Regal, his driver's-side door was yanked open from the outside. A giant body loomed in Omar's field of view, and a large, fleshy hand grabbed his left ear and twisted his head unnaturally. Spots formed in his vision and he felt the hand push his head, extremely strongly and excruciatingly painfully, toward the passenger seat.

The face leaned in, and, from his supine, forced, and twisted pose in the Regal, Omar could just make out his attacker's cloudy dark eyes as the interloper spoke in a familiar, slightly-Russian accented growl, "You piece of shit. I wanted to tell you myself. You allowed yourself to be tracked, you miserable fuck. You failed us. You failed *me!*"

Omar whispered through the pain, "Tracked? How?!"

"Lockwood. You let him escape!"

"No! He drowned! After he dove off the boat. We searched for him. That's not possible! I assumed he drowned!"

The Russian laughed mirthlessly, "Well, then, he's a fucking fish. Because he survived. And because he survived, he was able to contact the FBI. And they are onto you."

As he had been speaking, his tone had softened and his grip on the man in the Buick had lessened. Omar was able to breathe almost normally, asking with a raspy voice, "But you're here? Why? What about my flight? I don't understand."

"There is no flight, you fool. I needed to put you somewhere where I could get to you fast. To get to you to tell you this: I gave you Chicago.

All I wanted was New York; you demanded Chicago. I gave you what you wanted, and you failed."

Stealing a fast glance around the area, the big man leaned further into the car and pushed the man who had called himself Omar onto the center console. The Russian whispered, "And since I can't get what I want, and since I have no fucking doubt in my mind that when they catch up with you, you will fucking sing like a fucking canary, I wanted to make sure that would not be possible. Because, unlike you, I do not assume anything."

A black Smith & Wesson M&P22 compact pistol with a menacingly long suppressor extending from its barrel spat one shot, aimed at the center of Victor Wolford's face.

Anatoly Petrikov grabbed the keys to the Regal, slammed the driver's side door closed, carefully polished the door handle that he had touched, squeezed the fob to engage the door locks, and disappeared into the vast airport property.

CHAPTER
78

THURSDAY, 10:30 AM — FBI BOSTON FIELD OFFICE, CHELSEA, MASSACHUSETTS

WE FINALLY HAD A NAME, thanks to the passport that had been found in the Buick Regal, but the description of the dead man in the car did not match our sketch of Omar. However, working quickly and now comfortable with the OnStar data, Raiden had been able to backtrack the route of the Regal, discovering the vehicle's penultimate stop at a service station in White Plains, where we had been able to get access to the security cameras.

The driver exiting the Regal matched our sketches; it was Omar. The man reentering the vehicle matched the passport and, running the clear images from the White Plains cameras through our facial recognition system, we confirmed in short order that Omar's real identity was Victor Wolford.

Wolford's name was nowhere in any of our files, but after a Google search, I relayed what I found to the team in our ops center, "Victor Wolford was a jewel merchant. Specialized in diamonds. Originally from Nevada. And—this can't be a coincidence—he got his start in Chicago, then expanded to New York. Looks like he closed up in 2005 or 2006, because he disappeared from the news around then. All we got from our systems so far is a customs and immigration contact in January 2017 showing a departure from Newark, New Jersey, destination Athens, Greece. Then he drops out, off-grid."

"We'll find out more about him," Raiden said. "It's going to take some time, though."

"Yeah, that's all great, but what the fuck was a guy who was a what, jeweler, doing all this for?" Macallister helpfully asked, raising the question that was on all our minds. "This is gonna be some shit-show. You relay all that to SIOC yet?"

I responded, "Yeah, well, sort of. It's going in the case file as we speak."

I knew that the investigation would be taken over by Washington and then managed from there, and while even though it appeared that any imminent threat was contained, we had no idea what the motive was or whether this was part of some larger scheme. The FBI was on high alert and discoveries had started popping up quickly.

After the intercept at William and Wall Street, the two New York suspects had been taken to our offices at 26 Federal Plaza and the van had been impounded in the building's subterranean garage. Similar events played out some eight hundred miles to the west, as the two Chicago suspects were brought to our field office at 2111 Roosevelt Road, only three-and-a-half miles from where they had been captured. And an FBI forensics team was at JFK, first examining the area around the Buick and preparing to move that vehicle to one of our garages for extensive analysis.

By 10:30 AM, all four suspects apprehended in the vans had been fingerprinted and photographed. While the prints were being analyzed, the mug shots were sent electronically to the SIOC and to us in Boston. It had taken less than fifteen seconds to add those four printed photographs to our whiteboard, and to match them to our suspects. We had John and Seb in New York, and Bruce and Hans in Chicago, though we assumed that those were not their real names.

Raiden and her team, using the OnStar location history data, had efficiently assembled a timeline of the three vehicles' tracks, and, with SIOC linked in, she chronicled their travels:

"All three left Gloucester within seconds of each other shortly before 5:00 AM yesterday morning. They took different paths out of the town, but then all ended up on the same road, the Yankee Division Highway, eventually getting to the Mass Pike where we found them. Then they exited the Mass Pike in Sturbridge and took Interstate 84 through Connecticut. All three stopped for a long time at an industrial park in New Milford, Connecticut.

"The Chevrolet left New Milford early evening for the drive to Chicago. The GMC and the Buick stayed put, with the Buick taking a short trip to what appears to be the location of a restaurant in the evening. The Buick stops at the same point the next morning before driving toward New York, departing after the GMC van by several minutes and taking a circuitous route toward the City."

SIOC had instructed the local police in New Milford to secure both the industrial park and the restaurant, while agents from both our New Haven, Connecticut field office and from our New York office had been dispatched to the site. In the meantime, a cursory exam of the GMC van in New York had revealed that, though it appeared white, the door jambs and the exposed interior metals were silver. Our working theory was that the GMC had been wrapped in white automotive vinyl, most likely during the stop in New Milford where the suspects had presumably disguised the vans before dispatching them to their separate locations.

Agents would scour the warehouse site in New Milford, Connecticut, the boat in Gloucester, the vans in New York and Chicago, and the service station that the Buick stopped at in White Plains. The case had become a national counter-terrorism priority, with the full resources of the Bureau brought to bear on the investigation.

Most pressing was the question of what to do with the long, heavy boxes found in the vans. The suspect in Chicago said they were bombs. Were they? What kind? Nukes? What?

Both boxes had been sequestered and were being prepared for a multiday transport, to be moved only late at night, to TEDAC—our just-over-one-year-old Terrorist Explosive Device Analytical Center in Huntsville, Alabama, nine-hundred-and-fifty miles from New York and almost six-hundred-and-fifty miles from Chicago. It would be several days before we could confirm the composition of the packages and the type of weapon that they were assumed to be.

However, radiation samples taken directly from the outside of both boxes, and additional samples from Miles's boat, were already enroute to TEDAC by three of the FBI's jets, leaving from Logan Airport in Boston, from O'Hare Airport in Chicago, and from Teterboro Airport just outside New York City. The laboratory technicians at TEDAC would be able to measure the isotope signatures of the samples and, by tomorrow morning, we might have the identity of the type of radiation that was being emitted by whatever was hidden inside the long, ominous-looking boxes.

Meanwhile, the FBI spin doctors would also monitor the news and the media to ensure that the panic that the director feared would not materialize. Any questions about the activity on the streets of New York and Chicago were to be dismissed and explained away as merely a training drill. The facts of the case might be made public later, but not at the height of the investigation.

Additionally, our crisis management office had been partially briefed and was working with the director himself to figure out the arrangements and appropriate measures for George Lakeland's family. This was going to be a difficult matter to handle, especially since it needed to remain confidential at this stage.

And, we had a New York CIRG agent in intensive care. The bullet had hit Special Agent Rourke's exterior iliac artery as it transitioned to the femoral artery in her upper leg; even in the short half-mile trip to the hospital, she had bled copiously.

The FBI does not take a fallen agent lightly and that had only heightened the urgency of the investigation. But, even with that motivation, the evidence we had so far would take time to verify, and though the FBI is very, *very* good at checking every possible detail, and while we were confident that we had the mechanism of the plot well in hand, the motive was still a complete mystery to us.

Midday, Miles and I had returned to the conference room where this had all started, where Macallister and I had first interviewed Miles.

About twenty-four hours ago, Appleton had ghosted through the glass door when she had dismissed Miles as a lunatic and had told me that I was wasting time. Now, she had returned to the room to thank Miles, who was still wearing the now slightly smelly, borrowed chinos and button-down shirt from the Addison Gilbert Hospital. Naturally, she swore him to secrecy and offered him a ride home to Cohasset. Well, "offered" is the wrong word. She put it in no uncertain terms that two agents would drive him home, and then wait with him until the legal team could draft a nondisclosure agreement and have him sign it, in their presence. The agents were not to let him out of their sight. Except, maybe, for a shower.

"What about my boat?" Miles asked.

Appleton shook her head. "I'm sorry, it's evidence now. I spoke with our ERT men in Gloucester. They are going to have it hauled out of the water there, and they will continue to compile what they can for a complete forensic analysis. That will take some time, but we'll take care of it and we will get it back to you."

Miles nodded, dejected, but too exhausted to argue. "Can you at least get my stuff off the boat? My phone, passport, wallet, personal gear?"

"Of course. I'll have the team remove the smaller items and document them. We'll expedite that and deliver to you by sometime tomorrow," Appleton agreed. "It's the least we can do. Again, I'm sorry but the boat itself will be impounded for the time being."

"Yeah, I get it," Miles said.

Turning to me, he offered a hand, our eyes meeting. "Ben, thank you. Thank you for believing in me."

I laughed. "You're thanking me? Hardly appropriate. Without you, they would have gotten away with it. Amiright?" We both chuckled, dropping the handshake as the two agents that Appleton had assigned to escort him home came into the room. Miles turned to leave.

"Hey, Ben," Miles called over his shoulder as he and his agent escorts left the room. "Thanks for the beer! Next one is on me."

That seemed so long ago. I smiled, but my expression had quickly turned sour when Appleton asked, "What beer?"

I grimaced. "Right. Forgot to mention that. I got Miles a beer from the Harbor Cove Brewing Company for the ride back to Chelsea. He deserved it, but, um, there's one other thing. The restaurant owner, he was pretty adamant that Uncle Sam pick up the tab for all the people we evacuated out of his place, and to grease him to give us access to the security cameras without a warrant, I agreed." I pulled the American Express receipt out of my wallet and handed it to Appleton. "Can I expense this, please?"

The SAC glanced at the little slip of paper and then did a double-take, actually bringing it closer to her eyes as if she did not believe what it represented. "This is highly unusual, Mr. Porter," she scolded, looking directly at me, then back at the receipt. Slowly thawing, she smiled an ever-so-thin grin. "Okay, Ben, write it up in the expense requisition, attach it to the case file, and send it to me. I'll approve it." She handed the receipt back to me, turned, and glided out the glass door.

After Miles and Appleton departed, I thought I'd have the room to myself, where I could keep plugging away at the case file, but I was interrupted by a new visitor. It was Anastasia.

It's amazing how a crucible changes perspective, and there I was, standing face-to-face with this exotic creature who, prior to yesterday morning, I had never spoken to. I stood when she walked into the conference room. She approached me and took both of my hands into hers, our bodies scant inches from each other and our eyes locked as one. I savored the moment.

She broke the trance, murmuring softly, "Ben . . ." I waited. She leaned in, her lips so close to my ear that I could feel her breath. "Ben. You have *so* much potential. Real good work on this. See you around."

She dropped my hands serenely, slowly walked out the door. I was rooted to the spot, not sure if I should say something, follow her . . . or just do nothing.

Nothing won out.

I took a deep breath, sat down at the conference table, flipped open the screen on my laptop, and buried myself in my case file.

CHAPTER
79

AT 1:30 PM, AFTER I HAD scarfed down a cellophane-wrapped, mystery-meat sandwich and had just gotten yet another innumerable cup of coffee, Vanessa Raiden materialized in my conference room.

"Ben," she hissed, furtively glancing and then leaning her head closer to mine. "We gotta talk. Follow me."

Confused, but having no reason to object, I saved my file, closed my computer and, taking it with me, trailed her out of the room. She did not look back as she navigated the hall, finally stopping at the breakout area that Macallister, Appleton, and I had christened a day before. She sat on the sofa and I began to take my familiar, attractive, yet uncomfortable club chair, but she patted the firm cushion beside her. I obeyed, now more confused than ever.

"I don't know who else to tell this to," she said in a low whisper. She paused and it appeared to me that she shook, physically, before taking a deep breath.

"Okay, this is a lot. You ready?"

I nodded. *Ready for what?*

She paused again, taking yet another breath before continuing. "Alright, remember when we first got into the OnStar system? After you made the connection?" I nodded. "We were focused on the vehicles. We knew we could get location data from the vehicles and track them. They don't need to subscribe to OnStar because it's always on. It's always tracking. That was the priority and therefore we focused on that. I wondered why, because there's something else we can get from OnStar. We could get the emmy eye dee of the device that ran the app. Get it?"

I nodded. Bobbleheaded once again.

"Therefore, I—"

"Wait," I interrupted. "What's an emmy eye dee? Emmy identification?"

She spelled it out, slowly. "M. E. I. D. Mobile equipment identifier. It's like a social security number for a device. It's unique to the device. See the significance?"

"Not really. I mean, I get it, you can find the phone that was used to unlock the vehicle. But we already had the vehicle. Why bother with the phone?"

Raiden smiled. "Because that's what I do. But you're right, it had no real significance at the time, which is why I didn't work on it. I started on that after the vans were apprehended, and after we found the Buick at JFK. I figured someone should at least run it down and see if it went anywhere." The smile vanished from her face. "It did."

After letting that hang in the air for a moment, she continued. "It wasn't obvious at first. Like I said, the MEID is unique to every device. So, with that number, I could find out the type of phone, which, by itself, is not really important, except that all three MEIDs linked back to Google Pixel phones. They were all on the same cell network. The simple fact that they broadcast an MEID, not an IMEI, meant they were on Verizon, Sprint, or US Cellular. AT&T and T-Mobile use a different type of network which uses the other type of device identifier called an IMEI."

"Wait," I interrupted again. "I get the techno-geek-speak, but why is this important?"

"Well, I didn't know yet. What I was thinking, I could find out where the phones came from. And who bought them. Which I can still do. But before doing that, I wanted to see what the phones were up to. Like, if they had been used. To make calls."

"Of course!" I exclaimed.

"Shhh . . . ." Raiden whispered. I wasn't sure why the secretive nature of this conversation was necessary, but I also sensed we were getting somewhere important as she went on, softly, "All three phones initially geo-located in Gloucester, long enough to handshake with the network, establish a connection with OnStar, and then send the unlock signals through the app. Then all three phones were turned off. Are you with me?"

I nodded again.

"From matching the phone location to the vehicle location, I was able to easily figure out which phone went with which vehicle, but not at first. One of the devices came on, very briefly, at one of the service plazas on the Mass Pike. That device, and one other, were turned on in the early afternoon at the industrial park in New Milford, Connecticut. The place where I tracked them, where they had stopped for the day, presumably to disguise the vehicles.

"Anyways," she continued, "the important part is the device that was used to unlock the Buick, and that eventually ended up in Omar's car, received an incoming text message and then made an outgoing call to one of the other devices while both devices were at the Connecticut industrial park, before the receiving device traveled with the Chicago van."

"Okay," I said, "I know you're going somewhere, but let me make sure I have this straight . . . the forensics teams in New York and Chicago have searched the vans, we searched the men, and yet no one has reported finding a phone. Do we conclude that there is a phone in each box?"

"Yes! Exactly! If each box really is a weapon—and what else could it be?—I'd bet it is the arming device. So that the bomb can be detonated from anywhere. I would bet that *this* was a test call.

"Moving forward in time, the Chicago Pixel stays powered on and location data matches the OnStar vehicle data of the van traveling to Chicago. Omar's Pixel gets turned off but then comes back on the network late evening, in the same place in Connecticut. Omar's Pixel makes a second call, this time to the Pixel device that ends up matching the location of the van traveling to New York. A test call to the second arming device, logically."

"Whoa. Where are they now?" I asked. "Could the bombs still be detonated?"

"Both signals ceased just after we intercepted the vans. The cell signal is not powerful enough to penetrate the containment boxes in the transport trucks. Once the boxes get to TEDAC, they will be in a shielded location also. If the phone batteries last that long, they still would not be able to receive a signal.

"It's a really good question, but not what you need to know. Please let me finish," Raiden said gently. "Finally, the last device . . . Omar's device . . . remained powered on *after* making that test call. The location data from that device matches, exactly, the location data from OnStar for the Buick Regal. For a time, at least."

Raiden paused, her head hanging low. She breathed deeply again and slowly looked up at me, her face close to mine and her eyes glistening with tears, which confused me. "Omar's phone received one call. This morning, at 5:40 A.M. The call duration was under one minute. Then it was powered off."

I waited, and Raiden quietly continued.

"I traced the devices. Remember I said Omar's phone received a text? And then received that call this morning? Both came from devices which are most likely burner phones. Two separate numbers. Each one had only that one transmission in its entire history. Both devices followed the same pattern: both were first powered on immediately prior to making the transmission, and then were powered off immediately after and disappear from the network.

"During both transmissions, the cell tower data triangulates the location of the burner phones to the same place. To 201 Maple Street in Chelsea, Massachusetts . . . which is right here, in this building.

"The text, and the call to Omar . . . Both originated here, Ben."

I sat, stunned, immobile.

But . . .

"Hang on," I blurted. "That means . . ."

Raiden nodded her head, sadly, more tears welling up in her eyes. "Remember after you made the connection to OnStar, and we were all in the operations room? Anastasia told Appleton that we needed authorization and Appleton said that she'd go make a call. Then Anastasia said the server was down and she left the room to reboot it.

"See? Both the SAC and Anastasia were out of the room at the same time. And the call to Omar's phone was made during the time when they were both out of the room.

"Either Appleton or Anastasia made that call, Ben."

I remained in speechless silence seemingly forever, but it was probably only seconds, as I processed Raiden's words. Unbelieving but knowing that the electronic breadcrumbs couldn't lie, I asked anyway, "Are you sure? This is incontrovertible?"

Raiden wiped her tears, regained her composure, straightened up a bit, and replied, "Yes. I'm absolutely sure. I checked and rechecked. But—"

She suddenly stopped speaking, as we heard the sound of pounding footsteps approaching. It was Macallister, out of breath.

"PORTER! Fuck, I've been scouring the building for you. We gonna get a breakthrough! Follow me! Now!"

CHAPTER
80

WITH A QUICK GOOD-BYE glance at Raiden, while snatching up my backpack, I sprang from the sofa and chased Macallister as he literally ran to the operations center, briefing me in staccato sentences punctuated as he tried to catch his breath.

"New York called—fucking fifteen, twenty minutes ago—they got the guy John—he wants to talk—he wants a deal—right now."

We reached the operations room and stopped at the threshold, Macallister panting. And I thought *I* was out of shape? Macallister concluded, finally piecing together a complete sentence, "He's come to realize that he's in deep shit, now that in addition to being a terror suspect, he's also an accomplice to the attempted murder of a Federal officer. What questions do you want to ask him?"

Holy shit. What questions do I want to ask?

In the Chelsea operations center, I looked around wildly for Anastasia and Appleton, now knowing what Raiden suspected. Neither was anywhere to be found.

I figured Raiden would be steps behind me, but in the meantime, it appeared that Lewis was in charge. I still didn't know if *Lewis* was his first name or last name, but now was not the time or place to ask.

The technical team was restarting the secure video teleconference between us in Chelsea and SIOC, while also adding in an interrogation room at 26 Federal Plaza in New York.

As I scrawled questions on a legal pad and Lewis completed the connection wizardry, Macallister told me that the interview would be conducted by long-time Special Agent Jasmine Brown. She would have a tablet device in her hands and an earpiece in her ear, discreetly tucked under her hair. I could send her questions to ask via the tablet, or, if urgent, I could speak with her directly.

I looked around the room for my team. Miles and Vanessa, missing. Appleton and Anastasia, also missing—but under a cloud of suspicion. Just Macallister and me. As we took side-by-side seats at the table, with him at my right shoulder as we faced the camera and the big screens, he leaned in and whispered, "Ben. You got this. No one knows this case like you do."

I really appreciated that, and I steeled myself. *Here we go again.*

On the big screen, John was seated at a small table in a windowless room, facing Special Agent Brown, who had her wide, blue-blazered back and her frizzy black hair to the camera.

For once, the audio stream between us and SIOC was silent. Special Agent Brown began the interview. "You've agreed to provide information in exchange for leniency, for a plea, or for some other arrangement. You understand that we cannot agree to anything specific until we hear what you have to say, and until we have time to corroborate it. This interview is being recorded so that both you, and us, have a record of this agreement. Do you consent freely?"

The suspect nodded and then, looking directly at the agent, said, "Yes."

"Very well. Thank you. I will ask questions but first, I'd like you to explain, in your words, why you have consented to this interview."

The man nodded again and shifted slightly in his seat. Watching, I too, perhaps subconsciously, shifted as well, leaning in toward the screen.

In an accent that I placed as British, or perhaps Australian, he began, "I'm doing this because I'm not taking the fall for this cock-up.

It's a bloody farce. It's so bloody overcomplicated it's laughable. And that fucking Seb, who shot the FBI lady. I'm not going down for it."

I noticed Appleton had taken a seat next to Macallister as I fired off an instant message to Special Agent Brown, and I watched her head angle down toward the tablet ever so slightly as she paraphrased, exceptionally well I thought, the question that appeared on the screen in front of her. "Okay. Let's start at the beginning. Tell me about the fishing vessel in Turkey and Mohomed Yilmaz. Why him and why there?"

The suspect's eyes widened. *I got him.* Now's he's wondering how we knew about that. He scowled and said, "I needed a new job. One of my contacts reached me and told me to find a guy named Omar in Bodrum. I found him. An American. I figured right quick that Omar was not his real name, but in my line of work, you don't ask for real names. They had arranged to take Yilmaz's boat across the Atlantic Ocean, hijack a sailboat, and use the sailboat to enter the States."

I typed *why* and pressed send.

Special Agent Brown nodded and then asked, "For what purpose?"

"Omar had a plan to make a lot of money. When we succeeded, we would all get a cut. We're talking squillions. For each of us."

This wasn't making sense. *Fuck.* I have no business conducting an interview. All the same, something he said earlier was interesting, and as the mechanism of the plot had unfolded through our investigation earlier in the day, I thought I was onto something. I sent two words to Special Agent Brown.

She got the gist of my question right away, and smoothly asked, "Let's go back to your word *farce.* And *overcomplicated.* What do you mean?"

The suspect shook his head before answering, "The farce was the boxes. They are bullshit little bombs. They'd make a loud bang and if you were sitting on them, you'd probably get killed. But if you were fifty feet away, you'd be fine. They were set up to be like sparklers, like the ones you all use on your Fourth of July. A lot of sizzle.

"And they had little samples of radioactive medical waste in them. When you Feds got to the blast site, you would go bloody berserk thinking they were nukes. And that would get out on the news and there would be mass panic. Hysteria."

I sent three words to Special Agent Brown. *Where and why.*

She asked, "Where, specifically? And what outcome was intended by this?"

"The setup was easy. Get to downtown New York. If we were early, drive around a couple of blocks, stopping randomly as if we were dropping off packages, then go to Federal Hall and leave our big package on the sidewalk in front of the building at 9:30. Then we'd take off, ditch the van, and disappear. The Chicago van was doing the same thing at the same time. They would do a drive-by at their drop location, then make some fake stops, then go back to drop. They were putting theirs in front of the Mercantile Exchange.

"At 9:33, Omar would remotely detonate the two packages and they'd blow up."

With an exaggerated wave of his hands, the suspect stopped, perhaps to make a dramatic point. In a flash, I realized just how close we had been to the detonation time.

On screen, I watched Special Agent Brown scribbling on her legal pad, and I realized she was stalling for time. I composed a question on the tablet, and the experienced interviewer read it almost word-for-word, "I'm not sure I follow—why detonate a farce of a bomb, as you called it, in front of Federal Hall and Chicago Mercantile Exchange?"

"That's how Omar would make his money. Federal Hall is across from the New York Stock Exchange. Two bombs going off in front of two exchanges, and the markets would plummet. Fear. People would sell. They wouldn't know where the next one was going to hit. They'd hear on the news that radiation was detected and they'd panic. Maybe they'd assume there are more targets, London, or Tokyo, or whatever. Omar didn't care; he'd have shorted the market.

"And then, within hours, probably, you Feds would realize that the radiation had dispersed. There wasn't enough to be deadly. To calm the panic, you'd let everyone know that. You'd send agents in without masks. Hell, maybe you send in the mayor. Broadcast it on the telly and on the internet. People calm down. The markets would stabilize. Meanwhile, Omar makes a bundle, and no one gets hurt."

He sat back, crossed his arms over his chest, and closed his eyes.

This was incredible. Not only was the suspect claiming that they were going to detonate some sort of a fake dirty bomb in two American cities, but the plot was financially motivated? I was stunned and could not think of a question when the suspect spoke one last time. "I dunno how you caught up to us. But I want a deal. I am not taking the fall for Omar. Or for Seb. And I am not taking the fall for some bullshit dud bombs. You can disarm them with a screwdriver."

Stunned, we, too, sat immobile. One hippopotamus, two hippopata . . .

And the SIOC erupted into chaos.

CHAPTER
81

BY 3:00 PM IN THE AFTERNOON that Thursday, I was spent. Other than a brief nap, which I suppose gave me the clarity to figure out the OnStar link, I had not rested since getting to work the day before on Wednesday. The stress of the chase had taken its toll. And then, to hear Vanessa Raiden's disturbing discovery and to get that bombshell of a confession . . .

On second thought, maybe "bombshell" is a poor choice of a word.

Our suspect John had declined to continue speaking without an attorney, and in the chaos of the moment, Appleton had dragged Macallister to a private office for a secure conference with SIOC. The other three suspects had continued to remain silent, and each had been assigned a legal team. The FBI interviews, it does not interrogate. Building a rapport during an interview takes time, and it did not appear that we would get anything imminently from those suspects.

I desperately wanted to—needed to—track down Raiden, but she still had not returned to her usual workstation in the operations center, and I could not find her as I walked the halls alone back to my usual conference room, where Macallister and I had interviewed Miles yesterday. I sent her an email and an instant message through our system, but there was no response.

None of this made sense to me so, instead of typing as usual into my case file, I started scribbling questions and conclusions on a sheet of yellow legal pad paper.

Omar (Wolford) is a jeweler who had offices in both target cities. He must know his way around.

Omar (Wolford) plots to undermine the financial markets by bringing two weapons into the country on a hijacked boat? Why? For profit?

The witness had said that Omar had wanted to "short" the market. I didn't know what that meant, and I googled it. *Marketwatch.com* explained that "shorting, or short-selling, is when an investor borrows shares and immediately sells them, hoping he or she can scoop them up later at a lower price, return them to the lender and pocket the difference."

Okay, I thought, *that makes sense.* Omar detonates a bomb in front of two markets, panic ensues, people sell shares. It would be a risky move unless you knew exactly when a market would drop in price. And Omar had that advance timing knowledge; according to the suspect interview, the detonation was to take place at 9:33 AM.

He has created the weapons to be an imitation of a nuclear device using medical waste according to the witness. That must be the source the radiation signature that we found on the boat. Where did he get the medical waste?

His pieces are in place, but before he detonates the weapons, he gets his face blown off soon after receiving a phone call that originated from the FBI? Right after we figured out how to track him?

I looked at the sentences that I had written and instantly saw what I was missing. I scrawled, *He must be working for someone else! Is there someone above him? With the money to stake the markets and to make the trades, to pull off the transport and to buy the vans and phones. To buy the radioactive material. And who wanted to cover their tracks by eliminating Omar before we caught up to him?*

Vanessa Raiden had fingered Appleton and Anastasia. I couldn't bring myself to believe that one of them was somehow the mastermind of this whole thing. *Or could they be?*, I wrote, shaking my head *no* even as the ink dried on the page as the next thought coalesced in my mind.

Why did Omar use the sailboat to bring the weapons into the United States covertly? Why go to the expense and time of a trans-Atlantic journey? Why take the risk of the midnight hijack of a yacht? What about the hassle of coordinating logistics once ashore? All to transport what is essentially a cartoon bomb, with the intent to make a bang and to set off a Geiger counter?

My eyes blurred as I reread what I had written.

This was way bigger. I started to imagine possibilities and angles. When I briefed Appleton overnight after we had talked to the Coast Guard petty officer at Station Gloucester, who had literally watched Miles's boat on her screen as it returned to the United States, I spitballed the idea that terrorists could use a larger commercial fishing vessel to pull off the same ruse with an even bigger cargo and with even more men: hijack it a little ways offshore and casually bring it back to port. And, knowing what we knew, now, that gave me pause. There are literally hundreds and hundreds of ports up and down the east and west coasts of the United States. On a whim, I brought up the site that we had used yesterday, *marinetraffic.com*, and I was astounded by the number of icons gathered near the coastlines and crossing the oceans. Thousands. Ten thousand? More? Every one of them was a potential target. Every fishing boat, sailboat, freight vessel, ferry . . . thousands. How could you possibly keep track of every single one?

And, only one of them needed to be that trawler that had made the transit from Turkey, and only one of them needed to be a soft target to seize.

Wait a minute. Turkey. Why so far? Why start there?

Without conscious thought, but with the clarity that comes from a conclusion that you know is correct, my pen moved, and the words spelled themselves out on the yellow sheet of paper:

The bombs aren't fakes! The mastermind would tell Omar and his mercenaries that they were fake to convince them to work with him/her. But bringing them into the country that way, taking the long journey across the Atlantic to bypass border security? What about the dangerous radiation signature that was measured in Gloucester? That TEDAC concluded was weapons-grade?

The bombs must be real.

My mouth gaped open as I stared at my words.

I had to share this with someone. I had to find Raiden and run these theories by her. She'd been involved since almost the beginning. And since I couldn't find her, I knew I had to find Macallister. *He* was involved since the beginning. He'd had my back all along.

I folded my notes into a square and stuffed the paper in my pocket, grabbed my backpack and stood from the familiar conference table—but I was blasted by a sound—the jarring claxon of the building's alarm system, and then a robotic voice over the speakers scattered through the building, "*LOCKDOWN. LOCKDOWN. LOCKDOWN.*"

CHAPTER
82

WHAT THE FUCK? SINCE WE OCCUPIED this new building less than a year ago, that in-house crisis system had never been activated. Already tense as the investigation had reached a climax during the day and exhausted from the round-the-clock prep work associated with the canceled POTUS visit the day before, the agents and staff in Chelsea were wound tight. I hoped this was a false alarm, triggered in error, but my senses told me otherwise. Those senses had served me well these past two days, but, all the same, I had no idea what was happening.

And, apparently, no one else did either, as agents and admins moved to the core of the building, away from the perimeter rooms with windows and into the cube farm, as per the lockdown procedure. The claxon was finally silenced but emergency lights continued to flash their regular, red, double-strobe beat.

I waited.

Ten minutes passed, then twenty, then twenty-five. The emergency lights ceased their incessant flash and agents dispersed through the building, telling the confused staffers to return to their stations but not to leave the building. I had begun to walk back to my conference room when I heard my name called by an assistant who worked on our floor. "Porter? Ben Porter?"

I scanned the room, finally finding her standing by a cube outside Macallister's office, holding a phone handset loosely to her ear as she searched the room for me. Our eyes met and she whisper-shouted across the expanse, "Macallister is looking for you. He needs you in the server room."

Huh? But I'm looking for Macallister!

I didn't know that Macallister even knew where the servers were located. I'd only been there once, on a tour, after we moved into the building, to the over-air-conditioned room in the lowest level where the servers and our telecommunications systems hummed twenty-four-seven. I rushed to an elevator and pushed the down arrow button.

When the door swished open, I was instantly face-to-face with an agent who had his service weapon unholstered. He demanded, "Who are you?"

"Porter. Supervisory Special Agent Macallister sent a message for me to come down here."

I raised my ID lanyard and the agent examined it, saying, "Right. That way."

I followed his pointing finger through a corridor where I found three or four agents massed around a door. They turned to look at me and I preempted the question by holding out my ID and announcing, "Porter. For Macallister."

The group parted silently, and I passed through the door into a dimly-lit room to a gruesome sight, one which I had never seen before, wish to never see again, and will never forget.

A body dressed in woman's clothing lay on the polished concrete floor, face down, in a giant pool of blood that had trickled under a server stack, with hair splayed into the blood like an unruly floor mop. The left hand appeared to be reaching for a shattered laptop computer that also lay in the pool.

Macallister was standing to one side, clear of the pool, and he somberly looked at me, then looked down at the body.

I crouched, the bile rising in my throat as I squatted lower, hesitating, not wanting to see the face of the figure. I blinked, shutting my eyes tightly, and reluctantly opened them.

It was Vanessa Raiden.

✳ ✳ ✳

As Ben Porter had chased Bradford Macallister to the ops center, Vanessa Raiden had stood, tugged at her blouse, and wanted to go home. She had been on duty since 9:00 AM the previous morning. She had been an integral part of the investigation and the chase. And now, she had uncovered damning evidence that seemed to implicate either her direct supervisor or the field office's SAC. She needed a break.

Returning to her station was out of the question at the moment, as she was not yet willing to face Anastasia or Appleton, certainly not during an on-screen interview with a suspect. She needed a plan and time to think, and she decided to retreat to the over-air-conditioned server farm in the lowest level of the building, where the machines hummed purposely in a place that staff avoided due to the chill.

Inside the server room, she found a table to sit at in a far corner and she pulled a laptop computer from her messenger bag. Logging into the personal account that she had used to compile a trace of her cellular sleuthing, she decided to go over the data yet again. A single mistyped number or character in an MEID address would change everything. And she wondered, *Had I made a mistake? Had I jumped the gun and talked to Ben too early?*

Vanessa worked carefully, slowly, pedantically. One-by-one she reviewed the data points: fourteen hex character places for each phone in play, plus a checksum character, plus times and locations. It was tedious and she had lost track of time when, suddenly, the overhead LED light panels blinked off. The room went dark, lit only by the flickering indicator lights on the servers and by the glow of her laptop screen.

Confused, Vanessa unplugged the laptop from the wall charger and flipped it around, backward, so that the screen became a flashlight of sorts as she awkwardly worked her way back to the entry where the light switch was located.

With the door in sight, she felt a slight breeze on the sensitive hairs at the nape of her neck. The movement of air turned into a left arm wrapped around her shoulders from behind, the glint of a small silver wristwatch sparkling in the low light of the laptop screen.

The right arm from behind drew a razor-sharp blade swiftly across Vanessa's throat, slicing her carotid artery and her airway. She drew in an audible gasp from the rough tracheotomy as blood pulsed. Then both arms from behind shoved her with incredible force, knocking her to the floor. Vanessa's skull thwacked the polished concrete floor and cracked, and she lay unmoving, unconscious, until she bled to a silent death in a pool of her own blood.

Looking at her face, I started to hyperventilate, the pent-up exhaustion from the day comingling with fear and anxiety. Before I toppled face-first into the pool of blood, I felt a steadying hand on my shoulder, and I heard Macallister's voice, kindly and softly saying, "Ben, c'mon. Let's get you outta here."

CHAPTER
83

MACALLISTER LED ME TO A small office where I sat, head in my hands, slowly controlling my breathing and my emotions. He remained silent, allowing me the time to regain my composure.

I looked up at him, finally, and whispered, "We gotta talk. We gotta get out of here."

Of course, Macallister didn't understand, really, but I knew that the conclusion he reached was close enough for me when he replied, "Sure. It's been a crazy two days. Let's get some air."

We left the building as I racked my brain for someplace to go, someplace where we could talk, away from ringing phones and prying eyes and . . . from Appleton and Anastasia. "I really could use a drink, you know. Let's go to the Stationhouse. You okay with that?" I asked.

Macallister shook his head *no*, saying, "Not a chance. Ben, I know you're shook up. But we got a murder here. Right here in this building. We're not going anywhere."

"Please," I begged. "There's something you don't know. I can't explain it here. You have to trust me."

Looking down at me from his taller frame, Macallister hesitated, clearly torn. He was correct, of course; we really should not be leaving the building. But what I knew could clearly not be shared here. Not with Appleton and Anastasia around.

Macallister snorted one of his casual laughs, mirthlessly. "You've gotten this case right so far. Alright, let me in on the secret. I'll meet you there."

I could tell he was pissed off, but I didn't care. He'd understand soon enough.

We split for our cars, me to my Taurus and him to his Evoque.

The Chelsea Stationhouse was the place where Macallister had ordered our take-out dinner the night before, a fire station converted to a restaurant only a couple of blocks from our office. Macallister snagged the last spot in the parking lot and I slid the Taurus curbside on 4th Street.

Inside, we found an empty, polished mahogany, two-person high-top table in the bar area, and I took the seat which had my back to the wall and which gave me a view to the entrance. I've watched too many spy movies.

We ordered drinks; Macallister a fancy tequila on the rocks; me just a bottled beer. We looked like two bros out after work. Sort of, I guess. Tall preppy guy with his Range Rover key fob displayed on the table in front of him, and mildly-overweight stocky me with shifty, bloodshot eyes scanning for threats.

I took a swig from my beer and, dispensing with the pleasantries, I took a deep breath and dived in, watching as Macallister's face slowly lost color while his eyes never left mine. "Remember where you found me, before the interview? I was with Vanessa. She had just gotten done telling me that she backtracked the three phones that had been used to unlock vehicles in Gloucester. She concluded that they were not only for that purpose, but also that they were the detonation devices. There were what appeared to be test calls, made from the phone that Omar would have, to each phone that would eventually travel with each van. Calls made while the vans were in that warehouse in New Milford. And since, you know, we didn't find phones in the vans or in the Regal, Vanessa figured the van phones must be in the boxes and can only be the detonation triggers."

"And she thinks the bombs can still be triggered?" Macallister asked.

"Yeah, but no. That's what I thought too. But she said that the phones wouldn't work in the containment boxes. Anyway, that's not important, now. The key is that the phone that Omar had in his possession, the one that traveled the route of the Buick, made those two test calls. It received only one text, and then it received only one call. At 5:40 AM this morning. Right after I made the OnStar connection. Right after Appleton left the ops center to get authority to get into the OnStar system. Right after Anastasia left the ops center to reboot a server or something."

I looked at Macallister to make sure he was still following my narrative. He inclined his head to concur his understanding, and I stated, flatly, "Vanessa traced the call. And the text. Both came from separate burner phones. Both signals from those burner phones were triangulated to the location of our office."

"And now, Vanessa is dead."

Macallister sat back and took a long pull from the rocks glass. Setting it down with more care than necessary, his gaze dropped to his tequila. I waited.

Finally, he spoke. "Holy shit. Porter, that's—"

I waited again, watching his face set into a grimace as he reran the scenario in his mind. He picked up where he left off, "That's fucking unbelievable."

He crossed his arms over his chest and concluded, "That says we got a mole."

I nodded and added, "Yeah, and Anastasia was a no-show to the interview and I haven't seen her since. And Appleton was late to the interview. You'd think that Appleton especially would have been on time. Is it possible that the mole is also a killer? 'Cuz that's about when Vanessa would have been"—I stopped.

I couldn't bring myself to say *murdered*. I mumbled, "That's when Vanessa disappeared."

"Yeah. Looks that way." Pausing, Macallister contemplated his tequila again as I took a sip from my own bottle. He looked up at me and asked, "Listen, Porter. This is a really big deal, obviously. Other than what Vanessa told you, you got any proof? Did she show you anything?"

"No," I said, glumly. "She talked me through the process of identifying the signatures from the phones, and I could repeat what she said. But I have no idea how to do it myself. It was probably on her laptop. The one that was on the floor, next to her." In my mind's eye, I could clearly see that shattered computer in that pool of blood. I looked at my beer bottle and decided it wasn't going to taste all that good anymore, and I shoved it away from me.

He squirmed on his stool, awkwardly reaching into a pants pocket, and he pulled out his smartphone. Glancing at the screen, his eyes narrowed, he said, "Appleton. Texted me. She thinks I'm still at the office."

"You can't trust her."

"I know," he said. "But we gotta get access to those phone records. This is all hearsay at the moment. No offense, right?"

I smiled a thin smile for the first time in hours. "Nah." Thinking a moment, I added, "Maybe that guy Lewis can see if Vanessa left records on our system."

We both stood and Macallister tossed a twenty-dollar-bill on the table, saying, "Good idea. We're gonna stick together, okay?"

"Yup."

I knew Macallister, as a Special Agent, would be required to carry a weapon at all times, and there was no way I was leaving his side once we returned to our office.

CHAPTER

84

"WHERE'D YOU PARK?" MACALLISTER ASKED as we walked out of the door. "I'll walk you there."

"On Fourth," I replied, motioning to 4th Street to our left. Reaching my shit-brown Ford Taurus, I unlocked it, slid into the driver's seat, and started the motor, with Macallister standing next to my driver's side door. The hot July humidity had settled over Boston and had become almost insufferable, and I hit the buttons to roll all of the windows down while I waited for the pathetic air conditioning to trickle out its lukewarm air.

Macallister stated, "See you at the office. Wait for me in the parking lot there?" I nodded. The FBI Boston Field Office was maybe two blocks away, but I was aimed in the wrong direction. I'd have to circle the block.

"I'll see you there. I'm in the lot," Macallister said, pulling his key fob from his pocket and aiming it, sort of, through my window toward the lot. I watched, figuratively in slow motion, as his thumb squeezed the unlock button on the fob.

It happened in a split-second. To my right, a blinding flash of white light, instantly followed by a massively loud *BOOM*, and Macallister's blacked-out Range Rover Evoque exploded into a fireball.

My mouth drooped open as I stared at the growing inferno in The Chelsea Stationhouse parking lot. Macallister stood stock-still, his hand holding the key fob resting on the ledge of my driver's side window, his eyes staring over the roof of my Taurus as he watched his car burn.

Neither of us spoke.

Then, through my passenger side window, I saw headlights flash to life, on the far side of the lot on Everett Street. With a chirp of tire squeal, I watched a car that I knew all too well—the FBI's black Dodge Charger that I had driven during my investigation just yesterday, the car that Anastasia had given me the keys to—lurch forward and start to swing into the parking lot, it's menacing grill aiming directly at me.

Macallister saw it, too, and didn't hesitate. He literally dove through the open driver's side rear passenger window of my Taurus, yelling "Go! GO! *GO!*"

The black Dodge was forced to a stop by a group of people coming from the restaurant to ogle the evocative fireball in the lot, and I yanked the gear lever into Drive and stomped on the gas pedal. With Macallister still pulling his feet through the window, my Taurus shot onto 4th Street.

Which, fuck me, I realized was a dead-end street.

CHAPTER
85

MY TAURUS WOULD BE NO MATCH for the blindingly fast black beast in my rearview mirror—a mirror view partially blocked by Macallister who had dropped so unceremoniously into the rear seat and who was now yanking his suit coat aside to reveal his chest-holstered Glock Model 22 service weapon.

As we flashed by Arlington Street, I realized that I needed a plan. I scanned the street in front of me, seeing, only a short distance away, the elevated section of US-1 which created the fenced dead-end that I was aiming toward. I could swing an illegal left onto Walnut Street and try to lose the Dodge by merging onto that elevated US-1 roadway, but would that allow the more powerful Dodge to catch up on the multi-lane road? Or, maybe I turn right on Walnut and then right on Everett, and try to make a run for the potential safety of witnesses on that wide street . . . or even make it the three blocks back to our building.

I chose the latter, just as a gunshot rang out from the Dodge, shattering the rear window into a million tiny pieces and scaring the shit out of me, and I yanked the wheel to the right, tires screeching as I horsed my old Taurus around the corner on Walnut. Jamming my right foot to the floor, I glanced over my shoulder, to find Macallister now prone on the back seat.

Shit.

"Macallister!" I yelled.

"I'm hit," he said weakly. A bloodied hand rose from the back seat, clutching the unused Glock.

"Hang on!" I shouted, pulling the wheel to the right again, running a stop sign and hoping for a gap in cars on Everett as I swung recklessly onto the wider road.

The black Dodge matched my maneuvers and had closed the distance somewhat, though no more shots had been fired.

As soon as I had the Taurus mostly under control on Everett, I grabbed for Macallister's Glock, while realizing that on the straighter Everett, my chances of outrunning the Dodge were zilch. I had to make a new plan, and fast. We were not going to make it three blocks back to the office. We may not make even one block.

Up ahead, I saw the left-turn lane signal for Spruce Street flash from green to yellow, and I coaxed every last bit of power from my straining engine. A second after the light flashed to red, I carved the left turn to blaring horns. Behind me, I could hear squeals of brakes and a smash of metal-on-metal as the Dodge sideswiped an oncoming car.

I needed a crowd and a place to hide, so with the Dodge slowed somewhat in the intersection, I, too, slowed slightly, then turned my steering wheel to the right and jumped the curb into a bank parking lot, aiming for the much larger mall lot beyond, hoping to find safety among witnesses.

It was a bad call.

The right front tire performed admirably against the sudden onslaught of the concrete curb wall, but my left front tire hit that curb at an oblique angle and the inner sidewall decided against further punishment. I heard the tire blow out, and I felt the steering wheel shake and shimmy wildly. I kept the accelerator pinned to the floor and tried to careen across the bank lot. The Dodge had regained its speed and it, too, pounded over the curb.

I knew I was done. The Taurus still had its speed, but I didn't have control. I overcorrected the steering and the car corkscrewed, with the damaged left front tire catching a curb that surrounded the bank building, I felt the car lift to the right and before I even understood what was happening, the Taurus rolled onto its right side, finally toppling upside-down onto its roof, lazily rotating a half-turn as it bled off its momentum.

Amid the low, nails-on-a-chalkboard shriek of metal on asphalt, I could hear the Dodge growl to a stop beside the overturned Taurus.

It's a cliché, but I knew I could actually feel the adrenaline coursing through my body; my heartbeat racing and my breath shallow, as I searched for the safety switch on the trigger of Macallister's Glock.

Shapely legs—a woman's legs—appeared outside my window, then a torso followed quickly by a face.

Anastasia Volkov leaned close to my window, my body hanging inverted from the shoulder and seat belt but my mind as sharp and as focused as it would ever be.

"Ben," she hissed. "You have *so* much potential. Well, had. I'm sorry."

As a gun materialized in her hand by her side, without hesitation, I swung my own hand around and pulled the trigger on Macallister's Glock, again and again and again and again and again and again until the firing pin clicked hollowly against an empty chamber.

EPILOGUE
TUESDAY, SEPTEMBER 26, 2017

FBI BOSTON FIELD OFFICE, CHELSEA, MASSACHUSETTS

IN THE DARKENED F B I Boston Field Office operations center, Special Agent in Charge Jennifer Appleton, Supervisory Special Agent Bradford Macallister, and I sat side-by-side at the long conference table, facing the screens which showed a secure video tele-conference to the Washington, DC Strategic Information Operations Center, the helmet cams of two Critical Incident Response Group agents, and a camera mounted on the nose of a Blackhawk helicopter.

The scene and the characters set in front of me looked much like that of the chaos of that July morning, but now missing the hospitalized Anastasia Volkov and murdered Vanessa Raiden.

Raiden had been mourned, quietly, as the investigation remained tightly classified. Internally, she had been hailed as a hero, an exemplar of the culture to never stop investigating and to look at everything in excruciating detail.

I had learned well from Raiden: the truth can be found in the details. Laying on the table in front of us was a sheet of yellow legal pad paper, with several sentences scrawled on it in my handwriting. Many, many copies of this sheet had been made, and it had become an unofficial roadmap of our investigation. One by one, we crossed off my sentences as each and every fact was verified, my conclusions were vetted, and most of my questions were answered.

One mystery that remained unsolved was the fate of the fishing vessel. It never reappeared on the satellite images. It had become a ghost. We would find it, we hoped, eventually.

We did find, swiftly, what we had been up against inside the two long boxes that the fishing vessel had transported to Miles Lockwood's sailboat. The two bombs had been carefully disassembled, as instructed by the witness interview in New York, with a Philips screwdriver with a #2 head. The batteries in the Pixel phones inside had been exhausted, and there was no present danger of detonation.

One of my guesses had been correct. The weapons were every bit as dangerous as the initial report from TEDAC had led us to believe. By all accounts, they were, indeed, dirty bombs.

A "nuclear dirty bomb," or a "radiological dispersal device," is somewhat of a fantasy weapon; it is a conventional bomb with nuclear components. The idea of a dirty bomb is to use the detonation of the conventional bomb to spread deadly radiation through a large area. The mechanics, however, are not as straightforward, because by dispersing radiation, the effect of exposure is lessened.

In this application, though, it was the perfect weapon. The simple bombs transported in the vans had been cleverly fabricated, with enough radioactive material inside to have been disruptive. They would have caused the intended deadly effects, from the near-radius fatalities and short-term panic, to the long-term clean-up and decontamination of two urban areas.

There was no doubt that the detonation of these devices would have caused the panic Omar intended, and, as a corollary, the stock markets would have swooned.

Murkier was the involvement of Anastasia Volkov. The case against Anastasia was clear-cut, and there had been no investigation, other than the required proforma inquiry, about my actions in shooting her with Macallister's service weapon. Characteristically, Macallister had ribbed me over and over again on my marksmanship; I had emptied the fifteen-round clip of his Glock, yet I had managed to hit my target only . . . twice.

Fortunately, those two bullets connected and took her down. She was taken to the Massachusetts General Hospital and placed in the intensive care unit with critical injuries. If she recovered, she would stand trial for her involvement in the plot and for the murder of Vanessa Raiden.

We had found DNA evidence that implicated her in the murder case: a cell of Raiden's skin was found on Anastasia's watch, and a trace of the Russian metal from the watch was found in the blood at Raiden's throat, putting the two in the server room together.

The double shock of a murderer and a mole in our midst was compounded, of course, by the confirmation that she had been a conspirator in the attempted terror attack on New York and Chicago. We had a two-pronged investigation underway: the murder case and the terror case. We wanted to know "why," and we wanted to understand her motives. The Bureau assigned a team to dig through her past.

Thus far, we'd only been able to ascertain that her Ukrainian orphan backstory was bogus—there were no records of an orphan with her name or similar in the Ukraine who then emigrated to the United States, and her American adoptive family did not exist. That she was a ghost raised the obvious question: how did she get through our initial hiring process? And, even as the investigation team tried to figure out just who she was, another logical tangent of the investigation led to a new theory: that there was another inside connection that had facilitated her employment at the FBI—a second mole.

That alone was cause for colossal consternation throughout the Bureau, reaching way above my pay grade, and even above Appleton's status. A "mole hunt" is counterproductive to any institution, and though I was not in the inner loop of that investigation, I could easily surmise that it would explode into a major case in the very near future.

In the meantime, Anastasia Volkov's involvement in my case became quite apparent, at least with the benefit of the hindsight that we had now. She was a willing participant in the terror plot who, working from the inside, had subtly attempted to slow my investigation once she realized that I was making progress.

Indeed, she had cleverly been able to monitor every step I made by giving me that phone, the phone that connected me to her and passed on my every word and my every movement directly back to her.

Worse, we discovered that she had downloaded the files from the Harbor Cove Brewing Company's security cameras in a way that reduced their resolution, making it impossible for us to use our facial recognition software.

Critically, we learned that she had only opened one connection to OnStar, and we could have tracked all three vehicles simultaneously—another subtle roadblock that significantly hampered the speed of the investigation during its most critical moments.

One of the first items reviewed after Raiden's murder was the building's security system. It had been wiped, from key card access records to the always-on video surveillance of hallways, offices, exterior areas and, of course, the server room. But the deletion had been done hastily, and sloppily, and parts were able to be recovered. The computer forensics team concluded that Anastasia had killed Vanessa, and from that very server room, erased the security system. She then initiated a restart of the security system and fled the building during the reboot.

The in-car navigation system in the Dodge showed that she waited outside the building's perimeter for, presumably, me. She got a two-for-one, sort of, when Macallister and I left together for the Stationhouse. That she wired Macallister's car to explode, instead of mine, was just dumb luck. For me, that is. Not for her.

The FBI Behavioral Science profilers assumed, though we might never know for sure, that her outwardly apparent initial cooperation was to not only keep an eye on the investigation, but also because of my lowly status as an information management specialist who had been sent out into the field. She probably just figured I'd fuck it all up.

Ironic, huh? That I then had to shoot her, to save my own life.

And to save Macallister's life. He had been struck in his left shoulder with the bullet that shattered my Taurus's rear window, and though that injury was not fatal, there's no doubt in either of our minds that Anastasia would have killed us both after my disastrous swerve into that bank parking lot resulted in my upside-down, now totaled, Taurus.

On the plus side, after it got back from the body shop to repair the damage to its flanks, Appleton had assigned me the sweet black Dodge to use as my personal vehicle. She also said that she would promote me, and that plans were in the works, but given the unusual circumstances, those plans would take some time to put into effect.

Appleton had an alibi for the call placed to Omar at 5:40 AM; she had been confirmed by multiple sources and by electronic records as being on the phone with the Department of Justice to claim the "exigent circumstances" that allowed us to legally access the OnStar system.

It took days for the tech team to recreate Vanessa Raiden's analysis of the three Pixel phones that had been carried in the vans to New York, to Chicago, and to JFK and found in Omar's car. I did the best I could to explain what Raiden had told me and the tech team took it from there: first establishing that a text that originated in the vicinity of our Boston building was sent to Omar's phone at 6:56 PM the night before, and that a call from a different phone was made, also from 201 Maple Street, to Omar at 5:40 AM. And at that time, only Anastasia and Appleton had known about the OnStar discovery. The rest of us who knew about my OnStar revelation were all in the operations center at that time, and we could all alibi each other.

The call had to have been made by Anastasia.

At this point, and from the conclusions I had written down on my yellow pad, the FBI was convinced that Omar and Anastasia could not have acted alone. The team investigated every cell phone signal emanating from a radius around 201 Maple Street before and after 5:40 AM. That painstaking analysis and investigation uncovered a call placed from yet another burner-type phone at 5:36 AM, to a cell phone that had been on a yacht in Newport, Rhode Island.

One piece of the puzzle interlocked another, and archived satellite and security camera images revealed that the yacht in question, anchored in Newport on that morning, at that exact location, belonged to an oligarch named Anatoly Petrikov.

That was the easy part.

The hard part was, *why*, and, of course, was Petrikov involved? We dug deep into his past and discovered that Petrikov had an under-the-radar involvement with the Russian mafia based in Brighton Beach, outside of Manhattan. Back then, there was a tenuous link that was unable to be proven between him and a Russian gangster named Ivankov; when the gangster was arrested and subsequently deported in 1996, the trail went cold and the inconsequential Petrikov file had been closed.

Now, we realized that had been a giant mistake.

Unbeknown to the FBI, Petrikov had taken over Ivankov's position with the Brighton Beach mafia, and he built a highly-profitable operation fencing gems and stones in New York. Then, in 2005, as we learned through murmurs and whispers, he had attempted to broker the sale of a massive diamond nicknamed "The Creator." Problem was, he didn't own it, illicitly or legitimately, because it was property of the Kremlin. Not a group you'd want to trifle with, and that botched deal cost him his reputation and his standing.

And the jewelry expert who would vouch for the value of the diamond on behalf of Petrikov, and who would eventually be responsible for its sale, with a handsome commission? Victor Wolford. Who, when the transaction went south, lost his credibility and his credit, closed his businesses in New York and Chicago, and disappeared . . . until he turned up faceless at JFK.

Piece by piece, the puzzle took shape. Petrikov had the means to finance the operation, and both the Russian and the jeweler had the motive to wreak havoc in those two cities for their own personal gain. Could this all have been about cold, nasty revenge? With a side hustle in the financial markets for profit?

We couldn't ask Wolford, of course, so we thought we would ask Petrikov.

We had enough evidence that Petrikov was connected to the plot. We had the call placed from our Boston Field Office to his yacht. We had a flight plan for his helicopter from Newport to JFK on that fateful morning, as well as an image of Petrikov himself in the Terminal Four parking lot. We traced the isotope signature of the material to the Özel Amerikan Hastanesi in Bodrum, Turkey, where someone had acquired a large quantity of caesium-137 derived from calibration tests of the hospital's radiation therapy machines. And, to cap off the indictment, we triumphantly found records of a wire transfer from a Petrikov-controlled account to a bank in Greece; funds that we assumed were to purchase the caesium-137 and to pay for the operation in Turkey.

But much of that was circumstantial, and we wanted very much to discuss the matter with Anatoly Petrikov. However, we feared that if we knocked on his door and politely asked him our questions, he'd lawyer up and then flee to his native Russia. Given the serious nature of the terror plot charges against him, the Bureau and the Department of

Justice had authorized the operation that the three of us now watched, as the CIRG team covertly approached his yacht at this very moment.

By late September, summer is over, and the heat is much less intense, replaced by a refreshing coolness in the dark, early morning hours.

In the quiet Great Peconic Bay, stirred by the gentle night breeze, the reflections of tiny wavelets sparkled like millions of diamonds on the polished, anchored hull of a majestic, imposing, 235-foot, expedition-style yacht.

The glitterati had mostly left the area, returning to the City, leaving their staffs to clean up and winterize their summer-season Hamptons and Sag Harbor mansions and beach houses. The marinas and mooring fields emptied as the charter yachts and private vessels got under way for their annual migrations south.

A dull whomp-whomp-whomp of helicopter blades gradually increased in intensity, rudely disturbing the tranquil bay.

Low above the inland treeline, its underbelly, anticollision light blinking almost to the beat to the spinning blades, a Black Hawk helicopter appeared, making a direct and speedy approach to the bow of the massive yacht. With a deft pull-up and turn, the helicopter swept to a hover only fifty feet above the forward deck of the yacht, and four agents fast-roped from the chopper, swiftly and silently dropping from the helicopter to the yacht in a practiced maneuver. The instant their feet silently toed the teak decks, the thick, inch-and-a-half diameter braided ropes whipped up, carried by the rapidly ascending Black Hawk as it blended into the dark sky.

Special Agent Leroy Havens had a score to settle. His former partner, Heather Rourke, had been confined to limited desk duty. And, even though these types of missions were closely-held and classified top-secret, they both knew that this was related to the shot that almost killed Rourke in New York months earlier.

The layout of the yacht had been obtained from both the naval architect and the shipyard that built the vessel, and Havens and his team had committed it to memory. The oligarch's master suite was on the main deck, just aft of the sweeping windows that faced the expansive prow of the miniship where the agents now massed.

The team didn't bother with doors or halls or potential guards. Instead, they simply set specially-designed charges at the centers of two of the thick, tempered-glass windows; the charges superheated the center of the panes, creating a thermally-induced stress to the edge of the panes and causing the windows to spontaneously collapse into tidy piles of tiny tempered pieces on the decks and on the sills. At over five feet high and three feet wide, it was simple and fast for two of the agents to enter the suite by merely jumping through the open frames as the remaining men stood watch on the foredeck of the yacht.

The target had, of course, been awakened by the imploding glass but, twisted in the Egyptian cotton sheets, was helpless as he watched the two agents storm his suite.

Keying his collar microphone, Havens transmitted, "Target acquired."

The giant form in the bed actually laughed. "You think?"

Havens merely grinned. He and his team knew what was coming next.

Realizing that the oligarch would have private security on the yacht, the CIRG planning profile called for a quick entry to secure the target, and then a rapid deployment around the vessel to neutralize any resistance.

As the dozing sentinel watchman in the ship's wheelhouse, above the master suite, belatedly realized that the vessel had been breached on the level below, he signaled the alarm to the remaining crew. They all knew the consequences of failure if their ruthless employer was not adequately protected. But they were already too late.

Within the yacht, the guard crew attempted to fan out through the interior of the ship, taking positions outside the master suite and preparing to use an access hatch to the forward deck to create a perimeter around their employer's cabin. But, in the seconds that it took them to do so, the Black Hawk helicopter appeared again, this time with spotlights glaring from its underbelly, as two additional Black Hawks swooped in and flanked the first chopper.

From four locations near shore, four identical, black boats with twin outboards had each roared to positions that formed a quadrant around the yacht, also with spotlights glaring and blue-and-red strobe lights flashing.

Petrikov was surrounded.

The guardsman in the wheelhouse, however, feared Petrikov's retribution, and began firing, first at the small boats surrounding the vessel, then at the trio of Black Hawks. With their titanium-cored rotor blades, the helicopters were impervious to the small arms fire, but, yanking back on their collectives, the pilots of the two flanking Black Hawks walked the choppers backward, while the center Black Hawk fired a carefully-aimed shot from its 2.75" rocket launcher—a searing, piercing missile that impacted the wheelhouse windows, passed through the wheelhouse itself, killing the guard on its journey, and then connected with Petrikov's stationary Eurocopter EC155 helicopter on the aft pad.

The fully-fueled EC155 exploded in an inferno that could be seen clear across Long Island Sound, and the nine remaining men of Petrikov's useless security team dropped their weapons and surrendered.

In the master suite, Petrikov's eyes opened enormously wide as the rocket sliced through his yacht scant feet above on the wheelhouse deck.

As if the short firefight interlude hadn't happened, Special Agent Havens continued their conversation, casually smiling. "Yeah, I think so.

"Anatoly Petrikov, also known as Tony Petrikov, you are under arrest for crimes against the United States of America."

In Boston, we stood and cheered, clapping hands and clapping backs, and in the SIOC feed, we watched a similar scene.

Appleton extended her right arm and formally shook my hand, saying, very kindly, "Congratulations, Ben. Well done." High, and, as usual, faint praise, from the chill SAC, but I'd take it.

Macallister was more ebullient. He grinned broadly, offered me a casual fist-bump, and announced to the room, loudly enough that it was heard even in the Washington, DC SIOC, "Ben Porter has arrived!"

I smiled and allowed myself to feel the pride and warmth of a closed case. Yet, still, it gnawed at me. Sure, we solved this one, and prevented massive casualties, damage, and panic in two major cities, but only because Miles Lockwood dove off his boat and later gave us that crucial clue to follow the Automatic Identification System trail. That was just luck. Without that, Petrikov's terrorists would have succeeded in their deceptions, from their simple stickers to pose as everyday deliverymen, to their unprecedented use of a pleasure boat that broadcast their every move as they waltzed into the country unnoticed. They had no specialized technology or skills. They hid in plain sight, exploiting the false assurances that we all take for granted: that if something looks like whatever it is supposed to look like, it is invisible.

Thinking about my earlier analysis, when I had gamed out a scenario for Appleton that our maritime borders are easily penetrated to illicitly import weapons, or any sort of contraband, or people—spies or terrorists—I wondered, how do we guard against *that*?

Because, one of these days, we won't stop them.

THE END

THANK YOU

I HOPE YOU ENJOYED this story!

Reading and writing is fun and, to make it even more fun, and in the spirit of, perhaps, a tech company like Google or Tesla, I left you a half-dozen "Easter Eggs" in the text—six references to pop culture in music, movies, and television. Did you find them?

And, would you do me a favor?

Like all authors, I rely on online reviews to encourage future sales. Your opinion is invaluable. Would you take a few moments now to share your assessment of my book on Amazon or any other book review website you prefer? Your opinion will help the book marketplace become more transparent and useful to us all.

As an expression of my gratitude to you, please turn the page, where you'll find the opening chapters of *Threat Bias,* the sequel to *False Assurances.* Ben's story picks up where we just left off.

Thanks for reading!

THREAT BIAS

BEN PORTER SERIES – BOOK TWO

CHRISTOPHER ROSOW

PROLOGUE

AUGUST 2019

SATURDAY, AUGUST 3, 2019 — 9:15 PM — BURLINGTON, VERMONT

THE 12TH ANNUAL "Festival of Fools" had gotten off to a roaring, raucous start under sunny August skies the day before at noon, and the Festival had continued all day Saturday with a friendly and fun-loving crowd growing through the day. Now, with the sun set, the temperature was perfect as revelers crowded the Church Street Marketplace, a four-block long, pedestrian-only, brick-paved street at the core of Burlington. A hip and sophisticated city overlooking Lake Champlain, Burlington could be considered as the center of the arts in Vermont, but it was also the home of Ben & Jerry's Ice Cream, countless bistros, cafes, shops, and galleries, three colleges, and forty-two thousand people.

On four "pitches" on Church Street, buskers, or street performers, amazed the cheering crowds with their daring acts of acrobatics coupled with an eclectic and unpredictable mix of archery, ladder free-climbing, corny joke-telling, and juggling—not just with colored balls, but also with fiery torches and knives. The buskers' shows comingled with the music of two live bands and the din of outdoor diners enjoying a meal and more than a few drinks under a canopy of twinkling lights in the trees that dotted Church Street.

Two blocks away from the hullabaloo of the partying crowd and the antics of the entertainers, Suzanne Cahal snapped the turn-signal stalk upward in her Tesla Model X to signal a right turn, growing more and more frustrated by the minute as she carefully guided the spotless, white car from Battery Street to Cherry Street, scanning the sides of the road for that impossible-to-find prize at the Festival of Fools: a parking space.

Suzanne had circled for a solid twenty minutes, hoping to nab a spot and to meet her friends for the live band that had been scheduled to start playing their first set at nine o'clock, outside of a pub just off Church Street. Given the dearth of parking in Burlington, and with over a thousand people massed for the Festival, she was out of luck.

Approaching the intersection of Cherry and Church Streets, she slowed, now focusing on the bodies that ambled back and fro, crossing Cherry on a wide, brick-paved crosswalk. Unlike, say, the flatlander New Yorkers in the melee of their city, Vermonters don't hurry, enjoying the magic and the energy of their laid-back home state.

A Vermont-born artist who had recently sold out a show in New York, she was rightfully proud of both her new notoriety and of her new eco-friendly, hi-tech electric SUV. She gazed at the car's exquisite interior, the dashboard dominated by a large, vertically-oriented touchscreen that controlled every aspect of the car's features. In front of the steering wheel, even the display in the binnacle was digital; no old-fashioned analog dials to be found. The car was so new to her that she had not figured out how to use all of its features yet, especially the nifty Autopilot feature that would enable the car to almost drive itself. There was an app for her phone that she needed to learn how to use, and there were all sorts of clever ways to access her car. There would be time to dig into that later.

In the meantime, she was happy to enjoy this wondrous vehicle. Suzanne brought her Tesla to a gentle stop and waited, somewhat impatiently, as festival-goers slowly ambled their ways across the brick-paved crosswalk. Glancing at her silvery Swatch on her right wrist, forgetting, as usual, to scan for the time display on the giant screen in her Telsa, she drummed her fingers on the unworn leather on the steering wheel. She didn't fault her fellow Vermonters, taking their time and enjoying the festival, but she wanted to be part of it, too; to find that elusive parking spot and to seek out her posse of friends. "The drinks will be on me tonight," she thought, grinning at the prospect of being able to treat her group without worrying about every nickel.

Darting her eyeballs left and right, she tensed imperceptibly, realizing that there was going to be a break in the stream of pedestrians. She smiled, willing herself into patience for just a moment longer, and she inhaled deeply, holding her breath for a second more than necessary to better absorb the lingering new-car smell.

Suddenly, in the blink of an eye, the Tesla shot forward, its dual electric motors spinning all four wheels as the tires chirped on the brick pavers. The steering wheel spun rapidly, yanking itself from the light pressure that Suzanne had been applying and torquing the car right, onto the pedestrian-only Church Street.

The five-thousand-pound white projectile slammed into person after person, bodies tumbling off the shell of the car. Swerving around larger obstacles, the Model X twisted and turned, the windshield eventually spider-cracking as the long, angled hood lifted three men at once off the ground and launched them into the glass.

As she wrestled with the unresponsive, leather-wrapped steering wheel, Suzanne's screams of terror and abject panic were drowned out by the horrifying crunches of metal and rubber on bone as the SUV pounded over legs and arms. With the air suspension now at its maximum height, the car crashed through table after table at an outdoor restaurant.

The artist took her eyes from the carnage outside the windshield and looked down, dumbfounded, making sure that her right leg was not mashing the wrong pedal—but no, her foot was instinctively planted firmly on the brake pedal; the muscles in her calf straining as she tried to push even harder as, against all logic, the big car rocked and bobbled over the brick pavers.

The Tesla nicked the side of a food cart set up to serve sliders, toppling the cart and pouring hot grease onto its unlucky staffers. A child stood stock-still, frozen in the glare of the bright LED headlights of the white monster as it bore down on her and her two sliders carefully placed in a small, red-checked paper tray. Her mother stiff-armed the child out of the way, but not soon enough, and the little girl was caught by the front right bumper, her tiny body lifted by the dented and battered hood of the car, launching her over the vehicle as her two little sliders smacked into the mess of the windshield, ketchup blending with blood.

Suzanne's blood-curdling scream, inside the luxuriously-appointed SUV, may have matched the scream of the child's mother outside as the little girl's body disappeared behind the car's rear flanks.

For the briefest moment, the car slowed, but as the rolling weapon neared the next intersection at Bank Street, it rocketed back to speed, the torque-heavy electric motor allowing the car to reach sixty miles per hour in under three seconds as it aimed dead-center at the parked fire truck that had been positioned on the crosswalk to block off the street. With an astonishingly loud crash of metal-on-metal, the front of the bloodied-red-and-white Tesla collided into the side of the red ladder truck.

The Telsa's momentum pushed the massive mash-up sideways fifteen feet as the front half of the Tesla's roof sheared off under the raised bulk of the fire engine.

For a beat, there was silence, punctuated only by the creaking and popping of the twisted metal, and by the weak moans and cries of injured.

Then, controlled chaos, as first responders and Samaritans alike sprang forward to help the fallen, the shock of the moment dulled by the visceral need to react. Sirens and shouts created a cacophony of noise as the triage began.

Inside the topless remains of the Tesla, Suzanne Cahal's fingers still grazed the unworn leather of the steering wheel, but her decapitated head lay on the backseat, sightless eyes remaining open. Eyes that had processed sixteen seconds and three-hundred-and-eighty feet of horror.

Eyes that would see nothing more.

PART ONE
NOVEMBER AND DECEMBER 2018

CHAPTER

1

FRIDAY, NOVEMBER 9, 2018 —
FBI BOSTON FIELD OFFICE, CHELSEA, MASSACHUSETTS

MY NAME IS BEN PORTER. I'm twenty-eight years old.

I'm a Special Agent with the Federal Bureau of Investigation.

Cool, huh?

Yes!

If we've met before, you're wondering, wait, what? An *Agent?* This is new. And you'd be correct. I was sworn in as a Special Agent last week.

For those of you who I haven't met, let me give you the backstory.

The citizens of New York and Chicago still, to this day, have no idea how close they had been to a nuclear attack in their cities in July of 2017. And, can you imagine the fallout of a nuclear bomb detonating in the heart of two major American cities? Not only the weaponized kinds—the direct destruction from the devices exploding and then the indirect radiation hazard—but also the emotional fallout. The panic, the inevitable economic crash, and the uncertainty. Will there be more attacks elsewhere? Who's next? The ultimate damage, had the attack been successful, would not be reserved for the two target cities; it would be felt nationally, if not globally.

In short, the United States got lucky. Because there was every reason that the terrorists should have succeeded, except one.

Me.

Well, that's maybe a little bit cocky. Obviously, it wasn't *just* me. But it was me who believed the tale told by a sailor named Miles Lockwood, who played a critical role in stopping that nuclear attack. Initially, no one believed him until I got the chance to talk to him. That interview kicked off the investigation that would eventually become known as Operation E.T.

Huh? you ask, rightfully. As you might know, the FBI assigns a code name to each major case under investigation, because generally, it is easier and faster to refer to the name than to a file number. Some code names are randomly generated; some have a vague relevance to the investigation at hand. Originally, the terror threat case was proposed to be called "Operation Flying Lady," referring to the name of Miles Lockwood's boat, *Flying Lady*.

Apparently, someone in DC took exception to the code name, and upon further investigation (something we do very well, of course), it was discovered that the name of the boat was an indirect nod to the hood ornament on a Rolls-Royce.

This is where it gets a little weird, because, despite the staid attitude and stiff upper lip that one generally thinks of with Rolls-Royce, the flying lady hood ornament, officially called the "Spirit of Ecstasy," had been developed in the early 1900s by an English sculptor, who had scandalously (well, for the time) used his mistress as his model. And her name was Eleanor Thornton.

Betcha you didn't know that—that every Rolls rolling through Beverly Hills or Palm Beach is adorned with someone's mistress. Scandalous, indeed. Harrumph!

Few at the FBI knew that either, so when the Operation Eleanor Thornton code name was assigned by the wonk in Washington who did that research, we all, too, scratched our heads in wonderment that it was approved.

Nevertheless, the Washington wonk had selected a code name that was so *out there* that it was immediately recognizable, easily remembered, and, per FBI tradition, instantly acronymized, which is how, Bureau-wide, my terror threat case became known as Operation E.T.

The judgment call on my part to believe Miles Lockwood's story made me into an unlikely hero. When it all started, I was working for the FBI in our Boston Field Office as an Information Management Specialist—which means I was basically a data-entry guy, toiling in a cube and doing electronic case file management and intra-agency coordination work. On the morning of July 12, 2017, my direct boss, Senior Supervisory Special Agent Bradford Macallister, assigned me to interview Miles Lockwood.

By September of 2017, the active portion of Operation E.T. had been resolved. We had the mastermind of the plot in custody. A (then) sixty-five-year-old wealthy and powerful Russian immigrant named Anatoly Petrikov had been sequestered to a clandestine facility for questioning. We had discovered that his life in crime had not been limited to this case; he had been successfully eluding law enforcement since the early 1960s. With a rap sheet that grew by the week as our investigation continued, Petrikov was held as an unlawful enemy combatant, and his whereabouts were a closely-guarded secret.

Petrikov's primary accomplice, to our shock, was an Intelligence Analyst working in the Bureau's Boston office. Anastasia Volkov, a stunningly smart and good-looking computer and technology wiz, had been working side-by-side with me during the investigation. She had been assigned to the case by none other than my boss, Macallister. Of course, back then, he had no idea she was a mole working in cahoots with the mastermind.

Not only was Volkov currently in custody for treason, for her attempt to undermine the investigation and for collusion with an unlawful enemy combatant, she had also been charged with one count of murder. Volkov had been implicated in the death of Vanessa Raiden, a junior Intelligence Analyst who had also worked on the case, and who had exposed Volkov's role.

And, the accusations against Volkov didn't stop there. She was also charged with the attempted murder of Bradford Macallister and me.

Fortunately for both Macallister and me, and despite totaling my Ford Taurus after being chased through the streets near our office in Chelsea by Anastasia Volkov driving a souped-up Dodge Charger, I had shot Volkov before she had a chance to shoot me. Volkov had been taken into custody and sent to the Massachusetts General Hospital for treatment of my gunshots, which had come close to killing her. She was then transported to a secure medical facility outside of Washington, DC, and we have been waiting since for her to recover enough to stand trial as a coconspirator in the terror plot, as a traitor to the United States, and for the murder of Vanessa Raiden.

In the meantime, my trajectory from invisibility to prominence had attracted a lot of attention, most notably from the Special Agent in Charge (SAC) of the Boston Field Office, Jennifer Appleton, a cool, collected, sophisticated woman who was as feared for her unwavering attention to detail and procedure as she was admired for her poise, for her impeccable dress code, and for her conservatively styled, shoulder-length auburn hair that never stranded out of place. After we successfully apprehended Petrikov and Volkov, and we had resolved what was considered to be an ongoing threat, the SAC had congratulated me for my role in the investigation and then, in her usual chill manner, promised me a promotion.

And that promotion, dare I say, would be well-deserved. After all, I'd saved the world, or something like that. I was hoping for a nice raise, my own office, an expense account, and a company car.

Unfortunately, what I was offered was not nearly as comfortable.

CHAPTER

2

IN EARLY 2018, WITH NO thanks to the "promotion" from SAC Appleton, I found myself crawling through the partially-frozen dirt at the FBI Training Academy in Quantico, Virginia, enrolled in the Basic Field Training Course (BFTC).

It wasn't all about snorting dirt, of course; the BFTC is an extensive curriculum in law enforcement, and I spent over seven months learning how to become an actual FBI agent.

Seven months for training was a long time, and yes, it took me longer than the usual New Agent Training (NAT) progression, which typically takes approximately five months. Part of the extended time in training was my fault: I went into it a bit overweight and out of shape, so the physical part was tough for me. And I confess, despite the workouts, I'm still no superspy with chiseled abs; I don't rock a six-pack at my waist, though I am skilled at carrying one in a paper bag, in preparation for doing some twelve-ounce curls.

It also didn't help that my fitness regime (really, can I even call it that?) and my NAT schedule were interrupted on several occasions by obligations to work on the file for Operation E.T. Given my sort-of exalted status for being the sort-of hero of that case, the trainers at Quantico humored my superiors by allowing me to come and go as directed from the academy, but to my face, they cut me no privileges.

The NAT program is comprehensive: it covers everything from legal training to firearms proficiency, to the Tactical and Emergency Vehicle Operation Course (TEVOC). Ironically, had I taken the TEVOC before Anastasia Volkov chased me through the streets of Chelsea, I might have evaded her, and I might not have had the chance to shoot her, and then the case might still be open. Funny, right? Not in the funny, ha-ha way, but in the funny way the world works.

The training at Quantico was intense. I was initially part of a class of fifty wanna-be agents. You get assigned everything, from what you wear (polo shirt, standard issue), to where you sleep (dormitory, comfortable enough), and how you are labeled (my class was 18-4, which meant it was the fourth class to commence in 2018).

It's almost equal parts classroom work and hands-on field training, but it's all parts exhausting. Yet, at the same time, it's incredibly rewarding.

My first roommate, Abdullatif al-Hamid, was also from Boston. Turned out, I vaguely knew of him; he had graduated from our shared alma mater, Boston University, in 2009, three years before me.

We two NATs from Boston bonded. I'd ridicule my weight and my struggles with the physical training sessions. He'd say, "That's nothing, Ben," and he'd launch into a long-running mockery about his own name and how it would play during a pretend bust. Laughing, he'd boom out, "FBI! Agent Abdullatif al-Hamid!" And then, playing the part of his perp, he'd snicker in a meeker voice, "Duel a tiff what? What you say?"

We agreed that he would have to shorten his moniker for use in the real world, and eventually, the swarthy, bulbous-nosed, dark Middle-Eastern skinned Abdul Hamid and the stocky and mildly overweight me became good friends.

Despite his name, Abdul was American as apple pie. He was born and raised in Massachusetts to immigrant parents who had made a fortune selling perfumes or something. Abdul was one of those carefree guys who was nice to everybody. Not flashy, but not the quiet, studious type either. When I got called back to Boston for an internal interview related to the Operation E.T. case, Abdul remained at Quantico and finished out his training in the expected amount of time. He got assigned to the Bureau's Albany, New York, field office, only about three hours by car from my home outside of Boston. I hoped we would stay in touch.

On a chilly, dank November 1st, which was Thursday, last week, I finally graduated. My parents and siblings traveled from home in Rhode Island to Virginia to attend the ceremony. I was handed a shiny gold badge and a new credentials packet. My parents beamed. I couldn't believe it.

Only days prior, I had passed the final test. The dreaded pepper spray test. I didn't think I was going to make it.

Each NAT is required to pass the test, no exceptions. And it is brutal. Outside, you are hit with a massive dose of oleoresin capsicum, which is the scientific name for pepper spray. Your eyes burn in the most unimaginable, intense pain. And then you have to open an eye, or both if you dare, or must, in order to fight, as a trainer tries to wrestle your fake orange pistol from your holster, as the involuntary tears from the searing pain in your eyes drip down your cheekbones, and your nostrils contract as you try to avoid swallowing and, therefore, find it hard to breathe.

Let's just say it's nasty. And gross. And exceptionally painful.

I'd come a long way since starting the Quantico program, and I was in the best shape that I'd been in since, well, ever, and yet the pepper spray test attacks all your senses. The spray is debilitating, even though you know it's coming. Even though you've heard the stories of the NATs who got this far and couldn't make this final hurdle—and you did not want to be that trainee.

Fortunately, I was not.

It didn't really sink in that I had made it until the day after the graduation ceremony when each newly-sworn Special Agent visits the armory to receive their very own FBI-issued weapon, a Glock Model 22 pistol.

Holding the weapon in my hands was a transcendent experience for me. Bradford Macallister had passed me *his* Glock in the Taurus on that fateful day, and I had shot his weapon at Anastasia Volkov, saving my own life as well as Macallister's. And now I held my own Glock—a lethal version of the fake, orange toy pistol that I had defended during the pepper spray test.

I remember considering the gun carefully, under the fluorescent lights in the armory. I was once a data-entry guy, head down in front of a screen in a cubicle. Now, I'm an armed agent of the Federal Bureau of Investigation.

And I wondered if I would ever pull out that weapon and aim it at another human being. Someone who had me in the sights of their own gun. Someone like Anastasia Volkov.

I was assigned, as expected, back to Boston, where I was greeted by my colleagues earlier this week with a little party and with a lot of stories. I was on top of the world.

In the mornings, I'd wake up with a new purpose, look in the mirror, and beam. I'm an FBI *Special Agent*!

That feeling lasted for what, a week and a half? Until Tuesday.

Until that one person who haunted my dreams, that one person who once hunted me, reappeared in my life.

Anastasia Volkov.

And when *that* name resurfaced, that wondrous feeling of being a newly-minted FBI agent was dulled by the sensation that, once again, *I* was the target.

CHAPTER

3

TUESDAY, NOVEMBER 13, 2018 — WALTER REED NATIONAL MILITARY MEDICAL CENTER, BETHESDA, MARYLAND

FOR ANASTASIA VOLKOV, it had been a long year and a half since she had last tasted the freedom that most people take for granted. That was about to change.

Patience came naturally to her. She had learned long ago to suffer in silence, to wait out whatever it was that was difficult, and to persevere. That mental grit was, in her mind at least, her defining characteristic.

To others, it was not that. It was her striking looks, her olive complexion framed by her flaxen, long, straight hair. It was the hint of a Russian accent in her voice as she spoke. It was her computer sciences degree from the Massachusetts Institute of Technology. It was her aptitude for computers and for her intelligence. It was never her patience.

But it was her patience that gave her all of those things. The patience to grow into her physical looks while growing her mind, equally adept at the digital world as it was in the human world. The patience to observe and to learn. The patience to convince those who may have otherwise dismissed her as just another pretty face to realize that she was a force to behold.

And the patience to survive the past seventeen months, since Ben Porter had shot her, almost killing her.

She had pursued Ben Porter for a day and a half. First, by technology—giving him a phone that transmitted his every word and movement back to her. She could see what he saw through both the front-facing and rear-facing cameras on the device, and its sensitive microphone allowed her to hear everything he heard or said. When he looked at the screen to tap an icon, she could see his face. When he muttered to himself, she heard his thoughts.

She had given him her car to drive. A murdered-out Dodge Charger, with black wheels and black badging and black leather, customized for her with engine and suspension upgrades to go along with its menacing cosmetic enhancements.

It had been amusing to Volkov that her peers in the FBI all assumed that the Bureau had provided the car. Not exactly. She had procured it to her precise specifications, then altered the Bureau's electronic records to make it appear that it was an FBI-owned asset. If the time came to move on, she would simply change those records again. Child's play for the computer wiz.

And, on that Wednesday morning in mid-July, 2017, it had been greatly amusing to Volkov that Porter had been assigned to the case. Volkov had known, of course, that the assets of the Bureau would be stretched thin thanks to a planned visit by the President of the United States; that had turned out to be an excellent coincidence that distracted the Bureau from the plot she was working. What was even more excellent was the decision to send Porter out in the field to interview a sailor named Miles Lockwood, who had been picked up out of the Atlantic Ocean a few miles from Cape Ann, just north of Boston, and who had claimed that his boat had been hijacked off the coast of Canada and loaded with an ominous cargo.

While it was unfortunate that the sailor had escaped, it was controllable, especially with the inexperienced Porter assigned, for lack of any other options, to pursue a terror-threat investigation which had initially been considered to be a hoax.

The unfortunates began to accumulate, at odds with Volkov's initial expectations, and despite her best efforts to thwart his intuition and his investigation, he had persevered. Little by little, he put the pieces together. She had *grossly* underestimated him.

She reluctantly gave him credit for his patience, so much like her own.

She gave him no credit for his marksmanship, though. After she had chased his crappy brown Ford Taurus with her monstrous Dodge, boxing him into a turn that left the Taurus upside-down, he had surprised her one last time. Two times, to be precise. Two shots that connected with her body.

One bullet pierced her abdomen, below her heart, missing her lungs but damaging her intestines. Painful and debilitating, for certain, but treatable.

The other bullet was far more problematic. It passed partially through her neck, just barely clearing her jugular but carving a slice from her throat and airway, then burying itself scant millimeters from her spine.

Spinal injuries can be touch-and-go, and the neurosurgeons at the Massachusetts General Hospital Intensive Care Unit were hopeful that this particular patient exhibited quadriparesis, a condition shy of complete paralysis, otherwise known as quadriplegia. Volkov exhibited sacral sparing, and the reflexes in her groin, lower body, and extremities appeared to be preserved.

Immediately upon being admitted to Mass General, the surgeons performed a tracheotomy, connected her lungs to a ventilator, and inserted a feeding tube. And while the doctors at the Mass General ICU successfully patched her body where the first bullet entered, and while they were able to remove the offending second bullet in her neck, they had little choice but to merely wait for her spinal cord cells to heal themselves. In the meantime, because she couldn't move, her muscles were exercised for her, and because she couldn't speak, she was unable to answer any of the FBI's many questions.

The doctors at Mass General were puzzled at how this patient presented. Typically, after severe spinal cord injuries, reflexes disappear for weeks, even months. Yet Volkov, despite suffering from apparently profound weakness, had preserved reflexes. This observation was noted in her chart, but for privacy reasons, the chart was not shared with the FBI. Therefore, no one from the Bureau was offered the opportunity to review her file when the doctors declared that it was safe to relocate her, six months after the gunshot wounds. Volkov was transferred to a military hospital, the Walter Reed National Military Medical Center, a few miles outside of Washington, DC, in Bethesda, Maryland.

Little did the doctors know that their patient was a master at the art of deception. The patient was able to speak. She chose not to. She was able to move. But she allowed the nurses to work her joints and muscles without offering resistance. And all the while, she waited.

Anastasia Volkov would prove again that she was one step ahead of her foes. She was ready to get out, and when the doctors transported her from Mass General, away from Boston, away from Ben Porter and Bradford Macallister, she would seize the opportunity to plot her escape.

ACKNOWLEDGMENTS

FIRST AND FOREMOST: thank YOU!

I am grateful that you've taken your time to read this story. I'm of the opinion that storytelling, be it in words, pictures, music, song, or whatever, is what makes us human. I love stories, from "the fish I caught was thiiisssss big!" to "a long time ago, in a galaxy far, far away . . . ," and everything in between. Stories connect us and allow us to share a common bond. How cool is that.

This novel, and its companion, are the capstones of a multiyear journey. I started writing *False Assurances* in the fall of 2017, after sailing the Marblehead-to-Halifax race earlier that year on a boat called (you just might guess this) *Flying Lady*. Thanks to Dr. Phillip Dickey for taking me along as one of his crew for that race, and for allowing me to hijack his boat (name). That race was fairly benign, and none of this would have happened if I was not on-watch one night (or very early in the morning, as it were), a little bit bored, passing the time by fiddling with the AIS, and wondering, what if . . . ?

After writing maybe 20 percent of the story that I had in mind, the real world interfered, and I didn't pick up the text (er, open the Word file) until early 2019. The first person who read the completed first draft was my dad, and my mom read parts of it.

They say (whoever "they" are) that you need four kinds people in your life to attempt success: a mentor, a coach, a friend, and a cheerleader. Mom and Dad have always been my cheerleaders. I could not have accomplished this without their unfailing love and support. Thank you, Mom and Dad, from the bottom of my heart.

What started as a diversion, a fun distraction from work to create a story, took a turn when my father then introduced me to a figure who would become my mentor of sorts: James Patterson. His endorsement of the very first draft of the story was, perhaps needless to say, a huge boost. Now, granted, at the time, he also told me that part of the story was "goofy" (that section was cut, eventually), but his critiques were spot-on and taken with equal parts admiration and gratitude. I mean, *the* James Patterson? Really? Wow.

I'd be remiss if I did not acknowledge the work that the Patterson Family Foundation, and ReadKiddoRead, have done in bringing education and reading to everyone. As I wrote above, storytelling—and, therefore, reading—is fundamental to our lives, and few have been as passionate as James Patterson in advocating literacy. Thank you for your leadership, Jim. We are all beneficiaries.

My cheerleader Dad also passed a copy of the first manuscript over to Ted Bell, who said something like, it's good but it needs a lot of work. It did, and Ted was generous enough to introduce me to my coach, who has asked to remain unnamed. That person knows full well who that person is. Suffice it to say, that coach has been instrumental, and my appreciation is boundless for the advice, for the suggestions, and for the contagious enthusiasm.

We all lean on our friends, and I am fortunate to have lots of friends. In this context, several friends read drafts of the first book. Four of those people I had not met before, and they took their time to read and to offer thoughtful critiques: Bob Barnett, Amy Jurskis, Meg Butler, and Chuck Townsend. I hope you see the results of your comments, criticisms, and praise reflected in the stories.

In particular, former FBI agent Jim Elroy offered invaluable insight from inside the Bureau. Jim is writing a book about his decades of experience in law enforcement. He previewed one of his chapters with me, and now I cannot wait to read the entire book.

Friends need not be editors and beta readers, though, and in that regard, I must thank a group that inspired me, perhaps oddly: a building committee, who I met with every week, at 7:30 AM on Thursday mornings, for eighteen months. That group, and especially Mark Davis and Julia Gabriele, welcomed me kindly, and they motivated me, indirectly, to do more, and to reach above and beyond.

Last, but not least: my family. It should go without saying that this would have been impossible without you. You all took it in stride one night at dinner when I announced, well, I didn't sell the first book to the big New York publishers, so instead of giving up, I'm gonna double down, write a sequel, and independently publish both stories, at the same time. (What could possibly go wrong with *that* plan?) Not only did you take it in stride, you encouraged me to do it. Meghan, Connor, Keilan, Maggie—I love you all.

ABOUT THE AUTHOR

WHEN NOT WRITING, Christopher Rosow works in the design and construction space. And, when not working or writing, or enjoying time with his amazing family, he's probably found out on the water somewhere, sailing. He lives in Connecticut with his family, his dogs, and way too many boats.

www.ChristopherRosow.com

Facebook, Twitter, and Instagram: @RosowBooks